**"Let me make sure I've got this right. You want me to spend four months in *Marseille* overseeing *Oasis Natrun*."**

"I know it's a hell of a lot to ask," Dr. Kamal said, sounding wretched. "I mean—my nursing staff's fantastic, I'd never want to imply they're not competent to keep the place going, but I need a medical director who knows this stuff inside and out and—we have some particularly tricky clinical cases at the moment and I can't leave without being sure they're going to have an expert managing their care whom I trust without question—"

Oasis Natrun. The private and exclusive mummy spa and health resort. Where Greta had sent her own mummy patients who could afford a course of treatment, whenever she possibly could. Where cutting-edge therapeutic, restorative, and cosmetic techniques were being pioneered all the time.

Which was located in *the south of France*. Where it almost certainly was not currently pouring with rain.

"—Ed," she said, cutting him off in the middle of another compound-complex self-referential loop of apology, "I think the phrase I am looking for here is *oh God yes please*."

## Praise for Vivian Shaw

### *Strange Practice*

"*Strange Practice* is written with elegance, wit, and compassion. The prose is gorgeous, the wit is mordant, and the ideas are provocative. Also, there are ghouls."

—Laura Amy Schlitz

"An excellent adventure." —Fran Wilde

"An exceptional and delightful debut, in the tradition of *Good Omens* and *A Night in the Lonesome October*."

—Elizabeth Bear

"Shaw balances an agile mystery with a pitch-perfect, droll narrative and cast of lovable misfit characters. These are not your mother's Dracula or demons.... *Strange Practice* is a super(natural) read." —*Shelf Awareness*

"This book is a joy to read, unlocking every bit of delicious promise in the premise." —*B&N Sci-Fi & Fantasy Blog*

### *Dreadful Company*

"A playfully witty confection...framing London's supernatural residents as delightfully normative while still capably evoking the frisson of the uncanny."

—*Publishers Weekly* (starred review)

"Shaw's elegant writing makes this series a standout in the genre."

—*Booklist*

"There are...few heroines as well written and compelling as Greta Helsing."

—*BookPage*

"Makes you so pleased to be reading it that you are sorry to see it finish....A triumph."

—*SFFWorld*

"Fast-moving, funny, and irresistibly fun."

—*B&N Sci-Fi & Fantasy Blog*

# GRAVE IMPORTANCE

By Vivian Shaw

The Dr. Greta Helsing Novels

*Strange Practice*

*Dreadful Company*

*Grave Importance*

# GRAVE IMPORTANCE

A DR. GRETA HELSING NOVEL

VIVIAN SHAW

www.orbitbooks.net

Cover design by Will Staehle and Lisa Marie Pompilio
Cover art by Will Staehle

Author photograph by Emilia Blaser



Orbit
Hachette Book Group
1290 Avenue of the Americas
New York, NY 10104
orbitbooks.net

Simultaneously published in Great Britain and in the U.S. by Orbit in 2019
First Edition: September 2019

Orbit is an imprint of Hachette Book Group.
The Orbit name and logo are trademarks of Little, Brown Book Group Limited.

The publisher is not responsible for websites (or their content) that are not owned by the publisher.

The Hachette Speakers Bureau provides a wide range of authors for speaking events. To find out more, go to www.hachettespeakersbureau.com or call (866) 376-6591.

Library of Congress Cataloging-in-Publication Data
Names: Shaw, Vivian, author.
Title: Grave importance / Vivian Shaw.
Description: First edition. | New York, NY : Orbit, 2019. | Series: A Dr. Greta Helsing novel
Identifiers: LCCN 2019011181 | ISBN 9780316434652 (trade paperback) | ISBN 9780316434669 (ebook) | ISBN 9781478945178 (downloadable audio book) | ISBN 9780316434676 (library ebook)
Subjects: LCSH: Women physicians—Fiction. | Medicine—Practice—Fiction. | Patients—Fiction. | Cults—Fiction. | Murder—Fiction.
Classification: LCC PS3619.H39467 G73 2019 | DDC 813/.6—dc23
LC record available at https://lccn.loc.gov/2019011181

ISBNs: 978-0-316-43465-2 (trade paperback), 978-0-316-43466-9 (ebook)

Printed in the United States of America

LSC-C

10 9 8 7 6 5 4 3 2 1

*For my Uncle Tony, who did the* Times *crossword in ink.*

# CHAPTER 1

I've just had to rescue a *third* groundskeeper from drowning in the ornamental lake," said Sir Francis Varney over the phone, sounding put-upon. "I am beginning to suspect the wretched ornamental lake of harboring something unpleasant and tentacular that drags people into it—or possibly with this rain, everyone has become sufficiently wet and cold to develop suicidal tendencies. Also part of the roof's fallen in. Again."

It was pouring. Greta Helsing watched out of her office window as debris bobbed and swirled in the gutters of Harley Street—hardly gutters so much as small rivers, after the second week of practically ceaseless rain. Autumn this year had apparently given up on the mist-and-mellow-fruitfulness bit as a bad job, and gone straight for the Biblical aesthetic instead.

"Which part of the roof?" she asked. Varney's ancestral pile, Ratford Abbey, went by the much more stylish epithet of Dark Heart House, and was in the process of being renovated at considerable expense.

"The part over the green drawing room, which is not exactly benefiting from the experience. I rescued all the bits of jade and malachite that could be moved. At least the wellmonsters seem to like this weather; they're having a lovely time splashing around in the gardens."

"Well, that's something," said Greta. Dark Heart and its park had been pressed into service as a shelter for dispossessed supernatural creatures earlier in the year, and one of the species housed there was somewhat amphibious. "Is—"

Over the phone she could hear someone else's voice, and Varney's inventive cursing. "—Sorry," he said after a moment, "Greta, I've got to go, the stable block is apparently flooding—I'll call you later, all right?"

She could picture it, and bit her lip. "Yes, of course. Go sort things out, don't worry about me."

"I can't help it," said Varney, "I think it's a permanent condition. Talk soon."

*Click.*

She took the phone away from her ear, and it was probably only her imagination that the rain seemed even louder as it spattered against her window. Only her imagination, now that Varney's voice wasn't there with her. When she set the receiver back in its cradle, that sound, too, felt much too sharp.

*I could go home,* she thought. There weren't any appointments in her calendar, and it was extremely unlikely that anyone would bother slogging their way through this mess to come and see her, this late in the afternoon—

*But if they did,* she finished, not without bitterness, *they'd* really *need me, and anyway, being out in this weather appeals even less than sitting here and listening to the clock tick.*

She watched through the moving blur of rain on the window as a plastic lemonade bottle negotiated a series of rapids across the street, wondering vaguely if it was going to escape the maw of the storm drain in its path or simply vanish into the darkness of the undercity. Into the coigns and brick-arched vaults of Bazalgette's Victorian sewers, where anything might be waiting for it.

*I hope the ghouls are all right,* Greta thought, not for the first time. They lived in the deep tunnels under the city, in the places rarely if ever visited by humans; she knew they were more than bright enough to have evacuated the lowest-lying tunnels as soon as the weather really turned vicious, but it was still a present worry in the back of her mind. Presumably they could, if necessary, seek shelter in the cellar of Edmund Ruthven's house, as they'd done once before under rather different circumstances. Assuming the cellar wasn't already full of water.

She hadn't heard from Ruthven in several days, and allowed herself a brief flicker of resentment at the fact that he was hundreds of miles away, on the Continent, probably having an absolutely lovely time with his unsuitable boyfriend—and thus not around to let *her* stay in his Embankment mansion until the weather stopped being quite so vile. Resentful or not, the fact that he was not only traveling, a thing he hadn't done much of for about two hundred years, but doing so in the company of said unsuitable boyfriend, was something Greta found enormously pleasing.

She'd known Ruthven all her life—he was a friend of the family, had extended his generosity to her father before her—and for most of that acquaintance he'd been thoroughly single and stayed firmly ensconced in his large and luxurious townhome, the end of a block of buildings separating Inner Temple Gardens from the Embankment, stirring abroad only very occasionally on some philanthropic venture or other. It hadn't been until the previous autumn that he'd felt up to leaving London, let alone the country, for the first time in decades. Granted, the house had been partially destroyed by fire at the time and he'd had nowhere to stay, but still.

That journey—a holiday in Greece, one which he'd shared with Greta herself, along with Varney and another friend of theirs—had been the first of many, including the trip to Paris this past spring during which he'd met an equally stylish and sardonic vampire who'd come home with him after some complicated subterranean adventures. Which she didn't care to recall in close detail. It was much nicer to think about Ruthven's warm bright kitchen and the luxurious spare beds, plural, which he had available for guests; nobody did hospitality like a vampire.

Greta was, in fact, still so wrapped up in the thought of that luxurious home, and the way her old friend seemed to have lost decades off his not inconsiderable age now that he had someone to share it with, that it took her three rings to notice the phone's renewed demand for her attention.

"Dr. Helsing," she said when she picked up, aware that she

didn't sound quite as brisk and in charge as usual, not caring enough to really make the effort.

"Greta," said the voice on the other end, warm with relief. "Thank *God* you're in town. Are you terribly busy?"

She sat up. It had been at least a year since she'd talked to Ed Kamal, at a supernatural medicine conference in Germany; his job kept him too busy for much by way of socialization. "Ed? No, I'm not in the middle of anything, what's the matter?"

"I absolutely hate to spring this on you with no notice whatsoever, and I completely understand if you can't do it," he said, sounding both apologetic and hurried.

"Do *what*?"

"I—something's come up and I have to go back to Cairo, more or less immediately, and there's—no one I can really leave in charge of the spa, nobody with the experience to oversee the patients we've got, nobody who really understands the therapeutic regimens and the principles we're using—you're so good with mummies, and it'd only be for a few months, four at most—"

Greta stared at the phone, and then at the rain spattering against the windowpane. "Wait," she said. "Let me make sure I've got this right. You want *me* to spend four months in *Marseille* overseeing *Oasis Natrun*."

"I know it's a hell of a lot to ask," Dr. Kamal said, sounding wretched. "I mean—my nursing staff's fantastic, I'd never want to imply they're not competent to keep the place going, but I need a medical director who knows this stuff inside and out and—we have some particularly tricky clinical cases at the moment and I can't leave without being sure they're going to have an expert managing their care whom I trust without question—"

Oasis Natrun. The private and exclusive mummy spa and health resort. Where Greta had sent her own mummy patients who could afford a course of treatment, whenever she possibly could. Where cutting-edge therapeutic, restorative, and cosmetic techniques were being pioneered all the time.

Which was located in *the south of France.* Where it almost certainly was not currently pouring with rain.

"—Ed," she said, cutting him off in the middle of another compound-complex self-referential loop of apology, "I think the phrase I am looking for here is *oh God yes please.*"

The mummy Amennakht was over three thousand years old and on his third set of replacement fingers, but this didn't severely impact his typing speed. On a good day he was capable of about sixty-five words per minute.

It was useful to be able to work from home—he hated the word *telecommute*, he wasn't *commuting* at all, that was the point—when you couldn't exactly go out in public without people noticing certain peculiarities in your personal appearance. Nobody cared what you looked like when you existed solely as a source of e-mails and completed assignments.

(Sometimes, when he was feeling particularly philosophical, Amennakht reflected that in certain senses the function really did shape the entity: he *was* a Thing That E-mailed, and a Thing That Sent in Code, and he could *feel* the metaphysical parameters of that in a way that people who weren't largely made up of magic would never be able to manage.)

The other benefit of working from home was that you could fuck around on the Internet as much as you liked, as long as you were getting the job done, and no nosy manager could peer over your shoulder to read your RP posts or critique your Twitter banner image design. Amennakht had a couple of Slack channels open almost all the time, while he coded; he was expert at flicking back and forth between windows without taking his hands off the ergonomic split keyboard. Right now he was half paying attention to an ongoing conversation about the likelihood that anyone would ever design a functional fusion reactor while he slogged away in SQL. *Not in my lifetime, however long that is,* he thought, and smiled a little: his face creaked faintly. He at least *had* most of a face; he considered himself pretty good-looking, as Class B revenants went, even if he did need rewrapping rather badly.

He was halfway through a line when abruptly, *viciously,* a wave of terrible dragging weakness flooded through him. It felt like being pushed downward by a sudden G-force—the strength he was using to simply sit upright at the desk was not there, and he both felt and heard himself creak as he slumped forward—he felt like he was *falling*—

And just as suddenly as it had come, the feeling was gone. Well. Mostly gone.

Amennakht sat up again, slowly, with another creak. He

still felt faintly weak and dizzy, but the awful sensation of weight had disappeared as if it had never been there at all.

He looked around. Nothing at all had changed: same cluttered apartment overlooking Boston's Mattapan neighborhood, same stacks of magazines, same canopic jars sitting in a neat row on the mantelpiece. Nor did he himself look any different.

He saved his work—that was automatic, a completely ingrained habit—and then after a moment closed out of the fusion reactor discussion channel and opened a rather different one, with a more complicated name. There weren't many people on it at this time of night: mostly *his* people were either in various parts of Western Europe or in Egypt, and the time difference was kind of hilarious.

*Weird question*, he typed after a minute of staring at the screen, *has anyone else had a kind of... dizzy spell out of nowhere recently?*

Nothing. He went on staring, the dim pinpoint reflections of his eyes looking back at him. And then, from his friend Mentuhotep—what he was doing up at four in the morning London time was a mystery in itself—*You, too?*

A glossy black sedan slipped out of the usual chaotic honking mess of traffic on New York's Fifth Avenue to pull up precisely within the NO STANDING ANYTIME zone in front of the Metropolitan Museum of Art; the uniformed driver got out, as impassive and impressive as his vehicle, and came around to open the back door.

The woman who got out was no longer young. It was impossible to determine how old she *was*: behind the enormous sunglasses she had the kind of peculiar agelessness common to wealthy women with high-priced plastic surgeons at their beck and call, and yet the visible parts of her skin appeared neither artificially taut nor sagging. Her hair, cut and shaped expertly, was silver-gilt, the pale shimmer of electrum; her clothes and shoes, in shades of sand and beige, spoke of stratospheric price tags. The bag the driver handed to her, hooking the straps over one negligently outstretched wrist, was a cinnabar-red crocodile Birkin.

Without a word, she turned and began to climb the monumental steps—moving with perhaps more energy and confidence on four-inch heels than might have been expected.

Inside, the security officer whose job it was to peer into people's handbags attempted to stop her, and found himself transfixed with a hazel glare that felt like a physical blow—for only a second or two, before the sunglasses went back on and the bag was opened with an *I suppose I must put up with this ridiculous nonsense* sigh. He blinked hard, seeing afterimages, squinted past them into her bag, stammered out a *thank you, ma'am* that shook, and was extremely glad when she reclaimed her property and stalked on past.

Two people were waiting for her at the octagonal information desk in the center of the entry hall. "Ms. Van Dorne," said the taller of them, hurrying forward. "I'm so sorry about that—we do have to make sure no one is carrying anything dangerous—"

The woman cut him off with a gesture of one gloved hand—and did not pause, clearly expecting the others to keep up with her, turning to head toward the Egyptian wing of the museum. She was moving quite quickly, despite the crowd; it seemed as if people simply and instinctively got out of her way, parting to let her through. The others had a little more difficulty shouldering their way past tourists standing in line.

"As I said on the telephone," she said, still walking—*stalking* was more accurate—"my concern today is the integrity of your security systems in the areas of the museum where my artifacts are displayed. Unless I'm satisfied that they will be completely safe here, I have no interest in going any further with this loan agreement."

"Of course," said the museum's director, the taller of the two staff accompanying her. He glanced across at the chief curator of the Egyptian Art Department, who swallowed hard.

"We quite understand your safety concern, Ms. Van Dorne," she said, "especially in light of the recent series of antiquity thefts. Of course, all the incidents I'm aware of have involved private collections or auction houses, rather than museums...?"

"Precisely," said the woman, stopping to stare at a statue; the others had to stop as well. "Which is why I believe it's possible that my most valuable items will be safer *here*. Possible, but not certain. I understand you have installed a particularly sensitive security system for certain new acquisitions?"

"Yes, of course," said the chief curator, "I'd be happy to show you—just this way."

The curator led the three of them past the reconstructed Tomb of Perneb, into the smaller rooms deeper into the collection. They drew stares as they went: Ms. Van Dorne's heels clicked briskly against the terrazzo tile of the floor, and the silver-gilt hair and the huge black shades made a noticeable impression.

It was entirely characteristic of Leonora Irene Van Dorne, thought the curator, not only to keep her oversized Dior sunglasses on indoors, but to wear as her only visible ornament an absolutely exquisite three-thousand-year-old lapis scarab that the curator could not look at for very long without wanting to snatch it away and put it safely in a *case*. The last time this particular museum patron had been by to inspect the display of a donated artifact, several months ago, she'd worn a gold-and-carnelian pendant in the shape of a falcon, which the curator tentatively dated to the reign of Senusret II, 1897–1878 BCE.

Ms. Van Dorne *knew* it, too. That was almost worse: she wasn't just the kind of rich that liked to collect ancient Egyptian art and artifacts, she had *studied* them—on her own, of course, as far as the curator knew she'd never gotten a degree in it—and was considered something of an authority on Middle Kingdom jewelry. She *knew* the absolute irreplaceable importance of the pieces she was wearing, and did it anyway. They were her property: she could do whatever she liked with them, wear them to walk her dog or go grocery shopping or do whatever esoteric kind of yoga she undoubtedly did—no one that age should look that good, move that fluidly. She had to be in her late fifties at the least—the curator knew that for a fact, since the Van Dorne family was sufficiently important to have their own Wikipedia page—but she looked a hell of a lot younger than that.

*And now I'm just being catty,* the curator told herself. *So she looks great, so what? She's the kind of rich that can get her* everything *lifted, not just her face, which means she's the kind of rich that this place desperately needs, and she just happens to like playing the cultured philanthropist as well as the amateur scholar. You can't argue with endowment support at that level. You have to keep her happy, that's all that matters.*

Aloud she said, "And this is our most recently installed case. As you can see, temperature and humidity are under complete control as with all our other installations, but this particular case has certain security upgrades that we believe will meet all your requirements, Ms. Van Dorne, and set your mind at rest."

"You know," said Edmund Ruthven, leaning against a handy block of two-thousand-year-old stone, "you were absolutely one hundred percent right about this."

He had his hands in his pockets, sleeves rolled up, dark red silk shirt open at the throat, a wing of glossy black hair drooping over his left enormous silver eye, and could have stepped directly out of a fashion editorial; looking effortlessly chic and art-directed was one of the more irritating of the classic vampire characteristics. The Roman Forum provided a particularly effective backdrop at the moment: pale tumbled stone and ruined columns against the racing clouds of an autumn sky.

"Are you perhaps having some sort of cerebral incident?" said his companion, thinking how nice it would be if all the tiresome modern railings—and the tiresome modern human tourists—could be removed for the sake of aesthetics. "You *never* admit it when I'm right. What am I right about, anyway? Of the many things that come to mind just at the moment."

The companion's name was Grisaille, and he, too, looked intensely stylish with a cigarette carelessly held between two dark fingers and his long black coat rippling in the breeze. Unlike Ruthven's, his eyes had gone bright red during the change, and he didn't bother with contacts to camouflage this fact. He favored one shoulder ever so slightly due to an injury sustained that spring, in the catacombs under Paris, and only *partly* did so for effect.

"This," said Ruthven, gesturing. Grisaille watched as he flicked the hair back, and as it slipped down over his eye once more, very black against the alabaster of his skin. "Rome. All this. I haven't been here for centuries; I'd forgotten how much I like the place, even if it *is* lousy with churches. I was having a perfectly lovely time in Bavaria, but I'm glad you talked me into coming here after all." They had been in Italy now for two lazy, self-indulgent, and absolutely wonderful days.

"Oh, that," said Grisaille. "I'd about had enough of the old place, anyway—it was sort of nice to go back there, to see Ingolstadt again, see where it all happened, tying up loose ends, style of thing." He hooked two fingers in a sardonic air quote. "*Closure.* Consider me entirely closed. *Fermé. Chiuso.* And I wanted to throw sticks into the Tiber and get riotously drunk on partygoers in Trastevere and make everybody in the world die of jealousy."

His tone was light, as it almost always was; right now the lightness was very deliberate. About two hundred years ago he'd been peripherally involved in a very nasty situation featuring a school-friend's attempts to resurrect the dead, and his own failure to stop this friend from trying the unthinkable had been weighing on Grisaille ever since. This spring's events in Paris had made his life both simpler and more complicated—and introduced him to Edmund Ruthven and his big shiny silver eyes, which was an *excellent* complication.

Ruthven was watching him, head tilted slightly. "Well," he said. "We can certainly manage two out of those three, although I doubt my capability to make everyone in the world jealous. Just most of it."

"They will be jealous of *me*," said Grisaille comfortably, "the reason being *I'm* the one who gets to go back to the hotel with *you* at the end of the night and take off all your clothes, possibly with my teeth, and *they* do not."

Very faint color came and went in Ruthven's face. Grisaille grinned: it was always intensely rewarding to elicit that reaction. "Well," Ruthven said, "if you put it like that. Give me one of your cigarettes and let's move on before another herd of tourists is upon us; this place is filling up."

"Your wish is my command," said Grisaille, presenting his black cigarette case with a flourish. "Back to the hotel? The sun's beginning to get a little insistent, I think."

Ruthven nodded. "Back to the hotel. And...if you were

particularly moved to explore the logistical difficulty of undoing buttons with your teeth, I do not believe I would desire to stop you."

That faint brush of color high on his cheeks was back; he smiled, and Grisaille thought all over again, as he had countless times over the past six months, *I am in so much trouble here*—and a moment later *and I so* want *to be.*

# CHAPTER 2

Greta's clinic wasn't among the grandest and most ostentatious of the Harley Street premises: like most of the rest of the street, the first story consisted of pale rusticated stonework with a balcony running along the whole of the second floor, surmounted by an additional two stories of brickwork. Her reception and waiting area, exam room, and the surgical operatory took up most of the first floor—the equipment was so heavy, she hadn't much wanted to risk locating it any higher up—and her office was on the second floor, along with a small conference room, a kitchen, and storage; she had set up two private bedrooms on the floor above, for the infrequent times when she really did need to keep someone for observation overnight. The upper floors were accessible not just by the stairs but by a small neat elevator; her father had put the original in at great expense when he'd bought the place, and Greta's recent refit of the premises had included a replacement for the elevator as well as for her medical equipment: one more thing for which she had Edmund Ruthven to thank.

In fact, it had been Ruthven who'd introduced her to several of her extremely helpful friends, some of whom were currently sitting around Greta's conference table and drinking tea out of mismatched but cheerful mugs. Outside it continued to pour; two out of three of her guests were still a trifle damp from their travels, and the third only looked faintly smug about the fact that *her* hair not only didn't seem to get wet in the rain, but was—apparently of its own accord—absently tying and untying scarlet tendrils of itself around her hoop earrings.

"You do *know* how distracting that is, right?" Greta said, watching. Nadezhda Serenskaya, jobbing witch and general eccentric, grinned. Beside her sat her girlfriend Hippolyta, and on the other side Anna Volkov, Greta's part-rusalka nurse practitioner, who was also trying not to smile.

"It's easier to just let it do what it wants," Nadezhda said, "than try to keep it contained. It likes to take hairpins out and drop them on the floor with a clatter at the most inconvenient moments—it's got roughly the intelligence of a stunned iguana, but it's very determined when it wants to be."

Prehensile hair was not a trait Greta had encountered before she'd met Nadezhda, but it was apparently linked to the particular strain of magic Nadezhda's family had inherited; a strain which, fortuitously, seemed to work rather well with the ancient Egyptian magics involved in Class B revenant medicine. Nadezhda wasn't as good as an actual mummy would be, of course, in terms of the pronunciation and inflections of the spells needed during procedures and when placing amulets, but she was certainly good enough to satisfy Greta's need for the chanting side of mummy treatment.

It was one of the reasons she had been able to agree to take over for Ed at the spa for a few months: Nadezhda, Hippolyta, and Anna were entirely capable of running the clinic in Greta's absence. "Okay," she said. "*Technically* only Anna's supposed to be operating the equipment, if you want to get legal about it, but Dez, I know you know perfectly well how to work most of the stuff: use your best judgment. Hippolyta, you're going to be in charge of the administrative side of things, but at least I've got a decent computer system these days and it's not too excruciating to use."

Hippolyta Hollister was American and blonde and cheerfully sardonic and also, like Greta herself, entirely ordinary and human, without any supernatural abilities whatsoever. Greta found it somewhat refreshing not to be the only one. "I'm all over it, Greta," Hippolyta said, "don't worry about a thing. Your records will remain in tip-top shape, I promise."

"You're good at organizing things," said Nadezhda fondly. "Things, and sometimes people. There's appointments to be made and supplies to order and telephones to answer and peculiar people to greet; you won't be bored."

"Trust me," said Hippolyta with a smile. "I'm looking forward to this. Only I *am* gonna have to insist that we get this place a decent coffeemaker, stat. I can survive only so long on Starbucks."

"I'll allow it," said Greta. "Now, all my scheduled surgeries are going to have to be taken over by Dr. Richthorn in Hounslow; I've talked to him already and he's agreed to adjust his schedule to accommodate it, but all the patients need to be contacted about the change. Everything else you three can take care of here, I think, without too much difficulty, and you'll be able to call me pretty much whenever you need to, if I'm not with a patient. Anna will handle all the prescriptions. I've told the staff over at the Beaumont Street pharmacy that I'll be gone for a while and to expect a lot of scripts from NP Volkov instead.

"With regard to explaining the change in practitioners, Dez, I think it's probably best if you just do what you've been doing every time you step in for me: tell patients exactly what you are, a medically trained witch. Most of them will be absolutely fine with that, but if they're not, no one can argue with Anna's credentials. We'll keep the hours the same unless there seems to be a reason to change them."

She sat back, looking at the three of them. "Unless anybody's got questions, let's go show Hippolyta the rest of the place and how the computer system works—and then I've got to go, Varney's picking me up at three."

Nadezhda smiled. "I promise I won't let him see the hair doing its thing this time."

"See that you don't," said Greta, pink but smiling back. Varney had not reacted terribly well to Nadezhda's hair demonstrating its curiosity the single time they'd been seated together at Ruthven's dinner table, for which she couldn't really blame him, but it had still been hilarious to watch him flail at an importunate tendril trying to investigate his ear. "We're going straight to the airport, my flight's this evening, assuming it can take off in solid rain instead of actual air."

"Sun and fun in the south of France," said Anna. "You'd better send us *lots* of postcards, Greta. *Lots* of them."

"I'll see what I can do."

There was something pleasantly soporific about being driven through heavy rain; the rhythmic creaking of the wipers and the steady hissing of the wheels combined to make Greta feel drowsy and content. It was also nice not to be the one who had to drive in it.

Sir Francis Varney owned two automobiles: a small and intensely high-strung MG convertible and an elderly but dignified Mercedes CLA 250. He had only very recently reentered the world after spending a great many decades in hibernation, and the adjustment to the present day had not been easy—but once he had begun it, he had learned very fast how to pretend to be a person. She couldn't picture how exactly he had gotten a driver's license, or gone car shopping: Varney simply *did* things, quietly and unobtrusively, and at some point he had apparently determined that he should become a motorist, and proceeded to cause this to occur.

He drove well, Greta thought, watching the long mobile hands on the wheel and shift knob as he moved in and out of traffic. Not quite as effortlessly as Ruthven, who had apparently actually driven ambulances in the Blitz, but certainly well enough for her to feel confident enough to doze.

Which she did not want to do. It would be four months before she saw him again—that was the only real drawback to this whole business, really, the fact that she was going to miss the hell out of him—and she did not want to waste any of the time she still had in Varney's company.

Greta smiled at herself. It was perhaps not surprising that she should have reached her mid-thirties before experiencing actual romance; she lived a particularly strange life, in a liminal space between the mundane and the supernatural, and it had been practically impossible to find anyone with shared life experience, even if she'd had the time to spend on the search. Nor was it surprising that the person she'd happened to fall for was a vampyre: most of Greta's friends weren't human, one way or another. It was, however, amusing that someone as courtly and old-fashioned as Sir Francis Varney should have developed a thing for *her*: she was uncompromisingly modern, mostly practical, and devoid of glamour except for when Ruthven had done her makeup properly.

"You're very quiet," he said, glancing over at her. His voice was the most beautiful thing about him; tall and spare, long-faced, melancholy, he lacked the effortless style of the classic draculine vampires, but the voice was absolutely lovely. "Are you all right?"

Greta laughed. "I'm fine," she said. "Just thinking unimportant things."

"Worried about the clinic?"

"No. Not really; I know Anna and Dez between them can run it, especially with Hippolyta to back them up on the admin support—and it's not like it's the *only* supernatural-medicine care location in the metropolis." She yawned. "I don't particularly like Dr. Richthorn as a person, but he's perfectly competent and he was jolly kind to agree to take my surgeries for a couple of months. It's nice not to be the single care provider in a specialization."

"Speaking of which, Emily's getting along very well," he said. "Studying for the application to the Royal Veterinary College. Learning how to be a vet seems even more difficult than learning how to be a doctor."

"It absolutely is," said Greta. "Well, harder than being a *human* doctor. You have to learn so many different physiologies. I sympathize." Emily was a young vampire—very young, nineteen, and would remain nineteen for the rest of her existence—whom Varney and Greta and several other people had liberated from a bad situation in Paris earlier in the year, shortly after she'd been turned. Currently she was living at Varney's country house and helping take care of the rescued monsters while she adjusted to the limits of her new existence, with Varney as a sort of guide along the way. It had done Varney good as well, Greta thought, to have someone to *teach*: it was a lot harder for him to slip into his usual dolorous melancholia with someone young and energetic around the place. Even when beset by ridiculous weather.

"She is...determined," said Varney with a little flicker of a smile. "Most determined. You should have seen her stalking around with sandbags the other day, engaged in flood mitigation."

"How *is* the place, anyway?"

"Battered," he said. "And partly underwater. I keep wondering if this rain is quite natural."

"Natural?" she asked, raising an eyebrow.

"Non-occult in nature. It seems a little improbable that it should rain steadily for this long, without some sort of—I don't know, sinister *purpose* behind it. I mean, where does all the water even come from?"

"That's climate change for you," said Greta, who had in fact been thinking about arks not so long ago. "At least we aren't having hurricanes and wildfires and fifteen feet of snow, even if everyone is going to start growing algae if it goes on much longer."

"Climate change," Varney said disdainfully. "I don't know if that's worse or better than malign supernatural force. It seems *untidy*, man-made weather change. Humans shouldn't be able to have that kind of influence; they misuse it."

"They do," said Greta with a smile. Varney changed down to pass a particularly anxious driver, and she watched his hand on the gearshift, *how* he drove; pushing the knob down just with the fingers of his left hand, and then up into fifth again with it cupped in his half-closed palm. It was the gesture of someone entirely confident in their ability to do a thing, without having to think about it. She could clearly remember how *un*sure he had been of himself, back in the beginning, when they'd first met: he'd been wounded by a peculiar weapon and she had been called in to treat him, and the first thing he had done on introduction was instinctively lunge at her with his teeth bared. And then apologized profusely, in a fit of miserable embarrassment. That Sir Francis was a far cry from the one beside her, Greta thought, and then: *I'm lucky.*

Since that time he'd been involved in a rather complicated mess—the business in Paris, in which she'd managed to get herself abducted by the sort of vampires who wore body glitter unironically and called themselves the Kindred; Greta had extricated herself from that particular situation on her own, and had promptly gone right back down underneath the city with the aid of Varney and Ruthven and several others in order to deal with the coven and an associated tear in the fabric of reality. She tried generally not to think too hard about the tear in reality; that had been *weird shit* on a level difficult to comprehend, and had required the assistance of Greta's old family friend, the demon Fastitocalon, and a couple of jobbing remedial psychopomps with improbable names, and—all in all it was a pleasure to contemplate four months of just *doing her job* in one of the world's premier facilities for her particular favorite specialization, rather than getting involved in anything metaphysical. Going back to France wasn't something that frightened her, despite the previous experience. France hadn't been all bad; after the dust had settled, while Greta went about patching up their various war wounds, she and Varney had found themselves alone in a quiet corner long enough to kiss for the first time.

She'd been a little afraid that it had been nothing more than the aftereffects of desperation, that he would have thought better of the entire business; but when Francis Varney made decisions, he made them apparently all at once, and wholeheartedly. That had been the first of a great many kisses, some exploratory and uncertain, some rather more enthusiastic and inexact.

They were—taking it slow, however, physically, and she was surprised to find she didn't mind: being *courted* was something new and rather lovely in its novelty. She did, however, hope like hell that Varney could be convinced to visit her in the south of France at least *once* during this trip, and that perhaps the romantic surroundings might be sufficient impetus for him to lose his last inhibitions and take her to bed properly.

"Greta," he said, bringing her out of the reverie. "I—I'm going to miss you."

It sounded like an apology. Like a confession. She smiled, reached over to put a hand on his shoulder for a moment. "I'm going to miss you, too. You know that, right?"

"I—logically, yes, that makes sense, it's just—not so easy to believe in my heart. After so long. But I'm trying."

"I know you are," she said, "and I know it's hard. You've been alone for centuries and you've had a very thin time of it even when you *were* in relationships. It's all right, Varney. I do *know* it's difficult."

Varney looked over at her, faint color mantling his cheekbones. "That's so strange in itself," he said. "That anyone should know, or—or understand, once they *did* know, and not run the other way. I'm not used to it."

"*Get* used to it," she told him with a smile. "I'm not going anywhere. I mean. Other than to Marseille, but that doesn't matter, it's—I want to be something you *can* be sure of, no matter where either of us happen to be. Varney—*Francis*—I'm not going to think better of this, and decide to throw it over."

"Ever?" he asked, and then had to snap his attention back to the road.

"I'm pretty sure," she said. "Ever."

"Ah," he said, and navigated around a Rover that wasn't sure what lane it wanted to be in. "Well. That's—good. That's very good. I'm—glad to hear it."

Greta knew that tone, the retreat-into-impenetrable-politeness, and also what it signified, and she waited patiently. After several minutes he ran a hand through his hair and said all at once, a small dam breaking and spilling out the words, "That's awfully convenient, because I do not think I will, or *can*, change my mind, either, and—do you *like* diamonds, I know you don't wear big fancy rings because the settings catch on your whatsit, exam gloves, but—there are designs that wouldn't, and—*do* you like them, because that's the first thing that matters?"

Greta could feel all the little hairs on her arms and legs stand up at once, a long shimmer-wave of sensation; her face went hot for a moment. *This* she had not expected exactly, or—not for a long time yet, if at all. She had sort of known that one of the reasons Varney hadn't taken her to bed yet, other than his natural reticence and disinclination to inflict his dead and monstrous person upon the living, et cetera et cetera, was that he was almost certainly not very comfortable with sex outside of wedlock. Now, in the moment—despite all the time she'd spent turning over the idea and never quite being sure how she might react, if it ever happened—she found there was no hesitation whatsoever.

"Yes," she told him with a cloudless smile.

Being near a very happy vampyre was a little intoxicating. He kept a strong hold over his thrall—the sanguivore trait they used as a hunting technique, a kind of intense hypnotic control—but nonetheless she could *feel* the pleasure emanating from him. When he could look away from the road for a moment, she was a little surprised at how *much* his face changed, when he was this pleased with the world; he'd never be beautiful, not like Ruthven, but the joy lit his face up, transformed the sharp lines and hooded eyes into something quite different. Just for that moment Greta thought she saw the face of Varney as he'd been alive, all those centuries ago, before all the weight of sin and death and misery came down on him in their repeated waves.

"Then you shall have them," he said. "And—if it is not too disruptive to your patients and to your schedule at the spa—I should so very much like to bring them to you sooner rather than later."

"You are very welcome," she said, and felt that she was saying many things at once. "Please come, whenever you can, whenever you like; I'll miss you terribly."

All around them the ceaseless pelting of the rain, the swish-thump of the wipers in their Sisyphean task, the blurred tail-lights of other cars no longer seemed to matter at all: they might as well have been in a summerhouse on some long-ago estate, or in a gold-lit ballroom, or on the surface of the moon. Varney took her hand in his, lifted it to his cold lips, kissed it, feeling like a promise.

"Then I will," he said, and the world came back.

It was more of a relief than Greta would have liked, flying direct to Marseille rather than connecting through Charles de Gaulle. She *didn't* harbor ill will against Paris, but there was something undeniably unsettling about the idea of being so very near to the places where she'd been held prisoner not that long ago.

The flight was short and entirely uneventful: she spent it rereading articles on mummy medicine on her laptop. There was bound to be a somewhat sharp learning curve, despite her years of experience: she knew Oasis Natrun had absolutely up-to-the-minute equipment which put hers to shame; it would take her some concentrated effort to get up to speed, and she was looking forward to the opportunity to learn.

Ed Kamal was waiting for her in the airport. He looked exactly as he had in Germany: tall, rangy, the skin around his eyes perpetually darker regardless of his level of sleep deprivation. He wore a linen shirt with the collar open and the sleeves rolled up, the pale fabric a pleasant contrast to his dark skin, and looked less like a doctor and more as if he'd just come from a central-casting audition for Intrepid Adventurers; he smiled when he saw her, but Greta thought his mind was at least partly on something else.

"Greta," he said, and strode forward to shake her hand and

take her luggage, despite her protestations that she could manage. "Thank you so much for coming, I can't tell you how much I appreciate this—I couldn't leave the place in anybody else's hands, there simply *isn't* anyone I'd trust who could drop everything and come over to play locum for four months who knows anything about the specialty."

"It's my pleasure, Ed," she said. "Did you *know* it's been raining for approximately forever back at home? I notice that it is not raining even a tiny little bit in these parts, which feels like a gift. Really, I can carry that, it isn't heavy."

He gave a rueful smile and relinquished one of her suitcases. "Fair enough. This way—it's not a long trip, you should be able to get there in time to enjoy the sunset from the terrace."

She followed him. "I thought it was all the way up in the mountains above the town."

"It is," said Dr. Kamal, and she realized that instead of leading her toward the taxi rank or the airport's parking lot, they were heading for general aviation—the part of the airport that handled private aircraft.

She was beginning to get the idea that perhaps her mental image of the place they were heading lacked certain important details. Dr. Kamal grinned at her; the grin turned into actual laughter at her expression when he led her to a gleaming and very beautiful—and new—helicopter.

"You should see your face," he said.

"I didn't know Oasis Natrun had its own *helicopter*," said Greta, wide-eyed. "How much money do you actually *have*?"

"A thoroughly vulgar amount. Come on, let's get going. I

have to be back here for a flight to Cairo this evening; the schedule's pretty tight."

"Yes, of course," she said, and climbed in. The interior of the helicopter was configured as an air ambulance, to accommodate stretcher cases—or patients still in their original coffins, she thought, and had to smile—with several seats also available for ambulatory passengers and their medical attendants. It was undoubtedly the most elegant and well-appointed ambulance she'd ever seen, and she said so.

"It's necessary," Dr. Kamal said. "So many of our patients need absolute discretion and privacy; being able to provide secure and entirely confidential air transport to and from the facility has improved our services enormously. It's—like a great many of our large pieces of equipment—paid for with funds from a private foundation."

*Extremely*, Greta thought, and then had to swallow as the pilot pulled up on the collective pitch control and the tarmac fell away beneath them, frictionless, unnerving.

They didn't talk much on the short ride—for one thing, Greta was far too distracted by the scenery outside her window to hold any kind of serious conversation—but as the helicopter began to descend, Dr. Kamal leaned over to peer out of Greta's side.

"There it is," he said, and the warmth of pride in his voice was obvious. At first Greta didn't see what he was pointing out—the pale rock and scrubby vegetation below them looked like the rest of the landscape—and then, with the sudden shift of a magic-eye picture, the shapes resolved.

Oasis Natrun was partly *built into the hill.* Which made sense, when you thought about it—mummies were most comfortable in rock-cut tombs—and also significantly decreased its visibility. She couldn't see how far back the rock-cut part extended, but the surface section of the complex consisted of a series of round-to-oval pavilions connected with corridors and steps, cantilevered out from the hillside. All the colors had been designed to blend into the surrounding landscape. The whole complex was tucked into a triangular valley, the confluence of three streambeds meeting in a Y.

"There are major wards on every approach," said Dr. Kamal. "We have them checked weekly. No one who doesn't already know it's here is going to be able to see it. There's one road in and out, and it's gated several times. Seven, in fact."

Greta could see the road now, a narrow but very well graded pale ribbon leading down from a wide turnaround area, out into the rest of the world. A fleeting sense of claustrophobia closed over her, just for a moment—she would be isolated up here for four months, partly living underground—and then faded again.

The helicopter descended smoothly, so quiet inside that it was only by looking at the dust kicked up by the rotor wash that Greta could get an idea of how powerful a machine it actually was. They landed on the wide turnaround space, waiting for that dust to subside before climbing out, and Greta was only a little surprised when she checked her watch to find out that the whole ride had taken less than fifteen minutes. The sun was low in the west, but the light hadn't begun to change color just yet.

Dr. Kamal picked up her suitcases again and smiled. "Welcome," he said. "I hope you'll like it here, I really do—I'll introduce you to the staff and then I really must be going, I'm sorry to have to leave like this but I need to catch that plane."

"Ed," she said, smiling, "it's *fine*, I understand, and give me back at least one of my goddamn suitcases, okay?"

He smiled back at her, a crooked charming little smile, and handed over her bag. "Absolutely, Interim Medical Director."

"I like the sound of that," said Greta, and let him lead her inside.

*café.*, in Greenwich Village, all lowercase italic, punctuation included, was the kind of coffee shop that changed its menu frequently based on individual sacks of beans and featured more gleaming borosilicate glassware than a medium-sized laboratory. The baristas, achingly hip, had an average body-mass index of approximately sixteen and wore unrelieved black without even the slightest hint of a name tag. Either they had transcended the need for individual nomenclature or you were just expected to know.

All of which was largely lost on the two individuals sitting at a corner table, being stared at—partly because in this shrine to *Coffea arabica* they were drinking weak herbal tea, and not one of the esoteric hipster blends of it at that, and partly because they were both identical and exquisitely, alarmingly beautiful. It was a kind of beauty you didn't see outside of excruciatingly expensive fashion photography or runway shows. In fact, these two kept themselves in watery chamomile by having their pictures taken; they were very pale, with white-blonde hair and absurd white eyelashes that somehow avoided looking rabbity, complexions like translucent rose-milk, perfect and androgynous bone structure, vast violet-blue eyes. They were wearing slightly different variations on the theme of grey, long coats and sweaters, scarves, all of it the kind of fiendishly simple that spoke of *price upon request*.

They were either unaware of the stares or simply didn't care about them, locked in intense and largely inaudible conversation with one another. What little could be overheard was definitely not in English, which lent further credence to the assumption that they were models: models tended to be foreign. As it happened, these two weren't from *anywhere* around here; the language in question was Enochian.

"The land is full of adulterers," one of them was saying, looking peevish. "Adulterers and harlots and infidels and beggars and *demons*. And blasphemers. For because of swearing the land mourneth; the pleasant places of the wilderness are dried up, and their course is evil, and their force is not right."

"I saw one of them again today," said the other. "The demons. The one who has an art gallery. It was walking past a *church* and didn't even *look up*. As if it didn't affect it at all. As if it didn't *notice*. I hate it here."

"Sin of hatred," said the first one, whose name was Zophiel, the way one might say *you've got spinach in your teeth*. The second one, Amitiel, looked immediately contrite.

"I shall pray for forgiveness," he—they sounded a *little* more masculine than feminine, but still fairly vague on gender—said at once. "I am not worthy to conduct this great and glorious task that is laid upon us."

"All fall short of the glory of God," said Zophiel, nodding. "I confess I wrestle with the sin of hatred myself. It is a trial, to be in this world, even if the purpose *is* glorious and just."

"*And* a madman shouted at me," Amitiel added, wrapping his hands around his teacup. "About blasphemies and the end of creation."

"Courage," said Zophiel. "Many shall be purified, and made white, and tried; but the wicked shall do wickedly: and none of the wicked shall understand; but the wise shall understand."

Amitiel sighed, smiling a little. "It's always better when you tell me holy words," he said. "It—feels nice?"

Zophiel, who—like all of his kind—had an encyclopedic memory for scripture, reached across the table to pat his companion's hand. "It will be well," he said. "We are near to our goal, to accomplishing our mission, and then we will be able to return home and leave this terrible place forever. You know it was not simple fortune that presented us with the woman to use in our efforts; it was the providence of the Almighty, a sign of favor."

"Heaven will be pleased with us," said Amitiel, not sounding entirely convinced.

"Very pleased," said Zophiel. "Soon her greed and vanity will be her undoing, and with her will come about the end. Already she has caused so much damage to the world barrier;

it cannot be long before it is breached completely, and the great and terrible battle can begin."

"Tell me again about the end time," Amitiel asked, wide blue eyes beseeching. "About the battle and the righteous destruction?"

"Not now," said Zophiel. "Not here. There are too many humans listening. But—Amitiel, you are unhappy."

"I am weak," he agreed. "You can bear the iniquities of this world better than I."

Zophiel shrugged, a slightly constrained gesture, as if he was used to something heavy weighing down his shoulders which was currently in abeyance. "Praised be God, and not my strength for it—but even though this world is heavy with sin and wickedness, there are still places that should be holy. If besmirched, still holy of a sort. I will take you to this world's Rome, and perhaps being near this version of the Great Basilica will help you feel easier in your mind."

"You take great care of me, Zophiel," said Amitiel with a little smile.

# CHAPTER 3

She had thought the interior of the spa would be *oppressive*, or at the very least remind her unpleasantly of the time she had spent in another rock-cut complex underground, but whoever had built the place had taken the danger of claustrophobia into consideration. The surface sections of the facility were airy-bright, all pale golden wood and floor-to-ceiling windows and warm stone, accented with the deep blue of lapis and the red-orange of carnelian; but the parts of Oasis Natrun that were carved into the mountainside were not only high-ceilinged and cleverly lit, but also *painted* with exquisite care. *Tomb paintings*, Greta thought, and a moment later, *That's perfect.*

Ed Kamal had introduced her to the chief of nursing, Sister Brigitte, who was approximately eight feet tall and gorgeous; she wore white scrubs that didn't look like pajamas so much as some kind of ceremonial garb, brilliant against her deep brown skin. Greta had had to look quite a long way up to meet her gaze, feeling extremely small and unimportant, while Sister Brigitte gave her a narrow-eyed once-over; it was a considerable relief when she abruptly smiled and offered her hand. "I have heard good things about you, Dr. Helsing. Welcome to Oasis Natrun." Her accent was French, noticeable but not distracting.

Now—having seen Dr. Kamal off in the helicopter, which Greta still could hardly believe was real—Sister Brigitte was showing her around the facility.

"We have a nursing staff of twenty," she said, walking with Greta through the administrative offices into the underground section of the complex. It didn't *feel* underground; the corridor felt just like any corridor in a nicely appointed office building, except for those gorgeous mural paintings. "Six of those are nurse practitioners," Sister Brigitte continued, "which is why we generally don't have more than one physician in residence. At any given time we have up to ten patients—our capacity is fifteen—but generally it's closer to six, about evenly split between clinical and resort."

"What kind of cases do you see most often?" Greta asked.

"A lot of it's cosmetic and relaxation—we have a patient at the moment who's had a total rewrap and is on complete rest for a couple of days, and one who always comes in every autumn just for the hot sand treatment—but on the clinical side it's mostly reconstructive." She looked down at Greta with a sideways smile. "Your paper on the use of layered elastic bandage to replace missing muscle is required reading, by the way."

Greta went pink. "Oh, God, I wrote that *years* ago, the field's come on a lot since then."

"Nevertheless," said Sister Brigitte. "Would you like to meet the staff first, or tour the imaging suite?"

*Imaging suite*, she thought, and had to work hard not to wrap her arms around herself in glee. Even after her clinic's recent refit, she didn't have a ton of high-end equipment at home: being here was a little like being handed the keys to a Ferrari. Still—it could wait. "Staff first, I think. And the patients. How many do you have right now?"

"Seven," said Sister Brigitte, and there was for the first time a faint hint of concern in her voice. Greta looked up at her; the beautiful face was briefly clouded. "Three resort, four clinical. One of those is partly quarantined—canopic teletherapy for TB—and we have one complicated reconstruction case."

She'd never actually seen canopic teletherapy in practice—treating the patient's individually preserved stomach, intestines, lungs, or liver separately from their body—and the clinician in her was jumping up and down in excitement. Nonetheless, that brief expression of uncertainty on the nurse's face was bothering her. Greta had a feeling Sister Brigitte was ordinarily very certain indeed.

"Is something else wrong?" she asked.

"No," said Sister Brigitte, and then, "...not really. It's—you'll see, Doctor."

*That* wasn't ominous in the slightest. Greta raised an eyebrow, and then had to walk a little faster to keep up as Sister Brigitte quickened her pace. They had been walking through the rock-cut section of the complex; now Sister Brigitte led her back toward the external pavilions. "The nurses' ready room is this way, as well as the residential quarters—all the areas assigned to humans are outside the mountain; some people find it oppressive to spend all their time underground. You have a separate residence from the rest of the staff, but there's a state-of-the-art communications system in place so that you can be contacted if a situation arises that requires your attention."

*A separate residence*, she thought. *And it's probably luxurious as hell, given the fact that this place apparently has pots and pots of money. A holiday house in the south of France,* and *I get to do my favorite part of my job at the same time.* She couldn't help smiling, even though the chief of nursing's *you'll see* suggested that all was not completely well in the state of Oasis Natrun.

Sister Brigitte checked her watch. "It's eight o'clock," she said briskly. "The night shift's begun, but you'll get to meet most of the day shift, they're likely to be having dinner—which, of course, you can have brought to your residence, we have room service."

"I'll say hello now, and talk to all of them individually in my office over the next few days," said Greta. "And the administrative staff. I like to know all the people I'm working with, even if we don't interact all that closely."

Sister Brigitte nodded with a hint of approval. "It is—good to have you here," she said after a moment. "Dr. Kamal was so relieved when you agreed to come; he trusts you."

Greta could hear the unspoken *and therefore we can trust*

*you, too*, and smiled. "I am enormously happy to be here," she said. "For a great many reasons. And I can't wait to get started, so lead on."

After saying good-bye to Greta at the entrance to airport security—he'd been overcome by an attack of sudden, awkward shyness, not sure what to *do* after such an extraordinary experience as the one they'd had in the car—Varney had driven back down to Dark Heart in the pouring rain, glancing over every now and then at the empty passenger seat, running over in his mind the way she had sounded, saying *yes*.

Asking her had been the sort of almost-impulsive decision that had characterized a lot of Varney's more terrible life choices—he'd said it and then been flooded by a vast horrible wave of terror that had tightened his fingers on the wheel and lifted all the little hairs on the back of his neck—and the moment when she had *not* said *no*, where she had—*smiled* at Varney, the way she smiled sometimes that made him feel as if all the insides of his bones were glowing warm—she'd *smiled* and she'd said *yes* and that meant, didn't it, that meant that *oh God, could this actually happen?* To *him?*

By the time he got back to the estate, melancholy-grey through the veils of rain, Varney had almost convinced himself it was impossible. Almost, but not quite; the past year and a half had been so remarkably *different* from anything he'd ever experienced that he had begun to develop the edges of a different sensibility. Instead of always simply assuming the worst, he was sometimes—not always, but sometimes—capable of *noticing* that he was assuming the worst, and capable therefore of deciding not to.

He had spent the evening going through his collection of ancient jewelry: treasure he'd accumulated throughout the ages, which had been locked away in various chests for centuries, forgotten and cobwebbed. Half of it he barely recognized: old-fashioned rose-cut diamonds, a parure of garnets like frozen wine, emeralds, pearls, a pair of sapphire earrings he couldn't imagine where he had acquired, or when. None of it, of course, was any good for the purpose Varney had in mind, which was—well, causing a ring to exist that Greta could actually wear.

And that she *liked*. He'd stared at the heap of gems scattered across the table and it had glittered back at him, utterly unhelpful. He realized that he'd never seen her *wear* a ring—and then thought, as he so often had, *She hardly knows me.*

That had set off another cascade of catastrophizing; and Varney had retired that evening absolutely sure that he'd get a text from her in the morning to the tune of, *Of course I won't marry you, what the hell was I thinking*, and taken that down with him into disturbed sleep.

In the morning he'd had to deal with another handful of small domestic crises having to do with the monster menagerie he and Greta had rescued from Paris in the spring, and spent some time with Emily tracking down and capturing several escapees from the water-garden enclosures. It was difficult to focus on one's own personal shortcomings while trotting around in Wellington boots scooping small amphibious monsters out of the undergrowth, and by the time all of the creatures had been restored to their proper enclosures and the holes in the netting repaired to ensure they remained there, Varney's dolorous mood had lightened considerably. It had lightened further to discover a text from Greta waiting for him: *This place is brilliant but I miss you.*

Not, *Actually I'm not ready for this*, or *I've changed my mind.* Just *I miss you.*

And so having stared for a little while longer at the mismatched collection of gems on his writing table, Varney had shoved the lot of them into a small case and driven *back* to London—and miraculously enough found a place to park on Harley Street itself.

Inside Greta's clinic—he'd been there once or twice before, of course—everything was warm and bright and *dry*, cheerful, ordinary. The reception desk was manned, or womanned, by a blonde whom Varney thought he'd seen at one of Ruthven's parties a few months ago; there was no one else in the little waiting area, and he paused to set his damp umbrella in the holder by the door before approaching the desk.

She looked at him with a brisk talking-to-patients smile, which broadened after a moment or two in recognition. "Sir Francis Varney?" she said, his name sounding thoroughly foreign in broad American tones.

"Er, yes," said Varney, trying like hell to remember who she was and whether he ought to have this information at his fingertips. "I'm terribly sorry to bother you but I was wondering if, ah, Miss Serenskaya was available?"

"She's in the back," said the blonde. "Just a sec, I'll get her—did you want to hang your coat up?"

"I won't take up too much of your time," said Varney, very glad she hadn't asked him precisely why he'd come in. "Thank you so much."

"No problem," she said, and disappeared through the swinging door to the part of the clinic where medicine actually occurred. Varney hadn't been back there himself; the times he'd visited while Greta was working had been limited to bringing her pastries or picking her up in his car—she'd never gotten around to replacing the ancient Mini that had been effectively destroyed during that business with the Gladius Sancti last year—and he hadn't quite wanted to intrude on the business end of her job.

The waiting area was cheerful and pleasant: mismatched armchairs of varying size and shape sat along the walls, and a collection of brightly colored toys lurked in the corner to entertain small patients. He had enough time to wander over and inspect the magazines stacked on a side table before Nadezhda Serenskaya emerged in a white coat, most of her hair knotted neatly at the back of her neck. "Sir Francis," she said, smiling. "It's nice to see you. What brings you here?"

"I, ah," he said. "I wondered if I might speak with you for a minute or two about—well, about Greta."

Her eyes narrowed slightly, but the smile stayed. "Is anything wrong? We heard from her this morning. She's settled in over at the spa and apparently having a fantastic time in the not-pouring-rain repairing mummies—"

"No, no," Varney interrupted, "as far as I know, she's fine, I just—would like to ask your advice on a matter of some importance." He knew she'd been friends with Greta for years; if anybody could offer him useful information regarding her taste in jewelry, this woman could.

Nadezhda and the blonde, whose name Varney could not tease out of the recesses of his memory, exchanged a glance he wasn't sure he liked: there seemed to be rather a lot of communication going on in that brief visual exchange. "—Of course," said the witch. "Come upstairs, we can talk in the office."

"Thank you so much," said Varney, tucking the little jewel case under his arm.

The approach to St. Peter's Square in Vatican City is—in every universe—a triumph of design, engineering, and aesthetic manipulation. It does not matter that the pale gold massifs of architecture flanking the entryway have been partly taken over by expensive boutique shops; the effect of the lines of roof and balcony and window, creating perfect orthogonals that converge in the center of the distant basilica's facade, is unchanged. It does not matter that cars and souvenir-sellers and herds of tourists blur the hallowed emptiness of the vestibule that holds its breath just before the great, open, curving arms of the colonnade begin, spread in welcome; it does not matter that the space directly before the vast stairway leading up to the church itself is blocked off with movable barricades and folding chairs. The visual and emotional impact of Bernini's peculiar genius is exactly the same.

Almost.

Look, now, from the very top of the pediment surmounting the central third of the basilica's main facade, down into the elliptical space of the piazza. Look down at the pair of individuals standing just in front of the central obelisk, stolen from Egypt thirty-seven years after the birth of Christ. Observe the way in which they stand, shoulders slightly stiffened, as if to bear the weight of something heavy sprouting from their backs.

Observe, further, that while they appear identical in their achingly chic grey clothes, one of them looks as if it is going to cry, and the other, its arm around its companion's shoulders, looks as if it would like to hit something. Both of them are staring up at the basilica's facade with an air somewhere between puzzlement and frustration—and, perhaps, something quite like betrayal. Something about all this beauty is, apparently, *wrong*.

Watch as the tearful one turns to bury its face in the other's shoulder and is held close. Watch as the angry one strokes its companion's white-gold curls. It is impossible to make out what it is saying, from this distance: presumably some attempt at comforting, phatic utterance.

And watch as the weeping figure raises its head, and looks around. Even this far away it is easy to see an expression of determination on its lovely face.

A cloud passes over the sun; briefly, momentarily, all the warmth of mellow stone and tile seems to drain out of the day. It is over quickly, but a sense of chill lingers, even after the two figures in grey have disappeared into the drifting disorder of the tourist crowd; in the square, people shiver and pull their jackets closer around themselves, absently, unconscious.

Time passes.

About four hundred miles away, Greta Helsing stood in a pleasant high-ceilinged room furnished with comfortable chairs, looking through a glass dividing wall at something she'd hitherto only ever heard about. On the other side of the wall, in what looked like a perfectly ordinary clean-room laboratory, a counter ran the full length of the room; on this counter, surrounded by monitors and equipment, sat a large rectangular glass dish about four inches deep, full of cloudy liquid, and in this dish lay something greyish and crumpled and unmistakably organic. A tube led from it to a thin green cylinder marked O2.

A little farther down the counter, a beautiful alabaster canopic jar sat with its carved baboon-head lid next to it: the god Hapi, son of Horus, protected by Nephthys.

Beside her, Sister Brigitte was explaining, "Mr. Antjau is resting in his private room at the moment; when he feels well enough, he is permitted to visit them—only to view, of course."

"It must be an extraordinarily odd experience," Greta said. "So—tell me the sequence. Lab tests to confirm TB diagnosis, and then what—how do you get the lungs *out* of the jar?"

"Dr. Kamal has come up with a particular solution to rehydrate the tissue that maintains preservation," said Sister Brigitte proudly. "It's—"

"Glycerine, sodium bicarb, alcohol, and a dilute aldehyde," Greta said. "Possibly also various oils and spirits?"

The chief of nursing narrowed her eyes briefly. "Yes, in fact. It took several months of experimentation to get the correct proportions."

"It took me almost a year of messing around with it," said Greta, "but I eventually came up with something quite similar to soften skin and muscle tissue without compromising preservation. So after the lungs are soaked in this solution, you *very carefully* remove them from the jar?"

"Very carefully indeed," said Sister Brigitte, "and it is rather unavoidably unpleasant for the patient at this step of the process. Once removed, they are placed into a prepared tray, as you see."

As they watched, a nurse in cap and gown and mask and sterile shoe covers entered from a side doorway and came along to inspect the treatment setup. "The solution contains a combination of streptomycin and isoniazid," Sister Brigitte continued, "drained and replaced once a day until bacterial titers drop below detectability. As most of our patients are completely antibiotic-naive, we don't run into many difficulties with resistant strains: streptomycin alone knocks out a good percentage of our cases."

"Makes sense," said Greta. The *Mycobacterium tuberculosis* present in Mr. Antjau's lungs, like so many mummies', had last been active thousands of years before the discovery of any useful chemotherapeutic agents; it hadn't had the chance to mutate into drug-resistant strains. "What about all the other comorbidities? I've seen so many papers in ordinary human medical journals about evidence of silicosis in mummies. I don't suppose there's a damn thing you can do about it, though." Lung disease caused by inhaling fine sand or dust particles was practically unavoidable in an environment like ancient Egypt, Greta knew.

"There is very little that can be done," Sister Brigitte agreed with a sigh. "Mr. Antjau does show signs of silicosis, as have many of our other patients, but fortunately it does not seem to bother any of them very much; in a few cases we've had to do the Opening of the Mouth ceremony again, which can help a little."

"You have someone here who can do the ceremonies *properly*?" Greta said, trying not to sound overexcited. The spells and blessings were the most difficult aspect of mummy health care: Nadezhda's magic was better than nothing, but a properly trained and qualified priest would be ideal. "And who can do things like preparing that treatment dish properly before you put the patient's lungs in? You'd have to have it inscribed with the correct spells and so on to mimic the protective effect of the canopic jar, of course, and it's difficult to get them absolutely right."

"Yes," said Sister Brigitte, looking a little surprised—and pleased. "As it happens, our records clerk is a mummy who *was* a priest of Thoth once upon a time. We're very fortunate to have Tefnakhte on staff; he knows all the spells and can pronounce things properly, he's had his hands replaced so that he can do quite delicate inscriptions, and it's such a reassurance to the patients to have one of their own involved in the magical side of things."

Thoth, of course, was the scribe-god, also spelled Djehuty; Greta thought it was entirely fitting that a person sworn to the service of recording and measuring would end up in charge of a medical records office. Another thing they were doing *right* at Oasis Natrun.

She was trying quite hard not to smile like an idiot at the sheer excitement of being here—of getting to be part of this. It was difficult; her face already ached with the effort. The whole morning, so far, had been a series of delights: waking in the luxurious bed in her private residence, so unlike her flat in Crouch End, waking to find she was really still here and still *in charge of Oasis Natrun* for a whole four months; breakfast delivered to her door, exactly as she'd requested the night before; putting on the white coat with MEDICAL DIRECTOR embroidered on the left breast, settling into the office that was Ed Kamal's but would belong to her for quite some time—all of it had made Greta want to hug herself with glee. And they had a *mummy priest* available, she'd be able to perform quite complicated operations without worrying about the spell-blessing aspect of things, and—oh, so many small but cumulative excitements.

Witnessing canopic teletherapy in action was absolutely fascinating; but she did have things to do. Beside her, Sister Brigitte discreetly checked her watch, and Greta straightened up.

She could come back and visit Mr. Antjau's lungs *after* she'd visited Mr. Antjau himself. They weren't going anywhere without medical supervision.

Doing rounds briefly took Greta all the way back to medical school, years and years ago: that had been entirely different, a herd of medical residents trailing after the attending physician as they stalked through a ward from patient to patient. She'd realized quite quickly that she didn't want to work in a hospital, even if she did stay with ordinary human medicine rather than following in her father's footsteps: there was something unpleasantly impersonal about it, like an assembly line.

This was a much nicer kind of round. The spa had only seven patients; she didn't have to hurry from one to the next. There was ample time to sit with each mummy, talk with them about their diagnoses and treatments, listen to their concerns. She had seen the resort patients first, needing to spend less time with them: Madame Bameket (here for the hot-sand-natron treatment as usual this time of year), Mr. Djedkare (cosmetic patient; total-body rewrap), and Ms. Mayet (here to relax and enjoy the luxurious service)—the latter only to introduce herself and let Ms. Mayet know that she was available for consultation if desired.

The clinical patients, Mr. Nesperennub (moderate-to-severe fungal infection), Ms. Nefrina (tendon replacement, both forearms and wrists), and Mr. Maanakhtef (comprehensive reconstruction of left foot), took up the rest of Greta's day; Mr. Antjau was sleeping, and she had no desire to disturb him simply to say hello. Nesperennub had been very unwell indeed when he'd arrived last week, and the staff had taken one look at his cultures and got him straight to the linac room. Now he was just about ready to be discharged, spending another two or three days in the resort sector of the complex to get his strength back. Mummies were prone to fungal infections, especially in unsuitably damp climates: the ancient bandages offered a perfect breeding-ground for all sorts of opportunistic spores. Nefrina—who, like a lot of mummies, worked in IT—had had her left arm's tendons replaced and was ready to undergo surgery for the right arm, which Greta was looking forward to almost as much as Nefrina was. "I can't deal with not being able to type," she'd said. "I want to get this over with," and Greta had been able to reassure her that she'd be back up to seventy words per minute in a couple of weeks.

She saw Maanakhtef last. He was propped up on pillows in bed with his damaged foot resting on a cushion, loosely covered with a linen dressing, and smiled creakily to see Greta. "Come in, come in," he said. "So you're the Dr. Helsing we've all heard so much about."

His accent was vaguely German; she thought probably he'd woken up in one of the museums there. "Hello," she said, taking a seat by his bed. "It's an enormous pleasure and a privilege to be here, and I hope I'll not disappoint. I have Dr. Kamal's notes, of course, but if you'd like to tell me about yourself..."

Mummies in Greta's experience either absolutely *loved* to talk about themselves, particularly their myriad ailments, or clammed up like a sarcophagus at the slightest probe; luckily

Maanakhtef was the former type. She was treated to a complex and detailed description of how he'd woken up to the modern world with his foot already in mediocre shape, the victim of poor embalming practices that had resulted in one foot being twisted under the other inside his bandaging; how he had tried to ignore it, the problem steadily worsening, and when he finally did seek medical help, "I was told there was nothing to be done; the bones were too badly damaged to repair, I would simply have to have the foot off." It was difficult to tell through the wrappings, but Greta was good with mummy expressions by now, and she mirrored his look of horror.

"That's dreadful," she said. "I'm so sorry you had to go through that. In my experience there is very rarely *nothing* that can be done; I've rebuilt at least one patient practically from a skeleton, and parts of that were missing. May I see your foot?"

He was clearly enjoying this. "By all means, Doctor."

Underneath the loose dressing Greta could see why a less-experienced, or less-determined, clinician might have thrown up their hands in despair: four of Maanakhtef's metatarsals, the long bones of the foot, were simply *missing*, the damage clearly visible due to a certain lack of skin coverage in the immediate vicinity. The remaining bone was cracked in several places and looked as if it was about to fall to powder at the lightest touch.

Greta put on gloves and took the magnifying-lens glasses out of her white coat's pocket, turned on the little light attached to one bow. Through the lenses she could easily see the worn joint surfaces on the remaining bones of the foot, the residual deformation from all those centuries twisted at an unnatural angle. "Mm," she said, gently tilting his foot from side to side, examining the damage. "Dr. Kamal's notes say that he's 3-D printed replacement bones for you?"

Maanakhtef was watching her, fascinated. "Yes," he said, "only the surgery got put off because, well, apparently there's a lot of work that needs to be done on my foot before the bones can go in, and they didn't want to do it right away—that gentleman with the lung trouble was very bad, I gather, and took up lots of everybody's time..."

Greta took off the glasses and looked up. She remembered Sister Brigitte, the previous evening, saying, *You'll see.*

*See what?* Greta thought. Aloud she said, "There's something else, isn't there? I'm seeing a lot of damage here, but stabilization of the joints shouldn't take very long at all if I use the right impregnating resins, and the new bones could go in as soon as—oh, call it the day after tomorrow, so there's got to be another reason they put off doing it."

Maanakhtef looked away: the little pinpoints of light that were his eyes, just visible behind the bandages, blinked on and off a few times. Greta tilted her head. "Mr. Maanakhtef?"

"It's...rather embarrassing, actually," he said. "I've—only once or twice, it's not as if it happens all the time—had these sort of *attacks* of weakness? It's over very quickly, just a few moments of vertigo, and then I'm fine."

Greta frowned, the differential-diagnostic part of her mind spinning up. "When did this start?"

"Not long ago. Since I've been here, about two and a half weeks."

"Do you remember any kind of visual disturbances, sparkles or dark spots in your vision, or smelling anything strange just before one of the attacks?"

"No, not at all—they just sort of *happen*, out of nowhere. It feels as if I have no strength at all, and I'm extremely dizzy, and then it simply stops."

"And afterward you feel all right?"

"Yes, absolutely," he said, and then, "Well... perhaps a little tired and achy, but it's difficult to tell."

"I see," said Greta. Which she didn't, yet. "Well, it does make sense that Dr. Kamal didn't want to do complicated surgery until we've worked out what's causing these spells, but I think we can at least get started preparing your joint surfaces—that won't be too uncomfortable for you, and we'll be able to put your new bones in and get them all properly attached with tendon straps and everything as soon as possible."

"Do you think I'll be able to walk properly?" he said, sounding hopeful. By *walk properly*, he meant *lurch from foot to foot with his arms held out in front of him, groaning.*

"Absolutely," said Greta. "I think once the physical therapy is over, you won't need any sort of mobility aids at all, and your pain levels will be significantly reduced."

She was going over all the potential causes for vertigo in the Class B revenant in her mind even as she patted Maanakhtef's bandaged hand and stood. "Get some rest, all right? I'll see you tomorrow, and we can get started on those joints."

"Thank you, Doctor," he said, and the depth of meaning in the words made her feel warm all over.

"It's my pleasure," she said again. "I mean that."

"Yes," he told her. "I can see you do."

# CHAPTER 4

Leonora Irene Van Dorne lived in one of the last remaining Beaux-Arts mansions in Lenox Hill that had escaped subdivision into apartments; it appeared in the archives of the Museum of the City of New York as simply *the Van Dorne house*, complete with ancient gelatin-silver photographs of the interior as it had been in 1900, cluttered with knickknacks and oppressive with velvet hangings and William Morris wallpaper. Ms. Van Dorne's great-grandfather had built the house in the 1870s, and it had remained in the family ever since—although that venerable gentleman might not recognize it in its current state.

Ms. Van Dorne had turned it into a museum. A private one, to be sure, and one whose collection was among the most exquisite ever assembled. Other wealthy ladies of a certain age might collect porcelain, or David Hockney paintings; Ms. Van Dorne collected Egyptian antiquities, the rarer the better, and had them on display throughout her home. The cases which enclosed particularly valuable or delicate objects were custom-made for her by a company which did most of its work building bank vaults, but she was perhaps startlingly casual about her personal use of the objects that were sometimes stored within them. Particularly jewelry. This afternoon she had on part of a Middle Kingdom princess's burial goods, an exquisite cloisonné-inlay pectoral. The tawny gold and bright blue, turquoise, and red of the stones stood out vividly against her dark grey cashmere twin-set.

She was sitting at her desk in the third-floor study, the curtains drawn, the bright clear light of her desk lamp the only illumination in the room. On a soft leather pad in front of her sat a partially unrolled papyrus, a section of it sandwiched between glass. Her fingertip traced the hieroglyphics written on the unrolled section out of habit alone: she knew these words by heart.

Also on the desk lay a small faience *ushabti* figure, shaped like a man standing with his arms crossed on his chest. Ms. Van Dorne had selected it from among a mixed lot of similar figures she had purchased from a dealer: they were far from rare.

The papyrus, though. *That* was rare. She had bought it in another mixed lot at auction in the spring, and had only gotten around to examining it properly two months ago; had she known what she had on her hands *earlier*, well—

—well, she'd have been willing to pay a great deal more for it, had she known.

That discovery had not quite been by accident. Ms. Van

Dorne rarely dreamed, or rarely remembered dreaming, but one morning she'd woken with an astonishingly clear image in her mind: something important, something quite mind-blowing in its importance, in fact, hidden in the auction lot of papyri she was going through. In the dream she'd been here, in her study, looking down at the papyrus she had just unrolled, and the room had rustled and whispered with the sound of wings, although she'd been alone; she thought of the feather of Ma'at, the protective wings of painted goddesses guarding sarcophagi. She hadn't been able to make out what was written on the papyrus, and the sense that it was of vast importance had stayed with her on waking; it was so strong, so compelling, that she went to look in the crate containing the auction lot to see if it was actually there.

The sight of it was a shock, a hot-cold adrenaline rush, both frightening and exciting; and when she very carefully unrolled it this time, *déjà vu* very strong now, remembering doing this in the dream, she could quite clearly read what it said.

It was unlike any other Egyptian text she'd ever seen, and she knew almost all of them, some by heart. It wasn't part of the *Book of the Dead*, or any of the other commonly found texts she could recognize. It wasn't an individual king or governor's correspondence or edicts. It was—or it claimed to be—an entirely different kind of spell. *O beautiful one, beloved of Ra, that liveth forever, and dieth not, whose beauty is eternal, thou dost renew thyself—*

Ms. Van Dorne had read it several times, puzzling out the

odd phrasing, and had thought for quite a long time before selecting a small artifact from among the less important contents of her collection. It had been a cosmetic box, alabaster but not beautifully carved, and missing its lid. It had worked well enough nonetheless, when she spoke the words of the spell out loud. It had worked very well indeed.

She looked down at the *ushabti* figure on the desk now and picked it up: held it in her hand, the way she had held that cosmetic box, feeling the solidity and hardness of it, the way in which it took up space. An object made for a purpose, in another time.

An object which would *serve* a purpose, if not perhaps its intended one.

Her manicured fingers closed more tightly around the little statue, and she smiled.

It was possible, Ruthven thought, to actually *have enough* of shopping. Difficult—his tolerances were extremely high—but possible. It helped not to have to carry bags, of course; he and Grisaille had arranged for the great many things they'd spent the past hours purchasing to be delivered to their hotel later, and they had in fact shopped their way along the entire length of the Via Condotti, which was not an inconsiderable feat. Perhaps it was understandable that Ruthven thought he'd done enough of it for the present.

Grisaille, however, still remained engrossed in Prada. Ruthven murmured to him and got a distracted nod; smiling fondly, he left him to it, and made his way out into the afternoon. It only occasionally occurred to him that he, Ruthven, had grown *used* to doing things as part of a couple, rather than forging through the world entirely on his own, attempting to entertain himself by throwing money around; the experience of shopping with someone, rather than all by himself, was just pleasing in a dim, comfortable sort of way. After so long alone he had slipped into the rhythm of a shared existence with barely any difficulty adjusting; it was as if he'd simply been waiting all that time for the individual person who quite precisely fit.

He sauntered across the plaza toward the Spanish Steps, which really *were* as impressive as they looked in all the films. Ruthven was reminded of Montmartre, but the air was quite different; these stairs were the elegant side of baroque, a monument in themselves, curving and recurving in long elegant sweeps. He skirted the fountain in the middle of the plaza, and climbed partway up the lowest flight.

From here he could see directly down the whole length of the Via Condotti, ruler-straight, looking like an exercise in perspective drawing. Not for the first time Ruthven thought he actually owed the late and self-titled King of the Vampires something, after all: without all that business in Paris this spring, he would never have met Grisaille, and therefore would never have traveled to Rome; would not be standing here, with this incredible backdrop, looking, he knew, *intensely* stylish, and enjoying this view—

He *was* intensely stylish, and lots of people were looking at him, but suddenly he was very much aware of being watched. That crawling unease, out of nowhere.

Ruthven turned and found himself staring at someone all in grey: no, two someones, stalking rapidly toward him. Beautiful. Unearthly beautiful, all white curls and huge blue eyes, currently narrowed at him in an expression of violent hatred, which he couldn't make sense of. He'd never seen them before, he would have remembered these two—he actually looked over his shoulder, in case they were storming toward somebody behind him, and this was a mistake because when he turned back, the first of them was right there, much too close to him.

"What—" he began, but the person shoved him *hard* in the chest with its bunched fingertips, saying something in a language Ruthven had never heard, and a kind of shock raced through him: his slow heart juddered briefly out of time, the tips of his fingers tingling. It lasted a fraction of a second before everything went back to normal; in fact, it was over so quickly, he wondered afterward if he'd actually felt it at all.

The person who had touched him took its hand back, wiping its fingers on its coat with an expression of distaste, and turned to stalk away. Its companion put an arm around it, as if to comfort or reassure, and the two of them ignored Ruthven completely, heading on up the staircase as if the little encounter had never happened.

The people around them didn't seem to have noticed anything at all; nobody was pointing and staring at him, and while Ruthven would very much have liked to shout after the departing strangers "what the livid fuck was that about," he didn't particularly wish to die of embarrassment, and the latter took precedence.

He looked down at himself. The place on his chest where the person had touched him *looked* perfectly normal: there was no scorch-mark on his shirt, no stain of any kind. There wasn't any pain, either; when he prodded experimentally at the place, it didn't feel bruised despite how hard that shove had been. Despite the shock.

"What's the matter?" said Grisaille behind him, and Ruthven jumped.

"Where did you come from?—Never mind," he added quickly, but Grisaille never, *ever* let an opportunity like that pass him by, and was already drawling, "Well, when a gentleman and a lady love each other very much..."

"Shut up," said Ruthven, but he couldn't help a smile. Grisaille handed him the tiniest paper cup in the world, grinning back.

"Espresso," he said. "I thought you could use some extra energy, after all that shopping. At *your* age, one tires easily."

"You know perfectly well I'm only four hundred and thirty," Ruthven said mildly. "But thank you." In fact, the coffee did help clear the lingering unease from the earlier encounter: he felt better with the first sip, settled enough to mention it. "You don't happen to know a pair of unspeakably beautiful twins who for some reason hate me, do you?"

"That's both peculiar and specific," said Grisaille. "I think I need more information, although I am sure the list of people who hate you for having hair like yours is quite substantial. Why?"

Ruthven told him what had happened while the two of them sat on the steps. Grisaille listened with first interest and then intensity, and when Ruthven got to the bit with the shock, his eyes narrowed. "Let me see."

"I'm fine," said Ruthven, defensive. "It doesn't hurt, it didn't even leave a bruise—"

"Let me see," Grisaille repeated, and Ruthven sighed and undid the top button of his shirt despite the fact they were in public: he knew Grisaille wouldn't let this go, either. He held still while Grisaille peered closely at the skin of his chest, touched the place gently with his fingertips. The dissonance between that careful touch and the stranger's vicious shove made Ruthven close his eyes for a moment, and when he opened them Grisaille was looking at him with an expression he was not used to having directed at him: he knew quite well how it felt from the inside, sympathy and protection dissolving together into a vast wave of *care*.

"I'm taking you back to the hotel," Grisaille said, holding up a hand to stall Ruthven's protestations that he was absolutely fine. "I'm tired myself, and I want to look up some things on the Internet, all right?"

"I—" Ruthven stopped and sighed. It was strange to be looked at with that particular expression, and it was strange to be told what to do, and it was also rather lovely: the abdication of responsibility, being someone else's problem for a while rather than his own. That aspect of being in a relationship *didn't* pass him by without notice. "All right," he said, and didn't miss the flicker of worry that crossed Grisaille's face at the capitulation. "I'll be good. But I do want to go out tonight."

"Of course," said Grisaille, "the dissolute nightlife of Rome is at our disposal." He held out a hand to help Ruthven to his feet. "Untold perils haunt the streets, and so on."

"They're not untold," said Ruthven, and smiled for the first time in a while. "They're *us*."

In the great library at Dark Heart, evening was drawing in. Varney had lit a fire in the hearth against the constant drawing dampness in the air; outside the vast windows, the parkland was smudged into a grey-green blur by the rain. This part of the house was still in reasonable shape, but the far wing nevertheless had a patchwork of tarpaulins and plywood over parts of the roof, and Varney fancied he could hear the strange jangling concerto of drips into the thousands of buckets arrayed beneath, like a thoroughly modern and unpleasant piano piece.

He was on edge. The conversation he'd had with Nadezhda Serenskaya had been—encouraging, certainly, but he did not want to do what he was about to do for several reasons, and one of them was that he wasn't sure he could pronounce all the words correctly.

She'd given him a book and, humiliatingly, made him practice some of it, and judged him capable of performing the basic invocation it contained. "Better you should do it yourself," she'd said, "than having me play metaphysical phone operator; and you'll want privacy."

Now he took a deep, mostly unnecessary breath, and sighed it out. He picked up the piece of chalk she'd given him wrapped up in a silk handkerchief like a particularly valuable un-set stone, and—wincing at the necessity—began to draw a circle with it on the polished wood of his desktop. The chalk squealed thinly in his fingertips, making his teeth hurt, and he had to check with the book several times in the process of adding various small sigils to the rim of the circle.

They looked all right, Varney thought, sitting back, and then bit the edge of his thumb; face slightly twisted in distaste at the mess, he dabbed blood at five points around the edge of the circle, saying one of the strange words from the book at each dab. As he did so, he was aware that something was happening; he could feel a sense of gathering charge in the air, like the atmosphere before a lightning-storm, the roots of his hair trying to stiffen. He had a nasty blank moment before the final word he needed to speak came back to him, and he said it slightly louder, slow, hoping he wasn't somehow transposing syllables and calling down a plague of something other than just rain—and as soon as he had spoken the word, as soon as the last smudge of blood met the circle, an invisible shock-front raced outward from it like the pressure-wave ahead of an explosion. The flames in the fireplace blazed tall, roaring up the chimney; a quick flux of heat washed past him, and a hole opened up in the surface of Varney's desk, through which the transparent, staticky, grey-glowing image of a man's head rose.

It was buzzing, indistinct; after a moment the head tilted as if its owner were tapping on something, and the focus shrank into sharpness. It appeared to be the head and shoulders of a dark-haired man in his fifties, wearing an impeccable double-breasted pinstripe suit. Varney had last seen this particular individual in Paris, this spring, under very peculiar circumstances indeed, although the current situation was fairly high on his list of peculiarities.

"It's *el-epheth*," said the man in a cut-glass BBC accent, sounding brisk. "Not *al-epheth*, although it's easy to get wrong. Hello, Sir Francis, what can I do for you? I'm a little busy at the moment, I'm afraid."

Varney couldn't help remembering the *first* time he'd encountered the demon Fastitocalon, in the middle of the business with the Gladius Sancti: back then he'd been rather less self-possessed and rather more self-deprecating, as well as chronically ill. Now that the projection of his head had stabilized, he appeared to be in quite good shape.

"Ah," Varney said. "I'm sorry; I don't have a great deal of practice. Miss Serenskaya strongly suggested I attempt to contact you myself, rather than having her open the connection. I, ah. I have something I should like to ask for your advice on, Fastitocalon."

Fastitocalon narrowed his eyes. In the projection he was totally black-and-white; Varney knew that in real life the eyes were occasionally slicked with a faint orange luster. "Yes?" he asked. "I can give you ten minutes. What's on your mind?"

Varney took another deep breath. "I've asked Greta Helsing to marry me," he said, glad for once of his control over his voice: it sounded as graceful and mellifluous as he could make it. "And I should like to ask for your—*blessing* is the wrong word, *approval*, I suppose, and your advice on the design of the ring."

He had the pleasure of seeing Fastitocalon completely taken aback, just for a moment, and then the rather more significant pleasure of seeing him smile. "Goodness gracious me," said the demon, "I wasn't entirely sure if you'd ever get around to that; I'm terribly glad—she *did* say yes, did she?"

"She did," said Varney. It was impossible to hide the faint blush he could feel heating his face. "In a car, on the way to the airport—she's in France again, but don't worry, it's—she's over in some fancy resort for the undead gluing parts of mummies together, it's quite safe," he hastened to add. "I asked her if she liked diamonds and she said yes, she did, and I—don't know quite *what* she'd like in a ring, and so I went to ask Miss Serenskaya and she said that nobody has known Greta longer than you have, so..."

Fastitocalon's smile was thin, but real and warm. It was true: Varney knew he'd been a friend of Greta's father, Wilfert Helsing, and after his death had been the closest thing Greta had to family; had, in fact, taken it upon himself to watch over Greta and try to keep her safe. He'd been exiled to Earth sometime in the seventeenth century after a management shake-up in Hell, and had only just recently made his way back Below.

"Congratulations," he said. "To both of you. I've meant to

be in closer touch with her, but this job's taking up all my time, I'm afraid—Asmodeus left M&E in a hell of a state and there's mounting evidence to suggest something rather larger than sheer incompetence has been going on for a while now—but never mind that. Do you intend to have something custom-made for her?"

"Yes," said Varney, "I was hoping to be able to put some of my, ah, hoard of jewels to constructive use. I've had them for centuries and they do nothing but take up space and need polishing, and some of them might or might not be cursed. A bit. I'm not sure."

"Well, we can easily check on that for you," said Fastitocalon. "The jewelers of Dis are experts at identifying, tracing, and customizing curses, protective and otherwise. I have a meeting in five minutes, I'm afraid, but after that, if you'd like to come and chat with some of our people, I'd be happy to escort you."

"...to Hell," Varney said, not quite sure how he felt about that. "I'm—damned. Aren't I?" *Several times over*, he didn't say, *starting with the turning of Clara Crofton, centuries back.* It was something he tried not to think about, but could never entirely forget.

"To some extent all of us are," said Fastitocalon. "As a guest, you won't be set upon with pitchforks and torches, I can promise you that, and Sam is very much aware of how much you mean to Greta."

"And I'd be able to—leave, afterward?"

Fastitocalon smiled. "I give you my word. Besides, I think you'd like Hell, at least the nice parts of it. Nor will visiting Hell do anything to your pneumic signature if you have a safe-conduct pass."

Two years ago Varney would have recoiled at the very thought of visiting the underworld, even if he'd thought such a thing was possible; he'd always known he was bound for Hell in the end, but he'd certainly had no desire to see what awaited him below. He had to smile back, a little. "Very well," he said. "I confess the sin of curiosity."

"Jolly good," said Fastitocalon. "I'll be back in about two hours to fetch you, then. And congratulations again, Sir Francis. I'm so happy for you both."

He popped out of existence as if he had never been there at all, leaving only a faint wisp of smoke rising from the chalk circle on Varney's desk; and when Varney wiped away the remains of the chalk, there wasn't even a scorch-mark left.

*I'll be back to fetch you*, he thought, smiling at himself, thinking of all the dreadful plays in which the demon king waved his pitchfork at hapless idiots who had tricked themselves into trusting Hell. Varney had trusted Hell several times now, over the course of his acquaintance with Greta Helsing, and it had proven rather more worthy of that trust than had the world of men.

He sat there for a few minutes, listening to the never-ending rain, and then wondered what one *wore* to harrow Hell these days, and went upstairs to change.

* * *

Elsewhere, Greta Helsing was having rather a less exciting evening. She'd found it was actually hard to fall asleep without the constant hissing of the rain outside, no matter how tired she was; leaving the windows open to let the night breeze in brought with it the faint sounds of insects singing, leaves rustling, but not the familiar white noise of rainfall—and so she had brought an armful of reference books back to her private quarters to get some research done. She'd be awake until late, anyway, and the diagnostician in her was intensely curious about Maanakhtef's symptoms.

Sister Brigitte had looked briefly guarded, and then relieved, when Greta asked her about the strange episodes and what Dr. Kamal's approach to them had been.

"He's not the only one, I'm afraid," she said. "Poor Mr. Antjau had one not long ago, and—oh, several of our patients over the past two months, I should say. In most cases it's been just a brief moment of weakness and vertigo, but some of them have been quite exhausting and traumatic to the patient. Dr. Kamal wanted those cases to stay on at the spa for further observation, but no one has ever had *multiple* episodes until Mr. Maanakhtef, and the other patients—" She shrugged, her white scrubs rustling, still reminding Greta of some kind of ceremonial garb. "It is... financially unsustainable for most of them to extend their stay with us for very long, I'm afraid."

"I know," said Greta ruefully. "I've sent several patients to you, and it's not cheap. It's worth it, I know that, too. But

Dr. Kamal hasn't been able to work out what if anything the patients who experience these attacks have in common?"

"Other than being mummies, very little," said Sister Brigitte. "Different periods, different embalming practices, different origins—well, no, actually, several of them share tomb locations, but little else."

"They might be from the same cache," said Greta. The thing about burying your dead with ceremony and care and a lot of very easily liquidated treasure was that you inevitably developed a problem with tomb robbers; the trade had flourished for as long as people had been building tombs to rob. Over the centuries, Egypt's tomb robbers had looted thousands of burials, leaving the mummy behind and taking everything else they could carry and sell; these abandoned mummies were sometimes salvaged by priests and stored together in a secret cache to protect them from further desecration. It was a fortunate archaeologist indeed who happened to find one.

She might look up cache locations, actually. "Could you remind me where the library is?"

Sister Brigitte had shown her, and Greta had been pleasantly unsurprised yet again to find that Oasis Natrun had a very well-stocked catalog, including modern and historic volumes going back as long as the field of mummy medicine had been around. The field, at least in the West, was relatively new: there simply hadn't been much call for it until the early eighteen-twenties, when the fad for mummy unwrapping as parlor entertainment began.

Greta had treated several mummies who had actually *been*

unwrapped back in the Victorian era, the shock and horror of it bringing them to consciousness for the first time in thousands of years, and could roundly sympathize with those of them who wanted revenge. Being a human was, in general, not a thing she thought one should be proud of.

She was sitting now in the middle of the giant bed in her private quarters, the night breeze stirring her curtains gently, and reading *Diseases of the Mummy*, third edition, circa 1945. It was fascinating to see how the clinicians of the day had tackled—or not tackled—problems that she would have solved without thinking: at the time, tuberculosis chemotherapy was in its infancy, had only really begun in 1944, and the section of *Diseases* that included TB simply suggested treating troublesome symptoms empirically and having somebody recite appropriate spells. She wondered what the authors of *Diseases* would have made of canopic teletherapy, and had to smile a little.

*Also: modern dental equipment, dual-cure resin, elastic that won't go floppy or perish, 3-D printing, irradiation therapy for fungal infection, and a much better grasp of* what *spells and how to pronounce them*, she thought. It was a pretty good time to be a mummy specialist, even if you did have to deal with the nagging background tomb-robbing species guilt.

None of this was helping solve her current problem, though. She did find some references to vertigo in mummies, but all of them seemed to involve loose dried-up fragments of brain or linen packing shifting around inside the skull and causing discomfort and disorientation, and Greta *knew* Ed Kamal would have ruled that out first of all. It was easy enough to see inside somebody's head with the 3-D spiral multi-slice CT scanner, even if they were still inside layers and layers of linen wrappings, and a piece of loose desiccated brain tissue would have been obvious. Nor could there have been anything else in the skull that would suddenly start to cause disturbances, she thought; practically nothing would be able to get *in* there without the patient at least noticing it on the way.

*Ew.* She sighed, put the book down, picked up another. The idea that—how many was it, anyway, had Sister Brigitte actually given her a total number of incidents—the idea that a *lot* of mummies should suddenly develop some kind of intracranial foreign body without noticing was ridiculous. It wasn't mechanical, whatever it was.

Nor was it pathological, or at least she didn't think so. Mummies weren't really susceptible to pathogens except fungal infections; any diseases they had were ones they'd had as living people, like Mr. Antjau's case of antibiotic-naive TB, and most of those were barely symptomatic other than inflammatory arthritis. Dry rot, yes, and infestations of various unpleasant kinds, but a mummy didn't have a circulatory system to speak of—sure, the heart was there, the heart was of paramount importance to the ancient Egyptians, but the *rest* of the big veins were completely missing and therefore hemodynamic instability was completely ruled out as a cause of syncope...what *else* could possibly cause fainting, anyway... you couldn't *have* insufficient blood flow to the brain without blood or brains to do it with... this didn't make any sense...

Greta was only vaguely aware she was falling asleep.

She woke out of complicated dreams to find herself still surrounded by books, and wasn't at all sure for a moment where she was; then it came back, and she glanced sharply over at the clock on the nightstand, enormously relieved to find she hadn't overslept.

Nor had she come up with any solutions. At times in her life Greta had managed to fall asleep thinking about a problem and found herself waking up with the edges of an answer; not this time. She got out of bed, stacking the books neatly on the nightstand, and decided she'd skip breakfast in favor of information. It was definitely time for her to meet Oasis Natrun's records clerk.

Tefnakhte was among the most well-preserved mummies Greta had ever seen. He'd had his hands replaced at least once, and probably more than once judging by the deftness of his fingers, and his wrappings were exceedingly neat and even in color. He shook her hand, his grip firm and confident, offered her a seat. The office was also exceedingly neat, all his filing cabinets and bookcases presenting an air of methodical organization; the computer on his desk was a sleek iMac that couldn't be more than six months old.

"We keep up with technology," he said. He had clearly been unearthed by one of the British expeditions, judging by the accent. "When I first came here, we were still hard-copy-only, which as you can imagine dates me rather."

Greta laughed. "Twenty-first Dynasty? Your wrappings are in beautiful condition. How long *has* the spa been around, anyway? I hadn't realized it was quite so wealthy, either; the helicopter was a surprise."

"It was established in the early thirties," Tefnakhte said. "By a very wealthy gentleman who had fallen in love with Egypt and Egyptology, and built the original facility farther down the mountain; that building is still in use today as a boutique hotel for humans, as a matter of fact. He set up a private foundation and left his fortune to it as an endowment, which has been funding us ever since, and we've had several other extraordinarily generous donors over the years. The current facility dates to the mid-sixties."

"I'm embarrassed to say I didn't know any of that," Greta said, smiling. "Some expert I am. But it's an amazing place, and I'm so glad to be here. You're not just in charge of the records, though, right?"

"I also do the recitations," he said, a little self-conscious. "During procedures, and so on. It's helpful to have the spells pronounced correctly, and, well, that's difficult if you've never been fluent in Egyptian."

"It is incredibly difficult," said Greta, "which is why I don't do it at home; I have a witch friend do the chanting for me, but that's a far cry from having it done by an actual Egyptian priest. I'm looking forward to having you help me with Maanakhtef and Nefrina this week."

"You *are* operating on Maanakhtef, then," said Tefnakhte. "Dr. Kamal was hesitant about the surgery, I think?"

"So I gather, but I'm at least going to prepare the cuneiform bones and the articular surfaces of his metatarsophalangeal joints to receive the new bone and tendon replacements," said Greta, and then had to laugh at herself. "Sorry. Haven't had my coffee yet. I mean I'm just going to—"

"I know," said Tefnakhte, and she could hear the faint creak as he smiled behind the bandages. "Trust me, I've spent enough time watching and then writing down the names of the procedures; I've looked up almost every bone in the body, one way or another."

Greta could feel her face go pink. "Ah," she said. "Of course. I did want to ask you something in particular, though, about the procedures you've participated in since this idiopathic transient vertigo thing showed up."

"Of course," he said. "Let me guess: you want to know if I've done magic on them, and if so, what magic it is that I've done?"

She wasn't used to being so neatly and completely understood. Particularly by someone whose area of expertise was nominally quite a long way off from her own; then she remembered Sister Brigitte telling her that Tefnakhte had been a priest of Thoth, and a little of his detail-oriented sharpness made more sense. The ibis-headed scribe-god had always appealed to Greta as a thoroughly sensible deity.

"Well, yes," she said. "In fact. I wanted to ask about the spells you've done and what they're for and if you've noticed anything out of the ordinary during the spell-casting—can you *feel* it if something's gone awry with the magic?"

"To an extent," he said, "but no, in fact, there doesn't seem to be a correlation. There have been"—he paused for a moment, head tilted, accessing some inner memory bank—"fourteen patients who have experienced it to date. Of that number, nine have been here to undergo a medical procedure; of those nine, I've been present and active for six. Some of them have been very simple cases which didn't require any chanting or amulet replacement."

"So some of the guests who've had an episode have never even met you?"

"Exactly," he said. "And the *other* patients we've had come through the facility, who haven't ever experienced the attacks, I've been involved in approximately two thirds of their care. There's no pattern I can discern, and patterns are among the things I'm good at."

"And you didn't notice anything different magically about the ones you did see who had attacks?"

"I'm afraid not," said Tefnakhte. He sounded genuinely regretful, and Greta thought she understood: it would have been so much neater to have found an explanation, a thread to tie the instances together, because then perhaps something could be *done* about it.

It wasn't lost on her that this mummy was very specifically worried about the attacks. That he was taking it seriously, whatever it was, and minded not knowing the answers. She could sympathize.

"Have you ever been present when it happened?"

"Once," he said. "It was a little alarming, actually. The patient just sort of suddenly collapsed, and it was a good thing she wasn't standing up; she'd have shattered on the floor."

Greta winced. "And we can hardly require every guest to spend their entire stay lying flat on their backs lest they suddenly have one of these spells and injure themselves in a fall," she said. "This is—a problem, isn't it."

"I'm afraid so, Doctor," said Tefnakhte. "Dr. Kamal said before he left that he wouldn't trust any other physician with the spa. I think that goes for this mystery as well."

# CHAPTER 5

By the time they'd got back to the hotel that afternoon, Ruthven felt absolutely fine; the entire strange little episode on the Spanish Steps had receded into nothing more than a passing memory. He and Grisaille had gone out that night as they had done every night, and while he had certainly indulged in excesses, he hadn't indulged *excessively* in them, so waking up with a splitting headache to find that the room's light hurt his eyes seemed to Ruthven completely unfair.

He'd had a bad reaction to someone a few times in his memory—some vagary of blood chemistry or pharmaceuticals—but he couldn't remember drinking from anybody last night who looked suspicious. The pain felt like an iron band around his temples, *squeezing*.

"*There* you are," said Grisaille nearby. Ruthven opened his eyes again, shut them against the brightness of the room. "I was wondering if you'd ever wake up—what's wrong?"

Concern had rapidly displaced the mild amusement in his tone. "Ruthven, what is it, what's the matter?"

"Headache," said Ruthven between his teeth. "Can I have—lots of drugs, please?"

"Oh," said Grisaille, "yes of course, just a minute," and Ruthven heard him moving around; abruptly the overhead light went away, and that was so *much* of a relief. He could open his eyes; it hurt, but he could handle it, and when Grisaille came back with a handful of painkillers, Ruthven was able to smile at him.

"It's all right," he said, "I get these sometimes. Thank you," and he dry-swallowed the handful of drugs with a wince. "What time is it?"

"Late afternoon. You've been sleeping all day," Grisaille said, still concerned. "I thought you'd probably just had a bit much and needed to sleep it off."

"Apparently I did," said Ruthven, closing his eyes again. "Embarrassing old age, you know."

"Oh, hush," said Grisaille. "Do you want anything else?"

"Not right now," he said, willing the stuff to start working. "Sorry, I'm not terribly entertaining at the moment."

"You don't have to be entertaining," Grisaille said, "you have to be you, that's all, and—should I go away?"

Ruthven realized Grisaille had never actually seen him having one of his infrequent but dramatic headaches; they had only had about six months to learn about each other's faults and foibles. Nor was he himself used to the idea of anyone saying things to him like *you have to be you, that's all*; despite the pain, it was remarkably pleasant to be the object of that kind of plain and simple appreciation. That *care.*

"No," he said, "don't go away, please, it's all right, I'll be fine once this starts to work, I just can't be very conversational."

"You don't have to be," said Grisaille again, and took his hand; cool, smooth fingers. "You just rest, okay? I'm right here."

He smiled, and curled his fingers around Grisaille's, and let himself drift, feeling the edges of the pain already beginning to recede.

Tefnakhte had said that the spa was originally founded by a wealthy Egyptophile who wanted to do something more useful with his fortune than leave it to some distant cousin, and clearly philanthropic support continued to be *generous.* Greta made a mental note to go and see the original 1930s building when she got a chance, but right now she was a little busy being staggered by how *much* money the place must be bringing in. Not only did they have a spiral CT scanner and a wide-bore MRI, the clinic was also equipped with a fairly new Varian radiotherapy linac setup, which Greta knew for a fact started around six hundred thousand pounds and went up from there. She'd known Oasis Natrun had the capability to provide sterilizing irradiation therapy, but she'd been picturing something a little less impressive.

All her worries weren't exactly *forgotten*, looking through the windows of the treatment room at the machine, but there was a certain sense of childish glee nonetheless.

She made herself stop staring; she had work to do. Preparing

Maanakhtef's foot for the installation of the new phalanges wouldn't be difficult, but it required concentration. This wasn't a job for the full operating theater; she'd be using the smaller of their procedure rooms, equipped with a high-end dental operatory chair. That dental equipment was widely used in the field of mummy medicine had made sense to Greta from the beginning: what else was there that offered all the tools you'd need for delicately reshaping and repairing bone, after all?

When she got there, masked and gloved, Maanakhtef was already reclining in the chair with a blanket over him, and the nurse had set classical music quietly playing in the background. She smiled down at him. "How are you feeling?"

"Oh, quite well in myself, Doctor. Tefnakhte's been to see me and said some spells for the pain."

"Good. This will take about twenty minutes, start to finish, and you shouldn't have too much discomfort while I'm working, but if you do, tell me, and we'll get Tefnakhte back again." She nodded to the nurse, who was measuring out two-part epoxy resin into small beakers on the counter. "I'll want that mixed in about ten."

Maanakhtef creaked as he turned his head to peer at the beakers. "What's that?"

Greta settled on the stool by his foot and put on her magnifying glasses, examining the exposed bone surfaces. Good: not too much reshaping was necessary, just smoothing down the edges. "Stabilizing resin," she told him, "it'll strengthen your bones a bit and fill in the damaged surfaces. I've got all sorts of resins for all sorts of purposes, a little like the embalmers did, only I bet they didn't have mystic ancient dual-cure inlay cement."

She took down the drill handpiece and fitted the burr she wanted into it, and set to work. The sound of the drill was unavoidably a little upsetting to some people, but this one was quite quiet, a faint high-pitched whine. Maanakhtef was holding very still for her.

"That's a strange sensation," he said, sounding interested rather than distressed. "The vibration. I've never had it done before."

"In the old days we'd use a hand file," said Greta, carefully adjusting the curve of a bone's edge. "This is faster. I have to say I've rarely had the opportunity to work with equipment as advanced as this clinic's; it's a genuine pleasure."

"It does seem very advanced," he said. The German accent was incongruous coming from a mummy, but then again so was Tefnakhte's British version. "I've been *inside* several machines, which I understand is necessary to make new bones for me?"

"That's right; they had to scan both your feet to determine the shapes and sizes the new bones have to be. The machines take a great many pictures of you very quickly, and a computer sticks them together into a single composite image." She straightened up, turning off the drill. "Can I have that resin, please?—It's all very top-of-the-line equipment."

The nurse had the two-part epoxy mixed and ready, having watched Greta work and determined when she'd be likely to need it. Greta smiled behind her mask. "Thanks. Mr. Maanakhtef, this will feel quite warm for a minute or two; that's completely normal and will pass. How are you holding up?"

"Oh, fine, fine," he said, waving a hand. A few scraps of linen drifted to the floor; the cleaning staff were kept busy sweeping several times a day.

Greta nodded and began to paint the resin carefully over the articular surfaces of the bones she'd prepared. It would take about four hours to cure completely, at which point the impregnated bone would be much stronger and up to the task of forming a working joint. She paid particular attention to the one remaining metatarsal, which would have to take less strain when the new bones were put in but which looked extremely fragile nonetheless.

"I was chatting with Mr. Nesperennub in the sun lounge," Maanakhtef continued. "He said they'd done *magic* on him, which they don't, do they?"

"Only the kind Tefnakhte does, spells to enchant amulets and keep people safe during operations," said Greta, "and that's a quite different sort of power. Arthur C. Clarke once said that sufficiently advanced technology is indistinguishable from magic, and, well, I can see why Mr. Nesperennub might have gotten that impression. Back in the early days we'd have had to put him in a shielded room with a highly radioactive source for *hours* to knock out a fungal infection like that; with the linac it'd take—oh, thirty minutes, I should think, for whole-body irradiation, and you don't have to have bits of cobalt-60 sitting around the place being dangerous radiological accidents waiting to happen." She began to add a second coat to the remaining metatarsal. "When Ramses the Great had to go to Paris for treatment for the same condition, back in '76 or '77, I think he had to spend twelve hours in the chamber, poor king. It must have been unbelievably boring."

"I had no idea you *could* get rid of fungus without having to unwrap yourself completely," said Maanakhtef. "He seemed quite all right to me, if a little weak and tired, there was no... er... visible mildew."

"Oh, it works at once," she said. "The infection is knocked out immediately—along with any other form of life on or in the patient; they're completely sterilized. It takes a little while for them to get their strength back, but the cure is complete. It's extremely satisfying as a clinician. There," she added, sitting back and handing the resin beaker and the brush to the nurse. "That's done; it will take several minutes to dry and four hours to harden, and we can go ahead with the surgery tomorrow if all goes well. I've had a look at the bones they printed for you; they look beautiful."

His wrappings covered his mouth, but she could hear the creak as he smiled—and hear it in his voice as well.

"Thank you, Doctor," he said. "I shall look forward to having beautiful bones."

"Beautiful and *functional*," Greta said, grinning, and stripped off her gloves. She loved her job; she would never have been able to do it if she didn't. But sometimes—like now—she loved it *very much*.

* * *

The library at Dark Heart House looked out over the ornamental lake. It was looking a little less like an ornamental inland sea, Varney thought, now that the rain had finally backed off slightly; he could see all the way across the valley to the woods crowning the hill on the other side of his park, and even make out that the foliage had begun to turn. All the forecasts were tentatively hopeful about the idea of it not actually continuing to rain for the remainder of ever, but Varney had his doubts. It really did seem slightly sinister.

It was, however, pleasant to stand here in the warmth and light and comfort of his library, surrounded by books old and new, books read and unread, a room lined with words, and feel himself more a person of this world than he had done in a long time, possibly due to having recently and briefly *left* it. The familiarity of the things that were his, and that were understandable and reliable and real, was comforting.

The journey to Hell and back had been an interesting experience, and one he did not immediately care to repeat, but it had borne fruit nonetheless. In his pocket lay a small velvet box that felt much heavier than it ought to have been, given its diminutive size.

He'd come back very early in the morning to find Emily in the stables dealing with what appeared to be an outbreak of respiratory illness in the hairmonsters, and had helped her move the worst sufferers into the warmth and shelter of the house, without mentioning where he'd been; any questions had been driven out of both their minds by the unexpected discovery of a nest of very small screaming skulls in the breakfast-room wainscoting—they weren't uncommon in old houses, but Varney hadn't known Dark Heart had them—and in fact, both of them had been kept quite busy until late afternoon. Now, finally free to reflect on matters, he slipped his hand into his pocket and touched the velvet surface of the box. Was it the same kind of velvet a mortal jeweler's shop might use to wrap its boxes? Did the filaments of the fabric come from a subtly different source?

Fastitocalon had appeared without any fanfare whatsoever other than a faint and polite *ahem*, the equivalent of someone clearing their throat in the doorway to announce their presence: one moment Varney had been alone in his office, and the next he hadn't been, looking up at the tall, thin, pinstriped presence of the demon, double-breasted suit and all. He looked like a banker. The only visual tell that he *was* a demon lay in the fact that his skin was ever so slightly grey, as if he had a faint case of argyria, and that when he was really annoyed his eyes took on a faint orange iridescence like Persian lustreware.

The last time they'd seen one another had been in Paris, in the spring, and Varney had been in no real condition to say polite good-byes after a rather nasty little battle underground. It had been Fastitocalon, with the assistance of another demon and a couple of individuals Varney still had trouble thinking of as *remedial psychopomps*, even if that was what they had on their business cards, who had welded shut the weak place in reality caused by a series of extremely unwise summonings—how, Varney wasn't sure and didn't want to ask—and had promptly vanished back to Hell. Greta had told him afterward that Fass had not only gotten himself cured of the chronic ill health he'd been suffering the first time Varney had met him, back in London, but had also managed to secure a fairly important job in the infernal civil service.

"I'm sorry for taking up your time," he'd said last night, and Fastitocalon smiled.

"You are not taking up very *much* of it," said the demon. "And this is important. Have you got your jewels with you?"

Varney showed him the case: a tangle of gems, the collection of three centuries. "Good," said Fastitocalon. "I am entirely sure our jewelers will be able to put something together for you. Take my hand."

His fingers had been dry and smooth and slightly warm to the touch. Varney had just had enough time to close his eyes very tightly against the vertigo of translocation before both of them were no longer in the office at all, or even on the prime material plane.

Now, as the view across the park grew dimmer and dimmer—nobody had seen a goddamn sunset in weeks, it really was depressing—Varney turned the box over in his pocket and thought of Greta as he'd last seen her disappearing into the security line at Heathrow, and of himself as he'd been when he first met her, poisoned, sick and half-delirious with pain, snarling at the pale stranger bending over him on Ruthven's couch. That creature could not, he knew perfectly well, have countenanced the possibility of *visiting Hell* at all, except to stay there as a damned soul for all eternity. That creature would not have been able to imagine visiting Hell *to get a piece of jewelry custom-made*, the way one might pop into Garrard's with a handful of gems and order a bespoke tiara.

He smiled, without realizing he was doing it, and took out his phone to check the time. Just gone six; it would be seven in Marseille. He could at least try her; she might still be busy putting patients together, but he could leave her a message.

She picked up on the third ring. "Varney," she said, and he could hear the delight in her voice. "How are you? Is it still pouring?"

"Hello," he said. "I'm fine, and yes, although subtly less so than it was. We may not actually need to build an ark to house the monsters after all."

"I'm glad to hear it. Are they all right?"

"Mostly. Some of the hairmonsters seem to have caught colds, and Emily and I have moved them into the house—her entrance exam to the vet school is coming up and she's keen on any excuse to avoid studying—oh, and apparently we have skulls. I'm sorry about that, I had no idea."

"Skulls?" said Greta. "What *kind* of skulls?"

"The kind that scream. These are very little, still. I think they must have just hatched; they don't scream so much as squeak faintly. It's rather charming, although I expect they will become less so as they get larger."

"Screaming skulls are real?"

"Oh yes, I'm afraid so," said Varney. "Lots of the old places have them, you know. They only really make a fuss if you try to take them *out* of the house. Never mind the skulls, tell me about yourself, my dear, how is the job?"

"It's wonderful," she said, and he could hear the smile in her voice. "I can't get over how beautifully fitted-out this place is, Varney, they have equipment I've never even seen in person before, it's—they have a *lot* of money, and it's being well spent. And it's so beautiful here. I wish I could show it to you, I'm on the terrace watching the sun set—hang on a sec."

Varney waited. After a few seconds the phone vibrated, and he took it away from his ear to see that she'd texted him a picture: a gorgeous, improbable view down from a mountaintop to the glittering city caught in the lap between two massifs, like a crystal formation hugging the edge of the sea, and the sea itself a burnished sheet of rose-gold beneath a sky fading from aquamarine to violet, with wide strokes of gold across the depth of it.

"Good God," he said after staring at it for a moment, trying not to think *why would anyone ever leave that to come home?* "That's exquisite."

"And it isn't raining," Greta said. "It hasn't rained, in fact, since I got here. At all. I think it's a miracle. It's ridiculously lovely here, and the only thing that'd make it better is to have you with me. The work is—well, it's the kind of work I love most."

He could hear a faint undertone in her voice that spoke of unease, and wondered if she knew it was there. "Tell me about it?" he said.

"I can't go into much detail, but I'm doing a lot of reconstructive surgery," she said, and the unease was gone. "God, it's so nice to have all the equipment and supplies I could possibly need, instead of having to work out how to fudge it with what's available to hand. I have six different grades of dual-cure resin cement, Varney, and some of the replacement tendon and ligament materials are straight out of NASA—they won't perish or fail with use and age—and the scanners they have here are some of the best in the world; I can do non-invasive imaging in a quarter of the time it'd take me with less advanced technology. One of the patients is convinced his treatment was magic, and—well, in a way I suppose it *is* magic to be able to knock out a fulminant fungal infection with electron-beam radiation; the lines between magic and technology are increasingly blurred when you get this far up the sophistication scale."

Varney found himself grinning. "That's what Dr. Faust said about their whatsit, mirabilic resonance scanner. Magic and technology are often a matter of perspective."

Greta paused. "Dr. Faust?" He could hear the excitement and also the jealousy in her voice very clearly. "You met *Dr. Faust*? Varney, did you *go to Hell*?"

"I did," he said, enjoying it. "I had a very specific need that the artisans of Hell were more than capable of meeting. Fastitocalon came to get me last night and took me down there for a brief visit. He seems well, by the way, if extremely busy."

"I can't believe this," Greta said, "you went to Hell, that's—Varney, I'm dying of envy here, *why* did you go, what did you need done, did you meet Samael, isn't he terrifying, *tell me everything*."

He had to chuckle. "I needed a particular object made for me which I did not trust London's artisans to manage with sufficient elegance and skill and speed. Something small but quite important, which you will learn more about in due course."

"*Varney*," she said. He realized how unlike the old Varney it was to be able to keep secrets, and his smile widened. It wasn't an expression common to his face; he could feel it stretching the muscles.

"Which," he continued, "I have now in my possession; but while it was being made, I had some time to kill, and so Fastitocalon summoned an underling and assigned them to give me a short walking tour of Dis. It's incredible, Greta. It's like a series of very specific and bizarre fever-dreams, but not the kind that are frightening exactly."

"Did you take pictures?" she demanded.

"No. I did ask about that, and I was informed that the—thing, the image sensor—in my phone camera would pick up nothing at all, so I didn't try. But—picture a huge, huge lake on fire, with no smoke, no reek of burning. It looks a bit like a vast fire opal, only constantly moving, shimmering. The flames are small and blue and golden, and apparently demons can pick them up and hold them without harm."

"Lake Avernus," said Greta. "Fass has told me a little bit about it. The water's bottled and sold as a tonic."

"It is, and there's a great big white building that looks almost exactly like the Brighton Pavilion sitting at the water's edge which is the demon spa—"

"—where Fass went to get himself cured," said Greta. "I have *got* to see this for myself. Go on."

"The city itself is mostly white and crystal and gold," Varney continued, enjoying himself. "At least the downtown bits by the waterfront. I gather it is much less grand in the outlying suburbs. There's a big central plaza surrounded by eight huge glass towers that sort of—twist, like spiral horns, I can't describe it properly—and further back there's all sorts of much more old-fashioned architecture including an opera house and a university, which is where they do all the magic research business. I knew you were interested in the medical aspect of Hell, so I asked to see as much of that as I was allowed to."

"You are *exquisite*," said Greta. He could picture her, right now, picture the pale but present flush in her cheeks, the brightness of her eyes—they looked grey sometimes, but when she was excited, they were definitely blue—and the desire to hold her in his arms washed over Varney in an almost frightening wave. He was conscious of the kind of excitement he had not felt for centuries.

"—I try," he said, faintly unsteady. "I wasn't permitted to tour the laboratory facilities, but I did see some of the spa and the hospital, and I did in fact meet Dr. Faust. Who is—very human, still. I think you would get on quite well with him, actually."

"What's he like?"

"He shouts a lot, I gather," said Varney. "He is, I am told, in fact the only person in Hell who is allowed to shout *at Samael*, which tells you something. He only had a few minutes to spend talking to a visitor, but I mentioned that you were very eager to have the chance to visit yourself and discuss medicine, and he said he'd think about it."

"I love you," said Greta. "Enormously. Oh, Varney, thank you *so* much."

"My pleasure," he said, entirely honest: *I love you* still sent a deep sweet shock through him every time. "And Fastitocalon asked after you; I told him where you were and what you were up to, and he seemed very pleased."

"He looked okay? He's not overworking himself?"

"I couldn't say about overworking or otherwise," said Varney, "but he seems to be reasonably healthy, if a little short-tempered. He has new suits. They look exactly like the old ones, of course, except for not dating back to 1958."

Greta laughed. "He is probably going to look like that for all eternity; it suits him. I find it difficult to picture him ever having worn anything else, even back in the middle ages."

"The mental image of Fastitocalon in doublet and hose does rather boggle the mind," said Varney, bone-dry. "He's got lots of staff and I gather he's very busy with some sort of large-scale research project that may not be going tremendously well, but he didn't vouchsafe many details."

"Last time I talked to him about work was—right after the thing in Paris," said Greta. "I haven't heard much from him at all since then. He was having to clear up an enormous mess brought about by the demon who used to run Monitoring and Evaluation, who was doing a dreadful job of it and has since been turned into a large banana slug for crimes against the infernal civil service. There's some poetic justice in the fact that this demon happens to be the one who kicked Fass out of Hell in the first place. I don't know how much of a problem the M&E situation is, but that might be it."

"Could be," said Varney, thinking, *banana slug?* "He didn't seem in bad spirits, at least, despite how busy he is, and he was quite energetic and brisk. He brought me home again very early this morning."

"You still haven't told me *why* you went," said Greta.

"I have not," he agreed. "You'll see quite soon, I promise. I know you've only been there at the spa for a few days and it may not be possible to receive visitors while you're still settling in, but—do let me know when would be suitable for me to visit, if I may?"

"You *may*," said Greta firmly. "And—there's a couple of surgeries I need to do in the next few days, but after that, yes, please do come and see me? You'd be very welcome, everyone here is extremely pleasant, and I will arrange to come down to meet you myself in the helicopter."

"Helicopter?" he repeated. "Good heavens. You can't fly one, can you?"

"I cannot, but I can ride in it. Oasis Natrun has its own bloody helicopter, which delights me immeasurably. Please come this weekend, if you can? I want to see you so much."

"Of course," said Varney, "I'll—"

There was a commotion on the other end of the line, running footsteps, someone calling: *Dr. Helsing, Doctor, please come quick, it's Maanakhtef, we need you right away.*

"Of course," he heard Greta say, and then "Varney, I'm sorry, I have to go—"

"Go," he said, "I love you, dear," and heard the click as she hung up.

He closed his eyes, briefly dizzy with a sort of emotional water-hammer at the sudden end to the conversation, and his hand crept again to touch the velvet box, its strange but undeniable solidity.

*I hope you like it, darling,* he thought, *I harrowed Hell and brought it back*, and tried to squash a small but sharp wave of jealousy for Greta's patients and their monopoly on her time and attention.

*Ah*, he thought, not without bitterness. *There's the nasty vindictive creature I've always been. Not much is changing, after all, no matter how daring I have become. I'm still damned, and always will be, even if Hell let me go again; there is no getting around that awkward little fact.*

And it would have been very easy for Varney to descend into one of the spirals of self-disgust that characterized his particular brand of melancholy if at that moment something small and round and white that had been climbing down the velvet curtain had not chosen to squeak, and in doing so lost its grip on the curtain and fall, still squeaking, in midair. Varney's hand darted out, faster than a human's could have moved, that eerie vampyre quickness, and caught the thing as it fell; he opened his hand to find a skull the size of a walnut sitting on his palm and staring up at him with tiny empty eye sockets.

*Squeak*, said the skull, and Varney had to *sigh*.

* * *

She had been leaning on the terrace railing, looking down the lap of the valley to the city and the sea beyond, pleasantly tired but *satisfied*, enjoying the luxury of listening to Varney's voice on the other end of the phone. Until now Greta hadn't really had much time to enjoy the view from the spa's highest terrace, let alone lounge around on the comfortably cushioned chairs with a drink in her hand, and she had been thinking seriously about ordering one when the sliding doors behind her opened and running feet approached.

It was Sister Melitta, one of the shift nurses, out of breath. "Doctor," she said, "please come quick, it's Maanakhtef," and Greta's stomach sank like a stone. She said good-bye to Varney and hung up the phone, hooking her stethoscope around her neck as she ran inside, the nurse having to catch up with her. *What did I do wrong*, she was thinking, *what the hell did I do this time that I haven't done a thousand other times with the bone shaping and stabilization?*

Aloud she said as they hurried through the corridors, "What happened?"

"It's one of the spells, Doctor," Sister Melitta said. "It's worse this time, it's much worse, he was on his way back from the sun lounge when it happened and he—well, he *fell*."

"Oh, *shit*," said Greta, quickening her pace. Mummies were brittle. "What's the extent of the damage?"

"We aren't sure—Sister Brigitte is with him, she said we weren't to move him without you—"

*Good*, she thought, *at least that's something, he won't splinter any further, with luck I can stabilize him enough to get him on a stretcher.* She was trying quite hard to focus on the immediate situation rather than picking at the constant nagging awareness that she *didn't* know what was going on, what was causing this bizarre series of episodes, and it got a lot easier as she and Sister Melitta turned the corner and she got a good look at what they were dealing with.

Maanakhtef had been leaning on his crutches, of course; he wasn't allowed to put any weight on the damaged foot at this point. When the fainting spell had struck, he must have been taking a step forward, and in losing consciousness had slipped to the side as he'd fallen, landing with his back nearly flat on the floor and his legs twisted, the right hip uppermost. It was an enormous mercy that the crutches hadn't tangled themselves up with him; both of them lay safely flung wide on the floor.

Greta took all this in very quickly indeed, in a matter of a few seconds, and then she was on her knees beside the mummy. Sister Brigitte was kneeling by his head, her palms holding it completely still. "Doctor," she said tightly. "The skull's intact. This is what—"

"What Ed was worried about," Greta said. "Yes. I know. Thank you for your quick thinking." She bent over Maanakhtef and began very, very carefully to run her fingertips over his limbs, feeling for any give that should not be there, fractures in the bones beneath the fragile wrappings. She'd brought mummies back from much worse situations than this one, but Greta couldn't help thinking of how she'd reassured Maanakhtef just this afternoon that he'd be fine, that she'd take care of him, that she knew how to *fix* him, and it was painfully obvious that despite all her training she didn't, in fact, have a clue.

"One of you take notes," she said, evenly and clearly, to the other nurses gathered around. "And someone go get me a hard C-collar and a stretcher. Fracture of the left clavicle. Ribs two, three, and four, left side, broken. He landed on that shoulder, the scapula may be cracked—left humerus, too—possible hip fracture as well. I'm amazed the skull is sound and I want C-spine imaging *now*. Brigitte, you stay with me. Melitta, go power up the CT. Delphine, get Tefnakhte and page the imaging tech on duty."

When they were alone with the unconscious Maanakhtef, Greta sat back on her heels and took a deep breath. "Ed was right," she said. "I shouldn't have let him out of bed until this—whatever it is—is identified and controlled. We knew he'd had multiple instances of these attacks."

"All of which were transient," said the chief of nursing. "This one appears to have been prolonged and a great deal worse than the others."

"I can't help wondering if it's something I did today," said Greta. "I know it's ridiculous, but I can't help it. I asked Tefnakhte about the magic he's been doing on the patients, and he was way ahead of me—already had been looking for patterns and failing to find any, and if *he* didn't find any, I'm inclined to think there are no patterns to be found."

"I don't think there's any correlation between your treatment today and this episode," said Sister Brigitte. "You've done some procedures already and nobody's fainted afterward."

"I know. I just wish I had any idea what was going *on*." It was the worst thing, as a scientist. Not knowing why—and not having any idea where to start looking for answers.

Sister Brigitte was about to say something else—had drawn breath to say it—when Maanakhtef gave a very faint creaking moan, and shifted slightly. Brigitte's hands held his head and neck still, while Greta took his unhurt right hand carefully in hers, bending over him. "Maanakhtef," she said gently, "stay still, it's going to be all right. You've had a bad fall and you're hurt, but we're going to fix you. I need to make sure I know where all the damage is and then I will repair you. I promise."

"...Doctor...Helsing?" he said, a whispered creak. The bandaged fingers curled weakly around hers. "...Hurts."

"I know it does," she said, aching herself. "I know. But this I can fix, Maanakhtef. This I know how to repair, and we'll give you something to send you away again for a little while so that you don't have to feel it. Can you move your feet?"

He tried; the damaged foot she'd been about to repair obviously hurt to move, but he could get both of them to respond, and Greta relaxed a bit. "Good, that's wonderful. You're managing beautifully. In a minute I'm going to put something stiff around your neck to hold you steady while we get you onto a stretcher, and I'm sorry if it's uncomfortable but you won't need it for long at all."

"What...happened?" he asked.

"You had another attack," said Sister Brigitte. "A very bad one, it seems—and unfortunately it happened while you were upright. Do you remember anything?"

"No," he said, "just—this terrible weakness, all my strength gone, and then nothing."

She was about to ask more questions when the two nurses reappeared with a stretcher and a hard C-collar. "Mr. Tefnakhte is on his way to the imaging suite," one of them told Greta, without looking up to meet her eyes. "He says he'll do anything he can to help."

"Splendid," said Greta, and nodded for them to put the stretcher down on Maanakhtef's left side. She and Sister Brigitte got the collar fastened around his neck; she and the other two nurses knelt down on his right. "Brigitte, you're maintaining neutral inline stabilization. Melitta and Delphine, on my count, we're rolling him onto his side, in three, two, *one*."

They were as careful as they could be, and Greta had determined that holding his damaged left shoulder and side was preferable to rolling him onto it, but Maanakhtef gave a horrible stifled little groan nonetheless. Greta and the nurses got the stretcher flat against his back and eased him down to the floor again. "That's the worst of it over," she told him, taking his right hand and settling it on his chest. "You're doing extremely well, and in a few minutes we'll be able to give you something for the pain; you'll feel much better soon. Melitta, take the left side, I've got the foot of the stretcher."

As long as she was inside the clinical necessity of action, as long as she had no time to stop and think, Greta could set aside the awful sinking feeling of *not being in control*, of *not knowing what was happening and why*. As she and the nurses hurried Maanakhtef to imaging—as she watched Tefnakhte say several sentences in Egyptian, touching Maanakhtef's injuries with an amulet, and watched her patient visibly relax as his pain eased—as she stood looking over the imaging tech's shoulder at the monitors while the CT scanner spun around Maanakhtef and told the story of just how badly he'd been damaged, how much she would have to repair—cracked and broken bones, torn ligaments, sections of ancient muscle tissue destroyed, reduced to powder—she'd be able to hang on to her clinical compartmentalization; but she knew that as soon as it was over, as soon as she was done and all the repairs as complete as she could make them, she would need to find somewhere very private to do a bit of quiet, self-contained, discreet falling apart.

*Later*, she thought grimly, and went to scrub. *Later for that. Right now I have work to do.*

# CHAPTER 6

The time Grisaille had spent with Corvin and the vampire coven under Paris had encouraged nocturnal habits; it was only because he'd been cohabiting with Edmund Ruthven in the ordinary world that he had picked up the knack of walking abroad by day and sleeping at night.

Well, sort of night, anyway. They'd come back to the hotel around three, and—waking alone in the great bed, Grisaille could see the grey beginning of dawn. He frowned up at the ceiling, not sure what had woken him, head still muzzy with sleep, but when the sound came again, he was *completely* awake all at once. Awake and *worried.*

He didn't need to turn the bathroom light on to be able to see Ruthven being violently sick; in the dark, Grisaille's eyeshine was faintly reflected by the white tile as he knelt down beside him, putting a steadying hand on Ruthven's shoulder through another vicious, convulsive spasm of retching. Grisaille could feel him shaking helplessly, the silk of his pajamas damp with sweat, his breath coming in ragged sobs, and couldn't help but wrap his arms around him and try to ground some of the misery in his own bone and muscle, brace him through the force of it. He was murmuring useless phatic reassurances, barely aware of doing so—*I've got you, it'll be all right*—and not being even slightly sure he wasn't lying.

Ruthven had very clearly brought up everything inside him, but it seemed to take forever before the retching passed and he could hang exhausted in Grisaille's arms, gasping. When he found his voice, it was a hoarse wreck, acid-scoured, strengthless: "...I'm awfully sorry you had to see that."

Grisaille stifled an urge to shake him, and just sat back on his heels, cradling Ruthven against him. "Never mind *me*," he said. "What's—what *happened*? Did you eat someone you shouldn't?"

Ruthven shook his head, and then moaned, pressed his hands to his face as if attempting to keep his skull from bursting. "...headache," he managed after a moment. "This is... bad... but not unheard-of."

"*Another* migraine?" Grisaille demanded, and then bit his lip. "This isn't like you."

"It's rare. But... I haven't had one in years... I was probably due?"

"That's not how that works," he said, but the returning strength in Ruthven's voice was going some way toward reassuring him. "Are you finished, do you think?"

"Yes. It's—already fading." Ruthven leaned against him, still shivering. "I really am sorry to have woken you."

"Stop apologizing," Grisaille said, and kissed his temple very lightly before helping him up. He let Ruthven rinse his mouth out, not at all pleased by how hard he was leaning on the edge of the sink, before adding, "I'm taking you back to bed."

"I can walk," Ruthven protested, but Grisaille didn't give him the chance: very carefully, as smoothly as he could, he lifted him into his arms and carried him back to the bedroom, settling him against the pillows.

In the gathering light he looked absolutely dreadful, grey-white except for the bruised shadows under each eye, his face and throat sheened with sweat, but at least when he opened those eyes, he could focus on Grisaille; he had *some* vision back.

"You need a doctor," Grisaille said.

"Of course I don't, it's—just a migraine, there's nothing to be done about them, and anyway, it *is* passing." He sounded a little more like himself. "I need to sleep for about eight hours and then I will be quite all right again. Promise."

Grisaille sat on the edge of the bed and stroked a lock of sweat-damp hair away from his face. "Do you want to go home?"

"No," said Ruthven, and lifted a hand to capture Grisaille's fingers, pressed them against his cheek. "I do not. I want to enjoy the rest of my holiday, and go to see lots of museums, and—possibly not stay out all night engaging in riotous living?"

"I think riotous living is probably contraindicated," Grisaille agreed, "at least for now, and—can you take pills, or best not to try it just yet?"

"I think I can," he said. "I'd like to try, anyway."

"Right, then." Grisaille went to fetch a glass of water and the painkillers, still not quite able to relax. He'd never seen anyone that sick, except perhaps his old boss's consort in the middle of a junkie-blood overdose, and he knew for a fact that none of the people he and Ruthven had fed from recently had been carrying anything untoward in their bloodstreams: they'd *shared*, and Grisaille himself felt entirely fine, if seriously concerned.

*If he's not better when he wakes up*, Grisaille thought, *I am going to call someone.*

The Egyptian section of the Met represents one of the world's finest collections of Egyptian artifacts, including not only an actual Old Kingdom mastaba tomb from the Saqqara necropolis but also a temple that once stood in Lower Nubia; visitors can walk freely through both structures. They are among the most popular exhibits in the section, and often very crowded; Leonora Van Dorne ignored them completely as she stalked through the echoing halls, heels clicking sharply. She had much, much more interesting things to look at, and in any case, she found the wholesale installation of an actual historical structure in a museum to be somewhat lacking in taste.

She passed through the galleries, paying no attention to the stares she was receiving from other museum visitors, until she reached Gallery 128: early fourth century. Here was the famous Metternich Stela, as well as the Hermopolis Stela; here, fragments of statues displaying the smooth detailed modeling of the human form that characterized this period; here, smaller, complete statues like the figure of Horus protecting Nectanebo II; and here, in a very special case, a perfect tiny sculpture of a woman sitting on a block, hands resting calmly on her thighs, staring into eternity with a faint little smile curving her lips. GENEROUSLY LOANED FROM THE PRIVATE COLLECTION OF LEONORA IRENE VAN DORNE, the discreet plaque beside it read.

Ms. Van Dorne could see herself reflected in the thick glass of the case, her own face superimposed on the statue's tiny one; the smile was identical. *I know something you don't,* it said.

She was aware of footsteps behind her, but didn't turn around; not till the assistant curator actually reached her side did she move at all, and then it was only to turn her head to face her—and watched the woman go white and *stare.*

Her smile widened. "Yes?" she said.

The curator went on staring for a few more moments before blushing. "—I'm—I'm sorry, I—"

"Is something wrong?"

"I—no—that is—" she stammered, and then finally seemed to get herself under control. "You look *amazing.* I'm sorry, that was completely inappropriate of me, *wow.*"

She had, in fact, not been able to avoid glancing at herself in every reflective surface she passed all morning, and now she let a tinge of condescension into the smile, and watched the curator blush again.

"I'm so sorry. Forget I said anything. I—was there something we could help you with?"

"No," said Ms. Van Dorne, "I'm just visiting her. I approve of the security measures you have taken."

The curator's shoulders slumped a little. "Oh, *good*," she said. "I'm so glad. We followed all your instructions, of course."

"Of course. This is a similar case to the ones for the magical stelae, I see."

"It's very similar," the curator assured her, clearly relieved to have something to show off. Ms. Van Dorne followed her over to the two freestanding cases in the middle of the room, each containing a dark green stone slab about two and a half feet tall, densely carved with hieroglyphs and complex reliefs. "You can see the reinforced glass is the same thickness, and the chamber itself is locked with a multiply-redundant system and purged with nitrogen."

"Excellent," said Ms. Van Dorne, skimming the columns of incised hieroglyphs on the Metternich Stela: . . . *remove for me the poison of the bite which is in every limb of the patient, / so that your words are not rejected on account of it. / See, your name is called today. / May you create the raising of your renown, when you have lifted by your words of light. / May you cause the sufferer to live for me, / so that adoration is given to you by the populace . . .*

"It's a—" the curator began.

"A healing spell. I am familiar with the type of artifact," said Ms. Van Dorne, and had the pleasure of watching her blush again. "Sacred to Horus. They are covered with incantations to be recited to protect someone from harmful creatures. One would pour water over the stela and give it to the victim to drink, who would then be healed as Horus was healed from the scorpion's sting." She could remember the first time she'd come across the concept, and how neat she'd found it. How satisfying. Egyptian ritual was enormously satisfying, in a way no modern religion had ever seemed worth pursuing to her.

"Er, yes," said the curator, who was wearing a name tag; Ms. Van Dorne glanced at it.

"So, *Susan*," she said, still with that little smile, and rested her hand on the second glass case. "Tell me what's different about *this* stela."

*I know you know I know*, she thought. *And you're being tested.*

"This one," Susan began, faintly pink in the face, "is remarkable among magical stelae. To our knowledge, it is the only one sacred to *Thoth* rather than Horus that has ever been discovered. The rest of the known magico-medical stelae are often termed *cippi of Horus* and invariably feature some aspect of the story of Horus's poisoning and cure, but the Hermopolis Stela's inscriptions show the story from Thoth's point of view."

"Hermopolis," said Ms. Van Dorne. "Also called Khemenu. The center of the Thoth cult."

"...yes," said Susan. "As it happens."

"I'm surprised there aren't more."

"As far as we know, this is the only one ever found. That's not to say there aren't others—just that no one knows where they are."

"One of a kind," said Ms. Van Dorne, and ran her fingertips gently over the glass. "Immensely powerful, I should think."

"To the ancient Egyptians, certainly," said Susan. Her phone buzzed, and she took it out of her pocket, looking apologetic. "Oh. I've got to go, I'm afraid, I've been summoned to a meeting, but of course feel free to spend as long as you like—it's always so nice to see you—"

Ms. Van Dorne waved her away, distracted; she had begun to read the columns of inscription on the Hermopolis Stela, with a gathering sense of excitement. In the glass she could see her own face quite clearly, with the darkness of the stone as a backdrop, and she knew precisely why the girl Susan had reacted so sharply; she had lost not just a year or two, but something closer to ten. The woman looking back at her out of the glass might have been in her mid-thirties, and felt like it: the encroaching embarrassments of age were gone from her body as well as her face, leaving her with a kind of bright energy she had almost forgotten how to feel.

And that had been accomplished with such minor artifacts: ushabti figurines, amulets, cosmetic boxes. Nothing with *real* metaphysical significance.

*Imagine*, she thought, touching her reflection with a hand whose skin was firm and taut once more, the veins and tendons smoothly hidden, *imagine what I could do with* this *to play with.*

*How far could I go?*

Dawn had come and gone while Greta was working. In all it had taken nearly nine hours to repair the damage to Maanakhtef, while he was safely under the influence of

Tefnakhte's sleep spell: she'd had a second shift of nurses scrub in halfway through. The worst hadn't been the fractures. Those she could simply seal with dual-cure resin cement and reinforce with micro-mesh wrapping impregnated with more resin, not unlike fiberglass. The worst was definitely the powdered muscle tissue she'd had to replace with layer after layer of interwoven elastic bandage, re-creating lost tendons and ligaments with nylon straps, anchoring everything into the reinforced bones with tiny titanium screws. On the post-op scans his left side lit up like a tiny night sky with the individual screws glowing brightly against the dark.

No one else had had multiple instances of the fainting episodes. She had given orders that every mummy who had experienced it at all was to be on bed rest or in a wheelchair until they figured out what the hell was going on; she didn't want to have to spend another eight hours repairing someone who had collapsed and broken parts of themselves into powder.

She hurt all over. Her neck and the base of her skull were tight with a tension headache; the small of her back ached like a rotten tooth, her feet throbbed. The smell of resin and hot bone from the Stryker saw seemed to have coated the insides of her air passages with a thin but tenacious film.

Greta watched as the nurses wheeled Maanakhtef away, still under Tefnakhte's spell. He'd be under constant observation until he woke, and she was going to insist that a nurse stay with him for at least the next twelve hours. She stripped off her gloves, pulled the surgical cap off and shook out her hair, lank and limp, and tried to crack her neck.

She still didn't know what was happening.

That was the worst of this. Much worse than the work. Much worse than the difficulty of the work itself. The fact that she simply had no idea what was happening, and could not stop it, was absolutely worse than every other aspect of the situation.

At least Maanakhtef was stable, and no one else seemed to have gone into crisis while she was working. Greta thought she could maybe catch an hour or two of sleep, and make up for the rest of it with coffee, before going back to work; by her watch it was getting on for eight in the morning. She should call Varney back, let him know what was happening, tell him not to come over until she had a handle on the problem. She should call Ed in Cairo and tell him, too, and ask for his help, and that would be a great deal worse than talking to Varney; Ed might have to leave what he was doing and come *back* here because the person he'd left in charge had no fucking clue what she was up to and he'd clearly picked the wrong doctor to run the place...

*Oh, shut up*, she thought tiredly, turning off the overhead lights. There were still tiny scraps of linen wrappings all over the operating table, and they hurt to look at. *You aren't incompetent. You're just—currently unable to figure this out, that's all.*

*It comes to the same thing.*

She tossed her discarded gloves and mask and cap into the trash and left the operating theater, shuffling like an old woman, her back and shoulders one solid chunk of pain. Passing through the hallways took much longer than it should, but at last she found herself back at her personal quarters, and had to remind herself how to unlock the door. She'd just—fall over, for a little while, on the bed, and then get back to business. Yeah. That was the ticket, all right.

"Dr. Helsing," said the loudspeaker. "Dr. Helsing, there's a phone call for you."

It was probably Ed calling to ask what the fuck she was doing and why she hadn't figured it out yet. Greta stared blankly at the wall for a moment before hauling herself up off the bed and crossing the room to pick up the handset.

"Ed?" she said. "I'm so sorry—"

"*Greta*," said a voice she hadn't heard in a while. "Greta, I need you."

"Grisaille?" She sat down on the edge of the bed again, blinking. "What—"

"It's Ruthven," he said. Even over the phone the aching worry was very audible. "He's—he's not well, I didn't know what to do so I tried to call your clinic and they said you were away in France for four months and I finally got whoever it was to give me the number for this place and I need you, Greta, he's—he's very bad."

"What happened?" Everything had gone cold and clear and slow. She could still feel how much she hurt; she just didn't care.

"He's—he says it's migraines but I've never ever seen anyone this sick with them, he's had three in a row now and he can't *see* and he's been vomiting for hours and the pain is—excruciating to *watch*, let alone experience—"

"Wait," she said. "Back up. Tell me how it started."

"Out of nowhere," said Grisaille. "He was fine and then he wasn't fine at all, and it went away so I thought he was going to be all right and then he was very much *not*—and it's getting worse."

"Are his pupils even?" she asked sharply.

"I think so?" he said, sounding miserable. "It hurts him so much to open his eyes, though—the light is painful when he can see at all—"

"Any weakness down one side or the other? Can he stand up?"

"No, and yes, but it hurts more?"

"Where are you?"

"Still in Rome," said Grisaille. "He said he didn't want to go home, but—that was yesterday and it's worse now and I don't know what to *do*, I've never seen anyone like this—"

She closed her eyes tight. "You're going to get him here, is what you're going to do. You can't take him to a hospital, even a completely idiotic doctor would notice he's not alive, but I need to see what's going on inside his skull. This place has the best imaging suite I've ever seen, and I'm the medical director for the moment so I can admit a non-mummy patient if I want to. I don't care how you manage it, Grisaille, I have every confidence that you can get him here, and rapidly."

"Is it—do vampires *get* brain tumors, is that a thing that happens—"

"I don't know," said Greta, "but we have to find out. Throw money at the problem. He's got more of it than God; you can undoubtedly get hold of some of it. Just get him here, as soon as possible."

"Okay," he said, still sounding miserable and shaken but less lost. "I can—do that. Somehow."

"Good. Call me when you land in Marseille and I'll come down with the helicopter."

"You have a *helicopter*?"

"This place has everything," Greta said. "Including our own problems, but right now I want him here where I can see him. I'm going to call Varney and tell him what's going on."

She needed him. She'd been going to tell him to stay put, not to come over here until she had a handle on what was happening; but now, with *another* crisis looming over her head, Greta very desperately wanted Varney there with her, if only to reassure her that *he* wasn't mysteriously indisposed.

The trees in Central Park blazed under a clear autumn sky, vermilion and flame-yellow and bronze, reflected in the mirror-flat surface of the lake; and halfway across the elegant understated arch of the Bow Bridge, two angels were having their hair and makeup touched up mid-photo-shoot.

Amitiel and Zophiel held blankly still under the brushes and sprays, as expressionless and perfect as marble statues. They were wearing about thirty thousand dollars' worth of clothes and accessories between them, and this was only the second wardrobe change of the afternoon.

Only once had Amitiel forgotten about the wings. Their

mortal seeming wasn't quite infallible; they had to put a little effort into making sure their *reflections* were consistent with the disguise, and earlier he had forgotten briefly. Fortunately, the only person who happened to be looking at his reflection in the lake at the time had been a young man on the shore whose bloodstream was full of enough chemicals to make the idea of a white-winged seraph in Central Park appear perfectly understandable. Still, Zophiel worried.

They were so close now. So close. Both of them had felt it the last time the woman used the spell they had planted for her to find—that had been a significant level of mirabilic flux—and both of them knew it would not take so *very* much more of that to reach their goal, but they could not afford mistakes. Not now. It was not certain *enough* that the woman's sin of vanity would prompt her to use the spell enough times to cause the level of damage they required. And they could not return home with their mission half-completed; without that weakening of the border between worlds, the Archangel Michael of *their* Heaven could not hope to lead his army to invade and destroy the blasphemous creatures posing as angels on this side. It was up to them, a great and terrible responsibility to prepare the way for their Host; they had been vastly honored by the Council of Archangels with such an assignment, and Zophiel could not imagine failing to complete it as instructed.

Amitiel had seemed a little happier after the encounter with the abomination in Rome. That was good. All Zophiel had to do now was make sure nothing went wrong.

"Okay, darlings, let's get going here, give me *fierce* but *vulnerable*, all right? *Sell* it. Make me *believe*."

With uncanny grace, they took up their poses as the camera began its frantic clicking, and—not for the first time—the photographer thought to herself, *How the hell are they so fucking good?*

The first time Sir Francis Varney had ever flown had been to Paris, to rescue Greta, back in the spring, although she had turned out to be largely self-rescuing; this time, he thought as the plane made the long slow turn into the sunset for the approach into Marseille, he didn't know if *rescue* was precisely the term. It wasn't Greta herself in dire straits, precisely. It was—well, *everyone else*.

She'd sounded quite calm on the phone, but Varney recognized that particular tone: it was *okay, we're in a very bad situation, here's what needs to be done*—and he knew she'd be able to keep that up for quite some time, before the inevitable crash.

The box in his pocket felt slightly absurd, under the circumstances; one of their dearest friends was desperately ill, some unknown malady was attacking Greta's patients, and here he was showing up on her doorstep with an *engagement ring* in hand, as if anything about him *mattered*—

Varney closed his hands around the ends of the armrests firmly, and reminded himself that wallowing in his own melancholia was something of a luxury they could not necessarily afford just at the moment. The cabin tilted slightly as the pilot began the landing flare, and he was grateful for the distraction.

In the terminal he called her from one of the lounges, watching the last of the light fade from sea and sky, and received instructions. Grisaille had thralled someone into flying him and Ruthven the three-hundred-something miles from Rome, or possibly just chartered a plane, Greta wasn't quite sure and didn't care, but they were due to land in half an hour and Varney was to meet them and Greta, arriving separately in the helicopter.

"Of course," he said, and slipped his hand into his pocket, touched the ring box. "I wish there was more I could do."

"That's plenty," she told him. "Grisaille is understandably extremely upset and scared, and he'll need someone trustworthy there to help—and comfort. I can't think of anyone I'd rather have with them right now."

"Really?"

"Yes, really. You're immensely reassuring when you want to be, and excellent in a crisis. I've got to go. I'll see you soon."

"I love you," he said, wincing at how *young* it sounded when he said it.

"I love you back," said Greta, and hung up.

He had been told about Ruthven's condition, but nothing could have prepared Varney for the sight of him in a wheelchair, being rolled across the tarmac by a woman in the airport's flight services uniform, with Grisaille hurrying alongside. Ruthven was not white but *grey* and sweating, half his face hidden behind huge sunglasses that didn't conceal the twisted expression of agony. He was breathing in ragged gasps between his teeth, lips white and drawn back. The fangs were very evident.

Varney's first thought was *he won't even make it to the spa*, quickly followed by *what the hell is* wrong *with him?* Aloud he said, "Edmund, Grisaille, Greta's on her way," hurrying over.

Grisaille was an unpleasant ashy color himself. Varney could see the whites all the way around his red irises. "She has to fix him, Varney," he said, his voice not quite steady. "She has to fix him, he can't stand much more of this—"

"She will," said Varney. "If she can, she will."

He had never in his life been gladder to hear the thudding of a helicopter's blades approaching. It came down fast, faster than he had expected, the rotor wash blasting them with stinging force, and almost before it had touched down—a great sandy-gold thing, with the spa's logo on its side—Greta was jumping out and running toward them, bag in hand.

Varney was very grateful that only he caught the brief horrified look on her face; it was there only for a moment, and then gone as if it had never been, replaced with her calm clinician's expression as she came up to them. She'd raised her hands to her neck to grab the stethoscope, but clearly decided not to bother, simply bending over the chair.

"Edmund, it's me," she said, taking Ruthven's hand and gasping slightly as he squeezed her bones together in a tight grip. "I'm here, I've got you now. We're going to fly back to the spa and I will find out what's wrong and do everything I can to make it stop, all right?"

He didn't nod—Varney thought moving his head must make it worse, if that was possible—but Greta gave another little gasp as his fingers tightened briefly and let go. "Help me with him," she said to Varney and Grisaille, and, "Thank you, that's everything," to the airport services woman, whose dealing-with-rich-customers expression was much the worse for wear. Together Varney and Grisaille lifted Ruthven from the chair and carried him to the waiting helicopter, and Varney was only *mildly* surprised to find the thing was kitted out as an ambulance inside, complete with gurney and banks of monitoring equipment, crates of supplies. Greta nodded for them to set him down on the stretcher.

"Carefully. Very carefully. I know moving makes it hurt worse, Edmund, but you need to lie down. The rest of you strap in. Raoul, get us out of here as soon as you get clearance, expedite."

The pilot flashed her a thumbs-up, and Varney watched as Greta went through a rapid examination; winced when she took off the huge dark glasses to reveal Ruthven's eyes squeezed shut, the delicate skin stained violet with exhaustion and pain, winced more when he opened them at Greta's request and made a helpless little noise through his teeth, just a rag of sound. Whatever she saw seemed to reassure her somewhat, though, and by the time the helicopter lifted off, she was already starting a line in Ruthven's arm, clear fluid in a snaking tube, keeping both herself and her patient perfectly steady as the cabin around them shifted.

Varney glanced over at Grisaille, and wished he hadn't. The

expression on his face hurt to see: it was the terrible misery of someone watching their loved one in pain and being completely unable to help in any way. He wanted to say something reassuring, but—despite his beautiful voice, the most appealing thing about him by all accounts—for once, Varney had no words at all to give.

# CHAPTER 7

Swallowing hard as the helicopter tilted, carrying them away and up into the mountains, Grisaille had had a very horrible moment of thinking, *If this is the exciting world of interpersonal relationships, I should have stayed the livid hell away from it*, and immediately afterward, *I am a terrible person.*

*Not that that's news*, he thought bitterly now, pacing back and forth in the pleasantly appointed waiting room, arms folded tightly. It had been a very long day; it had, in fact, been part of the previous day as well. He couldn't remember exactly when he'd last *not* been worried.

Ruthven had slept, as he had foretold, and woken not magically restored to health but curled up in agonized dry-heaving, clutching at his skull and making noises Grisaille would very much rather not remember. The worst of the nausea seemed to subside, but the pain had continued, and Grisaille had registered with a kind of anguished fury that Ruthven couldn't see him at all; couldn't see anything but glittering, sickening, sliding patterns behind his eyes.

He'd called Greta. And as soon as he'd gotten off the phone with her, he had called a friend of his, who had called another friend, who had arranged it that when he got Ruthven to the Rome airport, they were taken directly to a tiny Cessna; and he absolutely did not want to remember that hour and a half in the air with Ruthven making small horrible choked sounds of pain against his shoulder.

As soon as they had landed at Oasis Natrun, there had been a phalanx of white-clad nurses waiting for them, and with Greta holding up the bag of whatever she'd been dripping into Ruthven's veins, the group of them had lifted the gurney out of the helicopter and hurried him inside, leaving Varney and Grisaille to trail behind. He'd demanded to be told what was happening, and a nurse who'd stayed behind had *not* told him anything reassuring whatsoever. The waiting room was pleasantly designed and furnished. Grisaille hated it on sight.

"What the hell is taking so long?" he demanded for the second time. He could tell very clearly that Varney was hideously uncomfortable, sitting upright in one of the chairs, and wished the vampyre would just fuck off and let him pace alone.

"The scans do take time, sir," said the remaining nurse, looking up from his clipboard. "Dr. Helsing and the team will tell us as soon as we have results."

"What are they *doing* to him?"

"It's a spiral CT scan," said the nurse. "That's computed tomography, a kind of X-ray—"

"I know what it is," Grisaille snapped. "How is it taking this long?"

"Sir," said the nurse, "it's been half an hour. I understand your concern, but please try to be patient. Mr. Ruthven is in excellent hands."

Grisaille made himself sit down by the force of will alone, and stared at the carpet, trying to think of something—anything—to distract himself. Song lyrics. The entire roster of the coven he'd been running with in Paris, including the truly stupid made-up names. The rain in Spain falls mainly in the plain. The catalog of Ruthven's gorgeous embroidered dressing gowns, all twelve of them, the first thing of his that Grisaille had worn, back in the beginning, a delicious shiver of intimacy—

It was no use. He was up on his feet again and pacing, wanting very much to put his fist through the tastefully painted wall, which wouldn't help, either, but might relieve his feelings slightly.

Grisaille had no idea how much time had passed when behind him Varney cleared his throat. "Could you tell me a little more about how it began?"

"Out of fucking *nowhere* is how," Grisaille said, coming to a stop and folding his arms. "He was fine, we were having fun, we were having a *lot* of fun, in fact, and then two days ago he woke up with a nasty headache and it just got worse and worse. He kept trying to tell me it was just migraines, that he got them every now and then, but if this is just a migraine, I am the president of Burundi."

Varney nodded. "It's certainly not like any I've ever seen," he said. "But you were—just getting on with your holiday, not doing anything out of the ordinary?"

"Not a damn thing," said Grisaille. "I thought it might be someone he'd eaten but we basically shared the same people most nights and I'm absolutely fine."

Something was kicking his brain, something about Rome, about the Spanish Steps; he reached for it, but just then the door opened and Greta Helsing came in, looking—drained, Grisaille thought. *Etiolated.* Oh God. What was she going to say—

"It's not a tumor and it's not subarachnoid hemorrhage," she told them, holding up a hand. "The scans are completely clear. There is nothing visibly wrong inside his head *at all.*"

She sounded almost angry about it. "That's... good, right?" Grisaille said after a moment.

"On the one hand, yes, nobody needs to go rent an emergency neurosurgeon who bills by the hour. On the other, it is very bad indeed because it means *I don't know what's wrong with him*, and therefore I can't *fix* it, which is a problem I seem to be having a lot of right now."

"I have to see him," Grisaille said. "Is he... conscious?"

"Mostly. Not comfortable, but conscious. I have managed to knock the pain down a bit by giving him an amount of morphine which I will not disclose, and he's profoundly stoned. Come on."

She looked from him to Varney; silently, the vampyre followed her, and a moment later Grisaille caught up. "You're sure about the scans?" he asked as they walked.

"I'm very sure. I did both T1- and T2-weighted MRI and spiral CT and he comes up green across the board. There's nothing in his head that should not be there," she said, taking them into a long ward corridor. Most of the rooms seemed to be empty; Greta led them to one of the few closed doors and pushed it open. Ruthven lay in a high-sided hospital bed with the head raised, covered with blankets, surrounded by stacks of monitors and equipment. A thin tube ran from a drip bag into one arm; wires stuck to his chest connected to one of the machines.

Grisaille had just about time to think *oh my God he looks so small* before he was across the room and taking Ruthven's hand.

He did look better; still pinched and shock-grey, but in less visible pain. His hand in Grisaille's was cool, no longer slick with sweat; when he blinked slowly up at Grisaille, his pupils were tiny black pinpoints, contracted all the way. The effect was both hypnotic and slightly horrible.

Grisaille tried to smile, squeezing his hand. "Hey," he said softly. "How are you doing?"

"The universe," said Ruthven in a faint, drowsy rasp, "is *hilarious* right now. Did you know that? You should probably know that."

"Good God," said Varney quietly, and then gave a faint sound as if somebody had jabbed him with an elbow. Grisaille didn't turn around to look.

"The universe has a pretty fucked-up sense of humor," he said. "That far I'll go. Oh, love, I don't know what to *do*…"

He didn't know what to do with the fact that he was now apparently the kind of person who said *love* as a matter of course, either; it was still new and strange and frightening, if undeniable. He'd never loved anything in his life before, except perhaps the pleasure of complicated thievery; never even known what it really felt like, and it had happened to him all at once, a dizzying landslide carrying Grisaille with it regardless of his intentions. He had already begun to fall even before the final and terrible battle underneath Paris, months ago; by the time he'd recovered from the consequent knife through his lung, Grisaille was helplessly in the grip of an entirely new kind of gravity, one that currently *ached.*

His fingers tightened around Ruthven's. Behind him he heard the door close as Greta and Varney gave them some privacy. Ruthven squeezed his hand back weakly.

"It's all right," he said. "I'm... fine, right now. Just fine."

"You are on enough drugs to run a small cartel for a *week*," said Grisaille, and found himself horribly close to tears. "Dr. Helsing says your scans look... normal. I don't understand."

"Neither does she," Ruthven said. "About me, or about her mummies. Not understanding has always bothered her, poor girl. She... *resents* it. Which is also hilarious at the moment."

Grisaille reached down to relocate the lock of Ruthven's hair that always fell over his left eye; cupped his palm to Ruthven's face for a moment, tracing the line of his cheekbone with his thumb. The unnerving silver eyes closed slowly, reopened. His lashes were thick and very black, resting in a delicate curve against the bruised stains underneath each eye;

Grisaille couldn't help being struck all over again by how lovely he was, even now, even in this condition.

This untenable condition. They had to *fix* him somehow. They had to. It wasn't anything growing inside his head; okay. So—

"Something else has to be wrong," he said. "Something that doesn't... show on her scans. You don't have a fever, it's not an infection—"

He heard voices outside in the corridor, in rapid conversation, and straightened up, still holding Ruthven's hand. The door opened to admit Greta, Varney, and... okay, that was a mummy. That was certainly a mummy. Holding a clipboard.

"It's not somatic," Greta said, sounding more brisk than she had. "We know that much, at least. Physiologically you're just fine, Edmund. Your BP is a little off, but nothing spectacular now that I've gotten the pain down a bit; your heart rate's back to low normal for a classic draculine, temp is fine, sats look good, respiratory rate's settled down. Your blood tests came back perfectly unremarkable for your species. I'd do a lumbar puncture to get a CSF pressure, but I am completely sure it would be normal too. You haven't sustained traumatic brain injury of any kind, nor do you have anything inside your skull that shouldn't be there. I can't find a single thing *physically* wrong with you that can explain these symptoms."

"Which means," said the mummy in a British accent, "that there appears to be something metaphysically wrong, which is a different problem altogether."

"Metaphysically?" Grisaille repeated, squeezing Ruthven's hand. "This is *magic*?"

"I think it has to be," said Varney quietly. Grisaille noticed he had his arm around Greta's waist, and that her left hand was in the pocket of her white coat. "And since none of us are any good at magic except Mr. Tefnakhte here—"

"—and I'm only useful in terms of ancient Egyptian magic, which is a very narrow specialization—"

"—we need assistance from someone lower down, as it were. It's time to contact Hell."

Standing outside Ruthven's room with Greta while Grisaille and Ruthven talked, Varney had simply opened with, "This is the worst possible time in the world to be doing this, but I'm not quite sure when we'll have another chance," and taken a small box out of his pocket. At the sight of it, a spike of adrenaline lifted the little hairs on Greta's arms and legs: glass-clear excitement in the midst of chaos.

She took the box with hands that shook ever so slightly, and opened it, not sure what she'd see—and drew her breath in with a gasp.

The ring had no protruding claw settings to snag on her exam gloves. It was a narrow band of white metal with a row of oval gems channel-set down the center; she took it out and turned it between her fingers, trying to identify the jewels. They were all in shades of blue and green save one single white diamond, and there didn't seem to be a pattern.

"One of the last times I was in the world," Varney said, "there was a fashion for something called a regards ring," and suddenly she understood, all at once, and looked more closely at the sequence of jewels. He smiled, that smile that lit his face, transformed him almost into a living man.

"It helps," he said, "if you know that aquamarine is a form of beryl."

Beryl, emerald, lapis, opal, something green that presumably started with a V, emerald, diamond. Greta slipped the ring onto her finger, and had to gasp again when it *shrank to fit her*, the entire object contracting in a way that was simply not possible—

"Where did you get this?"

"I had it made," he said. "At a jeweler's on Plutus Boulevard—" And got no further, because Greta had flung her arms around him and was holding on very tight.

"*That's* why you went to Hell," she said, muffled in his shoulder, "for me?"

"And the grand gesture, while well meant, is unfortunately somewhat overshadowed by the current situation," he said, rueful, stroking her hair. "But I wanted you to have it sooner rather than later."

"You went to Hell *for me*," Greta repeated, looking into his face. "I am *so incredibly jealous*—"

Someone behind them cleared his throat very dryly indeed, a papery sound. Greta turned to see Tefnakhte standing there with a clipboard in one bandaged hand.

"I hate to interrupt," he said, "but I think you're going to have to call for backup on this one, Dr. Helsing. The test results are absolutely conclusive."

He handed her the clipboard, and she flicked through the

printouts. "This makes no *sense*," she said, almost to herself. "None of it makes sense. It *can't* be."

"What can't?" Varney asked.

"The tests are as clean as the scans." Greta looked up at him, all her excitement gone, sunk into a miserable crawling sense of *not understanding*. "Nothing came up whatsoever. All his readings are clear. I'm . . . completely at a loss, except—"

She straightened up a little. "Except Clarke."

"Clarke?" Tefnakhte asked.

"Arthur C. He once said, memorably, that sufficiently advanced technology is indistinguishable from magic; I was just thinking of it the other day. If I can't find a scientific reason for Ruthven's symptoms, there must be an *un*scientific reason. I don't suppose your version of magic might—let you see what's going on, if you asked it nicely?"

"I'm afraid not," he said. "Mine is very specific to a particular religion, a culture, that no longer exists outside the mummy community. It's like asking a specialist in ancient diseases to diagnose something that's only been around for a few years."

Greta sighed. "I was afraid you'd say that. I need a witch."

"There might be a better option than witches," said Varney slowly. "Remember I told you when I was in Hell, very briefly, I was given a tour of the medical facility—"

"Right," she said as the obvious answer dawned. "Where there's a lot of advanced magical diagnostic equipment. I'm an idiot. I should have thought of that first thing. We debrief the patient, and then we ring up Hell."

"I could do the—the summoning thing," Varney said, tentative. "I have the pronunciation correct now, I believe."

Greta's distant mental link with the demon Fastitocalon meant that if she sent a sufficiently powerful message, he'd respond at once, but she looked at Varney, the unfamiliar heaviness of the ring on her left hand very much at the forefront of her awareness, and had to smile. "Yes," she said. "You could. It would be very much appreciated."

He smiled back. "All right."

The amount of morphine Greta had pumped into Ruthven was not precisely controlling the pain, just—masking it. He had read somewhere a description of pain like a jagged piling jutting from a beach, and the drugs simply bringing in the tide to cover it; when the tide began to recede, there was the pain again, a black rotten thing like a croggled tooth that had never gone away at all.

In the beginning he really had thought it was a migraine: the socket of his right eye had filled up with a familiar squeezing relentless kind of agony that felt as if it should be visible, lines of poisonous light shining through his skin, and the nausea and photophobia were just as familiar, if no more welcome. And it had gone away. Mostly.

It was when it came *back* that he began to be frightened, because it came back worse than before, much worse—he'd barely made it to the bathroom before being convulsed with vicious retching, each heave sending bolts of monstrous, astonishing pain through his skull; in the middle of it he'd been sure he was having a stroke—could vampires have strokes?—and then out of the fizzing blackness, cool hands steadying him, Grisaille's voice, and the awful realization that he was frightening Grisaille and could not *stop*—

—and after that he had lost track of time. Lying here half-listening to them talk, he had no idea how long it had been; hours, days, weeks, each felt as plausible as the other.

*I am going to die of this*, he thought, hazy, beyond the morphine. *I am going to die of this without ever knowing why*—and a slow moment later, *I hope it won't take long.*

Grisaille was still holding his hand, cool fingers curled around Ruthven's. The worst of this was knowing, knowing perfectly well, what it was doing to Grisaille, and being completely unable to make it stop.

They were saying something about magic. He could make out Varney's voice, and couldn't quite remember when the vampyre had joined the festivities. There had been—an airplane, and then night air around him, and voices, and another enclosed space, Greta Helsing out of nowhere, bending over him. Ruthven made an effort to think through the drugs, to pay attention. Varney was—chanting something, which made little sense, but then not much else was making sense just at the moment—

—and another voice, just as familiar, more impatient than Ruthven could remember hearing it: "... Sir Francis. What is it this time? I'm afraid I'm in the middle of something—"

Varney, cutting him off. "Fastitocalon, we need your help. *Edmund* needs your help."

A pause, and then he could feel a faint pressure-wave, as if a door had suddenly shut. Opening his eyes was terrible, but Ruthven did it, anyway, and out of the general painful brightness could make out a tall figure bending over him.

"...Fass?" he managed.

"Yes, it's me—what the hell's going on? Greta?"

"We were hoping you could possibly tell us that." Greta's voice, her clinical briskness. "Presented with acute and worsening migraine-like symptoms that refused to respond to triptans—onset, what, Grisaille? Two days? Three?—we got him in the scanner as soon as he arrived and every single test comes up completely clear. No physiological cause I can find, and believe me, I've tried."

"Mm," said Fastitocalon, and rested a cool hand on Ruthven's forehead—and snatched it away again with a rapid sequence of what sounded like invective in a language Ruthven had never heard. It wasn't exactly reassuring.

And the morphine was wearing off. Ruthven could feel it, feel the black jagged tips of the pain-pilings beginning to emerge. "...what?" he asked. "What is it?"

"It's very certainly not physiological," said Fastitocalon, sounding shaken, taking a step back from the bed. Ruthven closed his eyes again, shutting out the increasingly painful light. "It's a curse. Some kind of curse. I don't know enough to tell you what kind, or how, or why. He needs to see Faust right away, Greta."

"Can they fix this in Hell?" she demanded.

"You certainly can't fix it here," he said, which wasn't a *yes.*

Grisaille squeezed Ruthven's hand, and he squeezed back, weakly, the tide falling faster and faster now, exposing more of the rotten blackness of the pain.

"What do you mean, Hell," Grisaille asked on a rising note. "You're not taking him to Hell. Nobody is going to Hell."

"They're good with curses," said Varney, a little way away. "It's all right, Grisaille. I've seen their medical facilities myself; it's quite impressive."

"He'll be perfectly safe," said Greta. "And if anyone can help him, they can. Erebus General is probably the most advanced medical facility on any of the planes at the moment."

"I know it's an alarming prospect," said Fastitocalon, gentler now. "Believe me. But they're very good, and curses are absolutely a thing Hell's got experience dealing with—and I can tell you now that no matter how brilliant they are or what equipment they have access to, no human physician is going to be able to fix this."

"Can *you* do anything?" That was a different voice, one Ruthven didn't recognize: papery-dry. "I mean, you're—"

"A demon," said Fastitocalon. "One who spent rather a long time not quite being one, until fairly recently. I don't know. I—"

"*Try*," said Grisaille, and the ragged unhappiness in his voice hurt Ruthven even through the hugeness of the pain.

Fastitocalon said nothing, but that cool hand was back on Ruthven's forehead—wonderfully cool, he felt like stone, like dark water—and a moment later something a little like another of those pressure-waves touched Ruthven's face, and with it a shock-front of spreading chill raced through him.

It was over so quickly he scarcely had time to register the sensation—and after the chill an astonishing, ringing numbness, blank and stopped. The shock of it was enough to jar his tenuous grip on consciousness loose, and the last thing he thought before going away entirely was *oh God I'd forgotten how not to hurt.*

After Fass had done whatever it was he'd just done—Greta wasn't sure, but it seemed to have put Ruthven under anesthesia—he pulled out one of the grey glass rectangles she remembered from Paris as interplanar communications devices, memorably termed *hellphones* by Grisaille, and made a call. She was again struck by how much *better* he was than he'd been in London, how completely in control, although he had the faint preoccupied line between his eyebrows that meant he was either worried or in pain or both.

"Decarabia? Yes, it's me. Can you ring up Erebus General and let them know I'm going to be arriving shortly with a vampire—classic draculine, not lunar sensitive—who's got himself some sort of extremely nasty curse and will need immediate attention."

"Two," said Grisaille, and Fastitocalon looked at him, eyebrow raised. "You're going to be arriving with two vampires. I don't care what you are, nobody gets to take my boyfriend to Hell without me."

"...make that one cursed and one not apparently cursed sanguivore," Fastitocalon said. "Yes. Quite. Thank you." He hung up and put the phone away, sighing. "Greta, can you unhook all the tubes and wires and so on, please?"

She nodded, beginning to remove the various sensors taped to Ruthven's chest; the monitor squealed in sudden anxiety before shutting off. "I can't believe both Varney and Ruthven get to go to Hell before I do," she told Fastitocalon. "And I *can't* go with you: we have enough trouble here as it is, something mysterious is affecting several of the patients and I have no clue what's going on with that, *either*, and—God, at least Ruthven will be safe in Hell, won't he?"

"Safe as houses," said Fastitocalon, and when she'd finished removing Ruthven's IV line and the rest of the sensors, he simply bent and scooped the vampire up as if he weighed nothing at all. He lay in Fastitocalon's arms with no grace whatsoever, grey-white and deeply unconscious, and Greta's chest hurt sharply to see it.

"Hold on to me," he told Grisaille. "This will be unpleasant and disorientating, but the effect will pass quickly."

"I don't care, just—*fix* him," Grisaille said between his teeth, and took hold of Fastitocalon's shoulder. An instant later they were gone, with a small thunderclap of air collapsing into the space they had just inhabited.

Greta looked from Varney to Tefnakhte, whose wrappings made it very easy to look unimpressed by the situation. "Well," she said. "That's out of our hands. Time to get back to doing my *real* job—Christ, what time *is* it, anyway? How long have I been awake?"

"Nearly midnight," said Varney. "Can you get some rest *now*?"

". . . maybe," she said. "I have to check on Maanakhtef first. Tefnakhte, nothing else is on fire just at the moment, right?"

"Not as far as I know," said the mummy. "The night shift will take care of it unless there's a dire emergency. Go and rest, Doctor."

She nodded, and glanced over at Varney. "Wait here while I look at Maanakhtef for a minute and make sure he's doing all right, and then I'll show you the private residence," she said.

"I can stay in a spare room," he told her, "it's quite all right—"

"Please," said Greta. "I'd very much rather not be alone right now."

"Well," said Varney with the edge of one of those sunrise smiles, "if you put it that way, I suppose I can oblige."

# CHAPTER 8

Greta had been the kind of tired where she didn't even remember lying down; she'd simply fallen away from consciousness like a stone into black water, and it seemed that no time at all had passed between climbing into the bed and being shaken very gently by the shoulder.

"Nnh," she said into the pillows.

"Greta, love," said a beautiful voice, very close at hand, and she rolled over and squinted up at Varney, who looked intensely apologetic. "I'm so sorry to wake you—"

"What time is it?"

"Half past four," he said. "There's been a—"

"Who is it this time?" she asked, scrubbing at her face with both hands. "And how badly are they damaged?"

Varney paused. "Er. Well, yes, there's been another incident, and the patient is—not very well, I gather, but nothing like Mr. Maanakhtef—they're asking for you, though—"

Greta squeezed her eyes shut for a moment longer: her level

of fatigue had now reached the point where it was painful to keep them open. Then she sat up, took a deep breath, and got out of the bed. Varney watched, that expression of apologetic sympathy very difficult to look at, while she shrugged into her dressing gown and found a pair of shoes. "Go back to sleep," she told him, hooking her stethoscope around her neck. "No sense in *both* of us being awake at a truly ridiculous hour, if one of us *can* be asleep, then they *ought* to be—fuck, I need coffee—"

"I'm all right," said Varney. "And I can at least bully people into making coffee *for* you. Go on, I'll join you when you're free."

The thought of being able to get used to that, of having someone always there to *help*, of not having to do everything by herself all the time, was still delicious in its novelty. Greta couldn't help smiling at him before she turned to leave, despite the fatigue.

Sister Brigitte was waiting for her in the main spa facility, irritatingly perfect in her white scrubs; she seemed to be able to look like a statue of a queen no matter the hour of the day or night. "It's Antjau," she said without preamble. "He was in bed when it happened, of course, so there was no danger of a fall, but he's not strong."

Greta knew the TB treatment wasn't going as quickly as they had hoped, but he'd seemed to be making progress. This on top of his preexisting condition was absolutely not going to help. It was Antjau's second attack—she could remember Brigitte mentioning a previous instance.

"I have to find out what's *doing* this," she said almost to herself, and walked a little faster; Brigitte had to hurry to keep up. "This thing, whatever it is, coinciding with Ruthven's curse—it feels intentional. More than just terrible luck."

"The symptoms are completely different," said Sister Brigitte. "Then again—"

"—so are the species," Greta finished. "We're in totally uncharted waters here. I've never dealt with supernatural illness in vampires other than the standard reaction to sacral exposure—holy water, crosses, all that sort of thing, but I've never seen a *curse* in action before."

"Would your witch acquaintance have any experience with such a thing?"

"That's a damned good question," said Greta. "Soon as I've seen Mr. Antjau, I'll call her and ask. Thank you. I'm—not at my best right now."

"None of us are," said the nurse, ruefully. "You're doing quite well, in my opinion."

"I haven't been able to *do* anything about this," she said.

"But the work you did to repair Mr. Maanakhtef was remarkable, even if we don't understand why it's happening."

"...all right, that's fair enough," said Greta with a little smile. She was, in fact, slightly proud of the job she had done repairing and replacing all the bits of him that had broken on impact. "I just wish I hadn't had to. All right, let's see what we're dealing with here."

They had come to Antjau's room; Greta knocked gently. "Mr. Antjau? It's Dr. Helsing, may I come in?"

His *yes* sounded fairly awful: much raspier than most mummies, with a wheeze to it. Greta sighed, put on her brisk and sympathetic talking-to-patients face, and went in.

Antjau lay propped up with several pillows; the head of his bed was raised almost as far as it could go. She wasn't surprised to see the careful pattern of amulets tucked into the wrappings around his chest: Tefnakhte must have come to see him already. "I hear you've had another one of these attacks," she said, settling into the chair by the bed. "I'm so sorry. Can you tell me what happened?"

"I woke up," he wheezed, "and couldn't *breathe*—this terrible weakness in my chest—I could barely manage to push the call button—"

He was interrupted by a dry, rasping, crackling cough that sounded as if it hurt, pressing his hands to his chest. Greta bent over to get her arms around him, helping him to lean forward, carefully rubbing his back. He stiffened for a moment in surprise, and then leaned into her hands.

Every student of mummy medicine had to come up against a specific mental wall in the course of their research and discoveries: the point of *but that makes no sense*. Greta's own had been fairly early on: *How can they talk when they have no actual lungs in situ to do the breathing part with*, followed sharply by, *And how can they do literally anything, let alone think, with no brain?* Once she'd got past the no-brain thing and acknowledged to herself that, no, it did not make any sense at all but nonetheless was objectively true, she found herself able to look past the wall for the most part. Mummies were made largely out of magic, and magic did not have to make sense, even if the version of it Fastitocalon played with could be described in terms analogous to particle physics. Treating someone whose lungs were in another room exactly the way she'd treat someone who retained their originally installed equipment was second nature to her now.

When the fit passed, she let him lie back against the pillows. "That sounds like it's not even slightly fun to experience," she said. "I'm sorry—but I think we can make you a bit more comfortable.—Have you done anything to his lungs?" she added, turning to Sister Brigitte.

"The oxygen flow rate was increased," said the nurse. "It seemed to help a little."

"Good. Keep it turned up, and start him on a bronchodilator and benzonatate. What's the dose on the main cocktail?"

Sister Brigitte checked his chart. "Three hundred for the isoniazid and five for the streptomycin. We could go up."

"Leave the isoniazid, increase the streptomycin to seven hundred, check the titers more frequently," she said. "The sooner we knock out the infection, the better. I think we'll have you feeling better soon," she told Mr. Antjau.

"Will it happen again?" he asked. "The—the attack."

"I'm afraid I don't know yet," said Greta. "We're working on it. In the meantime if you start to feel worse again, ring for someone right away, all right? Did Tefnakhte's amulets make any difference?"

"A little," he said, poking at a particularly fine agate djed pillar. "The—having the words said helped more, I don't know why—just hearing the language spoken—"

"I'll ask him to come and check in on you regularly," she said, getting up. "And declaim."

That got a raspy little chuckle out of Antjau, and almost made him cough again; she could see the effort involved in holding it back, and sighed. "All right. I'll see you on my rounds, Mr. Antjau. Sister?"

Brigitte nodded. "I'll mark the changes on his chart and start the new medication."

"Excellent." Greta gave her a tired smile and left her to her patient, hoping against hope that she could find either coffee or a flat surface to pass out on for an hour.

At least one of those was forthcoming. Varney met her at the door to the nurses' lounge with a steaming cup. "How is he?"

"He'll do. I think the bronchodilator will help a bit, and the antitussive will definitely make a difference, but God, I wish I had *any idea* what's behind the attacks—"

Her phone vibrated in her pocket, and she sighed, fishing it out. *This* time it would be Ed Kamal calling to tell her off for being a useless excuse for a physician, no doubt.

It was not. Varney looked at her with an inquisitive eyebrow while Greta stared at the screen, which read EREBUS GEN HOSP/FAUST, J.G.

". . . I have to take this," she said, and thumbed the screen. "Hello?"

"Dr. Helsing?" said a female voice. "Please hold for Dr. Faust."

Greta looked around and to her relief saw an empty conference room, away from the comings and goings of the nursing staff. She nodded at Varney, and they went inside and shut the door—and she half-fell into a chair, her knees suddenly little sacks of water. This was something she'd always dreamed of, never thought could happen, and it was happening *now* at the most inopportune time it could possibly occur—

"Greta Helsing?" said a brusque voice in her ear, the accent faintly German. "Johann Faust. Calling about your vampire patient, if you have a few minutes."

"Y-yes," she said. "Of course. What—how's he doing, do you know what's *wrong*?"

"Yes and no," said Dr. Faust. "At first it looked like an absolutely standard self-referential escalating Type Two vengeance curse with a strong angelic signature, but then we ran him through the mirabilic resonance scanner a couple more times because of an anomalous reading and it turns out the signature doesn't map to any of the actual angelic strains that exist."

"Angelic?" Greta said, sounding stupid even to herself. "An *angel* did this to Ruthven?"

"Something that *looks* like an angel to the MRI algorithms," said Faust, "but if it's an angel, it's a type we've never seen before. Gabriel and his bunch wouldn't go in for this sort of thing, anyway; it's politically unwise and they don't get involved. It's a mystery."

"What looks like an angel but isn't?" she asked.

"You tell me," he said, sounding about as disgusted as she felt regarding her own medical mystery. "Anyway, he's responding well to treatment, the symptoms have mostly resolved, but the bad news is that the second he gets back on the prime material plane, it's going to snap right back on again."

"You mean he's...stuck in Hell indefinitely?"

"Until someone can find whatever cursed him and get them to take it off again—yes. I'm sorry, but that's the way of it."

"Does he know?"

"Yes. He took it rather well, all things considered, but I think part of that is sheer relief at not being in pain. His boyfriend is less sanguine about the prospect."

Greta pictured Grisaille's reaction, and covered her eyes with a hand. "Yeah. I bet. Is—can I talk to Ruthven? Is that allowed?" She had no idea how she could receive calls on a cellular network from a completely separate plane, but nothing else was making any sense lately, either. In a way it felt almost comforting that Faust was as baffled by Ruthven as she was by her mummies, and in a way it was a sinking kind of horror: there *weren't* any more advanced authorities to ask for help.

"You can have a few minutes with him," Faust was saying. "The symptoms have almost completely resolved, as I said; he's experiencing mild headache and moderate lassitude."

"I won't tire him out, I promise," she said. "Is he still in the hospital or have you moved him to the spa?"

"Hospital for now. If he continues to improve further, I'm happy discharging him to the spa, although most of the treatments they do that work best for demons won't do a great deal for him. But the beds are more comfortable and the food is better." She could hear background noises; he must be walking down a corridor with people in it, and closed her eyes to try to picture Hell's main medical facility.

Greta was aware of Varney being intensely patient and incredibly curious across the conference table, and gave him an apologetic grimace. On the phone Faust said something aside to a nurse, and then, "Lord Ruthven? I have Greta Helsing on the line. You can have ten minutes—"

Ruthven's voice in her ear. "Greta? Oh Christ, it's good to hear from you, I'm so sorry about everything—"

"*Edmund*," she said, rolling her eyes, "are you seriously apologizing for being cursed?"

"For making a colossal nuisance for you and—well, scaring everybody," he said. He sounded just like himself, if a bit worn. "And now apparently I'm stuck in Hell, which I could probably make some terribly clever jokes about if I thought hard enough."

"I've got Varney here," she said. "Shall I put him on, too?"

"Yes. God, yes," Ruthven said, and she put her phone on speaker and set it on the table.

"Now *both* of you have been to Hell before I got to," she said, "and I am envious in the middle of everything. Are you really feeling better?"

"I'm quite all right," said Ruthven, and then had to laugh a little. "Well. I'm not *quite* all right, but I can see and my head only aches in an ordinary sort of way and I don't want to be sick, so it's a vast improvement."

"I'm so glad," said Varney self-consciously. "I—you were in a pretty bad way when you arrived in Marseille."

"Thank you for helping," Ruthven said. "I—we—really appreciate it."

"*De rien*," said Varney. "I was very impressed with the facilities there on my quick visit. I know you're in good hands."

"Everyone's been very kind. Even if Grisaille has had to sleep in a not-very-comfortable chair thing in the corner of the room."

"My back will never recover," said another voice sepulchrally. Greta could picture Grisaille draped over the not-very-comfortable chair looking effortlessly stylish, and had to smile. "I shall demand to be known as the Hunchback of Victoria Embankment. That's if we ever get to go home, of course."

"Dr. Faust said the signature of whatever did this to you looks angelic but isn't," Greta said. "How is that possible?"

"Don't ask *me*," said Ruthven. "I thought angels were angels were angels, not that I've had the displeasure of meeting any. Except—"

"Except?" Varney repeated.

"I can't seem to remember it clearly," said Ruthven. "It's—something strange *did* happen in Rome, but I don't know what it was. Neither does Grisaille."

"Something on the Spanish Steps," said Grisaille. "That's all I have. I think you told me about it but it's like—oh, like a conversation you have right before getting extremely drunk, and all the details are gone."

"That must be when it happened," said Greta. "At least you

have that much. Up here I have *nothing* to go on with this weird micro-epidemic business, except that it seems to be getting worse."

"What micro-epidemic?" said Ruthven.

"There's been a rash of completely inexplicable sort of fainting spells affecting the mummies here," she said, blithely ignoring confidentiality protocol, too tired to think better of it. "And nobody seems to be sneaking around in the middle of the night cursing them—I think we'd know if something like that was happening—"

"I didn't faint," said Ruthven, "I just had the worst migraine of my life. Fainting would have been far, far preferable."

"You'd do it decoratively," said Grisaille. "Collapsing in an artistic fashion with your head pillowed on one out-flung arm, I have no doubt."

"Yes, and there would have been less being horribly sick," said Ruthven with feeling. "Is it just mummies?"

"So far," said Greta. "In a way it's sort of reassuring to know I'm not the only medical professional being completely stumped by something mysterious, and in another it's emphatically *not* comforting to consider that the best minds in Hell can't figure it out. I might ask Dr. Faust if he has any pointers, because right now I am at an utter loss."

"Fass diagnosed your curse," Grisaille said to Ruthven. "I was right there. It was alarming."

"Maybe he can diagnose this, too—but he seemed awfully busy with his research work," Greta said.

"He did take the time to come and fetch me for my visit to Hell," Varney put in. "Perhaps we can ask him—or one of the demon physicians?"

"Wait a sec," said Ruthven, "Faust is back—Doctor, Greta has a question for you."

"Make it quick," said Faust's voice. "I want my phone back and you ought to be resting."

She made it quick. Acute but transient idiopathic dizziness, weakness, collapse; attacks followed by varying levels of malaise and exhaustion; no pattern she or anyone else could discern; increasing in frequency, some patients experiencing multiple instances. Extremely difficult to map to any physiological issue, given the largely nonphysiological nature of the mummy as a species. "Which is why I am wondering if it's also magic in origin, but the closest thing we have to an ancient Egyptian magician can't find any answers, either."

"Mm," said Faust. "I'd like to have a look, get one of the patients down here and run 'em through the scanner, but frankly I don't know what that would *do* to someone whose functional presence in reality is based on a completely different belief system. The pneumic signature mismatch could be catastrophic."

"That's what I was afraid you'd say," said Greta, sighing. "The last thing I want to do is cut any of these people loose from the system of magic that sustains them. There aren't any *new* mummies being made. They're a critically endangered species as it is, and I won't do anything that might jeopardize the survival of any of them."

"Exactly," said Faust. "I'm sorry, I don't think I can help. You said you had an Egyptian magician?"

"Well, sort of. He was a priest of Thoth when he was alive," said Greta, and looked up; Varney was pointing at the conference room door, which had a window beside it. "And he's, uh, apparently right outside the room—just a minute—"

She got up and let Tefnakhte in. He was carrying his clipboard and looking, insofar as it was possible to tell, excited. "I'm sorry to interrupt, Dr. Helsing—"

"Not at all," said Greta. "Everyone, allow me to introduce the mummy Tefnakhte. We've got Ruthven and Grisaille on the line as well as Dr. Faust."

"Er," said Tefnakhte. "I'm not sure I—"

"What have you found?" she asked.

"Well. As this seems to be getting worse," he said, "I was thinking about what we might have done in the old days to find answers to an unanswerable problem."

"The old days?" said Faust.

"Twenty-first Dynasty," said Tefnakhte. "Anyway—well. When I was alive, praying to Thoth—Djehuty—for wisdom and guidance was one way to approach it."

"You were a priest of Djehuty," said Greta. "Is—can you just sort of *do* that, and if so, please will you do it at your earliest convenience?"

"It's not quite that simple," said Tefnakhte. "I mean, yes, I could offer up a basic request, but there's a difference between that and the kind of prayer that actually gets the god's *attention*. That asks for direct intercession. That's a little more complex."

"What do you need?" Varney asked. "I mean, if you can do this at all, what do you need?"

"A very rare kind of artifact," said Tefnakhte. "One with the right spells on it, that's been used for this kind of thing for thousands of years. Can't be just any version, it's—I didn't think I'd be able to find one, but I think I have."

"Where is it?" said Greta.

"That's sort of the problem," said the mummy. "It's in the Met. In New York. Where it's undoubtedly extremely well guarded and secure."

"And you have to actually be able to touch this thing, not just look at it through glass?"

"I'm afraid so," said Tefnakhte. "I have to—well, interact with it. Make offerings and so on. I need to actually have access to the artifact, and it's locked up very tightly indeed."

"Oh my God," said Grisaille. "Oh God, *finally* something is beginning to look up."

"What do you mean, look up?" Varney demanded. "This is *not* a positive development—"

"Do you *know,*" said Grisaille gleefully, "do you have *any idea* how long it's been since I got the chance to steal something priceless from a major world museum? This is fantastic."

"Hang on, hang on," said Greta, rubbing at her eyes. "Nobody said anything about stealing it, we just need *access.*"

"Oh, like they're gonna let an actual mummy lurch in there and open up the case if he asks nicely so that he can do weird arcane rituals *to an irreplaceable historical artifact,*" Grisaille said, and Greta could very easily picture his expression. "I'm sorry, I must have missed the part where members of the supernatural community were widely recognized and welcome in human society, silly of me."

"No, you missed the part where we know a museum curator," said Greta sourly. "He's with the British Museum, not the Met, but if *he* asks nicely, we might get somewhere."

"Cranswell," said Ruthven. "Remember? August Cranswell. You tried to get him drunk and waltz with him last time I had people over, and you got your feet stepped on for your pains."

"...oh," said Grisaille. "Well, fine, he can *help* me steal it. Even if he's the worst dancer in London."

"Let's start by giving him a call," said Greta. "Dr. Faust, I'm sorry to have taken up so much of your time, and thank you for getting in touch. On a more personal note: if this goddamn mess ever does get cleared up, do you think it'd be possible for me to tour your facilities?"

"Happy to," said Faust. "Nice meeting you," and the phone cut off.

"Well," said Greta, leaning back and looking at the others. She was reaching the stage of sleep deprivation where everything felt ever so slightly hilarious. "That was unexpected."

"Did you really just talk to people in Hell with your cell phone?" said Tefnakhte. "That was actually a thing that just happened?"

"I think so, or we're all trapped in some thoroughly complicated group hallucination," said Varney, "and I'd prefer to believe the former. Greta, do you want me to call Cranswell?"

"Yes," she said, making herself sit up with an effort. "Do

that while I do my rounds. Tefnakhte, if you have time, I'd like you to come along with me. Let's just hope nobody else has succumbed to totally idiopathic syncope in the meantime."

The hospital room in Erebus General was, Grisaille considered, upsetting in its ordinariness. You would have expected there to be some kind of visual indication regarding the fact it was *in Hell.* There wasn't a window, so the view of the burning lake and the white city of Dis wasn't available to orient the observer; the walls were that beige no-color that seemed to characterize all such institutions, the uncomfortable chair was unremarkable and upholstered in something that appeared to be dull pink vinyl, the various tubes and monitors hooked up to Ruthven seemed to be little different from the ones you'd see on Earth.

Grisaille was having trouble parsing that. Earth versus Hell. Actual Hell. The place where you went at the end of tragic operas. After the immediate and awful anxiety over Ruthven had begun to ease, as he'd begun to improve with startling rapidity, Grisaille had had more time to think about things, and he regretted this.

The journey here had been brief but unspeakable. He'd held on to Fastitocalon through a nauseating, dizzying white flash of sensation, being *twisted*, and then had to hang on a little longer while the sparkles obscuring his vision went away and the room stopped spinning. At least it *was* a room, rather than some terrible flaming wasteland pockmarked with pits full of sinners getting on with eternity. Grisaille hadn't had time—or presence of mind—to take in more than bright light and a smell of disinfectant, people crowding around them, someone barking orders—that had been Dr. Faust—someone else had brought a gurney, Fastitocalon set Ruthven gently down on it, and Grisaille had had to watch all over again as he was wheeled away. The echo was very strong: arriving at Oasis Natrun, arriving in Hell, and both felt like a bad dream.

*Don't worry*, Fastitocalon had said, putting a hand briefly on his shoulder. *He's in the best of hands. I've got to go*, and go he had, popping out of existence with a faint thunderclap, leaving Grisaille in what he realized was the waiting area of a busy emergency room. All around him people came and went, some in scrubs and some in ordinary clothes and some in—well, *robes*, and as he regained some measure of self-possession, he noticed that a lot of the people were also sporting accessories such as horns and tails and folded wings. *I'm in Hell*, he thought, *I'm actually in Hell and these are demons and I'm in Hell I'm in Hell I'm in HELL...*

By the time somebody in pink scrubs came up to him with a friendly smile, Grisaille had been very close to hysterics; the person, who appeared to be of indeterminate gender and relatively human except for their blank pupilless red eyes, had guided him to a chair and pushed a cup of what turned out to be very nice brandy-laced hot blood into his hands and told him to breathe. He'd demanded to be told what was happening to Ruthven, and the person—in a soothing tone he would under other circumstances have found unbelievably twee—told him his boyfriend was undergoing scans and would be moved to a room as soon as possible.

The brandy helped; the blood helped more, even if Grisaille didn't want to think about wherever it might have come from, and by the time the person in the pink scrubs came back to tell him Ruthven was out of imaging and already showing vast improvement, he could stand without his legs shaking very much at all.

The sight of Ruthven in the high white hospital bed, covered in tubes and wires, looking so *small* under all that technology, had given Grisaille a bad moment of *déjà vu*: he'd looked just the same in Greta's bizarre mummy clinic, however long ago that had been.

And then Ruthven had opened his eyes, and turned his head on the pillow, and *smiled* at him, and the awful tightness around Grisaille's chest had let go in a sudden dizzying rush of relief. He couldn't remember what he'd said—something utterly inane, no doubt—all he remembered was holding Ruthven's hand in his, resting his face on the edge of the bed, feeling Ruthven leaning over to stroke his hair, as all the terror and sleep deprivation of the past however many days and nights caught up with him all at once and took him *away*.

He'd woken up in the uncomfortable chair, for a long horrible moment unsure of where he was or how he'd got there, and nearly panicked all over again to see Ruthven lying with his eyes closed and his hands loosely curled on the bedclothes—but the steady, regular, slow beeping of the monitors reassured him.

That morning had come and gone with a series of persons

coming in and out of the room, occasionally wheeling Ruthven away to do some other arcane tests, and by the time Dr. Faust came in with Greta on the phone, Grisaille's desperate worry had turned into restless boredom. His excitement at the prospect of breaking into museums had been entirely genuine.

"So this Cranswell person," he said now, sitting on the edge of Ruthven's bed. "Other than being a shitty dancer, he's unknown to me. Fix that?"

Ruthven had closed his eyes, and Grisaille winced a little at how unutterably weary he looked, despite the improvement. *Let him rest*, he thought, *stop being insufferable*, and just as clearly heard the echo back: *I can't.*

"August Cranswell," said Ruthven, his eyes still shut, "is in his mid-to-late twenties and the latest and possibly last scion of a family I first encountered a very long time ago. The Cranswell dynasty shows up in the annals of classic horror lit due to an unfortunate experience with a sanguivore, which—from the description—seems to have been a member of the nosferatu subspecies. Unlike many other heroines in similar circumstance, Amelia Cranswell recovered fully from her experience and in fact insisted on returning to Croglin Grange, the house they had leased and into which the vampire had broken. Stop me if I'm boring you."

"*Boring* is not the word, dear heart," said Grisaille. "Complete tenterhooks. Go on."

"Due to some reasonably clever planning ahead, the second

time the thing crept over from the local churchyard to pick the lead out from between Amelia's windowpanes and let itself in—that's real, by the way, same thing happened to me—the family was ready, and drove it off with a bullet in its leg; and of course the next day they went and opened all the coffins and found the corresponding corpse and had a bonfire. The point is, they were brave and inquisitive and determined, and so were their offspring, and their offspring's offspring, and somewhere along the lines they switched from vampire *hunters* to vampire *scholars*, and somewhere further along the line one of them ran into me."

Ruthven opened his eyes and looked up at Grisaille. "I don't think I was living one of my best unlives at the time, but we eventually ended up friends, and that tradition has lasted. August Cranswell is the son of a British Cranswell and a Nigerian scientist; he is quite bright despite how hard he tries to obscure this fact and has a degree from Harvard; he is now well on his way from junior curator to full curator at the museum; and he was instrumental in stopping that business with the Holy Sword chaps last year. It was in fact Cranswell who smashed the possessed rectifier, even if a number of factors had to be in place for him to get the chance."

"And you think this kid will help us get the whatever-it-is out of the Met."

"No," said Ruthven, "but I expect him to give you a believable cover story."

"You're—okay with this?" Grisaille asked, suddenly hesitant. "Me leaving you here, I mean. I don't have to go—"

"You do," said Ruthven, "for any number of reasons, but to pick two completely at random: you hate being down here, and you're the most experienced thief we know."

"I don't—" he began, and had to stop, running a hand over his face. "Okay, I do hate it but that doesn't mean I can't—suck it up and be supportive?"

"Oh, Grisaille," said Ruthven, and held out his arms; there was something in the strength of that hug which went a little way toward reassuring Grisaille he really was approaching all right. "I am in good hands here. Even if they're slightly alarming hands. I'm—not thinking about being stuck here right now. I am thinking how nice it is not to hurt. *I* can't be of use to Greta and the others, but you can, and they need you. We need you."

Grisaille also was trying not to think about him being stuck here forever, and held him tight. "I'm not used to that. The—being needed." It was an admission he could not have made this time last year. "But I'd be lying if I said the chance to steal something priceless didn't make my heart go pitter-pat."

"I know," said Ruthven with a smile in his voice, and when he let Grisaille go and lay back against the pillows, it was there on his face as well. "Go and plan a heist, my dear. I am going to go back to sleep, in a strategic and forethoughtful kind of way."

Grisaille leaned over and kissed him. "Will they take me back upstairs if I ask nicely?"

"Flutter your eyelashes," said Ruthven, "and look demure, and—be careful."

"I will," he said, and although it hurt to leave him, all alone in the little hospital room surrounded by demons, Grisaille felt a stirring of excitement he hadn't experienced in years.

"Do you think that monster's dead?"

Amitiel was gazing dreamily out the window of their Greenwich Street loft, elbows on the windowsill, chin in hands. He wasn't bothering to wear the human-seeming, not when it was just the two of them together, and his folded wings nearly brushed the ceiling. More than once he'd knocked things over with them, or bumped into the overhead light fixtures, since they'd been here; Zophiel glanced up at the chandelier.

"Probably," he said. "I can't know for sure. It seems *likely*."

"I want it to be dead," said Amitiel. He turned and looked at Zophiel with wide golden eyes, pupilless and blank but nevertheless expressive. His real face was not so very different from the one he wore as a model. "*Something* went through the planes early this morning. I felt it. The disturbance. It wasn't our spell, either."

"I know," said Zophiel. Amitiel often seemed to need to talk things over very deliberately; he thought it might have something to do with how difficult the angel found it to *be* in this world, needing reassurance and clarification. "We both felt it," he said. "It woke me up."

"Me, too. You came to bring me tea," he said, with a smile so beautiful it would have been dangerous for a human to observe for any length of time. "That was kind."

"I thought you might have been—upset," said Zophiel.

"You're sensitive, and that was a strong disturbance." It had been distant but still powerful; he'd had no idea quite how far away, but if the monster had stayed in Rome while Amitiel's curse did its work, that would be over four thousand miles. Anything passing between planes sent a concentric series of ripples through reality, like a stone dropped into water, which creatures like himself could detect; the farther away from the point of transit, the weaker the ripple effect would be, and anything that could propagate over several thousand miles must have been a significant event. A monster being taken to Hell *might* do it, possibly.

"Anyway," said Amitiel, "it's helped, hasn't it? We're closer. Even if it wasn't the woman with our spell, it did *something* to the boundary. Weakened it further. Every little bit helps."

"We are closer," he said. "I can feel it. The thin places between worlds are getting thinner all the time. Soon it will tear open completely."

"And then we can go *home*," said Amitiel. "Home to *our* Heaven. The real Heaven, where they sing properly, not like this world's false version. I miss singing, Zophiel. I used to sing all the time. *Hosanna in the highest.* All day and all night. *Hosanna hosanna hosanna.*"

"I remember," said Zophiel. "The singing was so beautiful. And the chiming of the spheres as they rang."

"I miss that, too. And the walls made of jewels. *Battlements of rubies, gates of sparkling jewels, walls of precious stones.* Sometimes I was assigned to polish them." He closed his eyes for a moment. "I liked polishing things. And the manna. I like manna. I *miss* it."

Zophiel watched as the beautiful lips curved in a pout, and sighed. "I think it's stupid of the humans to call something *angel food cake* when it isn't angel food," said Amitiel. "At *all*."

His wings mantled in an avian equivalent of "humph," and Zophiel was not quite in time to tell him, *Mind the chandelier*.

It was a bit over one mile from the British Museum to Greta's clinic in Harley Street, and August Cranswell had set out on his own two feet, encouraged by the fact that it wasn't precisely *raining* at the moment, just sort of spitting aimlessly. When, about halfway there, the heavens opened up all over again, he was not so much surprised as resigned.

This was shaping up to be a profoundly strange afternoon. He'd gotten a call from Greta while he was down in the archives looking for a particular reference; by the time he got back to his desk and called her back, she'd left another two messages. He knew she was abroad doing something weird with mummies, so why she'd be calling *him* instead of the curators from the Egyptian wing was a puzzlement to Cranswell—but everything got clear in a hurry once he got her on the phone.

His specialty was fourteenth-century Britain, but he knew a little about Egyptian art and archaeology, and he had heard of the Metternich and Hermopolis Stelae. "You can't possibly be serious," he'd told her. "There's no way I can steal that thing. I'm not an international antiquities thief, I'm a junior curator with a couple of exhibitions on the history of London under my belt. You want somebody with a much more expensive car and bespoke suits—"

"We've got one," said Greta. "You remember Grisaille, right? Ruthven's new boyfriend, great hair, red eyes, morals of a cat?"

"*He's* a thief? Okay. Um. I can see that, actually. I thought he was a really high-class interior designer."

"The two often overlap," said Greta. "Point is, Ruthven is in trouble, and so are my mummies, possibly for connected reasons, and we need to ask a specific god for help who isn't reachable by any modern means. So if you could call out of the office for a few days, nip over to the clinic, and accompany him to New York City to come up with a good cover story to get him access to the artifact, I'd be profoundly grateful."

"I can't promise anything," said Cranswell, but he was having to work quite hard at keeping his voice even and level against a rising tide of excitement. "I mean. Of course I'll try."

"You've broken into your own museum to *return* stolen artifacts," said Greta. "All you have to do is run that sequence backwards. And this time you'll have Grisaille with you, rather than Fass, and Grisaille is extremely good at manipulating people for fun and profit. You might even have a good time."

"What's happening with Ruthven?" he asked.

"We're not sure. Well—he's been cursed, that's all we know. By something with an angelic signature that is apparently *not* an angel, which puzzles everybody. He's safe in Hell right now, undergoing treatment, and Dr. Faust seems to think that as long as he stays there, he'll be symptom-free. They're working on finding out where the curse came from and how to take it off again, which is apparently difficult because it's not associated with any of the angels Hell's aware of. Right now we have to figure out what the hell is going on with my mummy patients, and the way to do that is to get our hands on the Hermopolis Stela, so—"

"Ten-four," said Cranswell. "I'm on my way over there right now."

It had started pouring when he'd got to the corner of Cleveland and New Cavendish Streets, and he'd had to duck into a newsagent's to buy yet another cheap umbrella—his flat contained four of them already—but he was still fairly soaked by the time he reached Greta's clinic. Three of the people in the waiting room blinked at him as he let himself in: a tall, young black man with curly hair currently plastered to his head with rainwater. He had to wipe his glasses dry before he could get a clear look at the others.

One miserable-looking ghoul in an argyle sweater that did not suit them in the least; one greyish individual with what looked like folded wings humped under her shapeless coat; one teenage were-something with teal frosted lipstick and hair that had probably looked quite impressive when she'd left the house but currently was drooping out of its carefully arranged spiky points. And—one vampire.

Cranswell had seen Grisaille once or twice before, notably at one of Ruthven's shindigs, where he'd claimed to be able to drink gin by the pint and also to teach *anyone* to dance, and had had to admit defeat on at least one of those points; after that, things went somewhat fuzzy in Cranswell's immediate recall. But he couldn't have forgotten those bright red eyes, or the waterfall of faintly silvering dreadlocks that flowed down the other man's back. Or the way he—like Ruthven, like most of the other vamps Cranswell had met—exuded a kind of infuriatingly effortless style. *He* had apparently escaped the weather's latest fuckery.

"Um," said Cranswell. "Hi?"

"Mr. Cranswell," said Grisaille. "*Très* bona to varda your eek. Have you been briefed?"

Cranswell glanced around at the others in the waiting room, and was extremely glad when Nadezhda Serenskaya came out of the back with a clipboard and nodded for him and Grisaille to follow her. He could just about overhear the were-teenager muttering something about, *Hey, other people been waiting much longer'n he has*, before the door shut behind them.

"August," she said. "I've been on the phone with Greta and Harlach—he's the Hell surface op assigned to London—and you two are booked on the red-eye to JFK, leaving Heathrow in about three hours. When you get there, you will go straight to the Carlyle Hotel on East Seventy-sixth Street, where reservations have been made for you."

"We using our own names?" inquired Grisaille innocently.

"You can call yourself whatever you like as long as you've got believable ID in that particular name," said Nadezhda with an air that suggested she'd got limited patience remaining. "Cranswell, you need to be yourself, that's the whole point of having you along, although I've taken the liberty of slightly adjusting your CV and publications to indicate a focus in late-period Egyptian archaeology, specifically Thirtieth Dynasty. Take a quick look at Google."

Cranswell blinked at her, but pulled out his phone. Sure enough, a search for his name pulled up a long string of results in a discipline he'd hitherto been vaguely interested in but lacked a single academic credential to pursue. "How—"

"Witch, remember?" said Nadezhda, and he tried not to notice her hair was beginning to curl and uncurl itself irritably around one hoop earring. "Affiliated with demons. We can make you anything you need to be; all you have to do is sell it."

"Selling things isn't my strong point," said Grisaille. "Taking them away without paying for them is more in my line, you understand."

"Grisaille?" said Nadezhda. "Please don't take this wrong, I know you're under a great deal of stress, but shut up, would you?"

He mimed zipping his lips shut, and she gave him a tired smile. "Once you're in New York, you'll be operating on your own recognizance, but if you need help in a hurry, contact these people. They're the New York demonic surface ops and have been informed about what's happening."

Cranswell watched as she made a complex sigil in the air with one fingertip, and a moment later his phone buzzed with a text from UNKNOWN NUMBER: a picture of two dark-haired people, a woman in her mid-thirties of undetermined ethnicity and a fortyish man with curly hair and what would undoubtedly be described as a devilish gleam in his eye. Both were stunning; it seemed to be constitutionally challenging for a demon on Earth to appear anything other than stylish as hell.

"The woman goes by Glasya and the man calls himself Morax," Nadezhda said. "They will help you if you need it, but the general impression I got from Harlach is that they'd really rather not get involved. Their numbers are in the text, but if you're in dire straits and just yell their name three times, it's probably going to be good enough, given the heightened state of pneumic energy currently flooding the plane."

"There's a heightened state of pneumic energy?"

"So says Harlach, who has it from M&E downstairs. Fastitocalon's in charge of that department these days, and appears to be running it with considerably improved efficiency."

"How come *you're* so in tune with the state of Hell?" Grisaille wanted to know. "Also, when did you turn into Q?"

"You've only known me half a year, darling," said the witch. "It's entirely possible you haven't had the opportunity to experience the full variety of my capabilities. Also, I like demons. They buy nice rounds of drinks for the whole table, and don't mind importunate prehensile hair. You two should get going if you want to make it to Heathrow in time to catch that plane."

"How are we getting there?" Cranswell asked. "Are you gonna—what was that called, flip us?"

"I am not," she said. "For one thing, I have patients to see, and for another, you can almost certainly manage to get yourselves there on your own, like a couple of grown-up sentient beings, hmm? Tickets will be at the BA counter. I'll be in touch if anything changes."

"You heard the lady," said Grisaille, straightening up and tipping Nadezhda a lazy salute. "Best be toddling. Cheers, Ms. Serenskaya. Your capabilities are not in doubt."

# CHAPTER 9

Grisaille had his doubts about this.

He was a perfectly competent—nay, talented—thief; he had broken into and out of all sorts of places in his two-hundred-some years on the planet; he was a reliable second-in-command as long as the person he worked for wasn't an idiot—not that he'd had the best track record with that one—and he could tie cherry stems in knots with his tongue, but he was nobody's idea of a babysitter. The young man sitting next to him in the first-class cabin might be in his late twenties, but Grisaille would not personally trust him to follow simple instructions.

He'd spent the first half an hour in the air marveling out loud at the luxuries of first class. "The guy in front of me's reclined his seat and it isn't bruising my forehead!" he'd raved. "And the glasses are made out of *glass*!"

Grisaille couldn't remember a time when he'd had to fly coach. One of the things about being a vampire was that your bank accounts had such a long time to accrue interest; most of them who had a couple hundred years under their belts were independently wealthy to varying extents. He supposed he should feel sympathetic to people who couldn't afford nice seats, but all he currently felt was exasperated.

"Oh my God," Cranswell said as the flight attendant set a tray in front of him. "The cutlery is *metal.* And that napkin is made out of cloth. And—this is a *plate.*" He poked at the china with a forefinger, in wonder. Grisaille looked over his head at the flight attendant, giving her the hint of a shrug: *What can you do, he's an idiot, I'm so sorry.*

"And for you, sir?" she said. Grisaille smiled.

"Just the Château Faugères 2006, I think. Thanks so much."

"Of course," she said, and he could watch her go faintly pink. He knew exactly the effect he was having on her, and was—if briefly—enjoying himself; at least this museum business was something to take his mind off the concern for Ruthven.

He took the glass she offered, with another smile, and was faintly amused to see her simper slightly before moving on to the next row. Beside him Cranswell was now poking at the contents of the plate (seared fillet of Herefordshire beef with truffle taglierini, rosemary jus, grilled asparagus, and baby carrot), and drew breath to speak; Grisaille placed a hand gently on his wrist. "If you say something along the lines of 'this food is made out of *food*,' I am afraid I will have to stuff you in the overhead luggage bin for the remainder of this flight."

Cranswell looked at him, and grinned. "Fair enough," he said.

"Take it as read that I am basically in Cortez-on-peak-in-Darien mode right now about all of this."

"Wild surmise acknowledged," said Grisaille, and sipped his wine. Okay, so the kid knew his Keats. Fine. There *might* be hidden depths.

He just wished *he* didn't have to be the one to go fishing in them, right in the middle of a goddamn heist operation. Oh, well. If worse came to worst, they had the demons' numbers, and Grisaille smiled a nasty little smile to himself, picturing museum security's reaction to thieves escaping via translocation. *Explain that one to your bosses, ducky*, he thought. *Wouldn't I love to see you try.*

Around two thousand miles away, Greta Helsing straightened up and stripped off her gloves. "There," she said with satisfaction. "That at least is a job well done."

The mummy Nefrina peered down at her forearm, flexed her fingers experimentally. The replacement tendons Greta had installed were partly visible through the gaps in her remaining skin, very white against the mahogany-colored surface. They moved smoothly and easily.

"It feels odd," said Nefrina. "Being able to move my fingers again. When can I get back to typing?"

"I'd give it a week to settle," said Greta. "And for any adjustments to be made. Now, wrappings. Can I have the color sample book, please?" she asked the nurse, who was tidying away the surgical implements. "And if you could page Tefnakhte to do the spells."

The patterns of a mummy's wrappings, and the spells said over them at various stages of the process, held magical significance. Greta could do the rewrap job on her own, of course, but Nefrina's results would be noticeably inferior to what she'd get with the proper chanting.

She had no actual idea what time it was. The last time Greta had owned a watch had been before the Paris business, and it hadn't even worked; she had given it to a monster in exchange for getting her stolen earrings back, due to the fact that well-monsters liked shiny things. Ruthven had promised to buy her a new one, and had never gotten around to it, what with one thing and another. Greta's own sense of the diurnal cycle had ended up nonexistent during her captivity under Paris, and she was aware now of losing it again.

That was another thing to worry about. She tacked it onto the end of the growing, presumably endless, list, and set it aside to be dealt with some other time, looking up with a tired smile as Tefnakhte came into the room—accompanied by Varney.

She raised her eyebrows at the mummy, who looked faintly embarrassed. "Is it all right if Sir Francis observes?" he asked.

"Nefrina?" Greta said. "Do you have any objection?"

"No, that's fine, I just—kind of want to get this done with?"

"Of course. Here, based on the rest of your wrappings, I'd suggest either of these," she said, offering Nefrina the linen sample collection. "This one's too light, and the other one's much too dark, but either of these two ought to color-match quite well."

Oasis Natrun had its own linen-weaving shop, which turned out ream after ream of cloth in different weights, which was then dyed in various shades ranging from cream to caramel—and rolled around in a barrel full of rocks, to obtain the correct weathered texture. Greta had marveled at the scope of their operation, and then marveled all over again when she saw the jewelry production line halfway through a faience bead net. While Nefrina peered at the sample book, Greta looked up at Varney and Tefnakhte, who still looked a little embarrassed, and made a *go on, tell me* gesture with one hand.

"Er," said Tefnakhte. "It turns out that having *two* voices reciting the spells seems to have a beneficial effect—Mr. Antjau seemed to feel much better for it, anyway—and Sir Francis's voice, well—"

"Is mellifluous," said Greta, smiling. "Famously so. That's—I hadn't thought of it, but it makes sense."

"I'm finding the pronunciation rather a lot less challenging than I expected," said Varney, looking almost shy. "And it's... pleasant to be of *use*. To have something to do."

"Don't I know it," Greta said, and turned back to her patient as Nefrina appeared to come to a decision. "This one? Excellent. Since Sister Melitta is still busy putting things away, Varney, can you look in the cupboards and find me a box labeled 620C?"

The wrapping linen was packaged in individual rolls of fifty feet, unlike the original version, which could be over a hundred feet in length; the idea was for the replacement wrappings to be *modular*, allowing for one section at a time to be unwrapped if anything needed to be done to it. As she began to unroll the strip, as Tefnakhte and Varney stepped forward to watch closely what she was doing, Greta was aware of a certain kind of *comfort* despite all her aches and pains: a sense of rightness, of correctness, of *doing the job she was meant to do*, and doing it together as part of a team, with Varney there beside her.

Seen from above, Lake Avernus is roughly circular, its banks quartered by the mouths of the four rivers feeding into it. From farther up, the waterways of Hell resemble a crosshairs: Lethe, Acheron, Cocytus, and Phlegethon converge on Avernus, and the vast border-defining River Styx forms a circle intersecting with each. Beyond Styx lie the neighboring domains of Hades and Purgatory.

Each of the rivers of Hell has its own characteristic qualities. Lethe grants the drinker forgetfulness; Cocytus wails, which on the face of it would not seem to be of much use but in recent years has found considerable popularity as a source for mix samples for the more avant-garde infernal DJs; Phlegethon, the source of the lake's flame, burns; and Acheron, depending on interpretation, is a river of pain or a river of purification. In practice this last translates to *extremely astringent*, and Acheron water represents a widely used ingredient in some skin preparations.

Together, however, with the waters of Styx, the rivers that give themselves up to Lake Avernus commingle their individual qualities to produce a fluid of remarkable capability. Unlike mineral springs on Earth, the waters of Lake Avernus possess considerable *effective* therapeutic value—at least to demons. Taken internally, Avernus water has analgesic, anxiolytic, and antidepressant effects; applied externally, it stimulates circulation and wound healing, reduces pain, and induces a warming sensation. The flames are not exactly heatless but do not and cannot burn demonic tissue; they can be ingested without harm and produce a pleasant tingling sensation on the skin.

The Lake Avernus Spa & Resort has the monopoly on bottling and selling the lake water, although there are no penalties for individual demons who wish to collect the water for their own use. Nor is there official oversight or control of access to the waterfront except on Spa property, which is limited to the section of shore immediately surrounding the Spa complex and its grounds and gardens. Critics of the Spa are quick to point out how much it shares architecturally with the Royal Pavilion at Brighton.

Ruthven thought he was probably a terrible person for not minding how much he liked it.

Dr. Faust had examined him with brisk no-nonsense competence after Grisaille had left for Earth, and pronounced him well enough to be transferred to the Spa, "although you're not to try anything energetic," and Ruthven had assured him of his total lack of desire for energetic pursuits. He was feeling so much better that the memory of his previous agony seemed increasingly improbable, but he certainly wasn't *well*; all he seemed to want to do was lie around and doze, and possibly read books, and drink fortified blood. It had come as some amusement when he realized that he was, in fact, displaying almost identical symptoms to those of an unscrupulous vampire's victim.

He still couldn't remember anything about how the actual curse had *happened*. The blank spot in his memory was apparently intent on remaining blank; Faust had said it looked like the work of an angel, but not one they recognized, and Ruthven wasn't sure he wanted to think about that very closely. Neither the thought of random angels wandering around putting curses on people nor the idea of *strange* angels, from somewhere *else*, was particularly comforting. Nor did he have any idea why an angel should single him out for any such attention; he couldn't remember doing anything particularly offensive to any members of the heavenly host, even back in the day when he'd been rather less circumspect in his predations. It made no *sense*, and Ruthven didn't like things that made no sense; in this he and Greta were of one mind.

He was lying on a remarkably comfortable deck chair, covered in a blanket, on a balcony overlooking the lake, vaguely wondering what time it was. The sky in Hell was never blue, exactly; it was a sort of dim red-gold vault high above the surface, faintly gleaming. The daylight here seemed to come out of the air itself, without bothering to involve a sun of any description—it hadn't rained once since Ruthven had been here, either—and it did change color as night drew on. Anywhere near the lake never got completely dark, of course. The dancing opaline flames didn't give off a brilliant glow, but their light was always present.

It *felt* to Ruthven as if it were late evening, getting on for nighttime. Which meant there would be a nurse arriving sometime soon with his blood. He found he was looking forward to it, and both despaired of himself for turning into such a pathetic lump and was rather glad that his appetite existed at all, after several days of violent nausea.

He watched the little sailboats that had been scudding about far out on the lake coming in to the marina, one by one, tying up; watched the demons climbing out of them, some laughing together, some holding tails or hands or both. Presumably boating on Lake Avernus was a popular date activity; Ruthven, like most sanguivores, got seasick on a wet pavement, and had never been able to see the appeal of messing about in boats.

Someone was coming. Ruthven's senses were somewhat blunter down here than they were on Earth, but even so, his hearing was acute. There was a faint clear chiming sound, very sweet, that he'd noticed a few times during his stay so far; it came and went apparently at random, and Ruthven couldn't work out where it could be coming from; it didn't seem to be directional in any way, as if it came directly out of the air itself. He'd have to remember to ask the nurse—and wondered, not for the first time, what the nursing staff were saying about him, amongst themselves. Wondered if they'd ever had cause to treat a vampire before, and if they minded.

"They don't," said a voice behind him, and Ruthven blinked, sitting up and looking over his shoulder. Fastitocalon stood there, grey suit immaculate as always, holding two glasses; he came forward and handed one of them to Ruthven. Cut crystal, brilliant as diamond. In fact, down here, it *might* be diamond. This time there was no bendy straw. "They're fascinated, in fact."

"Since when do you make a habit of casually reading my mind?" Ruthven asked without much rancor. Fastitocalon pulled over another deck chair and sat down.

"I'm not, actually," he said. "You're thinking extremely loudly; it's impossible not to overhear. How are you feeling?"

Ruthven rolled his eyes. "I don't think loudly, I think at a perfectly normal volume, and it's nice to see you properly, Fass." The last time he'd seen the demon had been through a haze of pain and morphine in the hospital's emergency department.

"It's nice to see you, too," said Fastitocalon, leaning back in the chair with a sigh. His own glass contained something pale-gold and clear, with bubbles in it; after a moment Ruthven realized there was a tiny flame flickering from the rim. A garnish. "I haven't had time to come and see you before now."

"Work being extra busy?" said Ruthven, eyebrow raised. They'd put something pleasant in the warmed blood, something a bit like brandy; it felt very nice indeed. "You look tired."

Fastitocalon did. Vastly better than the last time Ruthven had seen him on Earth, without the too-thin, worn, unwell expression, but tired nonetheless, and the worry-lines in his forehead were deep. "Work hasn't *stopped* being busy for months. There's so much data to sift through, I have a team of demons working on it in shifts."

"What data?" Ruthven was peripherally aware that Fastitocalon was in charge of some enormous complex project that had to do with the past administration of the M&E department, but that was about all he knew.

"Well. You remember that awful business in Paris, with the reality rip."

"In excruciating detail," said Ruthven.

"Yes. Quite. So after that, an inquiry was launched into the entire department's failure to do its bloody job right, and a lot of rather worrisome things came to light, including the behavior of the department head, and I ended up in charge instead of Asmodeus, who is currently a slug. It turned out that not only had M&E been run incredibly poorly in terms of its surface operative training and placement, in some cases not run at all, but the data analysis side of the department had basically been spending the past fifteen years sitting around, picking their noses, and occasionally submitting made-up reports on the data analysis they weren't doing. Sam was livid."

"I can imagine," said Ruthven. "A *slug*?"

"A banana slug. About so big." Fastitocalon sipped his drink. "I am told he exercises the privilege of continuing to wear his crown despite the transmogrification, which was graciously granted him upon sentencing, and please do not ask me how. The point is, we have *years'* worth of data from the surface placements that has barely been looked at, and my people are having to sort through all of it to see what we've been missing. The extent to which reality has been—*corroded* isn't the right word, or *dissolved*, but you get the idea—indicates that this trend has been going on for quite some time, and I, or rather we, need to find out when it started and *where it began*. And who's doing it. If it's something from outside our universe."

"Is that why the—thing, the whatever it was in London, was able to come through and take up residence in the shelter?"

"Yes, and why that wretched vampire's repeated monster-summonings were able to cause that much damage in Paris; both of those were made possible by whatever's behind this, even if they had no idea it was responsible. Reality's been badly weakened on purpose, and that entity in London won't be the only thing coming through from somewhere *else* if the fabric tears open. If it isn't already. Somewhere, someone's doing something they should not be."

"And your people on Earth now are trying to find it?" Ruthven didn't like the idea of *somewhere else*, especially if the thing they'd encountered under London was a representative example.

"We're spread thin, and I simply don't have the personnel to replace all the operatives, even if it badly needs to be done, and in any case I can't spare a lot of people to analyze the *new* data. Sam says the priority is finding out the scope and extent of this trend; if the people on Earth become aware of any emergency, they will notify us at once, and that's the best I can manage."

Ruthven stared into the depths of his glass, thinking about

the awful *otherness* of the thing under London, its inherent alien quality, thinking about the timeslips in Paris. That sensation of sliding, helpless *destabilization*, the edges of everything too fluid, too vague.

If both of those instances were due to the same underlying problem, what else must have been going wrong, all this time, all over the world, and *who was responsible for it*?

"This is probably a stupid question," he said, still looking into the glass. "But what happens if reality does... fall apart?"

Fastitocalon gave him a long look. "It's the end of everything," he said. "End of *this* world, anyway. State of total entropy."

"Would we know it was happening?"

"If the collapse was gradual? Yes. We wouldn't enjoy it, either; better hope it goes with a bang and takes everything with it in an instant. What a cheery sickbed conversation this is, to be sure." He took another sip of whatever he was drinking, and Ruthven noticed the little flame garnish moved itself around the rim of his glass to get out of the way.

"I think I'd rather know about it than not," said Ruthven slowly. The demon's desire to change the subject was obvious, and he lay back, looking up at the vault of sky above them for a long moment before speaking again. That faint chiming sound was back, barely on the edge of audibility. He wondered again what it was; there was no breeze to stir a windchime. "But regardless, I can see why you've been working so hard. And why you've always loved it here." He gestured to the lake, the view, the general surroundings. "It's beautiful. I mean, I knew it was, you'd said so, but..."

"Words don't do it justice," said Fastitocalon with a tired smile. "It was always beautiful, you know. Even in the very beginning, when we were all treading water and trying to work out what had just happened to us and what we were going to do about it, long before we'd built the towers of Dis, when it was just a wilderness—it was beautiful."

Ruthven blinked at him. "That's right," he said. "I keep forgetting you actually Fell."

"Oh, yes." He swirled his glass, drank the last of it. Ruthven watched, feeling faintly hysterical, as he scooped the tiny flame off the rim with his fingertip and popped it into his mouth, the way a man might eat the last olive from the bottom of a martini glass. After a moment he glanced over at Ruthven. "What?"

"You just ate a flame," he said.

"They're quite nice," said Fastitocalon, "although I don't recommend you try one; they don't do any damage to demons but I've no idea what effect they have on the undead."

"They don't burn you?"

"No. Incidentally, the main effect they *did* have, back in the beginning, was to bleach all our wings white. Some of us, the ones with complicated plumage, were quite annoyed about that."

Ruthven stared at him a moment longer, and then leaned back against the deckchair and laughed helplessly. Despite the ominous conversation, despite the lurking fear, he laughed: everything in the universe, as he had told Grisaille back in

Greta's clinic, was *hilarious*. After a moment Fastitocalon joined in; and a couple of demons walking along the promenade looked up and wondered what in the Spa could possibly be that funny.

The jet lag coming this way was far easier than the kind you got heading east, Cranswell thought. It was unsettling to have taken off around eight p.m. and landed at half past ten, the seven hours of the flight collapsed to two, but he'd had absolutely no trouble falling asleep the moment he faceplanted onto the hotel bed; and this morning he'd been up with the dawn.

He had, in fact, been so very awake that he'd taken the opportunity to slip out and go for a quick walk in the waking city, while it was still quiet. He loved the sense of vast waiting potential at this time of day, a whole microcosm's worth of people and machinery and ideas gearing up to begin their work; it always felt almost electric. Mostly he couldn't be bothered to roll out of bed before seven a.m., but on those instances when he'd had to be up very early, Cranswell had enjoyed watching London waking up. New York was no different.

(Sure, they were here to commit antiquities theft on the orders of a witch with prehensile hair, but he could have a good time *beforehand*, couldn't he?)

By the time he'd got back, Grisaille was beginning to stir, but Cranswell had had time to shower and dress and order and mostly consume room service breakfast before he appeared. It had taken two cups of black coffee before Grisaille progressed beyond monosyllabic into sardonic, and Cranswell thought he could see how he and Ruthven would get along like the proverbial house on fire.

The Met didn't open until ten, and they spent some little time strolling along Fifth Avenue and looking at the trees in Central Park; they were a riot of autumn color, brilliant against a white sky.

"So what's the plan?" Cranswell asked, leaning on the wall separating the park from the sidewalk. "I mean. We're here to case the joint, right? And figure out how the hell to get the thing out of there?"

"That's what that unfortunate phrase *means*," said Grisaille, lighting a cigarette. They were black and smelled of cloves; Cranswell wasn't even slightly surprised. Grisaille's wardrobe appeared to be limited to black, grey, and very dark red. "And yes, in effect. We go and look at it and I come up with a way to pull this off. The easiest is probably to arrange for it to be moved, and nick it in the process, rather than trying to get it out of the case our own selves."

"Which is why I'm here," said Cranswell. "Me and my nice new doctored expertise in Egyptology. You want me to convince the museum they need to move one of their most prized exhibits for reasons."

"Something like that," said Grisaille, not sounding happy about it. "Perhaps you need to examine it in the conservation department, or run tests, or whatever it is curators do. I thought you mostly hung pictures on walls and frowned at people."

"That's art gallery curators," said Cranswell. "An easy mistake to make. I think they'll let us in now, it's after ten."

"Wait a few more minutes," Grisaille said. "Never be the first one to enter or the last to leave, because people tend to *remember* you, and it's easy to find on the security footage. Best to attach yourself to a random group. And don't look self-conscious and don't look exaggeratedly casual and don't say anything unless spoken to."

"...you realize now I'm *going* to look incredibly self-conscious," said Cranswell, beginning to wish he hadn't had breakfast after all.

Grisaille flicked away the butt of his black cigarette. "No," he said, "you're not," and looked Cranswell full in the eyes—his were so *weird*, they looked like red contacts—and all of a sudden Cranswell felt entirely calm. Grisaille's pupils were expanding and contracting in a slow pulse, hypnotic, fascinating.

Then he blinked, and the effect cut off. Cranswell's equanimity remained.

"...you just thralled me," he said.

"I absolutely did," said Grisaille. "Come along, let's go experience some culture."

Cranswell had spent some time in America, growing up; he'd been to the Met once, when he'd been quite little. All he could clearly remember was a vast echoing open space, and a lot of columns, and some statues with no clothes on. This time it was a rather different experience. This time he wished very much they weren't here on a mission, because he wanted to see *everything.*

Grisaille paid cash for their entry stickers, and Cranswell could tell he was doing the thing vampires sometimes did where they made themselves *less noticeable*; a tall slender dark-skinned man all in black with long dreadlocks and bright red eyes was difficult to ignore, but as he watched, the cashier didn't even stare, barely looking up from the till to hand him his change.

"This way," said Grisaille, looking at a map. "Stick close to me and no one is likely to pay us much attention." He led Cranswell through a huge doorway into a gallery largely taken up by what looked like an actual *tomb*, but didn't stop to let him read anything about it; didn't stop to look at anything, in fact, passing through room after room until they came to the one he wanted. It was smaller than several of the galleries they'd passed through, high-ceilinged, almost square, with a doorway in each soft-ochre-painted wall; a piece of stone frieze hung opposite a little case containing a red stone statue of a kneeling figure; headless statues and statueless heads were arrayed around the walls, and in the middle of the floor were two tall thin glass cases on plinths, and inside the cases—

"Wow," said Cranswell softly. "They're beautiful."

He'd had a chance on the plane to read through the documentation on the two stelae; he knew enough, or hoped he knew enough, to casually pass as someone who'd actually spent time studying these particular artifacts. It helped that he had a good memory for detail.

The Metternich Stela had vanished for two thousand years before being discovered during the construction of a Franciscan monastery in Alexandria; the Hermopolis Stela had turned up during an Egyptian University expedition in the 1930s at Tunah al-Jabal that uncovered a maze of underground streets and catacombs connected with the Thoth cult. It was so far unique, the only one of its kind to have been found, and now Cranswell was going to have to figure out a way to get it out of here. How much did it even *weigh*?

"It's remarkable, isn't it," said somebody quite near, and Cranswell jumped, turning to see a woman in sand-colored silk next to him, looking at the thing in the case. "The only one of its kind."

"That we know of," said Cranswell, and was a little surprised to hear how confident he sounded despite the fact she'd said the very thing he'd just been thinking, right out loud. Grisaille's thrall was doing the work of a dose of Xanax. Where *was* Grisaille, anyway—he'd been right there when they came in, and now he couldn't see him anywhere. With an effort he forced his concentration back to the woman.

She was in her mid-thirties, with a quietly expensive haircut and quietly expensive clothes, and Cranswell thought the makeup was probably pretty pricy as well. And she was smiling at him. In a slightly peculiar way.

"Do you think there are more?" she asked, and *boy*, was he glad he'd just reread the background materials this morning over breakfast.

"It's an enticing idea," he said with a smile of his own. "That there are other treasures like this out there to be found. It's *possible*, of course, but between the German expedition in '29 and the Egyptian University dig that started a year later, I think it's unlikely that particular stone remains unturned."

She nodded. "In my opinion, if such a valuable object had existed, it would have been kept somewhere safe."

"Such as the catacombs they found in the necropolis on the west bank," said Cranswell. "The Egyptian University archaeologists were there from '30 to '39; I believe they would have found a second stela, if there was one there to find."

"I'd agree with you," she said, and held out a hand. The lapis scarab set in the ring on her third finger was too huge and dramatic to be anything but real. "Leonora Van Dorne."

"August Cranswell," he said, and shook her hand. "I'm with the British Museum."

Ms. Van Dorne nodded. "I thought so. A pleasure to meet you, Mr. Cranswell. Is this your field?" She gestured at the cases, the vast blue stone of her ring brilliant under the spotlights, and he thought, *Either she's a jewel thief, or she's unspeakably rich, or she's married to some incredibly unethical archaeologist who gives his wife things that should be in museums.* On the whole, he thought option two was the most likely.

"Not specifically the magico-medical stelae," he said. "Late period, Thirtieth Dynasty. You?"

"Oh, I'm just an interested amateur," said Ms. Van Dorne, and smiled that slightly peculiar smile again. "And something of a collector, as well."

Cranswell revised his assessment: *incredibly rich jewel thief?* "Something like this would be the gem of anyone's collection," he said casually, "but of course it belongs on display."

"Of course," she agreed. "That's why I occasionally lend out some pieces of my own for the museum to show the public. That statue, for example." She nodded at a small, beautiful figure of a seated woman, carved from some dark smooth stone.

"This is yours? It's beautiful," said Cranswell, and was extremely glad he'd caught a glimpse of the legend without seeming to. "Thirtieth, obviously?"

"That's right," said Ms. Van Dorne. "I have several other Thirtieth Dynasty pieces, in fact; I intend to lend them my Horus-protecting-the-pharaoh statue when this little one comes off display; it's much better than the one they already have in their collection." She paused, head tilted. "If you'd like to see them, I'd be happy to show you."

*I am being hit on by a woman wearing a ring that is probably worth nearly a hundred thousand dollars,* Cranswell thought. *How is this my life?* Out loud he said, "I'd love that, actually. I'm only in town for a few days, but I'd hate to miss a chance to view a private collection like yours."

Ms. Van Dorne smiled, reaching into her handbag, and handed him a card. "Come by at four this afternoon," she said. "We'll have coffee."

"Thanks very much," said Cranswell, looking down at the card: LEONORA IRENE VAN DORNE, and an address and number, nothing more. When he looked up again, she had gone.

What was it with people vanishing today, he wondered, and even as the thought crossed his mind, a section of the wall beside the doorway stopped being the wall and started being Grisaille. It was rather as if he'd stepped forward out of the surface, all at once, and Cranswell realized he'd been there all along: he'd simply jacked up the *don't notice me* effect all the way.

"Well, *that* was fascinating," he said over Cranswell's startled yelp. "I suppose Serenskaya and Helsing were right: you *are* going to be useful, after all. Did you see that ring?"

"How could I miss it?"

"My poor little fingers were itching," said Grisaille, coming over to the stelae in their cases. He wiggled the members in question, and grinned, an expression Cranswell was coming to realize meant that he was getting ready to happen to someone. "This job is getting more interesting by the hour."

In the Met's Great Hall Balcony Café & Bar, a pair of angels were not having a good time.

Zophiel and Amitiel were not tremendously good at thinking; thinking was not what they were *for*. Nevertheless, at the moment, it was necessary.

"It's one of the Commandments," Amitiel was saying. "That's—it's the *rules*. We can't break the *rules*. I mean. That's why they're the rules. Because you can't break them."

Zophiel was tearing a croissant into smaller and smaller

pieces. "I *know*," he said, "but…the purpose of our mission would be attained sooner rather than later, we'd *really* damage the barrier, surely that's a greater good? Can one do ill in order to do good?"

"That's *theology*," said Amitiel, wide-eyed. "We're not allowed to do theology."

"I know," said Zophiel again. "I know. And—one of them's a monster, we can't possibly *help* monsters, it—goes against nature…" He trailed off wretchedly. On the one hand, if the monster and his friend *did* steal the artifact for Van Dorne to use Zophiel and Amitiel's spell on, it would undoubtedly be enough to achieve the angels' actual objective, the destruction or at least critical weakening of the barrier between this world and their own next door, so they should help; on the other hand, stealing was against the Commandments, and anyway, the monster was monstrous, and Zophiel was not happy. "When this is over, I am going to have to do so much penance," he said. "Being in this dreadful world is making me have sinful thoughts."

Amitiel reached across the table, touched his hand; he stopped destroying the pastry and sighed. "I suppose we could…do nothing?"

"We're not supposed to interfere," said Amitiel. "Just—let it happen as God wills. Anything else is dangerous."

Zophiel looked up with an unhappy smile. "You're right. Of course you're right. I was just so *eager* to bring about the end of our assignment that I let doubt into my mind."

"You've been working so hard," said Amitiel. "Taking care

of me. Talking to the model agencies and the photographers so I didn't have to—I know I'm slow—"

"You're not slow," said Zophiel. "You are as the Lord created you."

Amitiel smiled at him, and it was nothing more than bad luck for the art student on the other side of the hall who happened to be looking that way; on the other hand, the retinal afterimage of that blazing beauty would fade in an hour or two.

# CHAPTER 10

Greta leaned back in her chair and stared at the ceiling. On the table the conference phone squatted like a small alien spaceship, its red telltale light steady. It was around midday in New York, but here the last of the sunset was fading in the west, the sky visible through the conference room's blinds a deepening blue.

"Well," she said, "at least nobody could accuse the pair of you of wasting time. What do you hope to get out of visiting this woman?"

"Information, maybe," said Cranswell. "Or she might have something we could use?"

"She's either a thief or the next best thing to one," Grisaille drawled. "A *collector.* I could see it going a couple of ways. Anyway, we don't have a better plan yet."

"The thing is really well secured. It's under constant surveillance and the case is as robust and difficult to crack as any I've seen," said Cranswell. "Probably has vibration sensors or a built-in scale to alarm if the weight changes. The only way to get in there without just smashing-and-grabbing is probably to have the museum do it for us."

Greta sighed, looked across the table at Varney and Tefnakhte. "Great. Not that I'm surprised, exactly, but great."

"Which is another reason this Van Dorne person might be of use," said Nadezhda from London. "If she's friends with the museum—"

"Way ahead of you," said Grisaille. "We just have to convince *her* that she wants to convince *them*, and I've been practicing my thrall like a good little bloodsucker, haven't I, Cranswell?"

"What I don't really get is how the hell we're supposed to physically move it," said Cranswell, ignoring this sally. "I don't know how much it weighs but it's *big*, it's like nearly three feet tall and pretty solid, with a heavy base. What exactly is the—uh—"

"Extraction plan?" said Grisaille. "That, I think, is going to have to be up to the fine folks representing Hell to the New York constituency."

"I gave them Glasya and Morax's contact information," Nadezhda said. "It might be worth giving the pair of them a ring just to advise what you're up to and request help, Grisaille."

"I think I'll do that," he said. "In the meantime we'd best be toddling if we are to rendezvous with the Van Dorne at her palatial abode on time. Will keep you apprised."

"Good luck," said Greta, and there was a click as he went off the line. "Anyone else got anything new to report?"

"So far having Sir Francis assist me in the chanting seems to have a beneficial effect," said Tefnakhte. "And there have been no new episodes among our patients."

"Good," said Greta. "Dez, you're not seeing it too, are you?"

"I haven't had any mummy patients yet," said Nadezhda. "Which isn't to say that it is not happening among London's Class B revenant population: just that it hasn't been reported to us."

"Keep an ear out," said Greta. "It'd be useful to know if this is limited just to Oasis Natrun, but I think it may not be."

"Got it. Anything else?"

"I think that's it. How's the clinic in general?"

"Oh, ticking right along," said Nadezhda. "Hippolyta's making all sorts of friends with the patients as they hang out in the waiting room, and between me and Anna, we haven't had any difficulty keeping up. They miss you, of course."

Greta had to smile a little. "Tell them I miss them, too. If Krona comes in, say hello for me and tell him he is to *listen* to you about his arthritis, he's the most stubborn old wight I've ever encountered but his daughter's quite sensible and will pay attention to what you tell her."

"All right," said Nadezhda. "We had Ms. Montrose in yesterday, bringing her baby in for a checkup; she asked us to pass along her regards." Sheelagh Montrose was one of the city's more urbane banshees, whose tailored coats almost completely hid the hump of her folded wings; she had quite a nice speaking voice except when she got profoundly irritated with someone. "I'll let you go, but call us if you need anything, all right, Greta? We'll get through this."

"I know," she said, trying to sound as if she believed it. "Thanks, Dez. Good-bye for now."

"Take care." Another click, and the red eye on the phone base went out.

"We *will* get through it," said Varney, reaching across the table to take her hand. "Right now it's time to stop for dinner. You haven't had anything but coffee for most of the day."

"Neither have you," she pointed out. "For at least two days. You ought to go down to the city and find someone to eat, Varney. I need you to take care of yourself as well as the rest of us."

He went faintly pink. Unlike Ruthven, Varney was a vampyre, and had specific dietary requirements vis-à-vis victims' virginal state that couldn't be met at Oasis Natrun other than by snacking on the nuns, and that was somewhat impolite. "I'm quite all right," he said, "but... well. If you're sure you don't need me for a little while, I might slip out for a bite."

She smiled at him. "Go. I'll see you later tonight, if you can come with me and Tefnakhte while I do my night rounds. Can I see you do the bat thing?"

Ruthven never let her see him turn into a bat; she held out little hope that Varney might, and wasn't particularly surprised when he demurred; she walked him out, though, and spent a few minutes looking up at the vast deep-blue bowl of the sky. The stars were brilliant here, without the faintest wisp of cloud to blur them; they were high enough up over the city that the light pollution didn't have much of an effect, and the air was crystal-clear. In London it was apparently still raining on and off, although the unrelenting deluge seemed to have passed off; there were fewer halfhearted ark jokes being made on the morning news. Everything *except* this mysterious illness—and Ruthven's mysterious curse—seemed to be steadily improving.

She turned Varney's ring on her finger, still vividly remembering how it had felt when the metal shrank itself to fit her, warming to her blood-heat. Remembering how it had felt to understand that he had gone to Hell for her, and come back again with this in his pocket. Just for a moment, despite the fatigue and worry, despite her gnawing awareness that she didn't know what was happening or how to fix it, just for a moment Greta Helsing was something close to simply and powerfully *happy*.

Ms. Van Dorne's address on East Sixty-eighth turned out to be about a ten-minute walk from their hotel. Grisaille was in no mood for window-shopping, despite the riches on offer up and down Madison Avenue—the thought of it brought back Rome, vividly and awfully, how much fun they'd been having before Ruthven fell ill—but he let Cranswell stare at the shopfronts as they made their way south; and since they in fact had over an hour to kill before turning up on her front step, he agreed to stop at a little French café just down the street to fill Cranswell up with food again. Grisaille kept forgetting how often humans needed to *eat*, although he was fairly sure Cranswell could have got along quite well without spending so much time doing it.

Cranswell had called their new acquaintance and asked

if he could bring along his colleague and traveling companion who, while not an academic, was a fellow collector and would very much appreciate the opportunity to see Ms. Van Dorne's treasures; she had acquiesced immediately, sounding as if she'd been expecting something of the sort, with a smile in her voice. That hadn't gone very far toward reassuring Grisaille about—anything, really—but they were committed now, and he wanted to know what her *deal* was; there was something very unusual about this particular human which he couldn't quite put his finger on.

He sipped his espresso, deliberately not watching Cranswell engulf a ham-and-cheese panini, and wondered what Ruthven was doing right now, and if he was all right, and whether he was bored to death yet—and had to stop thinking about that. "So go over it again," he said to Cranswell to distract himself. "What are we going to tell her?"

"Rash of antiquities theft," said Cranswell through a mouthful, and swallowed. "Strongly suggest she advises the museum to move the Hermopolis Stela off display for safety's sake. And also see if she owns anything like it herself that might mean we don't need to get hold of that piece in particular."

It was a lot easier to nick things that weren't already in museum-quality locked cases, Grisaille had reflected, and he was fairly sure he could thrall the Van Dorne into letting them waltz out with something of metaphysical significance, if the opportunity presented itself. If not, well. They might be able to get her to do the hard part *for* them, since she had an in with the museum.

He'd called up the demons, as suggested. Neither of them had sounded particularly thrilled to hear from him, but both had agreed to help if necessary. The woman was a gallery owner somewhere in Soho and the man was a theatrical producer, and both of them were so very *New York* that it hurt. Grisaille had been put faintly in mind of the useless Irazek, from that spring in Paris: a demon who had gone entirely native, rather than doing his actual job. Hopefully these two were better M&E operatives than Irazek, but mostly what he needed them for was going to be exfiltration—even if they did manage to get their hands on the stela, and even if he, Grisaille, could lift the thing, he was not going to be able to stroll onto a plane with it tucked under his arm as carry-on luggage: getting it out of the country was going to be a trick and a half unless they called in paranormal assistance. He didn't know if demons could flip people and objects all the way from New York to Marseille, but he imagined he was going to find out.

"Come on," he said to Cranswell. "Finish your coffee and let's get going before we're unfashionably late."

It wasn't the most imposing private residence Cranswell had ever been to—that would definitely be Ruthven's Embankment mansion—but Leonora Van Dorne's gorgeous Beaux-Arts home was a close second. The curved glass in the bow window, the carved stone cornucopias spilling their wealth of fruit and flowers, the iron lacework of the balconies, spoke very firmly if decorously of *more money than God.* When Grisaille rang the doorbell, he was surprised that Van Dorne herself came to let them in; he'd been expecting a servant, possibly one in uniform.

Out of the museum she looked even more impressive, despite the fact that without her four-inch heels she'd have come up to Cranswell's collarbone. She smiled that rather unsettling smile. "Mr. Cranswell," she said. "So nice to see you again. And you would be Mr. Grisaille? A pleasure."

Grisaille shook her hand firmly. Cranswell had been briefly afraid he'd do something Gallic such as attempt to kiss it, but he had apparently decided to go for *charming and urbane* instead. "The pleasure is mine, Ms. Van Dorne. Thank you for your kind invitation."

"Of course," she said, and stood aside to let them into an entry hall that reminded Cranswell vividly of certain stately homes he had visited: the walls were pale dressed stone, the tapestry hanging on one wall should probably itself have been in a museum, and the beamed ceiling was pure Jacobean.

"Is that..." he said, and trailed off, staring at a carving on a plinth—or a fragment of a carving, in yellow jasper: a woman's face, the enigmatic curving smile familiar. Very familiar; he'd seen something very much like it in the museum that morning.

"Queen Tiye," said Ms. Van Dorne. "The Met's version, of course, is generally considered a fine example, but I prefer the original. This way, gentlemen."

While they were still trying to process that remarkable statement, she led them up the stairs and into a vast high-ceilinged room still full of light despite the lateness of the afternoon, and this time both Cranswell and Grisaille were lost for words.

There were treasures *everywhere*. More statues and statuettes stood on the mantel, in cases, on tables; framed sections of papyri and facsimiles of tomb paintings hung on the walls; a glass-topped curio table displayed royal jewelry, rich gold and carnelian and lapis and turquoise vivid against the softness of black velvet.

"Please, look around," she said, still smiling. "May I offer you some refreshment? Coffee—or wine? I have quite a nice little Sancerre."

Cranswell had done just enough cramming on the way here to be dumbstruck at some of the things she had casually lying around. "Um," he said. "I—that sounds lovely, actually—"

"I'll be just a moment," said Ms. Van Dorne, and left them alone together—and Cranswell and Grisaille shared a wide-eyed look. *Jewel thief*, he thought, *has to be a jewel thief, there's nothing else she* can *be, right?*

"Well," said Grisaille out loud, "this is quite the little collection, I must say. Do tell me if you recognize anything."

"I'm looking for stuff that's sacred to Thoth," Cranswell said, still staring around himself. "We might have come to exactly the right place."

Ms. Van Dorne closed the door behind herself and smiled, leaning against it with her arms folded. Just lately it seemed as if things she wanted kept simply falling into her lap.

She stayed there, listening, for a few minutes before fetching a tray from her kitchen; returned soundlessly, her heels deliberately silent on the parquet floor. The taller of the two men, the one with the long dreadlocks, was draped elegantly in a chair, the westering sun catching the planes and angles of his face to good effect; the younger one jumped guiltily when she came in and pushed his glasses up his nose, trying to look as if he hadn't just been considering running his fingers over a falcon statuette on the mantel.

"That's the Horus I mentioned this morning," she said. "One of the finest examples yet discovered, I believe."

"Er, yes," he said. She handed around glasses, sat down on the ottoman, ankles crossed decorously, and waited for him to make a mistake—aware of being observed quite closely by the other one, with the French name and the ostentatious colored contacts. *Gay*, she thought, *obviously, but these two aren't together; there's something else going on here. And neither of them is an Egyptologist, or hasn't been one for more than a few days.*

She didn't have to wait very long. "So, um," Cranswell said after a gulp of wine, "you must be concerned about security, what with a collection like this one?"

"Oh, I have an excellent security system," she said. "My cases are made by the same company the museum uses, in fact. It's second to none."

She watched that one go home, and mentally wondered at the choices made by whoever had sent *this* kid to play this particular game—and was not at all surprised when the other one winced ever so slightly. He was the one she'd have to be careful with, Ms. Van Dorne had known right away, but she'd let the kid spin himself a little more rope first.

"So the recent rash of antiquities theft doesn't concern you?" he asked.

She let her eyes widen. "Oh, no. I made absolutely sure the museum's precautions met my standards before I agreed to lend them my little statue. One can't be too careful these days."

"One can't," said the other man. Grey-something. *Grisaille*, her mind supplied. Ostentatious contact lenses, ostentatious name, British accent. She wondered if he was supposed to *be* somebody, and smiled: a deliberate smile.

"It's important to take one's own advice," she said, "wouldn't you say? Since neither of you is telling the truth, I think I ought to insist."

The younger man—his name probably *was* Cranswell, nobody would make that up—went ashy-grey, staring at her. "What—what do you mean, the truth—?"

"You are no more an Egyptologist than I am a long-distance runner," said Ms. Van Dorne, although she thought that she could probably at least manage a half-marathon in her current rejuvenated state. "Oh, don't panic. I know you're a thief."

He went even greyer. "I don't know what you're talking about—"

"Which is extremely convenient," she continued, "because there happens to be something I'd like you to steal for me. And I think you already know what it is."

The last time Ruthven had been seriously ill had been while he was alive, and he didn't have too many very clear memories of the experience; he'd died in the late sixteenth century. Nevertheless he thought that it was probably a good sign to have progressed from *sleeping all the time* to *being really bored and irritable about everything*, even if it did mean he was having to put some effort into not snapping at people.

Faust agreed. The doctor came to see him midmorning, the day after Fastitocalon's visit, and told him he was continuing to improve.

"When can I have my clothes back?" Ruthven wanted to know. Faust chuckled.

"At the pillow-hurling stage, are we? Want to get up and stop being treated like an invalid?"

"Rather," he said. "I mean—I do appreciate it, everything you're doing for me—"

"But you've had enough of lying down and doing what you're told. Understandably. Well, my lord, I think that barring any return of pain or nausea, you are probably cleared to get up and walk around a bit, if we can find you a suitable escort. I'd detail Fastitocalon, but he's busier than I am these days and he doesn't need any more things to worry about—I'm not entirely happy with how he's doing, either—so I'll see if I can find someone with more free time."

"I don't know any other demons," said Ruthven. "Wait. Is Irazek down here, and is he a slug, too?"

"Irazek," said Faust, looking as if he was trying to recall the name.

"Shortish, orange hair, little horns to match, freckled, incredibly bad at being a surface operative? He was involved in the Paris thing a few months back."

Faust snapped his fingers. "Oh, *him*. Yes, he's down here, and currently bipedal, although no longer employed in M&E. I think he's working in a bakery."

"He was definitely a better baker than a surface operative," said Ruthven, bone-dry. "Fass had quite a few piquant observations to make on the subject."

"I don't blame him," said Faust. "I'd say a good two-thirds of Asmodeus's hires are some level of incompetent—it's to be expected when they're working for someone both incompetent *and* corrupt—and poor bloody Fastitocalon's the one who's got to clean up the mess while trying to do eighty years' worth of data analysis all at once. Don't envy him the job, I can tell you that for free."

"Can I... I don't know, help somehow? At all?"

"I doubt it," said Faust. "But I'll ask. Are you any good at math?"

"Not the way Fass is. I can do basic stuff. Pattern recognition's more what I'm good at."

Faust looked at him. Ruthven could see where the woodcuts had got it right: the engagingly ugly bearded face, the intense brown gaze, the shapeless hat. He was wearing a dark medieval gown without the fur trim common to the illustrations, and on him it somehow looked as imposing and impressive as a standard doctor's white coat would have been.

"I'll see what we can do," he said. "And I will have your

clothes cleaned and pressed and returned to you. But take care, my lord. You're not quite back to a hundred percent yet, and you need to be a bit careful not to tire yourself out."

Ruthven sighed, running his hands through his hair. "Fine," he said. "I'll do my best. And—thank you."

He meant more than just *for seeing if there's a job around here I could do*; he meant *for fixing me*, and knew the doctor understood.

Grisaille closed the hotel room door behind the room-service waiter, and turned the bolt. Behind him Cranswell was face-down on the bed, with a pillow pulled over his head.

"Unless you emerge," Grisaille told him, running a thumbnail around the foil on the top of the bottle he'd just had delivered, "I am going to drink all of this myself. I'm just saying."

Cranswell said something too muffled to understand, but after a moment he did take the pillow off his head and sit up, hair rather hilariously disarranged. "Don't you dare," he said. "I need that for medicinal purposes. I thought I was going to fucking keel right over when she said *you're a thief*."

"I know," said Grisaille. "It was extremely evident. You went rather a remarkable color." He uncorked the bottle and poured them each two fingers of cask-strength Connemara. "Anyway, as it turns out, we didn't have to convince *her* to help us after all."

"Do you trust her?" said Cranswell, taking the glass in both hands.

"Do I look like a *complete* idiot?" Grisaille inquired. "She's a fucking snake, and I still can't figure out what it is about her that's pinging all my senses—it's almost as if she's not quite human, but she *smells* human, if you know what I mean."

"Not in the least," said Cranswell. "She's—unsettling, though. I mean. That smile. There's something wrong with it."

"You didn't recognize the smile? Look at any of those statues we saw today." Grisaille knocked back his whiskey, refilled the glass. "Anyway, we're on. In a minute I'll call the home office and let them know."

"I hope she's going to be *able* to convince them to move the stela," said Cranswell. "I mean, yeah, she's super influential and she said she knew the director and gives them a ton of money and lends them her artifacts, but—I don't know if *I* would be willing to take a rich patron's word for it that one of my prize pieces was in danger of being stolen and I should have it taken off display."

"It's a neat little balancing trick," said Grisaille, sitting down. "Warning them something's going to be stolen so that it can, in fact, be stolen. Self-referential, with built-in credence; why would she tell them it was in danger if she was the one who intended to take it, after all? I think it'll work. I have about—call it eighty percent confidence."

"That's twenty percent of *oh shit*," said Cranswell. "I'm not wild about the odds."

"You don't have to be," said Grisaille. "All you have to do is follow the plan and avoid fucking up."

"She's not going to be happy when we don't turn up at her place in an unmarked van bearing her newest prize."

"Words cannot express how much I don't care," said Grisaille, pouring himself a third drink. "Presumably the New York demons can handle getting it, and us, the hell out of here."

"I'm just picturing it," said Cranswell. "I mean—it's kind of a pleasant mental image. The hustler becomes the hustled."

"Come to think of it," said Grisaille, transferring himself to the other bed, glass in hand, "the reason this has worked so far is that you are absolute shit at lying. She saw right through you probably from the moment you bumped into her at the museum."

Cranswell glowered at him and went to fetch the bottle. "Thanks," he said sourly. "Really makes me feel good about myself, you know?"

"Oh, shut up. If you were any good at deception, we'd still be trying to figure out how to get the stupid thing out of its stupid case. I'm, in my own peculiar idiom, attempting to give you a compliment."

"Were you? I couldn't tell." Cranswell sighed. "This better *work*."

"Relax. I said, I'm pretty confident it will."

"No, I mean—the thing itself. It better summon up Thoth or whatever it's supposed to do and get the answer they're looking for. I'm going to be so pissed if we went through this whole mess and it turns out to be the religious equivalent of ASK AGAIN LATER or ANSWER UNCLEAR."

Grisaille couldn't help picturing a mummy shaking the stela like a Magic 8 Ball and peering at it. "You and me both," he said. "What time is it in Marseille, anyway?"

"Um," said Cranswell, counting on his fingers. "Two in the morning."

"Maybe I'll wait till tomorrow to call them." Grisaille sighed. "And it is entirely off-brand for me to be sensible, but I should point out that you ought to have more for dinner than whiskey. Even very delicious whiskey. I need you functional in the morning."

"Can we order more room service? I don't feel like dealing with humans right now."

"I never feel like dealing with humans," said Grisaille, and tossed him the menu. "Knock yourself out, but keep the garlic thing in mind, okay?"

"Garlic soup with garlic bread and extra garlic, check," said Cranswell. "Fine, fine, okay, I'll tell them I'm hideously allergic to it when I place the order. What about you?"

"What about me?" Grisaille drained his glass, laced his fingers behind his head. "I might go out to eat, actually. Sample the local cuisine, or at least the locals."

"You might as well," said Cranswell. "Since we're here. Be a pity to waste the opportunity to try new things."

"Couldn't have said it better myself," he said, and sighed. "Next time it's somebody else's turn to save the world, I'm not cut out for it, even if I am extremely good at stealing things. All this metaphysical bullshit is not really my scene." He couldn't stop thinking about Hell, about Ruthven in Hell, and what his long-term prognosis was likely to be. Sure, the city had been weirdly beautiful, and maybe he could get used to it, but he didn't want to have to try.

"Mine, either," said Cranswell. "I had enough of that last year with those mad monks and the giant evil lightbulb, which honestly I still have trouble believing is a thing that actually happened."

"Yeah, what *did* happen with that? Ruthven doesn't talk about it much," said Grisaille, glancing over. Cranswell finished his drink, set the glass down.

"I hit it with a sword," he said. "Some kind of—*thing*, entity, I don't know what, that basically fed off hatred and fear and bad emotions, had come to hang out in this glass rectifier thing in the Underground and was making people do bad shit, beaming out its mind-control rays or whatever you want to call it, and I guess it found this weird little secret society and decided to use them as henchmen to fuck with the city and hunt monsters as well as humans. So we went down there and it was—yelling at us, inside our heads, pulling out all the bad memories, and—I hit it with a sword and broke the rectifier, and *really conveniently* the Devil showed up and caught the thing before it could escape."

"The Devil," Grisaille repeated.

"Yup. In a white dress, with wings, the whole deal. Then he made the wings disappear and turned the robe thing into a suit, and brought Fastitocalon back to life, and—it was all kind of trippy, to be honest with you."

"It *sounds* trippy," said Grisaille. "Fastitocalon was dead?"

"Yeah, he got killed by one of the monks during the attack. Actually it was Greta who saved the day; she managed to turn the power off for a second so we *could* get close enough to the thing to smash it. But you can see how I'm not really so hot on the magic stuff." He shrugged. "Like I said. Let's hope this thing works, that's all."

"Yeah," said Grisaille, thinking about their friends, thinking about Paris, about things he'd done and not done, and the associated guilt—and then deliberately *not* thinking about it; he couldn't afford to go down one of his infrequent but profound spirals right now. "Well. Order room service, and leave the window open for me, okay? I'll probably be back late."

"Okay," said Cranswell. "It'll be over tomorrow night one way or another, won't it?"

"Oh, yes," said Grisaille, about, well, eighty percent sure he wasn't lying. "It'll be over, all right."

# CHAPTER 11

It made such a difference, having his own clothes back. The Spa-issue pajamas and dressing gown had been perfectly acceptable, a vast improvement over the hospital gown, but Ruthven had knotted his tie this morning with a sigh of relief. He looked like *himself* again, even if he did still appear somewhat more cadaverous than sleek.

Dr. Faust had apparently had a word with Fastitocalon, as he'd promised; as soon as Ruthven's breakfast things had been cleared away (coffee and spiced blood, he still didn't know where they were getting the blood and still didn't *want* to know), an orderly had arrived with his clothes and the news that somebody would be waiting at reception to escort him to Fass's office. As he'd expected, *somebody* turned out to be Irazek, who gave Ruthven a slightly anxious smile.

"Lord Ruthven," he said. "It's a pleasure to see you again. I'm so sorry you've not been well—are you sure you feel up to this?"

"Entirely sure," said Ruthven. "Drop the 'lord' and lead on. I hear you're working in a bakery these days?"

Irazek had grown his hair out a bit; it almost completely hid the little carroty-orange horns, exactly the same color as the hair itself. He had been quite helpful in the end, during the Paris business, but he was definitely better off outside the ranks of Monitoring and Evaluation.

"Yes," he said, "Naberius's, on Plutus Boulevard, it's quite well known. Er. I'm sorry we don't—carry anything that would fit your, um, dietary requirements—"

Ruthven laughed. "Never mind. I am sure you make the best pastries in Dis. Is there some sort of map of the city I could have a look at? I barely have any idea of where anything is."

They were crossing the vast crystal-and-white plaza that separated the waterfront from the eight glass towers, each tapering to a point. The towers had astonished Ruthven when he'd first seen them from the Spa balcony: they looked like snaking rays of the sun, like stylized flames, twisting as they rose in a close arrangement, the tallest of them seeming to touch the distant vault of the sky. He knew he'd been *in* one of them—Erebus General took up most of Tower Three—but it was still a shock to see the whole complex from the outside.

"External Affairs has all kinds of maps," said Irazek, "I'll find you one. M&E is in Tower Six; it's this way."

He led Ruthven past the cluster of bars and restaurants that surrounded the base of the towers; one or two of them were open, serving breakfast to newspaper-reading demons at little tables outside. It made Ruthven think of Rome, and that sent a spike of *longing* through him: he missed Grisaille so much it hurt, a depth of feeling he hadn't had for anyone in hundreds of years. If ever. He closed his eyes for a moment.

"Lo—Mr. Ruthven?" said Irazek, and Ruthven shook himself out of it, reached for a smile.

"Sorry," he said. "I'm all right. Momentary aberration. Tower Six, you said?"

"This way," Irazek said, not looking all that convinced.

Tower Six was the tallest—Samael's penthouse apartment and boardroom took up the top several floors—but the rest of them were plenty tall enough. Looking up at them, following the helical twist of their structures, vast columns spiraling into the sky, made Ruthven briefly dizzy.

Inside, the reception area was sleek black and silver, glass and chrome, and the demon at the desk looked up from a scarlet computer and gave them a practiced smile. Ruthven noticed they had not only very pointy teeth but also pupils shaped like hourglasses, and was only faintly discomfited.

"Um," said Irazek, "hi, this is Lord Ruthven, Director Fastitocalon is expecting him?"

"Of course," said the demon. "You'll need a visitor badge, my lord, or the portal wards won't let you into sensitive areas; please wear it at all times." They handed Ruthven what might have looked like an ordinary ID badge, clip and all, except for the fact that it was matte black and completely blank.

"Thank you," Ruthven said, and clipped it to his lapel. The receptionist turned and gestured at a bank of elevators behind them.

"Elevator six," they said, "you'll want the thirtieth floor."

"I should be getting back," said Irazek, "um, give Director Fastitocalon my best regards?"

"I will," Ruthven promised. He could clearly remember his own surprise this spring at Fastitocalon's apparent restoration to well-being and administrative competence; during the course of their previous acquaintance he'd been plagued with chronic ill-health and exiled to Earth, but a prolonged sojourn at the Lake Avernus Spa had seemingly *fixed* him. Ruthven thought it had probably come as something of a surprise to the rest of the M&E staff as well.

The elevator buttons appeared to be made out of jewels; everything else was rather upsettingly ordinary. On the thirtieth floor he stepped out to find himself in a reception area that could have been in any large and expensive office building in any large and expensive city on Earth. Glass doors separated the space from what looked like a corporate cube farm, full of people busily working away on computers, hurrying back and forth, and Ruthven thought things were getting faintly surreal. He wanted someone to saunter past carrying a pitchfork, or laugh diabolically and flap their leathery wings; all these people seemed to be interested in was the mounds of paper on every desk.

He introduced himself; the receptionist paged Fastitocalon, and he had to wait only a few minutes before the latter appeared, threading his way between the cubes. He looked somewhat less pristine than he had at the Spa, shirtsleeves rolled up and tie loosened, but he gave Ruthven a weary smile.

"Hello—sorry for the lack of fanfare, we're all working flat-out, I'm afraid."

"I can see that," said Ruthven. "Tell me quickly what's happening and what I can do to help?"

"Step into my office," said Fastitocalon, pushing the glass doors open. "And mind the Bosch-ear demonlets; we've got an infestation at the moment."

"Bosch-ear demonlets," Ruthven repeated slowly.

"Exactly what they sound like. They're ears on legs. It's a little startling if you're not expecting one." He was leading Ruthven along the corridor between groups of cubes, pausing every now and then to look at someone's work and tell them to adjust something. Ruthven realized that the stacks of paper weren't just printouts: they were *graphs*, sheet after sheet of a red-ink trace on blue ruled paper, and he knew where he'd seen that particular type of graph before.

"These are the essograph traces that never got properly analyzed," Ruthven said. "The data you were talking about. How much of it *is* there?"

"A very great deal," said Fastitocalon, quellingly, and nodded to an open door with DIRECTOR stenciled on it. "You see why I'm in something of a rush. We need to know what's in those readings before we can have any real idea of what might be happening, and why—before anything *else* goes dramatically wrong. London was bad enough; Paris was worse. I've still not quite got my strength back after repairing that particular thin stretch of reality, and that was with quite a lot of help."

Ruthven could clearly remember how violent the burst of energy had been when Fastitocalon had tack-welded shut the damaged section of space-time. He was about to follow him when something ran over his foot; he yelped and looked down to find not a mouse but...

Okay, that was an ear on legs.

"I'm sorry," Fastitocalon was saying, "the bloody things are everywhere—"

"No," he said, raising a hand. "Actually it helps. The—the weirdness. It's a little reassuring."

Fastitocalon looked at him, eyebrow raised. "Feel free to adopt as many as you like. Do you want coffee?"

Ruthven bet it was absolutely awful coffee, from an *urn*, with powdered creamer, and somehow with that thought, the absurdity of the situation slipped over from upsetting into something like exhilaration. When in Rome, or when in Hell...

"I'd *love* some," he said, and smiled.

"I'm no good at this," said Greta Helsing, passing a hand over her face. They were back in the conference room, with its flying-saucer phone squatting in the center of the table. The telltale light was dark.

Varney and Tefnakhte looked at one another—she could feel the glance, and resented it enormously—and Varney began to say something about how yes of course she was when the phone rang. Greta leaned over and pushed its little button.

"Grisaille?" she said.

"*C'est moi.* Has anything earth-shattering occurred on your end?"

"Not so far. There was one brief episode of the fainting, but only one. What happened with the woman?" She'd looked up Leonora Van Dorne on the Internet after Grisaille's previous call, and hoped like hell that American aristocracy was vulnerable to vampire thrall.

"Funny you should ask. We trundled on over to her adorable little *enormous fuckoff mansion* with our metaphorical hats in hand and practically the first thing out of the Van Dorne's rosy lips was, *I know you're thieves.*"

"Fuck," said Greta, but he cut her off.

"It gets better. So the kid and I look at one another in some considerable dismay and I get ready to drop a ton of thrall on her and leg it, when she comes out with, 'And there's something I want you to steal for me.' My dears, you could have knocked me over with a *feather.*"

"Lots of stone feathers in her collection," said Cranswell's voice, and Greta could picture Grisaille's eyeroll. "So it turns out that Van Dorne wants the stela thing, *too,*" Cranswell went on. "It's the only one in the world, so she has to have it, apparently. I mean, I'm not surprised, she goes around wearing irreplaceable Middle Kingdom jewelry like it's mass-produced Tiffany; she has a kind of cavalier relationship with the whole 'this thing should be in a museum as opposed to in my living room' concept."

"What did you say to her?"

"What could we say?" Grisaille told her, and now she could

picture his *who, me?* expression. "I believe the general thrust was something along the lines of, 'Yes of course, ma'am, it'd be our pleasure to assist you in this matter, there's just the little problem of how to winkle the thing out of its current setting without causing alarm and consternation on the part of the museum authorities,' and get this, she was all, 'Nonsense, don't worry about that, I'll make some phone calls and the item will be taken off display for safekeeping because as a prominent collector and personal friend of several auction house directors I've received credible threats that someone will try to steal it.' "

"Good heavens," said Varney. "I don't think I can remember ever encountering a more brazen bit of effrontery."

"It rather took the breath away. So we, as in Cranswell and I, will make our way unto the museum's loading dock tonight in the guise and seeming of armored-van personnel, complete with armored van accessory, and if we have even the slightest bit of luck, we'll have the thing out of there and into our custody in no time at all. It will undoubtedly disappoint the Van Dorne when we fail to arrive at her prearranged location, poor lamb, but the case can be made that this experience serves as a lesson on morality."

"I get to drive the van," said Cranswell.

"Yes, you get to drive the van. The rest of it's all details with which I won't burden the home team. As soon as we get the magical MacGuffin safely away, I'll ring up the New York demon types and ask for a lift back here, and that, I believe, will be all she wrote. Do I have the green light?"

Varney and Tefnakhte looked at Greta. After a moment she sighed, pushed her hair back. "I don't know why everyone seems to think I'm the one in charge here; we're all equally making this up as we go along."

"Because you are," said Tefnakhte mildly. "Interim Medical Director Helsing."

"That's facile and you know it. Oh, hell. Yes, Grisaille, you have the green light, but be bloody careful, all right? Both of you. Get out of there if it starts to go wrong, your safety is much more important than a carved bit of stone, even if it is a very significant carved bit of stone."

"To hear is to obey," said Grisaille. When he was under stress, he got a lot more facetious, Greta had observed. "I'll text before we go into action. It'll be about ten o'clock our time, I'm afraid, so you might not want to stay up waiting."

"You think any of us are going to be able to sleep?" said Greta, bone-dry. "You just concern yourself with getting in and out safely."

"I will," he said, and she could hear how tired *he* was underneath it. "Ta-ta, darlings."

The light on the phone went out. Greta stayed where she was, staring at it, for a few moments before leaning back in her chair and letting out a deep breath.

"Well," she said. "This is certainly the most *eventful* week I've had in, oh, must be getting on for seven whole months now."

"Do you think he can pull it off?" Tefnakhte said. "And I'm sorry, it's the pattern identification habit, but doesn't it seem awfully strange that we *and* the woman should both want to steal the stela at the same time?"

"Of the strange things that are currently happening," said Greta, "that's pretty low on my list. We can worry about the Van Dorne and what to do with priceless stolen artifacts after we solve the actual problem at hand."

Varney and Tefnakhte looked at one another again. "What?" Greta demanded.

"You," said Varney with a smile in his voice. "Being actually rather good at this."

"I'm not, it's just what has to be *done*, that's all. And right now what has to be done is more coffee, and possibly even a shower, and food, and then I have to get back to my actual job, which does not seem to have stopped being necessary."

It was inconvenient, Grisaille thought, that of the vampire traits he'd ended up with, *turning into mist* was not an option. He could do the bat thing, but he was no good on eagles, mist, or big black dogs with glowing scarlet eyes, which were the other traditional options. Mist would have made the infiltration part of tonight's festivities a lot easier.

As it was, he'd still found his way in bat shape through the ventilation system, which was designed to keep objects the size of human beings out but posed little difficulty for *Desmodus rotundus*. Cranswell was outside in the armored van and matching uniform which Ms. Van Dorne had arranged for them—Grisaille had been not at all surprised that the Van Dorne could get hold of specialty rolling stock on very little notice, since she probably spent a lot of time trundling priceless artifacts back and forth from auctions, or possibly other people's houses, late at night—parked in the loading dock, waiting. From where Grisaille stood in the vast glass-walled atrium of the Sackler Wing, he couldn't quite see the van, because part of a two-thousand-year-old temple was in the way.

Despite his worry over Ruthven and his general desire to get this over with, Grisaille couldn't help a certain excitement. It had been ages since he'd had a chance to steal things; in fact, the last item he'd personally lifted from a museum was a large ruby ring originally belonging to a fourteenth-century bishop, and the only regret he had regarding that particular incident was the fact that he'd stolen it *for* someone who had turned out not to deserve it in the slightest. This time, even though it was ridiculously fraught, he was at least stealing something for a relatively good reason.

He was fairly sure he'd be able to carry the stela himself if necessary, but it was far preferable to have the museum's own movers put it in the truck for him, for several reasons. Van Dorne had called him earlier to confirm the specific time when the thing would be taken off display—thus confirming that she had, in fact, arranged for it *to* be moved—and he'd been slightly impressed by her determination. It really was going to be a pity when she figured out they weren't going to show up.

Grisaille still couldn't work out what it was about her that bothered him so much, apart from the sheer bloody-minded greed; that was practically vampiric, anyway. It was something about the way she smelled that wasn't *quite* human, or wasn't just human; he wondered if she was part-something, like Greta's half-rusalka nurse. Her eyes were peculiar.

He was running through the potential species that might have intermarried with old-money New York families when a faint change in the air gave him the cue he'd been waiting for. A few moments later he could hear footsteps, and smell slightly anxious human wearing deodorant that clashed with their perfume: the curator, here to oversee the process of moving the stela. She'd arrived before the movers. Excellent.

Grisaille took a handful of change from his pocket and tossed it into the reflecting pool with a splash that sounded very loud in the silent museum; and retreated into the darker shadows of the temple proper. He had his *being inconspicuous* effect turned up all the way, and the security cameras would be able to pick up only a faint dark blur; the motion sensors blithely ignored his presence.

The faint gasp, and a moment later the sharper hint of surprise and fear in the air, told him everything he needed to know. *This* part Grisaille was going to enjoy, even if he was undoubtedly going to end the evening with a vicious headache; it was worth it.

What the cameras saw: a minute later, a youngish woman creeping through the doorway from the study gallery, eyes wide in the dark, and holding her ID badge up to the nearest camera. The motion sensors went off, but in the security control center the guards on duty recognized Susan Blake, who'd just come to talk to them about the planned move, and who was supposed to be in the Egyptian section tonight.

Later, those guards would be asked some serious questions about why they hadn't *kept* closely watching that particular channel.

Susan Blake looked around, trying to find any sign of whatever had splashed in the pool—that hadn't been her imagination, she'd *heard* it—and caught her breath in a sharp gasp when something rustled inside the darkness of the temple itself.

God but this place was fucking *spooky* after dark—she knew better than to let herself start thinking about the blank-eyed gaze of thousands of carved smiling faces, and what she'd do if those sculptured staring heads suddenly turned to look at her as she passed by, but there was *something* in there and she had to find out what it was; that was her job.

She took a step closer, and then another step, peering into the deeper darkness, and froze in blank stomach-dropping terror when two round points of red light suddenly looked back at her. Quite close up.

*An animal, it's an animal, somehow something rabid got in here—*

And then a pleasant, cultured voice said, "Excuse me, miss, I wonder if you could help me," and Susan Blake stopped thinking altogether.

Afterward, of course, she would have no memory at all of ever entering the Sackler Wing, or of leaving it—flashing her badge at the cameras again—and returning to Gallery 128 to await the movers; in her mind there was no discontinuity at all between her arrival at the museum and her arrival in the square high-ceilinged room that held the stelae. It was strange that only the Hermopolis Stela was to be moved, but those were the orders she had received and passed on. Only once did she catch a glimpse of something strange out of the corner of her eye: something small and dark that seemed to flitter rapidly past, high up near the ceiling; she blinked and it was gone.

The movers were museum employees, like herself; she checked their IDs even though she knew the security guards would have already done so at least once. Everything seemed to check out, and she felt strangely calm and serene as she went through the process of disarming the security systems and unlocking the case. Quite unconcerned. Everything was for the best, in the best of all possible worlds.

Cranswell was sitting behind the wheel of the armored van, tapping his fingers on the curve of its rim, staring out at the flow of traffic on Fifth Avenue. He had never in his life felt so *exposed*; he was absolutely sure that at any moment someone was going to knock on the window with a flashlight and demand his license and registration, which was why he jumped quite high and bit his tongue when somebody *did* knock on the window. Not so much knock as scrabble.

"...Jesus fucking Christ," he said unsteadily, reaching over to roll the window down far enough for an annoyed bat to scramble through. "What's happening? Did it work?"

"Yes, it's working," said Grisaille, his voice recognizably his but quite a lot higher and squeakier, and then there was a rather unpleasant noise and a sequence of shapes Cranswell would really rather not have seen. "Where's the other uniform?"

"Can you maybe *not* traumatize me twice in rapid succession?" said Cranswell, reaching between the seats for a folded coverall. "Just as a matter of courtesy?"

"I'm a vampire," Grisaille told him, wriggling into the coverall. He did not look even slightly like someone who worked for a secure transport company, but then again neither did Cranswell. "I'm supposed to traumatize people. Anyway, look sharp, they'll be coming out any minute, all nice and neat and aboveboard, with the MacGuffin in a crate for safekeeping, whereupon you will have the curator sign a clipboard in an official sort of way, and as soon as she's gone, I'll thrall the living hell out of the movers and off we'll go."

There was a faint edge to his voice that Cranswell hadn't heard much. "Are you okay?" he asked. In the darkness Grisaille's red pupils were quite wide, and very hard to look at; they painted the dashboard very faintly scarlet with their light. He could remember the first time he'd seen Ruthven's eyes do that, on their way down to the deep-level shelter back in London; it never got any less eerie.

"I'm fine," said Grisaille. "Except for the fact that performing that much profound thrall multiple times is a little like lifting weights with your brain, and I do hope they get a move on because I may shortly start to lose vision in my right eye."

"Oh," said Cranswell, and then, "*Oh.* Shit. I'm sorry—I didn't know you got migraines, too—are you going to be okay to do this?"

"I don't make it a matter of casual disclosure," said Grisaille. "Shut up, will you, there's a good co-conspirator, and keep your eye on the mirrors."

Cranswell looked at him a moment longer before sighing and returning his attention to the loading dock behind them, and was enormously glad to see the door had begun to rise.

In fact, Grisaille could still see out of both eyes while he and Cranswell came around to the back of the van to help load their precious crate and secure it safely. He could still see well enough to observe the departing curator, and to note that her off-the-rack pantsuit did not suit her in the least, and that her shoes were all wrong; it wasn't until he turned back to the two movers Cranswell was keeping distracted with conversation, said "Look at me," and proceeded to drop half a ton of thrall on the pair of them that his vision on the right side went entirely to fizzing sparks. A bolt of really quite extraordinary pain shot through his head along with the sudden eclipse, and for a moment he thought miserably of Ruthven blind and grey with something very like this, wondering if he'd actually hurt himself by pushing that much power all at once.

*You haven't given yourself a stroke*, he thought viciously, *you can still move both sides of your body, so bloody well move it into the van and get out of here.*

"Grisaille?" Cranswell was at his elbow, ignoring the movers, who were standing stock-still with completely blank expressions, to match their completely blank recent memories.

"I'm all right," he said between his teeth, shaking his arm free—which sent another spike of pain through the bone cradling his right eye—and turned to make his way to the passenger side. "Let's *go.*"

He didn't want to remember much of the ride that followed; he spent it staying as still as possible with his eyes shut tight, hanging on to the door handle hard enough to leave dents in the plastic. It seemed to take forever, an endless miserable cacophony of car horns drilling through his skull, but eventually he realized the van was no longer moving.

"Where are we?" he said without opening his eyes.

"I don't know. Somewhere in Hell's Kitchen, I think." Cranswell didn't sound as if he was having the time of his life, either, Grisaille thought, and could scrounge up a few scraps of sympathy for the kid: driving in New York was horrible at the best of times. "Come on, I think we have to be touching the thing to bring it with us when the demons do their—whatever it is."

Getting out of the van required Grisaille to open his eyes, which was as unpleasant as he expected, the right one still useless and silver jagged scotomata beginning to drift across the left. It didn't matter. Nothing mattered other than getting the fucking thing *out* of here and back to Marseille, where it would no longer be *his problem.*

He made his way carefully around to climb into the back of the van, where Cranswell was already crouching next to the shipping crate. "You're going to have to call them," he said. "I don't think I can look at screens at the moment."

Cranswell didn't reply, getting out his phone. Grisaille sat down beside the crate, leaning against the wall, and closed his eyes again. At this stage the pain came in waves, a kind of sickening rhythm, pulsing in the rim of his eye socket like a poisoned heartbeat. Over it he could hear the kid talking—presumably he'd gotten through to the New York demons, or at least one of them, good, that was good, they might make it out of here after all...

He had no idea how long it was before a brief sudden pressure change made his ears pop. Two people suddenly appearing in an enclosed space would do that, Grisaille thought, and opened his left eye just enough to make out a tall man and a curvy woman, both in black.

"—this is completely irregular," the woman was saying. "I'll be filing a complaint, this sort of thing is *not* on the list of surface operative duties."

"Oh, surely you can spare the poor mortals a moment of your time, Glasya," said the man, who sounded as if he was enjoying this. "Precious as it may be."

"I was in the middle of an *opening reception*," she said. "Maybe *you* can randomly disappear at any hour of the day or night to go ferry stolen objects around without having to make excuses to your guests, Morax; with *your* undemanding schedule I wouldn't be surprised. Let's get this *over* with. Also one of them's a vampire, not a mortal; get your taxonomy right at the very least."

"Touché," said the man. "Where are we going again?"

"Marseille," said Cranswell. "The place is just outside of Marseille—here's a picture, they said that would help you get us there?"

"Of *course* we need a picture, don't be ridiculous. Very well. You, take my hand and touch the crate thing with the other. You—wake up, whoever you are, vampire, we're doing you a *favor*—"

"He's not okay," Cranswell said. "I'm sorry about your reception and we really appreciate your help but can you go easy on him?"

"There is very little I enjoy more purely and delightedly than being talked about as if I were not present," said Grisaille with delicate precision, "but as you say, let's get this over with." He managed to detach himself from the wall and get to his feet, accompanied by another burst of pain, and held on to the crate with one hand; his other was taken by Morax in a warm, not unfriendly grip. He could feel it, a slight shock, when the demons clasped *their* hands together, closing the circle.

"Hang on tight," said Morax. "This is going to be somewhat disorienting," and a moment later all the world *slid* into blank and spinning white.

Back in Central Park, several hours later, two very confused museum employees woke to find themselves lying on a bench with a cop standing over them, still holding the nightstick with which she had just prodded them awake.

"You can't sleep here," she said, and proceeded to inform them of the rules and regulations governing public spaces—most of which went over their heads—while they looked at one another.

"Okay, was it just me," said one of them slowly, "or were that guy's eyes actually *glowing red*?"

# CHAPTER 12

She'd expected Grisaille to *call* before showing up.

Greta had been asleep for all of four hours—long enough to render her functional, not even close to long enough to put much of a dent in the sleep deprivation she'd been stacking up for days—when the panicked voice on the intercom tore her awake. Beside her Varney sat up with a hiss, and she was glad whoever it was hadn't actually come to physically wake her, because his eyes were glowing red and his teeth were on display. She'd seen that herself, the first time she'd met him, and the nursing staff didn't need any *more* reasons to be panicked.

"—they're here, Dr. Helsing, there's—you're needed—"

"All *right*," she said, dragging her hands down her face. "I'm coming, I'm on my way, hang on," and she struggled out of bed and put her dressing gown on. Varney was still sitting up, but the light show had died away; he looked faintly embarrassed. "Go back to sleep, love," she said. "I don't know what's gone wrong now."

"I don't think I can," he said, and sighed. "Go on. I'll be there in a minute."

Greta nodded, and hurried out.

The bedside clock had read half past four, which fit with the timeline Grisaille had given them, so presumably the plan had worked—at least in part—but she had no idea what to expect as she made her way from the director's residence to the spa proper—

There was a group of people in the entry foyer, gathered around something on the ground: mostly her nurses, but there were two dark-haired people she'd never seen before in her life, one of whom simply popped out of existence as if she had never been there at all—obviously a demon, Greta thought, must be the ones who flipped them back—and Cranswell, looking exhausted and unwell but *there.* As Greta approached, he looked up, and the others moved aside for her to see Grisaille crumpled on the ground next to a packing crate stenciled with the Metropolitan Museum's logo.

"What happened?" she said, kneeling down beside him. The last time she'd seen Grisaille looking anything close to this bad was after he'd had a knife through his lung, back in Paris.

"He had a migraine," Cranswell said. "Um. He said he couldn't see out of one eye?"

Greta stared at him. "Nobody *cursed* him, did they?" *Please*

*God*, she thought, *please God, don't let there be an epidemic of cursed vampires on top of every other bloody thing that's going wrong.*

"Not as far as I know," said Cranswell, "he, uh, had to thrall a bunch of people and he said it was like—lifting weights with your brain? And then the thing with the demons happened—that sucked enormously and I nearly puked but he just collapsed as soon as we got here."

"He'll be all right," she said, rolling Grisaille onto his side, heavy with the helpless weight of unconsciousness. He'd almost certainly be sick, but this was at least a natural consequence of overexertion rather than something that would require evacuation to Hell. Which reminded her, she should probably try to get in touch with them to reassure Ruthven his boyfriend wasn't languishing in durance vile in a New York holding cell.

She looked up at the remaining demon, a man with dark curly hair. "Thank you," she said. "We all appreciate your help a great deal. Could you get a message to Monitoring and Evaluation saying that the plan was successfully executed?"

"Not a problem," he said. "Fantastic place you've got here."

"You aren't seeing us at our best, I'm afraid—Sister, go and fetch a gurney, Grisaille ought to be in bed. Can I offer you some tea or coffee, Mr.... ?"

"Morax," said the demon, and handed her his card. "And thanks, but I ought to be going. That's quite a heavy load you people had us transport, do you mind if I ask what's in it?"

"A priceless work of art," said Greta, "the only one of its

kind ever to be discovered, which we plan to use to speak with an ancient god."

Morax laughed, raising his hands. "Okay, okay. I get it. Not my business. I'll let Downstairs know you all pulled it off successfully, whatever it is. Nice meeting you, have a great night, *ciao*."

He vanished with a faint thunderclap of collapsing air, and Greta looked down at the card in her hand: *ah*.

"I wonder how many of the world's theatrical producers happen to be demons undercover," she said as the gurney arrived. "Probably quite a few. Help me lift him, will you?" she added to Cranswell.

"Is he really going to be okay?"

"He is. He won't like waking up, but he'll get over it. Thank you both so much, Cranswell. I hope I'll never have to ask anything like that of you ever again."

"Me too," he said with feeling. "I want to sleep for a week."

"That can probably be arranged. We can get you a ticket back to London in the morning—well, actually, it *is* morning—never mind, Varney'll arrange it."

"I kind of want to see the spell thing," he said. "Like—I want to know if it works. And that sculpture is amazing, I never got to see it outside the case."

"Well, you're welcome to stay and watch. We've got lots of spare beds." Greta rested two fingers on the pulse in Grisaille's throat, nodded at the nurse to take him away. Cranswell watched him go.

"He's weird," he said. "But kind of amazing."

"That's a decent summation," she said. "I want coffee. Do you want coffee?"

"Of *course* I want coffee," said Cranswell, and gave her a wan but relatively cheerful smile. She was reminded of waking up in the Savoy, after the business with the rectifier, and finding him scarfing down room service breakfast as if he hadn't just spent twenty-four hours in the middle of a dangerous existential crisis; there was something comforting about Cranswell's ability to bounce back from dramatic and perilous situations.

"Come on," she said. "And tell me all about it."

Leonora Irene Van Dorne knew almost to the minute how long it would take the pair of thieves to collect the crated stela, load it into the truck she had obtained for their use, and drive it to the secure location where she had arranged for them to deliver the goods.

Waiting by the phone for the call from her security people, she watched the hands on her Patek Philippe move, with the expressionless faint smile of a Late Kingdom statue.

Ten minutes past.

Twenty.

She watched traffic pass by on Sixty-eighth, headlights splashing the houses on the other side of the street. Thirty minutes.

At thirty-five minutes past their ETA, she picked up the phone and dialed a number from memory. It was not, in fact, the number of her security agency.

Two rings before the other end picked up, with a double click that she knew meant the line was secure. "Richard?" she said calmly. "Van Dorne. I have a job for you. Two men flew into JFK recently from London, one named August Cranswell and the other going by Grisaille, first or last name unclear. Cranswell claims to be with the British Museum, the other one has no known affiliation. Almost certainly on British Airways. Find out if they had return tickets."

She tapped her fingernails—long, now, and natural, stronger than they had been for years—on her desk blotter. "No. Let them go, if they're going, but find out where, and call me back."

Ms. Van Dorne hung up, and made two more calls, to underworld fences of her acquaintance, requesting them to alert her if a priceless Thirtieth Dynasty stela showed up unexpectedly; when she set the phone down, the faint enigmatic smile turned into a rather less enigmatic and more unpleasant one. She was not worried about the safety of the stela; whatever else August Cranswell might be, he hadn't lied about his appreciation of the thing's beauty and significance. She was, in fact, not worried about a thing—except how messy it was going to be when she caught up with the pair of them to regain what ought to have been her property, and even that would be someone else's problem. Everything was, really, when you got right down to it. The only things that mattered were her collection, not how it was obtained.

She stroked the stone-and-gold confection of her Middle Kingdom pectoral, and smiled into the dark.

* * *

Farther south, in their loft on Greenwich Street, the angels had been woken unexpectedly—they went to bed early, as was virtuous and correct, the only people who stayed up late were undoubtedly up to no good—and Amitiel was pacing up and down the apartment hugging himself, knocking things over with his wings, and chattering happily. Zophiel, however, was sitting on their achingly stylish couch with a confused look on his face.

"It's not her," he said. "The magic stela thing is—gone—but—*she* doesn't have it."

"What? How?" said Amitiel, tilting his head. White-gold curls bounced.

"I can't see—oh. Oh. *Oh.*"

"Oh?" Amitiel came to sit beside him, put a hand on his knee. Both of them were in pale grey silk pajamas. "What is it?"

"I couldn't see *because* there's been a—an incursion. Huge. Two demons, right *here*, right here in this awful city, it's—*they* have it, the echoes were interfering with my perception—oh, Amitiel, the monsters and the demons have the magic stone, everything's going wrong—" He sounded miserably confused. Thinking really wasn't what they were *for*.

"But the—the incursion," said Amitiel, looking into his face with huge violet-blue eyes. "That's weakened the wall more, surely? That's—better than nothing, even if *she* isn't using the stela as we intended?"

Zophiel blinked. "It *has*. Weakened the fragile places.

That was huge—the demons left and came *back*, that's set up echoes—"

"Then that's all right, isn't it? Surely? The woman still has the spell, she still needs to use the spell or—"

"Yes," said Zophiel. "She still needs to use it, and more now, to keep the effects she's achieved—even if she doesn't have the special stela to use it on, she still has to *use* it, and she has hundreds of objects in her godless house to drain."

"Then this is just a setback, isn't it?" said Amitiel. "We'll still get there, the barrier will be breached, our heavenly hosts will be able to pass through to destroy *this* world's blasphemous mockery of Heaven, it just—will take a little longer."

Zophiel sighed, and leaned over to rest his head on his compatriot's shoulder. "You are wiser than I," he said. "Your faith is greater, and faileth not."

Amitiel put his arms around him, sheltered them both in the white curves of his wings. "Have courage," he said, "we are so close, Zophiel, you've worked so hard, soon we can go *home*."

"Home," said Zophiel with another sigh. "To the *real* Heaven, *our* Heaven, everything white and gold and pure and holy, and the host singing on and on, for always, and—nothing sinful, nothing stained—everything *righteous* and *true*…"

"Soon," said Amitiel with the surety of unshakable faith. "Soon the day of reckoning will be at hand, and the unrighteous will go down quick into Hell, for wickedness is in their dwellings, and among them."

The Hermopolis Stela had been hastily set up in the spa's sunroom, as far away as possible from the heavy imaging equipment, in case there was some kind of interference between the CT or linac and Tefnakhte's magic. It stood on a low table, a narrow thin tongue-shaped piece of dark greenstone frosted pale with line after line of delicate incised hieroglyphs. The relief carving of Thoth with crocodiles under his feet and a serpent in each hand was exquisite, even after so many centuries, as precise and unmarred as it had been the day it came from the sculptor's workshop.

Varney, Greta, Cranswell, and Sister Brigitte watched as the mummy Tefnakhte—stiffly, unavoidably stiffly, but with about as much grace as a mummy could hope to muster—genuflected before it. He was wearing jewelry over his wrappings, pieces Greta hadn't seen before, and the pinpoints of his eyes behind the bandaging were brighter than usual.

In his dry, raspy voice, Tefnakhte began to chant, reciting his spell in Egyptian, the vowels and consonants strange and incomprehensible to Greta, even after so much exposure. She knew perfectly well she'd never be any good at languages, and mostly managed not to mind, but there was a crawling kind of unease at not knowing what was being said. It was some small comfort when Varney's cold, smooth hand slipped into hers, squeezed it gently.

*This isn't going to work*, Greta thought as the strange words went on and on, accompanied by what looked like ritual gestures. *This isn't going to work, we sent them to New York to steal this thing for no reason and I'm still no closer to finding out why any of this is* happening, *I don't know what else to do—*

And the air *changed*. Pressure, like a wave; the shimmering, crawling sense of electrical charge, the roots of Greta's hair trying to stiffen, sending goosebumps down her arms and legs. The air tasted metallic, strange, and then *hot*: hot and dry, sun-warmed dust and stone.

She looked up at Varney, saw the same apprehension on his face, and squeezed his hand again—and returned her gaze to Tefnakhte and the stela in time for the strangest sight of her life. Between the mummy and the stone slab, something she couldn't quite see was taking shape in the air; it looked like blurred lines of ink, shifting and swirling, as difficult to follow as the jagged patterns of a migraine aura.

Tefnakhte's chanting took on a triumphant note, and he stepped aside as the *thing* taking form clarified itself a little. It was still hard to look at, like a magic-eye picture right before the illusion slid into place, and it seemed to be more than one thing at once, flickering in and out of perception: the form of a man, bare-chested, copper-skinned, in a white linen kilt, his dark hair in a mass of neat tight curls with golden bands around them, *and* the form of a bird, an ibis, black and white and bald-headed with a long curving beak, *and* the form of a man *with* that bald inquisitive head and long beak, black liquid eyes examining them with interest.

And behind it all, shimmering in and out of visibility, ink.

Liquid ink, spread on the air as if the air were parchment, and could hold it.

*That's a god*, Greta thought dimly. *That is a god who was last worshipped long before the birth of Christ, standing in the middle of the sunroom, looking at us. Looking at* me.

*What do I look like, to those eyes?*

Tefnakhte said something to the god, and this time she did catch one word: *Djehuty*.

"*Huu*," said the god, a soft birdlike sound, and replied in the same language, and then looked from the mummy to the rest of them. He closed his ibis eyes for a moment, and reopened them, and Greta could have sworn for a moment she saw the reflection of the moon in those clear dark pools. "Where... is this place?" he asked in quite passable English, the pronunciation rapidly improving. "I have been asleep for... a long time, I think."

"A very long time," said Tefnakhte. "O noble Ibis. O god who longs for Khmunu, O dispatch-writer of the Ennead, the great one of Unu—"

"You speak with a strange accent," said the god, "and you consort with the dead. Has so much changed?"

"More than you could imagine," said Tefnakhte, sounding less in control than Greta had ever heard him. "I—we—have summoned you to beg for your advice, O Djehuty."

"*Huu*," he said again, and stepped down off the platform on which they had set the stela, turning to run a long finger down its face. "I remember these. It has been—" He closed his eyes again, and was to Greta's eyes for a moment not a mostly man-shaped creature at all but moving, shifting columns of handwritten calculation in the air. "—a very long time indeed."

"We need your help," said Greta, still blinking against the instant of vertigo that transformation had induced. "This place is a—a hospital for mummies. I'm a physician, I treat them—"

"But you are human," said the god, and tilted his ibis head. "Come forward."

Greta let go of Varney's hand and took an unsteady step toward the god, and in a single too-quick motion, he reached out his hand and set his palm against her chest, flat on her sternum, between her breasts. Behind her, she heard Varney's sharp gasp.

Once before, she had looked into the eyes of another being of great power and felt his blazing, merciless attention, a searchlight reading everything written on the inside of her skull, *knowing* her, all there was to know. Djehuty's hand over her heart felt a little like that, only kinder; she could not have pulled away if she'd wanted to, his palm was fast against her chest, *warm*, like sun-heated stone, like desert winds, and all that she was, all that she had been and wanted to be and could hope to become, was drawn out of her through that contact, examined, tabulated, and *recorded* in some unknowable library of the mind.

He nodded once and let her go, and she stumbled backward

into Varney's arms; he caught her, steadied her while she remembered how to breathe. The place where the god had touched her felt icy cold without that strange warmth.

"Greta Helsing," said Djehuty. "Your heart does not rise up against you as a witness, nor does it make opposition against you in the presence of the keeper of the balance. I will go with you to visit your patients."

"...oh," said Greta, still a little dazed. "I'd appreciate that a great deal."

"Can you heal *other* dead people?" said somebody behind them, and she turned in Varney's steadying grip to see Grisaille, grey in the face, leaning against the door frame. "'Cause I'd really appreciate a jolt of the good old-fashioned godly magic right about now."

"*Huu*," said Djehuty. "I will see what can be done."

The thing about money was that it made everything so *simple*. What might have posed an insurmountable obstacle to someone with limited funds simply found itself thrust aside by the oncoming ram of Leonora Irene Van Dorne's personal bank account and the personality behind it. *No, there were no more first-class tickets to Paris available at all out of JFK, the representative was sorry, it was simply not possible* turned into *Um, well, perhaps it might be possible to arrange a first-class ticket if Ms. Van Dorne was willing to—okay, would that be miles or credi—okay, what was the number?—um, well, your reservation is confirmed, please enjoy your flight, we'll make sure the gate agent knows to expect you—*

Money was also among the reasons it had taken her only about four hours from the time she'd made the first call to the time she was settling into her seat: Ms. Van Dorne had acquired a thoroughly efficient network of people whose purpose was to find things. Things, and sometimes people.

August Cranswell did, it seemed, actually work at the British Museum, but his field wasn't even close to late-period Egyptology. What was interesting about that was the way in which someone had gone through recent search results and deliberately adjusted them to imply that he *was* a scholar of ancient Egypt; her people hadn't been able to immediately identify the method whereby this had been done, but it went back only a few months. Their journey to New York to obtain the stela had clearly been planned ahead of time.

She wondered how they'd planned on actually pulling it off, prior to meeting her. Without her help, there wouldn't have been an easy way to get in, snatch the thing, and get out before security caught them, and Ms. Van Dorne was absolutely sure that at least Cranswell was not an *experienced* thief. His friend with the long hair and the Goth contact lenses, though. That one felt different. That one had felt a little bit dangerous, in a way she rather found attractive.

And the other thing about Ms. Van Dorne's network of associates was that it served as something of a who's who of thieves. She had met only two or three of them, but she knew the names of every high-end professional art thief currently operating in the fields she was interested in, and "Grisaille" was not one of them. The prearranged return tickets to France had been stupid of them, too: she'd found out quite quickly where they'd been planning to go.

*Where are you from?* she thought as the runway fell away beneath her window, as the hand of inertia pressed her back against her seat. That accent hadn't been French, despite the French name. *Where are you from and what do you want with that piece?*

She knew what *she'd* have done with the stela, if she hadn't meant to use it for her peculiar and secret beauty routine: she'd have had a copy made and store that in her private vault, and put the real thing on display; if anyone ever came looking for it, she'd assure them she didn't know it was hot, that she'd bought it in good faith, and that she knew it was sufficiently valuable to need to be stored securely, so she'd had a copy made to put on display—she could, of course, give them the original, which was in her vault, *this way please, gentlemen, I'm mortified, of course, it must go back at once...*

Leonora Van Dorne smiled, and reclined her seat, and ordered champagne from the flight attendant when she came round to be obsequious; and it wasn't until she reached out to take the glass that she realized the veins and tendons in the back of her hand were much too visible. Much too visible, and the skin was—the skin was slightly *wrinkled*—the skin was *spotted brown—*

"Is something wrong, ma'am?"

"Oh—no—not at all," said Ms. Van Dorne through a fixed and artificial smile, and took the glass with a hand that only slightly shook, thinking, *My ring, the lapis scarab, it's the only thing, I'll have to use the scarab, it's so small it won't be powerful but it's something—I can go to the restroom, I can do it quickly, I know the spell by heart—*

Her hand, her *crepey, aging* hand, crept up to her chest, and touched warm gold and polished stone: the Middle Kingdom pectoral, which she'd *forgotten she was wearing*; and with a kind of angry miserable certainty, she knew what she had to do.

Greta wished she could have given her patients more warning, prepared them for the sudden appearance of an actual living god at their bedsides; but there simply wasn't time.

She took him—and the others, who trailed along as if unable not to follow—to see Antjau first. The mummy's shock upon seeing Djehuty made her heart hurt—it set him off into a wracking fit of coughing, which sent scraps of linen raftering to the bed linens, to the floor—but just as he had done to Greta, the god set his narrow brown hand on Antjau's chest, and his coughing stopped at once.

"This is a disease I know well," said Djehuty. "It meant death."

"It's treatable today," Greta said, feeling absurd. "We've got his lungs in another room undergoing therapy, he's responding quite well—I can show you if you like—but he's had one of these attacks recently on top of the TB and it knocked him back a bit."

"*Huu*," said the god, and blinked his large black eyes. They had the nictitating membrane common to birds, which Greta found both disturbing and logical. "Let me see."

Greta stepped back from the bed; that strange charged feeling had begun again, some kind of potential energy building up. Djehuty was bending over Antjau, hands hovering over rather than touching the bandages of his chest. As far as she could tell, the mummy was too awestruck to do anything other than lie perfectly still and let himself be—what, examined? Assessed somehow?

She wasn't precisely surprised when Djehuty did that dizzying phase-change again, turning to ink, rapid calculations on the air. It was incredibly hard to look at, because he was still *there*, still a physical presence, visible at the same time as the brushstrokes of his analysis, like two layers of holograms seen at once. It went on for longer this time before he settled back into one consistent form and took his hands away.

"This is strange," he said. "Very strange. I must see the other patients who have experienced the unknown sickness."

That wasn't reassuring in the least. Greta nodded to hide her reaction. "Maanakhtef had a particularly bad episode; he was walking when it struck and he—well, he collapsed, and broke." Not just breaking a bone; parts of him had gone to *powder*.

"Take me there," said Djehuty, straightening up. "I must see them all, to be sure of my calculations."

"Of course," she said, and was glad when Varney came silently up and slipped his arm around her shoulders. She was so tired, and so completely at a loss, and for a moment the simple kindness of the touch brought a prickle of tears to her eyes; she swallowed hard, blinked several times, and the threat receded. "This way."

She led the little group from room to room, visiting each patient who'd suffered an episode. At each bedside Djehuty repeated his peculiar analysis, without saying anything other than a few words of comfort in Egyptian, which clearly did for her mummies what a good shot of scotch did to Greta. *If nothing else*, she thought, *at least he can give them that*, and was grateful to the god despite her exhaustion and concern.

When he had finished the strange round, Djehuty beckoned to Greta. "I would speak with you alone."

"Anything you can say to me you can say to my team. There's a conference room big enough for all of us," she said, appalled at her own daring, and for a moment the black bald bird-head turned to look at her, eyes narrowed—and then he clacked his beak once, managing to convey exasperation and patience at the same time.

"Very well," the god said, and gestured for her to lead the way.

The ordinariness of the conference room with its long table and the flying-saucer speakerphone sitting on one end, the quiet framed prints of tomb paintings on the walls, looked absurd with Djehuty in it. He sat down, steepled his fingers, and obviously decided to make an effort to put them at their ease: all the other forms flickered out of being, leaving him simply man-shaped.

"Good eyeliner," murmured Grisaille, sitting down beside Greta across the table from the god. "I mean, excessive, but good."

"Shhh," Greta said, glad of Varney settling on her other side. Tefnakhte, Cranswell, and Brigitte joined them, and the silence waiting for Djehuty's diagnosis felt almost as electric as the performances he'd shown them hitherto.

"It is indeed magic," he began. "What has occurred to these people is without a doubt the result of a spell being worked; the result of the spell is to consume the energy, the spiritual force, of an object sacred to the individual, and in doing so draws that force from the individual themselves."

"Like the teletherapy," said Greta. "What happens to Antjau's lungs in another room happens to him."

"In a sense," said Djehuty. "What you are doing for Antjau is to heal part of him and in doing so provide healing to the whole entity. What has been done to your patients is—destructive. A small fraction of their *selves* is being destroyed, somewhere else in the world. Deliberately."

"How do we find and stop them?" Varney asked.

"Patience," said the god. "I have not finished. The magic that is being done to effect these little destructions *is* magic, and it is made to look like magic in the Egyptian fashion. What it is not is *from this Egypt*."

"How can you have more than one Egypt?" Cranswell wanted to know. "For that matter, how do you *know* it's not from here?"

"I am the scribe," Djehuty said simply. "I am the keeper of

the balance and the book of life. I *wrote* the magic of Egypt, but I did not write this spell. I tell you I know this is designed to look as if it is from *an Egypt*, but it is not from this one."

"'There are other worlds than these,'" Greta murmured. Something was kicking her brain.

"Countless, perhaps. I cannot say."

"How do we stop it?" said Tefnakhte. "How do we—find who is doing it, and why?"

"That I do not know," Djehuty said, sounding tired for the first time. "I cannot follow its threads back to the source; its ways are not my ways."

"What about our patients?" said Sister Brigitte, entering the conversation for the first time. "Can you help them?"

"To some extent," he said. "But I cannot stop this from happening. Not even I can do that."

"Then we are out of options entirely," said Varney, and all the beauty of his voice seemed to have drained away, leaving only a melancholy heavy and dull as lead.

In Hell, in the M&E bullpen, underneath the din of calculating machines clattering and demon claws typing and voices in intense consultation, amid the drifts and heaps of graphic recordings of essograph traces, Ruthven stared at the papers he held, and at his notebook half-full of neat little pencil notations, and back at the papers again.

Fastitocalon had set him to look at the *recent* esso traces, going back only several months: the recordings that should have been reported monthly by the surface operatives, and in perhaps a third of the cases *had* been so reported. Those that hadn't were assigned to the operatives originally appointed by Asmodeus, and Ruthven had a fairly good idea of Asmodeus's management style and oversight of employees by now. The other demons under Fastitocalon's overview were working through the backlog of the past several decades of unanalyzed data, and every now and then the general background noise was interrupted by an excited shout as someone found a significant data point and hurried over to add it to the whiteboard that held their running tally of discrepancies.

Ruthven had said to Fastitocalon that pattern-finding was more his speed than crunching numbers, and even so, he'd had to go back several times and make sure he wasn't cognitive-biasing his way into a false assumption—and then he'd turned the page in his notebook and begun to draw a rough, not-to-scale graph based on the results listed on the whiteboard. Meta-analysis in real time.

Ninety years ago, nothing. Ordinary background noise. Eighty years ago—a couple of incidents, unexplained excursions that didn't correspond to known and assigned trips between planes. Still could have been nothing more than static, statistically insignificant—but the rate had continued to increase gently but steadily over the next half a century. Something or someone, or several somethings or someones, was making it a habit to pass between planes quite often, without explanation, and in doing so was wearing down the fabric of reality bit by bit. Translocation alone shouldn't have caused that kind of deterioration: this seemed to be *intentional.*

And then fifteen years ago, the rate had started to go up sharply. Ruthven didn't know what had changed—but it seemed fairly clear that Hell either wasn't paying any attention or was fully aware of the incursions and failed to report them. Monitoring and Evaluation should have raised the alarm decades ago, even under the inefficient oversight of Asmodeus.

*Asmodeus*, Ruthven thought, and then dismissed the idea: *Asmodeus might possibly be behind this, but what the hell he'd get out of destabilizing* his own *reality, I don't know; that seems incredibly stupid even for him.*

He flipped back through his own notes. There was the incursion of the—entity, the *thing* that had appeared in London last year; there was the sudden spike of repeated summonings due to the vampire Lilith's monster menagerie this spring; the intense peak of energy that marked Fastitocalon's tack-weld job to repair that tear in reality—and a little after that, *another* series of repeated metaphysical disturbances, centering on—

He looked at the coordinates for the recent series again, typed them into the computer terminal at the desk he had borrowed, and was not as surprised as he'd have liked to be to find out they corresponded to Manhattan's Upper East Side. Where Grisaille and Cranswell had gone to fetch the magic stone from the museum.

Something or someone was systematically damaging the structure of this particular world's basic underlying fabric, if he understood it right. And had been doing so for the past eighty years. Perhaps it was more than one group of people, working over time; perhaps it was using different individual tactics in a long game played over decades.

Ruthven just wished he could come up with a reason *why.*

He got up, a little dizzy but only a little, and collected his notebook and the stack of esso traces, going to knock on Fastitocalon's half-open office door. "Fass?" he said. "I rather think you need to see this. Right now."

# CHAPTER 13

This time there simply weren't any flights Ms. Van Dorne could bully, intimidate, and overpay her way onto: no one was leaving Charles de Gaulle for Marseille for several hours due to a line of thunderstorms sweeping their way across the country. They had circled for almost an hour before finally being given clearance to land, and coming down through the brief gap in storms had been one of the more unpleasant experiences she'd had on a plane in years.

She was pacing around one of the observation lounges, the view obscured by pouring rain lit by the occasional stuttering flash of lightning, wondering if it was worth actually trying to *charter* a flight south, knowing that if commercial airliners weren't being allowed to take off, personal jets wouldn't be given clearance, either. *Goddamnit*, she thought, *I have to—find something else to juice, this won't last long—*

It wasn't just the horror of her visual decay that she needed to *fix*, either. She had been a smoker for years, and the process of quitting had been miserably difficult; she had recognized something like the crawling discomfort of *withdrawal* in her own distress on the plane.

The moment in the tiny bathroom when she'd had to close her hand around the gorgeous, brilliant goldwork and inlay of her princess's pectoral, close her hand and close her eyes so she didn't have to see all that irreplaceable beauty crumble to dust, had been awful. She'd gone through the words of the spell fast, from memory, and felt the immediate jolt of energy and strength wash through her. The simple relief of looking in the mirror and *watching her face transform*, watching the age spots on the backs of her hands fade and dwindle to nothing, watching the sagging skin of her throat firm and smooth itself back to beauty, had also cleared her head, resolving that nervy irritable crawling sensation. Letting the faint grey dust of what had been her favorite piece of jewelry, her personal connection to that long-ago royal princess, swirl down the tiny steel sink had felt like losing part of herself, though, and even now her hand kept straying to her chest, expecting to feel warm gold and polished stone, and being reminded over and over again that it was gone.

(She was trying not to wonder how long it would last, and what the hell she was going to do when it wore off; the aging seemed to come on faster every time, and the jolt of energy the spell brought never seemed to last as long.)

Another crack of thunder came, closer now, and the rain hurled itself against the windows like a living thing trying to get in. Nobody was flying *anywhere* until this little lot moved on.

She looked away from the window, back into the airport proper, and happened to glance past one of the directional information signs guiding passengers to ground transport. Taxis, buses, rail—

Rail. She could take the RER into Paris and get on a *train*—of course, it'd only take three hours or something—she'd get to Marseille and find a hotel room and work out what to do next when she *got* there, and she would find something to juice if she needed it before she found the stela, anything with votive power would do to keep her going long enough...

For the first time since she'd seen the wrinkles beginning to reappear, Ms. Van Dorne felt as if matters might once more be under her control. She straightened up, settled her handbag more comfortably, and stalked off toward the rail connection, Louis Vuitton suitcase in tow. She was going to find her stela, and she was going to bloody well *use* the thing, and she would never again have to see her face sag and shrivel and droop with age: she would never, ever, ever grow old.

The world felt different with Djehuty gone. Different in a way Greta hoped she'd be able to stop noticing at some point: it was as if there were less air in the air, as if some indefinable warmth and richness were suddenly gone.

At least he had helped some of her patients, she thought, rubbing at her temples. At least they seemed a little cheered up, even if nobody was much closer to finding the answer to the fundamental problem. There was no way to trace the energy spell, whatever universe it was from; it seemed to happen at random, unpredictable, and now Greta knew (without wanting to) that it wasn't limited to just her patients at the spa: this was probably affecting mummies all around the world. And it wasn't just the spell itself; there were deeper ramifications.

"Grave goods," Tefnakhte said. "It has to be draining the energy from grave goods. Our—there are so *many*, and they have been so widely spread over the millennia—each tiny object that's part of a burial is effectively part of *us*—"

"Why, though?" Greta asked. "Why now? There has to be some reason behind it. If this really is from another world, why are they doing it, why now, what's the *point*?" Whatever it was that had been kicking her brain was still doing it, and she couldn't quite see what it was.

"Remember Paris," Varney said quietly. "Remember the summonings," and Cranswell nodded.

"Oh, no," she said. "No. It—can't be happening *again*."

"What about Paris?" Tefnakhte asked.

"This spring," Greta said. "There was a—very stupid vampire who for not-very-good reasons was summoning small monsters, over and over and over again, and each little conjuring weakened the fabric of reality just a little more until it was beginning to tear open, but, Varney, she's *dead*, and this isn't summoning anything from anywhere to anywhere else, it's just—draining."

"But the repetition," said Varney. "What if *that's* the point?"

Greta thought despairingly, *I want six months of my life in which the phrase "fabric of reality" simply never, ever crosses anybody's mind; is that so much to ask?* Out loud she said, "Hell needs to know about this, if they don't already."

"Can you call them?" said Grisaille from the doorway. She turned to look at him; he was still greyish and looked like thirty miles of bad road, but he'd lost some of the shocked expression. "And—find out how Ruthven is?"

"I can try," she said, and got out her phone. She had no idea how Faust had managed to reach her, but she scrolled back through her recents until she found the number.

Of course the country code was 666. Of course.

"Dr. Faust's office," said a bored voice on the other end after two rings. "How may I direct your call?"

"Hi," she said. "This is Greta Helsing, on Earth. I'm sorry to call your office but I don't have the number for Monitoring and Evaluation. Would it be possible for you to transfer me?"

"Greta Helsing," said the voice, and then, as if its owner had just made a mental connection, "You're *the* human? The one Dr. Faust was talking about?"

"I have no idea why he'd be talking about me, but I did speak with him recently regarding a patient of mine who'd been transferred to Hell." Greta felt faintly hysterical: how was this conversation actually happening, and why didn't it strike her as more improbable than it did?

"Of course I'll transfer you, one moment," said the demon, and there was a series of clicks. She looked at Varney and

Tefnakhte and Grisaille, and wished enormously that she had never answered her office phone that rainy afternoon; never found her way here, never become part of this whole wretched, stupid, miserable situation.

Of course, then someone *else* would have had to be.

"—Greta?" said Fastitocalon's voice in her ear. "What on earth are you up to? We just had a massive incursion spike on the Côte d'Azur essographs, something *huge* just came through and it's set up a standing wave, we're a little busy—"

"We summoned a god," she said. "We had reasons."

"You *what*? Bloody hell, Greta, are you *trying* to rip the world wide open?"

*Oh, fuck,* she thought, a cold bloom of realization all at once. *What have I done, what have* we *done, why didn't I think of that, the danger of it—*

"I'm so sorry," she said, achingly tired, doing everything wrong. "We—I—didn't think it through, we were trying to find out what's hurting my mummies—and he told us several useful bits of information, key among which is that it's sucking out a little bit of energy, or life force, each time, and that it's being done by a spell that's designed to *look* as if it's Egyptian—but it isn't from *this world*."

"Ah," he said in a somewhat different tone. "That changes things a little."

"Changes *what*?"

"Edmund's been helping out with the data analysis," he said, "and has found what I believe to be credible evidence that this goes back almost a hundred years—the slow weakening of reality, and just recently a series of repeated attacks which appear to be located in North America, not unlike the pattern of summonings we saw in Paris."

"You think that corresponds to this energy spell?" Greta asked. "Like, every time a mummy has one of these magical attacks, reality gets ever so slightly more foxed around the edges?"

"Something like that," said Fastitocalon, sounding very tired. "It doesn't make sense from the interior perspective; even someone as bloody-minded as Asmodeus would be unlikely to try it because damaging one's own reality is an excellent way to stop existing, but if the spell is from *somewhere else—*"

"Where else is there to be?" Greta demanded. "Djehuty said—oh, that there were other worlds than these, or something, but it makes no sense—*shit*, that's what it was—Faust said Ruthven's curse was made to look angelic in origin but *not* due to any of the angels he could identify." She snapped her fingers. "Maybe the spell and the curse are from the same place? How does that even work?"

"When I am not in the middle of attempting to avert apocalypse, I will be glad to draw you quite a lot of diagrams of applied relative cosmology," said Fastitocalon. "And yes, if Faust can't identify it as being from this world, it might well be from somewhere else. This does change matters. We need Heaven in on this one, and that means Samael has to make a call."

"Ask him about Ruthven," Grisaille said. While Greta had been talking, he'd drifted over to the table and now leaned on it with both hands, intently focused. "*I want to know about Ruthven.*"

"You said Edmund was helping you in the office?" Greta said, waving a hand at Grisaille: *Calm down.*

"Yes, he's been quite helpful. He demanded to be given something to do. Now if you don't mind, I've got to get off the phone—"

"Grisaille is asking after him," she said. "Meaningfully."

"Oh, for—look, I'll send someone up to fetch him, I can't be having with lovelorn vampires, and one *more* brief disturbance won't tip us over the edge. I'll be in touch. Stay safe," and he was gone. Greta looked up at Grisaille with a shrug.

"Get packed for Hell," she said. "You get a front-row seat to this whole mess, apparently."

"My nipples explode with delight," he said solemnly, and despite how old and worn and exhausted Greta felt, she discovered she was still able to laugh.

The train from Paris had taken Leonora Van Dorne through the center of the thunderstorm-front into bright sunshine as it raced south, and despite her grief at losing the princess's pectoral and her shock and horror at having to use it at all, she was considerably cheered up by the improvement in the weather.

It was a little over three hours from Paris to Marseille, which gave her time to make several more phone calls. Checking in with her network to see if anything had shown up on any of the international stolen-antiquities lists; contacting the Marseille airport to inquire about chartered flights, and after some chatty conversation determining that they handled a lot of one-way charters but one private concern kept their own helicopter registered at Marseille Provence Airport and was always flying in and out as it suited them. Her notebook, open on the tray table in front of her, listed the names of the charter companies.

"I've been thinking of doing the same," she said in flawless but accented French. "It's just simpler to have one's own, don't you think, rather than having to arrange it separately every single time one wishes to visit Ibiza or Rome for the weekend—it's good to know you handle other private individuals' aircraft with discretion—"

"Oh, no, madame, Oasis Natrun's not an individual, it's an exclusive wellness facility," the representative had said, with the faint emphasis on *wellness* that implied *place for rich people to dry out*. "Very private, you understand."

"Of course," she said, and smiled. On the notebook page, her pencil printed the words OASIS NATRUN in block capitals, and circled the name twice. "Thank you; you've been very helpful."

That had been an hour ago. Another few minutes of concentrated work on the phone and online had given her an address, flagged with multiple warnings: the entry was gated and guarded, only preapproved clients were allowed to visit. *If you had to ask, you weren't supposed to know*, Ms. Van Dorne thought with her enigmatic smile curving at the edges. That type of rule applied to other people, not to her.

Now, as the sunset started to fade from the sky, she turned

the nose of her rental car up into the hills above Marseille. It was about a forty-minute drive if she was in a hurry, and at this point she could take her time and enjoy the scenery, secure in the knowledge that she knew where she was going, even without knowing precisely what she'd find. She wasn't worried about the gates; she'd figure those out as she got to them, or simply drive through. At this point she didn't mind making a little bit of a mess; somewhere in the back of her mind Ms. Van Dorne was aware that she had left objectivity behind in New York City, and did not care. She had already come so far and done so much to get her hands on that stela; giving up now was not in her nature, even if it meant she had to break not only laws but objects.

It turned out she didn't have to do anything at all. The first of the gates, at the turnoff from the public road onto the facility's private drive, looked fairly solid, and she rolled the car up to it prepared to stop and get out—but the gate's bar simply slid smoothly upward with oiled ease to let her pass.

As if it had recognized her. As if she carried some sort of—opening device, or talisman.

That sent a little finger of doubt down her spine, but it was rapidly subsumed under a sense of satisfaction, of *rightness*: of course it would let her in. She deserved to be here.

There were seven gates, as described in the *Book of the Dead*. Ms. Van Dorne was faintly amused by that, and also mildly glad they hadn't gone with the twelve gates mentioned in a lot of tomb paintings. Every gate opened for her as if she was expected, soundless and smooth.

*Wellness facility*, she thought, changing down as the road grew steeper. *What kind of wellness facility is used as a staging ground for international art theft? What other treasures might there be lying around up here in the middle of nowhere that I might decide I want?*

She was almost upon the place before she saw it clearly: a series of mid-century modern pavilions set into the edge of the hillside, the tilted windows only just catching the last of the dying copper-rose light of sunset. There was a terrace with deck chairs on it, and as she came around the last curve of the road, she could see the polished ochre fuselage of the helicopter squatting on its pad.

Ms. Van Dorne parked the now-dusty rental Mercedes in front of the main entrance, without bothering to make any attempt to disguise her approach, and got out. She'd traveled in what was for her casual wear—narrow Prada slacks, a cashmere twin-set, a Hermès scarf tied over her hair, huge Dior sunglasses—and she could see herself reflected in the glass doors. *Not bad*, she thought. *Not bad at all.*

*Now to reclaim my property.*

Knowing what was causing the attacks of faintness, even if they couldn't *stop* them, was in fact a weird kind of comfort. It meant that Greta could go ahead with surgeries she'd been putting off until they could find some kind of etiology, and—as she'd said herself—her job still needed to be done, whatever the condition of the universe.

Maanakhtef's replacement metatarsals had been printed

weeks ago and the final preparation and sanding was complete; all Greta had to do was install them. She was nearly finished with the attachment points for his new tendons and ligaments when raised voices in the hall outside her operating room filtered through her concentration.

"—Dr. Helsing?" someone asked. "I'm so sorry to disturb you—"

"Then don't," she said between her teeth. "Hand me that micro-driver."

"It's—there's a trespasser—"

"Ask Varney to tie them in a knot, and *hand me that micro-driver.*"

The tool was set in her outstretched hand; she bent closer to Maanakhtef's foot and fastened another three tiny titanium screws into place, securing his new transverse metatarsal ligament to the replacement fourth metatarsal. Only when she was sure it was solidly attached did she straighten up and take off her magnifying glasses.

Sister Melitta was standing just inside the door, actually *wringing her hands*, a thing which Greta had never seen anyone do outside of fiction. "Tell me what's going on," she said.

"There's a woman here," said the nurse, "who doesn't have clearance, who's not on any of the lists, but she just—*drove up the road*, bold as brass, and the gates *opened* for her—"

"What does she want?" Greta's eyes narrowed.

"As far as we can tell, she wants the stela," said Sister Melitta. "She seems to think it belongs to her."

*There is no way*, Greta thought, *that the Van Dorne woman could possibly have found her way here. No way at all.*

She *sighed*. "Scrub in and put a temporary dressing on his foot. I'll deal with her and *then* finish the job. Maanakhtef, I am *so* sorry about this."

Mummies didn't really need much anesthesia; Tefnakhte had chanted a spell to send him into a kind of twilight doze. He woke enough to mumble something that sounded like *of course*.

Sister Melitta looked almost comically relieved to have something to do—and to be excused from dealing with their unwelcome visitor. Greta stripped off her gloves, tossed them in the disposal, and left her to it.

In the entry foyer she found Sister Brigitte towering over a stranger, accompanied by several other nurses. Sister looked thoroughly relieved to see her. "Dr. Helsing," she said. "This—person is not authorized to be here."

Greta nodded, and she stepped aside. The stranger was about as tall as she was, dressed expensively, wearing what looked like a genuine lapis scarab in an enormous ring.

"I'm the medical director here," she said. "What do you want?"

"'Medical director,'" said the woman in an American accent of the type Greta thought of as transatlantic. "Cute. I'd never have come up with an Egypt-themed detox facility, but clearly you people are making it work—Ah," she added, looking past Greta, who turned to see Cranswell in the doorway. "Mr. Cranswell. What a pleasure it is to see you again."

Cranswell had gone a very horrible unhealthy color. "What are *you* doing here? How did you—did the demons bring you, too?"

"Demons?" said the stranger, and laughed. "Oh, dear. I'm so sorry, I didn't realize; you really do manage to seem quite normal most of the time. Where's my stela?"

"It's not your stela," said Cranswell. "It's not ours, either, but we needed it."

"So do I," she said, "and I made it possible for you to get it out of the museum, so hand it over—"

"This is her?" Greta said ungrammatically. "This is Van Dorne?"

"Yeah," said Cranswell. "God knows how she got here, we didn't leave a postcard with the address or anything—"

"You didn't have to, dear," said Van Dorne, and then all the color slid out of her face at once, leaving the expertly applied rouge standing out like fever spots.

Greta and Cranswell turned to find Tefnakhte, with his clipboard, in conversation with Varney, just coming through the door. "What..." Van Dorne said, strengthless, sounding as if she'd just been hit quite hard.

Well, there went their cover. Still, Greta couldn't help a nasty little flicker of satisfaction. "What seems to be the matter?" she inquired. "Are you quite well?"

"That's—that's—a—"

"A mummy?" said Greta, tilting her head. "Yes. Yes, he is."

"That's not *real*, they're not—" She was still grey-white, and beginning to sway. Behind Greta, Tefnakhte handed Varney his clipboard and lurched toward them.

"Oh, I assure you they are," said Greta. "This is Mr. Tefnakhte. He's a records clerk here at Oasis Natrun. He's also been dead for several thousand years. Tefnakhte, Ms. Van Dorne, of New York."

"Pleased to meet you," said the mummy in a whistling creak quite unlike his ordinary voice. Greta could tell he was enjoying himself.

Van Dorne stared at him in horror, taking off her enormous sunglasses; they could all see quite clearly when her eyes rolled up and she crumpled—

—into the arms of Tefnakhte, who looked extraordinarily smug.

"Can someone take a picture?" he asked. "I can lurch."

"It's... it's done," said Zophiel, his voice soft and strengthless, sitting up in bed. It was full dark: sometime in the very small hours of the morning, the traffic outside as quiet as it ever got, and both of them had been torn out of sleep by the echo-shock of something *huge* passing through the planes, followed by a shimmery unreal sensation of imbalance, something teetering on the edge of collapse. "That was enough to damage the last of the barrier—but *we* didn't do it, it wasn't the woman with the spell, something *else* used that stone's power—"

"But it was done," Amitiel said beside him. Zophiel wasn't quite sure when they had started sharing a bed, but it seemed entirely correct somehow, looking at his fellow angel. His eyes were *huge*, luminous violet-blue in the dimness of the room. Both of them were giving off a faint pale light. "After so long," Amitiel added. "I can *feel* it, Zophiel, that—there's almost nothing left of the barrier between worlds—it's *done.* Even if we didn't do it in the end, our work is done. The Archangel can lead the host through to bring down devastation on the other Heaven—we can go *home*—"

"We can go home," Zophiel repeated wonderingly, and all at once dropped his human seeming completely: the blue irises of his eyes flared bright gold and spread into pupilless cabochons, blank gold from lid to lid, and his vast white wings came into being, folded around both of them; a bright circle of light settled just above his white-gold curls. "Oh, Amitiel. It's been so *long*, in the wrong world."

"Take me there," said Amitiel, and clung to him, his own wings and halo visible. "Take me home where we belong."

"Yes," Zophiel said very gently. "Yes."

He closed his golden eyes and *twisted* one hand slightly in the air, and a small thunderclap knocked the alarm clock off the nightstand as the two angels disappeared, leaving only a faint gold shimmery dust where they had lain.

Somewhere rather different from Greenwich Street, Ruthven was watching another angel: this one on a large viewscreen, glaring at the Lord of Hell.

He had only been allowed into Samael's enormous all-white boardroom because Fastitocalon had let him in—along with a gaggle of staffers and several of the archdemons who ran other departments in the infernal civil service. Ruthven was having that creepy *discordant* feeling again: this was too normal for the setting; why wasn't anything on fire or reeking of brimstone?

"—hardly feel that this matter is of the significance you claim," the angel was saying. It was inhumanly beautiful, which Ruthven was beginning to understand was par for the course, but it also wore an expression as if something in its vicinity were giving off an unpleasant smell. "It's our understanding that your people sorted out whatever that was in Paris earlier this year."

"The point is we shouldn't have had to," said Samael with awful patience. He was leaning against the table with one hip, arms folded, wearing a beautifully cut white silk suit with no shirt, the jacket unbuttoned. Ruthven thought probably nobody else in all the world *other* than the Devil could have pulled off that much look. "My people, as you say, sorted it out with what was in effect an emergency tack-welding job, which staved off the immediate danger; but the overall source of the disturbances is *external*. Which means you're also in jeopardy, and that despite our vast and storied list of differences, we may need to collaborate on this one."

"Heaven," said the angel, "does not *collaborate*. If the danger exists, we are more than capable of handling it ourselves."

"Let me ask you a question," said Samael. "When was the last time you actually had direct contact with Himself? I don't mean just the praying and so on, all the hosannas and that sort of phatic repetitive stuff, but actual interaction with the divine? Was it about eighty years ago, by any chance?"

The angel went a whiter shade of pale, and its golden eyes narrowed. "I would *expect* nothing more than gross discourtesy and insult from *you*, traitorous scum. This conversation is over." It reached for something, and the screen went blank.

"That's a yes," said one of the archdemons. There were eight of them, apparently, who together with Samael made up the Council of Nine, the body in charge of the infernal civil service. Ruthven thought this one was Ahriman: exquisite Persian features, very long dark hair. The only visibly demonic attribute was the bright red eyes, which made Ruthven think of Grisaille, and hurriedly redirect his attention to the conversation going on. "There is nothing quite so defensive as an angel who doesn't want to let on they have no idea what they're doing," Ahriman added. "And if God's really adopted a hands-off management style they're not about to admit it to the likes of us."

"It doesn't help that Gabriel's in charge," said Samael. "Some of the others are a bit more reasonable, but Gabriel is the prig of all prigs. Well, at least we've warned them to some extent." He sighed, detaching himself from the table. "Back to work. Fass, I want to see your data myself."

Fastitocalon nodded. "Of course. It looks—more bad news, of course—it looks like a good third of the current surface ops have gone native in the *abandon one's responsibilities* manner, but I can't replace them at the moment. If we get through this, I'm going to enjoy firing them one by one."

"Quite right," said Samael, walking, so that Fastitocalon and Ruthven had to catch up. "I'm beginning to think I didn't really do Asmodeus justice with the slug. I might reopen the case and see if I could adjust his sentence to something more fitting, such as a hagfish. Lord Ruthven, are you sure you ought to be out of bed?"

Ruthven blinked. "I'm fine," he said. "I'm quite all right now, and—I want to help?"

"He's already been quite useful," said Fastitocalon. "He noticed the pattern before anybody else did. Let him stay."

"By all means," said Samael, rubbing at his temples. Outside, distant thunder muttered. "One feels somewhat out of order asking one's guest to lend a hand in an ongoing existential crisis; it's bad manners."

"The guest is volunteering," said Ruthven, faintly amused—and the amusement vanished behind a sudden bright-hot spike of shocked *gladness* as they turned the corner and saw none other than Grisaille standing beside Fastitocalon's office, looking awkward and exhausted at the same time.

Ruthven had been told not to do anything energetic, but there was nothing on this or any other plane that could have stopped him *running* across the remaining distance between them and wrapping Grisaille in an almost painfully tight embrace.

"—Hello," he said. "I *missed* you. What's happening on Earth?"

"You would not believe some of the things I've seen," said Grisaille, muffled in his shoulder. "Do they have booze in Hell?"

"More of it than you can imagine," said Fastitocalon mildly, joining them. "Was the trip down awful, Grisaille?"

"Not as bad as from New York," he said, still attached to Ruthven. "But not a lot of fun. Thanks for sending someone to come get me."

"Of course. There's a nice little bar just at the foot of the towers if you want to go and catch up and get pleasantly inebriated—"

"Yes *please*," said Grisaille. "Right now."

Greta had let Tefnakhte lurch around *briefly* with the Van Dorne in his arms, partly because he did it so well and partly for the same reason she'd let Ruthven give her a makeover for the opera in Paris: he was so clearly having an absolute ball. After a few minutes, chronicled on Tefnakhte's own phone, she told him to put her down on the couch in the reception area and had one of the nurses fetch a smelling-salt ampoule.

"So tell me what you want with the Hermopolis Stela," she said when Van Dorne had gasped and shuddered her way back to consciousness. "You can't possibly exhibit it in your house, and why bother stealing it if you're only going to lock it up in a warehouse somewhere?"

Greta was sitting in a chair beside the couch, watching Van Dorne attempt to pull herself together. After a few moments she pushed aside the now-disarranged wing of silver-gilt hair and stared at Greta with peculiar hazel eyes.

"That was a *mummy*," she said.

"I believe we covered that," said Greta. "Yes. That was a

mummy. In fact there are several on the premises. Not that anyone is going to believe you if you go back to the city and start telling people about it."

"That was *real*. They—they move? And talk?"

"And pay quite a lot of money to come up here and have me, or an equivalent person, fix them when they are ill or damaged, which a lot of them seem to be just recently. I am, in fact, not finished with a surgical procedure I was performing when you showed up uninvited and unannounced, so you will understand my lack of patience," said Greta. "What do you want with the goddamn stela, and how did you trace the thing *here*, anyway?"

"Greta," said another voice behind her, and she turned to see Varney in the doorway, looking at his phone with narrow tin-colored eyes. "Something's off here."

"That's a bit of an understatement," she said, bone-dry.

"With her, I mean. I looked her up. According to this, if she's really Leonora Irene Van Dorne, she was born in 1954."

Greta had turned back in time to see a shocked blush flare and fade in the woman's barely lined face. She would have put Van Dorne in her mid-thirties at most, so where the hell were the other thirty-something years? No plastic surgeon was that good.

"Huh," she said slowly.

"You're not a vampire," said Varney, slipping his phone into his pocket and coming to loom over the couch. "I'd know. So what *are* you?"

With the *are*, he widened his eyes slightly, and Greta—even out of direct line-of-sight—felt the faint silvery dissociation of his thrall. Van Dorne's face went blank.

"I'm an amateur Egyptologist," she said dully. "And a collector."

"So what's with you failing to age?" said Greta. "Did you unearth some kind of mystic ancient time machine?"

"Not a time machine," said Van Dorne. "A spell."

Greta looked up at Varney, a sudden yawning pit of horror opening up before her. He put a hand on her shoulder.

"And how did this spell work?" he asked, and perhaps only someone who knew him as well as Greta could hear the effort with which he was keeping his voice calm and gentle.

"Drew...power, energy, force...from artifacts," said Van Dorne, sounding vague. "I have lots of them—little things that don't matter, ushabtis, cosmetic jars, amulets—*oh*—my *pectoral*—on the *plane*..." Her hand went to her chest as if to grasp something that was no longer there. "It...they *crumble*..."

Greta had been this angry only once before in her life; it felt like a ball of burning metal in her chest, rapidly heating from dull red to an incandescent white. Varney's hand on her shoulder tightened slightly. "Where did you find the spell?" he said, and yes, all right, they *did* need to know that and *then* perhaps she could hit Van Dorne very hard, even if she didn't know how to punch somebody. She'd figure it out.

"In a dream," Van Dorne said. "In a dream. A papyrus. Just a thing I'd bought...in an auction lot...and never got around to looking at. I dreamed of it... exactly as I found it... the picture was so clear..."

"Did it look different from the others?" Greta asked sharply.

"No," she said. "Just exactly the same... only the text was different."

"Egyptian, but not a text you recognized."

"Yes," said Van Dorne. "I translated it... and thought it was just another spell... and after a while I *tried* it..."

"And it worked," said Varney. "Obviously. But it wears off, doesn't it?"

Van Dorne nodded unhappily. "Faster now."

"She wanted to destroy the fucking *stela* to zap herself back to sweet sixteen," Greta said flatly. "I can't believe this. Varney, snap her out of it. I think it's time Ms. Van Dorne met a few friends of mine."

Varney closed his eyes, cutting off the thrall; Van Dorne gave a faint sigh and seemed to come back to herself, blinking at them. "What just happened?"

"You painted your self-centered awfulness in some pretty broad strokes," said Greta, getting up. "Come with me."

She waited for Varney to haul the woman to her feet—who the hell wore four-inch heels to travel in, the rich truly were a different species—and then led the way out of the reception area back into the clinical side of the spa, heading for the inpatient ward. The bright-hot ball of anger in her chest pulsed like a second heart, nearly in time with her footsteps.

"What *is* this place?" Van Dorne managed. She was being

propelled along by Varney's hands on her upper arms, without much choice in the matter.

"I told you. Private mummy spa and resort. Right now it's not really all that recreation-oriented, as you'll see in a minute." Greta stopped outside Antjau's room, checked the charts on the door. "This is Mr. Antjau, undergoing treatment for tuberculosis, which as I'm sure you'll agree, is bad enough without *you* sucking all the juice out of something that belonged to him."

"What—" said Van Dorne, but Greta was already knocking on the door; at Antjau's weak "Come in," she opened it. Ignoring the gasp behind her, she crossed the room to Antjau's bed—still piled high with pillows, the bed's head raised to help him breathe—and stood beside it. He looked a little better, she thought: Djehuty's visit really must have done him good.

"Mr. Antjau," she said in a rather different tone than the one she'd just been using, "if it's not too much trouble, I'd like you to tell Ms. Van Dorne here about the fainting episode you experienced a little while ago."

"Oh...certainly," he said, sounding puzzled, but obliged. Greta watched Van Dorne, arms folded, while the mummy's whistling creak of a voice described the sudden terrible weakness and dizziness, the inability to breathe, having to struggle even to push the call button. Van Dorne's expression went through a series of changes—shock, disbelief, a kind of horrified guilt that settled into nausea.

"And this happened twice," Greta said when he'd finished. "Thank you so much, Mr. Antjau. We'll leave you to rest now."

"Is something happening?" he asked.

"I believe we may have discovered the cause of the attacks," she said gently. "Which means I can stop any more of them from occurring."

Antjau curled a shaky hand around her arm. "Really?" he rasped.

"Really," said Greta, feeling Van Dorne's stare. "Get some sleep. Sister Brigitte will be here to check on you in a little while."

"*Thank you*," he said, and squeezed her arm for a brief moment before letting go.

Greta rejoined the others, shut the door behind them. "That's *one* of the patients your little stunt has hurt. There are quite a few others to visit. Maanakhtef, for example. The second time you used up something of his, he collapsed on the floor and shattered most of his left side. I had to spend nearly nine hours repairing the damage, and some of it I couldn't: some of him had *turned to powder*—if you're going to be ill, kindly do it in the washroom. End of the hall."

# CHAPTER 14

Amitiel and Zophiel had been separated from one another on their return and, in fact, had spent the time since they had regained Heaven in isolation, all-white cells with no decoration at all other than a golden crucifix on one wall, without furniture. From time to time they were interrogated by other angels—identical, all of them, impossible to tell apart but for their voices and the cloaks some of the higher-ranking individuals wore.

Being back in Heaven felt wonderful, of course. Back where they were meant to be, in God's presence; the constant nagging awareness of being surrounded by the other world's sinners and filthiness was gone, but in its place the angels had begun to notice a different kind of discomfort: something that might be described as *boredom*, or as a desire for one another's company, which they had never felt before: being in Heaven, being in the brilliance and glory of His regard, had always been more than enough joy to suffuse their consciousnesses, and now...

Well, now it felt as if they'd *lost* something.

Zophiel could picture Amitiel sitting disconsolately on the stone floor of his chamber, looking up every time somebody came in; could picture the other angels speaking sharply to him, asking the same questions over and over again—*the plan was not executed as intended, another power's manipulation of magic caused the rift, why was this allowed to occur, control over the matter was lost, why were you unable to perform the duties you had been assigned*—and Amitiel not being able to answer. Or—not being able to answer *satisfactorily*.

He was very much aware of an uncharacteristic desire to *be with* the other angel, to—comfort him, to curve a wing around him in protection. Zophiel didn't know why exactly, only that it seemed necessary, and that the people asking them questions were *unkind* in some way, which was an absolutely strange thing to think about the heavenly host, about the high-ranking angels who had sent them out to complete God's mission in the other world.

They had been brought ambrosia and nectar, and it was just as lovely as Zophiel remembered, but he found himself missing the quite ordinary and not even slightly glowing-gold herbal tea he and Amitiel had drunk in the other world's New York, and not knowing how to ask for such a thing: he should not *want* anything but nectar and ambrosia; it was as if something was wrong with him that he had not noticed going wrong, and did not know how to fix.

He wasn't sure exactly what was going on. Back on the other Earth, he and Amitiel hadn't really considered this part very clearly, what would happen *after* they had weakened the barrier sufficiently for the invasion to occur: it wasn't their job, what they were *for*—that was the business of the Archangels, with His blessing, who had come up with the plan. All they had thought about was following orders: making it possible for the next stage of the overarching plan to take place, not the logistics of how that stage would be carried out. Nor had they thought there would be so many *questions* to answer.

He was kneeling on the floor of the cell, wings folded quietly, looking up at the crucifix on the wall with blank golden eyes, when the door behind him opened again. "Zophiel," someone said. "It is time. You have been granted the gift of permission to witness the glory of our hour of triumph and righteousness."

Zophiel rose, knees aching a little—that was another thing, he had never experienced discomfort or fatigue in Heaven before—and let the other angel take his arm; the touch was cold. "Is—where is Amitiel?" he asked.

"Amitiel will be granted permission also," said the angel, sounding as if it didn't necessarily agree with the decision, and walked him briskly down the white-on-white corridor.

"May I see him?"

"There is no need," said the angel, and Zophiel was slightly horrified to find a spark of resentment somewhere inside his own chest, where it did not belong: there was no such thing as resentment in Heaven, what was *wrong* with him, was he *broken* somehow—had the mortal world left such a taint on him that it could not be removed?

The angel took him up a flight of steps and out to a pearl-and-agate balcony, crowded with other angels, their wings brushing together as they talked in an undertone. He knew where he was now: this was one of the galleries overlooking the central courtyard of Heaven's jeweled city. Above them the ruby battlements glowed like wine; the walls of many precious stones caught the clear endless light in a vast panoply of color against which the white wings of the angels were brilliant, snow-pure, giving off their own faint shine.

Down below in the courtyard stood massed ranks of angels dressed in white and gold, wearing breastplates of electrum; each held in its lovely hand a golden sword, and at the head of the ranks stood the Archangel Michael. His armor was even brighter and more beautiful than that of his soldiers; he was difficult to look directly at for very long.

It struck Zophiel—perhaps for the first time—that there would be a great deal of violence. He had known they were preparing for a holy war, a righteous crusade, but until now the actual ramifications of that had seemed—academic. Distant. Now, as he looked at the swords, it was suddenly very present indeed.

As Zophiel stared down at the host of Heaven, a movement out of the corner of his eye caught his attention: he turned to see Amitiel standing on a different balcony across the courtyard, waving at him, and watched as the angel standing beside Amitiel caught his forearm and forced it down again. Again that spark of resentment flared and faded inside his chest.

The Archangel was saying something. A speech. Zophiel

found it difficult to pay attention to, although the words were the sort of thing designed to strike fire and determination into the listeners' hearts: righteousness, triumph, the downfall of all things evil and sullied and made unclean. *The great day of the Lord is near, and hasteth: the sun will be turned to darkness and the moon to blood; the enemies of the Lord who take His name in vain and profane the very thought of Heaven in their iniquity will be driven into utter darkness, and the world made pure.*

Zophiel watched as the Archangel raised his golden sword, as the host of angels raised theirs in response, and although he knew what was coming, it was still a shock to see every blade burst into flame at once: a thousand brilliant bars of light raised skyward in salute.

*We march forth*, said Michael, and the army raised its massed voice; as one, every angel turned, and the footfalls in unison as they began to march out of the city shook the paving stones beneath Zophiel's feet. Michael spread his wings and sprang into the air, flying to take up position at the head of the marching column, flaming sword in his hand—

—and Zophiel looked across the courtyard at Amitiel, and recognized the look on his face; it was the same one he was wearing himself. Puzzlement and confusion. They were the only angels in all of Heaven who were silent in the midst of the vast and many-voiced cheer.

*What is wrong with me?* he thought again, and could not excise the image of those flaming swords raised in salute: could not unsee the brilliant coruscating light of all those blades. Could not unthink the clear and present realization that swords were meant to slay, that every last one of them would be slicked over with golden ichor by the time this was complete.

What happened to angels, when they were killed?

He and Amitiel had had almost a year to think about this part, and somehow he had failed to spend much time considering what it would actually mean, to—invade another Heaven, to slaughter its inhabitants, to destroy what was so obviously a false and profane facsimile of *their* Heaven, the only true Heaven, where things were right and just and correct; they had spent so long on the false and profane Earth without giving any thought to the next phase of the plan.

*I'm not supposed to think*, Zophiel told himself. *I'm supposed to—adore. That's what I'm for, I'm an* angel*; when can I stop thinking and just* be *again, just float in His regard, do His bidding—*

He looked around at the rest of the rejoicing host, and with dawning horror began to realize he no longer felt like *one of them.*

That he no longer belonged.

He had wanted to come home for so long, so very badly, and his hands tightened on the pearl parapet at the thought that perhaps it would—perhaps it *could*—never truly be his home again.

Grisaille had had enough single-malt by now to be actually enjoying himself, despite the fact that *he was in Hell* and the lake over there was actively on fire. Ruthven looked like himself again, not the grey-pale ghost he'd been when they first got here, and reluctantly Grisaille had to admit Hell had done him quite a lot of good.

"So you're helping with the whole *who's fucking with reality this time* analysis?" he asked. They had found a quite nice little café in the ground floor of one of the towers and were sitting outside under a red umbrella. Demons came and went around them without paying much attention. It felt a bit like Paris had done, except Parisians tended not to have wings or tails as a matter of course.

(The ears on legs were freaky. There was no way around that. They were also extremely *cute*, which Grisaille found amusing: they ran around a little bit like pigeons, in flocks, and wore very small medieval-looking hose.)

"It was either that or die of boredom," said Ruthven, and swirled his drink. "And I'm good at spotting patterns. Fass let me help, and I found some evidence that shows this has been going on for eighty years or so, but recently seems to have accelerated a lot, presumably due to whatever's attacking Greta's mummies."

"What does that mean?"

Ruthven sighed, and was about to reply when abruptly, suddenly, the perfectly pleasant day *changed*. Black clouds poured up the sky like ink; a rapid rising wind swirled leaves across the plaza; a brief flash of lightning was followed by a crack of thunder that left Grisaille's ears ringing. He stared at Ruthven, who stared back and got to his feet.

"Come on," Ruthven said. "I have a feeling something's just gone rather dramatically wrong."

Back on the thirtieth floor, the previously chaotic M&E bullpen had gone into full crisis mode: alarm sirens were going off, teleprinters rattling out loop after loop of data on ribbons of paper, demons rushing around shouting into their phones. Nobody noticed Grisaille or Ruthven in the slightest.

"What the hell is going on?" Grisaille said over the background din. He was just drunk enough to be faintly dissociated from how frightened he thought he probably ought to be.

Ruthven seized his hand, tugged him back out of the chaos, into the elevator once more, thumbed the button for the sixtieth floor. "I have a feeling the weather in Hell might have something to do with the mood of its ruler," he said as they rose with stomach-dropping rapidity—one of the walls of the shaft was glass above the fortieth floor of the tower and the view of the plaza falling away beneath them did not do Grisaille's head any favors—"and I want to know what's got him this infuriated all of a sudden." Rain lashed the glass wall, curtains of it drifting across their view; the burning lake didn't seem to take any notice, merely a bright smear through the blur.

Grisaille wondered, slightly hysterically, if he was perhaps hallucinating all of this and would shortly come to his senses, but he hadn't drunk anybody's actual blood in—however long it had been, let alone got himself a bona fide junkie. The faint *ding* of the elevator drawing to a halt was absurdly ordinary under the circumstances, but when the doors opened on a white-on-white corridor full of hurrying demons, he stopped and stared until Ruthven grabbed his hand again.

"This way," he said, "Samael's conference room, I'm pretty sure that's where he'll be—"

In fact, they could hear him before they got there, the beautiful bell-like voice raised. Nobody was watching the door, and they were able to slip in, and stop, staring at what was on the massive screen at the other end of the room. The crowd of demons around them was frozen in horror; Grisaille had no idea who any of them were, but a few seemed clearly important.

"—don't know where they're coming from—" what looked like an *angel* was saying on the screen, wide-eyed. It had a halo. In the background were yells, screams, the sounds of a struggle. "They're angels but they're not *us*, they're not from *here*, there's so *many* and they've all got *swords*—"

"Fuck, fuck, *fuck*," said the Devil, running his hands through his curls. "Of course they're not from your Heaven, they're from a different *universe*. I told you, I *told you* something was happening, Gabriel, you absolute idiot, I *warned you*—all our monitors are going mad, the point of origin's expanding, it's an interreality septal defect of massive proportions and it's only going to get bigger—think of a balloon bursting in slow motion—"

"What are we supposed to *do*?" the angel almost screamed. "God's not *answering*, what are we supposed to *do*?"

Samael's hands closed in his hair, tight, for a long moment:

when he let go and opened his eyes again, he seemed to have regained some control over himself.

"What you're going to do is fight back," he said. "For as long as you can. Where's Michael?"

"I don't know! I don't know where anyone is!" There was a crash in the background, and the angel's terrified face vanished briefly in a cloud of dust, the whole picture shaking. "They've broken into the administrative center!" it managed between coughs. "Samael, *help*!"

"I'm going to," said Samael, and a moment later the screen went blank white and then fizzing with static, the idiot noise of an open carrier wave. He turned to see the crowd massed at the room's entrance, and Grisaille saw with a kind of dim, sick-feeling shock that his eyes had gone blank scarlet from lid to lid and were giving off visible light.

"Right," he said. "Things are about as bad as they can possibly be. A foreign force of angels has broken through from the neighboring universe and is laying waste to Heaven, and it's anybody's guess whether we're going to be able to stabilize reality before our erstwhile colleagues get slaughtered. We can't rely on help from *this* universe's Most High, who as far as any of us can tell, seems to have gone on an eighty-year sabbatical, so we're all there is, and we'll have to do. Fass, you're on monitoring and intelligence; deputize whoever you need to and run the simulations in real time, I want to know what that rift is doing. Ahriman, you're communications—set up a direct line and give me visual to Heaven as soon as possible; send out a mass announcement through all broadcast structures that combat volunteers are urgently needed. Meph, I want you to get in touch with Faust and tell the hospital to prepare to receive evacuated casualties; you're my liaison to the medical center. Beelzebub, Mammon, you're with me; get started immediately preparing volunteers as soon as they arrive. Ozymandias, you're infrastructure, you have the best supply-chain management capabilities; get started sourcing equipment and weaponry right away. Any questions?"

Grisaille was still *just* drunk enough to give in to the urge to raise a finger. "Is this the end of the world?" he asked. Heads turned to look at him and Ruthven at the back of the crowd.

"We're going to find out," said the Devil. "Okay, people, *go*."

The first real intimation Greta had of things going very badly wrong was the earthquake.

It was the first earthquake she had ever experienced, and she hadn't known the south of France even *had* them. That it had chosen to occur right when Greta was finishing up her interrupted work on Maanakhtef's foot was, she thought, a clear and present proof of Sod's Law.

She managed not to hurt him, at least—she had snatched her instruments away as soon as it began—but the sterile tray with all her *other* instruments had slid to the floor in a musical crash, along with several of the jars on the counter. Greta cursed; the nurse let out a yelp, and Maanakhtef made a surprised creaky noise.

She couldn't help thinking of him falling and *shattering*, of how much work she'd had to do to repair the damage Van

Dorne had caused by proxy, and got up to page the nurses' ready room, picking her way through broken glass and scattered instruments. It only took a moment to order a wellness check on every single patient, but actually *doing* it would take more time.

"What happened?" Maanakhtef asked, drowsy and confused.

"That was an earthquake, and I have no idea why. And now I need a new set of instruments out of the sterilizer, Sister, and call the janitor to clean up this mess." She was *going* to finish this surgery, no matter what. And as long as she was working, she didn't have room to think about the larger, looming problem of *what the hell to do about the stela and the woman from New York*.

The nurse hurried to obey.

Ruthven had been down here long enough to be utterly unsurprised at the efficiency with which Samael's conference room was transformed into a command center. Banks of monitors were being set up at the ends of the table, some of them already scrolling data. The main screen was showing standby blue as of yet, but the peculiar grey glass ring Fastitocalon had set in the middle of the table was clearly the source of the slowly turning model of the inter-universe rift made out of cyan light hovering above it.

He and Grisaille had made themselves scarce, getting out of the way while the other members of Samael's Council of Nine sped off to do his bidding, and had then simply made themselves *unnoticeable*, standing in a corner and watching as demons hurried in and out with equipment. Impenetrable IT jargon in Hell sounded a lot like impenetrable IT jargon on Earth, it turned out.

Samael had been busy directing the team on where he wanted which monitor, and then had had a brief talk with Fastitocalon when the latter arrived with the grey glass projector, looking exhausted. Neither of them had looked particularly happy about whatever conclusion they had reached, especially when Fass tapped the glass thing in a specific pattern and the blue-light projection sprang into being. The rift, modeled in cyan-blue 3-D wireframe, looked to Ruthven like any other tear in any other fabric, and that somehow made it *worse*. It was the—mismatch thing again. Too ordinary to be as vast and cosmically significant as it was.

Fastitocalon had done something to the projector, and the image changed; the rift began to heal, its edges drawing together seamlessly until there was nothing left, just faintly glowing air above the table; he tapped it again and the rift reappeared, tearing open much faster than it had closed. He ran through the simulation several more times at Samael's request, slower or faster, stopping here or there to enlarge a point.

Ruthven *wished* he knew the beginnings of any of the mathematics necessary to understand what was going on, but was not about to interrupt them to ask. Eventually Samael had seemed satisfied, and Fastitocalon had hurried out again, back to his own office, leaving the Devil briefly alone.

He was standing with his back to them, tapping his fingers

on the table, which appeared to be made out of a single vast cultured pearl, thirty feet long. "You might as well stop being invisible," he said without turning around. "I know perfectly well you're there."

Ruthven felt his face go briefly warm, but he and Grisaille stepped away from the wall, dropping the *don't notice me* influence all at once. "Sorry," he said.

"Don't mention it." Samael turned, looked at the pair of them. "I can't imagine any of this is particularly pleasant or entertaining, and I do apologize for the inconvenience; if I were you, I'd just go back to the café and get quietly bombed out of my mind and let us worry about this war."

Ruthven and Grisaille looked at one another. "Actually," Ruthven said, in the same tone he'd often used to tell Fastitocalon to stop apologizing for *being unwell*, "I was going to ask if there's anything at all we could do to be of assistance."

"No," said the Devil, and passed a hand over his face. The weary, resigned expression was incongruous on those exquisite features, Ruthven thought. "There's not a—damn. Wait. Yes. There is. Go over to the hospital, report to Faust, see if he can use a couple of spare pairs of hands—I'm betting he'll need them when the casualties start coming in."

Ruthven shared another look with Grisaille, but just nodded. "Of course," he said, and managed to squash the urge to salute.

The short journey over to Tower Three took them several minutes longer than it usually might, simply because of the volume of traffic: demons hurrying in all directions, most carrying equipment and supplies. The plaza was thronged with what had to be volunteer reinforcements, and as Ruthven and Grisaille went past, skirting the edge of the wide expanse, a couple of rather larger demons started shouting them into some semblance of order and rank. It was a relief to get inside away from the noise, but as soon as they reached the hospital itself, more chaos became evident.

"Gets things done fast, doesn't he, that Sam," said Grisaille, in an undertone, as they stood to one side to let nurses roll enormous, presumably medical machinery past. "Not a person for whom one would wish to dillydally in the course of one's duty."

"Dillying or dallying would seem to be ill-advised," Ruthven agreed. "It's the most efficiently run small country I've ever encountered, and the majority of citizens seem to *like* it. There's malcontents, there's always malcontents, but they're pretty rare. Did you notice the one item of social architecture this place *doesn't* have?"

"A monorail?"

"I speak metaphorically. And I missed it, too, at first. There's *no police force.*"

Grisaille blinked at him. "Really?"

"They don't *need* one. Roll that around in your head for a bit."

One of the nurses who'd been pushing the machine came back over to them suspiciously. "What are you doing here? You're the vampire, aren't you, the one with the curse."

"Vampires plural," said Grisaille. "Sorry for the lack of notice, it's *très* poorly bred of us, I know, but we've been dispatched on the direct order of the Adversary to lend a helping hand with the wounded warriors. Mop a brow or two. Roll the odd bandage, sort of thing."

The nurse's eyes, which were slit-pupiled and green, narrowed. "Stay there," she said. "I'm going to get Dr. Faust."

"Splendid," said Grisaille, and the eyes narrowed further before she turned and strode off. Ruthven elbowed him. "Ow!"

"Do you *have* to be intensely witty at inopportune times?"

"I can't help it, it's in my nature," said Grisaille, and fluttered his eyelashes. "To thine own self be true."

Ruthven knew the facetious byplay varied directly with Grisaille's levels of stress, and sighed, slipping an arm around his waist. "I know. It's all—a lot."

Grisaille leaned his head against Ruthven's shoulder. "It's a *lot* a lot. Maybe we should've taken his first suggestion."

"No," said Ruthven, "*not* having something to do would make it worse. You know that."

"I hate it when you're right."

"I know."

Leonora Van Dorne could not clearly remember a time when being what and who she was had not possessed a single ounce of weight. Even her earliest memories were tinted with the awareness that, if she simply complained to her father, whoever was thwarting her desire would *stop doing so*, and it only grew more and more clear as she got older: she was meant to be in charge. Other people were for doing what she wanted them to do, the way small furry squeaky things are meant to be eaten, and sleek sharp-toothed things are meant to take their meal at ease.

As a young woman, she had been aware of being beautiful, and used it like a calculated battering ram, triangulating her approach for the most effective attack. She had been the kind of beautiful that starts with good bone and is heightened with exquisite, deliberate skill: expensive skin care, the best stylists, the *only* clothes; expertly applied makeup, the catalyst of just the correct piece of jewelry to bring it all together in a collective well-aimed blow. Her appearance had always been her foremost weapon, with her intellect coming next, and the enormous expanse of her wealth backing the first two up with endless, endless ammunition.

And so when she had begun to see the first horrible hints of aging—when she had seen a faint shadow in sidelight under her eye, a place where the skin had begun to *lose its elasticity,* and far, far worse, when she had seen the hint of *wrinkles* in the skin of her throat, the beginning of *crepe*—she had thrown everything she had at the problem to make it go away. Surgery, more expensive skin care, facials. It had worked for a while.

The moment when she first saw the sagging in skin that had been artificially pulled taut by sutures and firmed by chemicals, when she knew it was no longer her battle to win, had been terrible. The knowledge that she had lost the thing she valued most, and that attempting to carry on as if it had not gone would only invite ridicule, was a blow that saw her barred up in her house for a week, ignoring phone calls, pacing through her lovely rooms in black despair.

But she was a Van Dorne, and Van Dornes did not give up: they regrouped. She had spent the latter half of that week intently focused on creating a new Leonora Van Dorne, one that *had* crow's-feet, one whose jawline was *not* that of a twenty-year-old coed, one whose hands were no longer smooth with the taut skin of youth but showed the veins and tendons underneath. This version dared the world to tell her she was old, because old did not matter when you were *brilliantly rich* and also the classier sort of eccentric.

She'd always loved Egyptian art, but now she threw herself wholesale into the study of it. Taught herself Egyptian, slowly and painfully, from the books written by the people who'd worked it out themselves and changed the world. Traveled, collected, wrote articles. Learned to think of people dead for two thousand years as something quite like friends. Became an unofficial-yet-recognized authority. That authority, and the wealth to back it up, had settled into the place where her beauty had once been, as her sword and shield against the world. All the determination that had been her driving force for her entire life had been focused on this one pursuit. It had worked. For decades, it had worked.

But then she'd found the spell. And the spell had *really* worked.

And just like that, those decades of self-creation crumbled under a desperate drive to regain what she had lost, to see again in the mirror the self she still secretly felt she was, coupled with a gnawing, growing need for the rush of energy and euphoria the spell brought; and so she had used it, again and again, so many times she didn't remember them all, each time destroying a small and irreplaceable piece of the past. Each time destroying—she knew now—a piece of a *person*.

How mummies could be, could exist, Van Dorne didn't understand, any more than she understood how magic words could make her young again; but sitting very still in a chair in the room she'd been locked in, she thought now that there wasn't any difference at all.

Helsing—was that really her name, a ludicrous name, and that hair, had she had it cut with garden shears, and whoever had told her she didn't need to wear makeup had been lying—had taken her to see four other mummies after she'd—well. After the first one. All of them had been *people*, in a way Van Dorne didn't see many humans as being. All of them had lived in the world she'd spent so long studying and imagining. They had seen the faces that inspired her own statuettes. They had *been there*. They had been part of it. And now they were here, desperately fragile, needing to be repaired all the time to stay functioning, and—she barely recognized *empathy*, it wasn't an emotion she'd had much cause to explore, but she thought she understood a little of what that might feel like.

She was thinking about this when the first earthquake struck, rolling the chair she sat in a little way across the floor. Van Dorne had been to California more times than she could count, and had been through a few earthquakes in her time; she recognized the sensation at once. Through the locked door she could hear running feet, voices raised in sharp concern, and thought unbidden, *One of them fell, when I—when I did it that time—and the doctor had to rebuild half his side—*

Van Dorne had had a lot of plastic surgery. She knew about rebuilding oneself. *I hope no one broke this time, even if it's not my fault, I hope, I hope, I hope.*

It was only about twenty minutes later that the second earthquake arrived, much worse than the first: she scrambled under the desk as it went on and on and on, sending cracks through the walls and plaster dust pluming down from the ceiling. The window cracked with a single sharp note but did not shatter—

—and the door frame, into which the lock's tongue fitted, first bent and then broke. Van Dorne watched, staring, as the bright metal of the still-engaged lock caught the light, swinging free.

The second earthquake frightened Greta in a way the first had not. They were sitting in the conference room when it hit, trying to come up with something, *anything*, to deal with the current situation vis-à-vis stolen art objects and magic spells, and one of the light fixtures fell and shattered on the table, making her scream a little despite herself. "Get under the table," said Tefnakhte sharply.

"What the fuck is going on?" Cranswell said over the rattle and clatter, eyes wide, as he pushed his chair back and climbed under the table's edge. "What's happening?"

Another musical crash told them the second light fixture

had followed the first, and a moment later the window joined them. Glass scattered; huddled under the table next to Varney, Greta was glad of its protection. The jagged, unsteady motion was making her feel slightly sick. "I don't know," said Tefnakhte, "but it's not *normal—*"

The shaking stopped. She stayed perfectly still for a long moment, waiting to see if it would start up again, but the ground seemed to have settled.

When she did crawl out, the room was noticeably dimmer: too dim, even without the overhead lights, and Greta looked at the shattered window. The sky outside was darkening rapidly; a rising wind stirred her hair.

"It's going to rain," she said, sounding inane even to herself. "It hasn't rained the whole time I've been here—"

"That's not ordinary rain," said Varney behind her, and she'd heard that leaden heaviness in his voice only once or twice before, in very bad moments. She turned to look at him; his pupils had shrunk to tiny dots, the metallic dark grey of the irises like twin mirrors. She could see herself reflected in them, small and distorted but present, and behind her the gathering darkness as the storm approached.

"What do you mean, not ordinary rain?" Cranswell came to join them.

"I can smell it," said Varney, and a moment later so could Greta, faintly: not the wild sweetness of petrichor, but something much sharper, coppery and unmistakable.

She could feel it very clearly when her adrenaline dumped all at once, a cold-hot shock up and down her arms, a dropping weight in her stomach, a distant roaring in her ears. *That's impossible*, she thought. *That doesn't happen, none of this can happen—*

She remembered telling Grisaille *you get a front-row seat to this mess*, and thought now, as the first spatters of blood began to hit the broken window, *apparently so do I.* Her own voice sounded very far away, distant, almost unconcerned, when she said out loud, "Does anyone have any idea what we're supposed to do now?"

"Yes," said Leonora Van Dorne behind them, calm and composed. "I do."

# CHAPTER 15

"What do you mean, *you* do?" Greta demanded at the same time Cranswell asked, "How the hell did you get out?"

Van Dorne looked different, Greta thought. Something close to *serene*, despite the current situation. "That doesn't matter," she said, and turned, walked away into the uncharacteristic dimness of the entry atrium.

Greta followed, making her way through broken glass and furniture, and one glance upward was enough to tell her *why* the atrium was dim: the great central skylight was dark red. It was raining quite hard, the sound of raindrops on glass both absurdly familiar and somehow obscene: thicker, heavier than water. Beyond, in the corridors leading to the exam rooms and patient ward, they could hear rapid voices. The nursing staff must be quite busy, she thought and, past the adrenaline, could manage to summon up some gratitude for their hard work.

The others joined her. Van Dorne was standing under the red skylight, with a peculiar half-smile on her face: after a moment Greta recognized it from God-knew-how-many Egyptian statuettes.

"I know what to do," Van Dorne said again. "It's the only thing, in fact. I caused this. That I did not know I was doing it is not an excuse."

"What are you *talking* about?" Greta said, staring at her. Djehuty hadn't said anything about the magic spell causing rains of blood. "Van Dorne—"

"I can never undo all the damage, I know that. But I *can* return what was stolen, at least to some extent." She brought her hands up, held them like a pair of scales, nearly even. "If not the objects themselves, the historical artifacts, then the force they contained. A kind of balance restored, at least."

An uneasy suspicion was unfolding in Greta's mind. "Don't," she said. "Whatever you're about to do, *don't*—"

"Too late," said Van Dorne, that weirdly serene smile more statue-like than ever, and closed her eyes, rapidly whispering something. She crossed her arms over her torso, like a pharaoh, fists clenched, trembling slightly—and then slammed her palms flat against her chest.

There was a faint shockwave, and the lamps flickered for a moment before coming back up, and by their light they could see a rapid and horrible change overtaking Van Dorne. She seemed to *shrivel*, shrinking inside her clothes, the flesh dwindling from her to leave bone and skin; wrinkles arrowed across her face like cracks across a dam, deepening and deepening;

her closed eyes shrank into their sockets, her hands nothing more than dry and twisted twigs, her silver-gilt hair draining to white and then coming out completely in great clumps, and *still* she stood there—on and on and on, from wizened to *desiccated—*

—and then abruptly it was all over; her clothes crumpled in a heap, empty; a faint bitter dust skirled across the floor, and was gone.

They stood, silent, stunned. The only sound was the hammering of the blood on the skylight overhead.

"What just happened?" said Cranswell eventually, sounding very sick.

"She turned it back," Tefnakhte said, as if he was trying hard to make himself believe it. "She—used it on herself. The draining spell."

"So—wait, does that mean..."

"All the mummies whose grave goods she drained have that back," said Greta. "Right? The—the energy, or whatever it was, that she stole."

"I think so," said Tefnakhte. "I think the patients who've suffered the episodes will be feeling quite a lot better just now."

Greta looked up at the skylight. The sound of the rain had not changed, hammering on the glass with an insistent rhythm, hard as pebbles. The crumpled heap of Van Dorne's empty clothes lay in the center of the atrium floor, an awful kind of anticlimax.

"She seemed to think the—uh—the whatever's happening—was because of her," Cranswell said, staring at the heap. "Like her doing that would fix it all somehow, take things back to normal, so why is it still *raining blood*—"

"There's something else going on," said Greta. "There has to be. More than just her stealing energy—unless it's like the summonings in Paris, what she's done has *damaged* things enough to bring on catastrophe—"

The sound of the rain changed abruptly, and she looked up again. "I think we should move right now, everybody. Get back."

They were all sufficiently on edge that they didn't ask why, simply obeying, and Greta was awfully glad of it: just then the sound from the skylight intensified, followed by a crack, and then a violent crash as the glass failed completely under the onslaught of hail, spilling an unspeakable torrent of glass and blood and knots of ice the size of Greta's fist into the center of the atrium. The coppery stink of blood was immediate and all-encompassing; the downpour didn't seem to be letting up at all.

Raining blood. Greta was a scientist, and had spent quite a lot of time training herself to accept the inexplicable when it was objectively true; her work with mummies relied on her ability to circumvent the *but that can't happen* instinctive response. Here was incontrovertible evidence, splattering on the floor tiles, of something which could not be happening, and Greta did not have to work very hard at all to acknowledge that it *was*.

This was happening. She wondered if the frogs were next, or ought that to be locusts? A lifetime spent in study, and she didn't even know the right order of operations for the ending of the world. Was the red rain falling on London, too, swirling in the gutters and dripping from umbrellas? Had the Thames gone scarlet and slow? Had the earthquakes toppled St. Paul's dome, sent the great hoop of the Eye spinning free, shattered the Shard?

It wouldn't matter, she thought, that Ruthven couldn't come back from Hell; quite soon there would be no Earth for him to go back *to*, and all his beautiful things in his beautiful house quite vanished, along with Dark Heart, along with all the monsters they had rescued from the Paris catacombs, and Emily, and everyone she knew and had ever known: all her friends, Nadezhda and Anna and Hippolyta and the ghoul-chieftain Kree-akh and *everyone*. All of it gone. The understanding unfolded like a poison flower, realization after realization: *I am going to die, and my friends are going to die, and the places I have loved are going to die, and the rest of the whole world is going to die, right in front of me, and I can do nothing at all to save us.*

Greta reached for Varney's hand. If this really was the end of everything, at least she was with him; and there truly was nothing more she could do. All her skill and knowledge and experience was no longer relevant.

It felt strangely freeing, in a way.

Faust had been too busy to ask them questions other than *what medical training do you have*, and since Grisaille had once been a medical student and Ruthven had driven ambulances in the Blitz and had been pressed into service as a de facto scrub nurse, Faust hadn't had to do much on-the-spot instruction. The initial chaos Grisaille had perceived was actually not a disordered mess of activity; after he'd been watching for a little while, he could determine that the groups of nurses and technicians were setting up individual triage stations.

Listening to the chatter around them, and watching the live feed of Samael's makeshift war room on one of the large monitors hung here and there on the walls, Grisaille was putting together a mental image of how the infernal civil service worked. The eight branches were under the oversight of the eight archdemons: infrastructure was Ozymandias's division, Beelzebub ran operations, Mephistopheles was health and sciences, Ahriman communications, Azazel arts and culture, Belial external affairs, Mammon budget and finance, and Fastitocalon—in place of Asmodeus—was in charge of monitoring and evaluation. At the moment all of them seemed to be working together as a remarkably well-organized group, and Grisaille was *aware* of the fact that he found this comforting.

A little while ago the monitors had blanked out and lit up again to show a single shot of Samael, head and shoulders, with a chyron running along the bottom of the screen to reiterate his statements: *Attention all citizens, I am afraid I must declare that as of this moment Hell is at war*, the beautiful voice steady and serious but entirely confident. Grisaille had been impressed despite himself at the Devil's skill with rhetoric;

Samael's speech had not been long, or fear-mongering, or falsely enthusiastic. He had simply told his people that a foreign armed force had invaded Heaven and was causing mass destruction; that Heaven lacked adequate defensive preparation or disaster management capacity; that therefore in order to preserve the vital and necessary balance between Heaven and Hell, he was providing them with reinforcements. He had concluded by offering reassurance: *We are in no immediate danger here. I ask all citizens of Dis and Oldtown and the surrounding areas to remain calm and follow instructions given by the Department of Operations.* A pause, then, *This situation is bad, but not impossible, and I will do everything I can to keep you safe, informed, and secure*—talking directly to the camera, and even Grisaille, interloper and noncitizen, had felt the warm regard of the Devil's attention, a personal assurance, Samael would take care of *him* specifically, it would be all right. Grisaille had been manipulated by experts before, but he was aware of standing in the presence of a master, and minded it less than he thought he should. The situation was, in fact, being handled.

(He was trying not to think about the fact that the situation *being* handled was not something he could really wrap his head around without wanting to gibber and hide under a desk, and that would be more unhelpful than Grisaille felt like being at the moment.)

He and Ruthven had been given scrubs and gloves and caps and gowns. As they sat out of the way, waiting to be needed, Samael's words still on his mind, Grisaille looked at his lover and was struck all over again at just *how* beautiful he was, despite the incongruity; the long eyebrows, black as ink-strokes, the huge silver eyes with their dramatic dark rims, heavy eyelashes; a short, neat, elegant nose, high cheekbones, and a mouth Grisaille had often wished he could draw: the delicacy of it, the sharp Cupid's bow of the upper lip.

"What?" said Ruthven, aware of his scrutiny.

"You," said Grisaille. "Just you."

Ruthven smiled a little. "You know, if this really does turn out to be the end of it all, I don't have much regret. Everything's worth it, to have had this little time with you."

Grisaille was horrified to find his throat closing with the threat of tears, and looked away, but when Ruthven took his hand and squeezed it gently, he squeezed back—wishing he were the sort of person who could *say* the right words, wishing a lot of things all at once. Wishing he'd had more *time*.

"There they go," said a nurse, and he was almost grateful for the excuse to redirect his attention back at one of the wall-mounted monitors: it had returned to a shot of the plaza covered with neatly arranged battalions of demons, disappearing group by group. Ahriman's communications department was maintaining a live feed on the main broadcast channels, which Grisaille wasn't sure was entirely wise; the rest of the population of Hell might not find it comforting to watch the battle play out in real time.

"They still don't have visual of Heaven," someone said. "Must be the connection's damaged on their end—that should be an easy fix, soon's our people get up there—"

Everyone, doctors and nurses and technicians and volunteers alike, was watching intently. The screen split to show Samael's war room as well as the plaza, and Grisaille found himself wishing they had sound—and a moment later wished they *didn't*, because the feed of the plaza flickered to bright static and then to a shot of somewhere he didn't recognize at all, with a blurt of raw noise. The picture shook, smoke drifting across it, but Grisaille could make out what looked like ruined battlements in the background before a demon's face, indistinct behind a full-face breathing mask, suddenly took over the shot. "Sir!" she yelled, before communications cut the feed to the broadcast channel, "it's worse than we thought—there's got to be a couple *thousand* of 'em, with flaming swords—they've knocked down half the citadel, send more—"

That half of the screen went blank abruptly, and then the command center shot cropped itself to show only the table and the demons around it, rather than the big main screen on the wall—*that's a mistake*, thought Grisaille, *that looks like they've got something they want to hide, that's not a good look if you want to maintain people's trust*—and then cut out entirely, going to standby color bars for a few moments. In the hospital, everyone was talking at once, and it took them a little while to *stop* talking even after the screens lit up again with what looked like a perfectly ordinary news show desk, with a conventionally attractive demon behind it.

*Oh my God they have news anchors in Hell*, Grisaille thought absurdly, and was *enormously* glad when, a moment later, the first casualties started to arrive. Watching people pop into existence was even more disturbing than watching them disappear, especially when they had large white wings and were lying limply in someone else's arms, liberally splashed with what looked to Grisaille like gold paint, but at least it was something immediate to focus on rather than existential lunacy.

"Casualty!" the demon carrying the—angel, all right, fine, Grisaille accepted that it was a fucking *angel*—yelled, and a moment later a couple of nurses were there with a gurney, rolling it away to be seen to just as another couple of demons arrived with wounded angels, and another, and another: a steady stream of casualties, all splashed with that strange gold liquid, which Grisaille realized belatedly must be angel blood. The sound of the news show on the monitors was completely blocked out behind the cacophony of screams and groans and nastier noises, coupled with the raised voices of the medical staff.

"Here we go," Ruthven said, catching his attention. "Look sharp, this is only going to get worse," even as somebody rolled a moaning angel on a gurney up to them and immediately disappeared back into the chaos. Grisaille glanced across the gold-soaked heap at him, and just before Ruthven pulled up his mask, he gave Grisaille a smile.

They did a rapid examination: the angel had broken one wing in three places, one due to what looked like a machete cracking the bone—*no, a sword, it's a fucking sword wound,* he thought—and had lacerations all down its side; golden blood was oozing from some of them, but others appeared to be partly cauterized.

Oh, right. *Flaming* sword.

"What's your name?" Ruthven asked the angel gently, running gloved fingers down the other wing's long bones.

"Iofiel," it managed. "Hurts..."

"I know," Ruthven said, "we're going to give you something for that, and get you sorted out, Iofiel. It'll be all right."

"No it won't," the angel moaned, "they're—*angels* and they're *killing everybody in the name of God*, why has He forsaken us—"

"Not everybody," said Grisaille, fetching the morphine. "There's more help on the way." Samael had said God was—what, AWOL? Presumably this was a *different* God, the one from the next universe over, with a somewhat more direct approach to things.

Iofiel looked up at him with blank golden eyes, rimmed with tears. "Who are you?"

"We're volunteers," he said. "That's—it, really."

Ruthven took the syringe Grisaille passed him, and gave the angel its injection, and together they began to clean and stitch the worst of the wounds—the wing could be dealt with later, right now they needed to get this done as quickly as possible so they could move on to the next casualty, and the next, and the next. Very soon Grisaille stopped really seeing the individual angels at all: there were only wounds under his hands, gold-drenched body after gold-drenched body, broken bones and torn flesh, and some of it he thought could be mended and some of it could not, and he didn't have room to *think* about that right now: he was back in Ingolstadt, in anatomy class, and not surprised at all that angels should have muscle and bone and blood vessels just like humans; he might never be surprised again—

"—What's wrong?" said Ruthven, not to him, and Grisaille did look up from the wound he was cleaning, and realized that the background noise had changed: not just the cries of the ruined angels, but a steady chorus of coughing and sneezing underneath it, as if some irritant gas had been released into the vicinity.

He straightened up, looking around, and stared. Almost every demon, doctors and nurses and technicians alike, seemed to be in some level of distress: puffy-faced, their eyes streaming, some of them sneezing and coughing helplessly into their elbows, as if—

"Oh, bloody hell," said Faust over the noise, shouldering his way through the ward. He, too, was liberally splashed with golden blood, his surgical gown covered with it, gloved hands solid gold to the elbow. "Uphir, Varamas, Decarabia, you're done, get out of here, go mainline antihistamine until you can breathe again, don't argue with me. Kharath, Muphas, Nyctur, Jopharel, take a break. Someone hack the building's emergency protection system and get the smoke fans turned on to ventilate this floor. *Now*, people." He clapped his hands.

"What's going on?" Grisaille asked as the three worst-affected demons were helped away by colleagues and the activity of triage began to resume. Faust sighed.

"Demons are allergic to angels," he said. "It's a bloody nuisance, is what it is, but some of them are worse than others and I don't have enough pairs of hands to spare, they'll just have to do their best, and the smoke-evac fans will help a bit."

Grisaille and Ruthven looked at each other. "You need—doctors who *aren't* demons," Ruthven said.

"Yes, and where d'you think I'm going to find 'em in the middle of a damn war?"

"I know where you can get at least three," said Ruthven. "Right now. Page Fastitocalon and tell him to get hold of Greta Helsing and her clinic staff."

Faust stared at him. And then, without a word, turned on his heel and set off toward his office at the other end of the ward, moving *fast* for a stocky, middle-aged man.

They had retreated to the rock-cut chambers—not because of the hail, or the rain, as both of them had passed off within half an hour of Van Dorne's awful exit, but because the clearing night sky had been *wrong.* Instead of the vast scatter of diamonds she'd grown used to seeing overhead, the sky had been empty pure black from edge to edge, save only one point of light that Greta could not look at without wanting to scream. She couldn't identify what it was about the single star that was so terrible, but all of them had felt it: being anywhere its light could reach was unspeakable, having that *wrong* illumination touch their skin was not to be borne: a single glaring eye in the vault of heaven.

All of the mummies were out of bed. Antjau, still wheezy but much better, and Maanakhtef, limping slightly on his repaired foot, and Nesperennub with his sterilized and pristine wrappings; Bameket, Nefrina, Mayet. Tefnakhte was wearing all his jewelry again. Some of the nurses were crying, others praying in a constant muttering undertone, rocking back and forth with rosaries dangling from their folded hands. Two of them had fled in the spa's livery car, and Greta had no idea if they'd managed to make it down to the city, and if so, what they'd found there. She wondered vaguely what Ed Kamal was doing in Cairo, if that terrible star was looking down at him, too, shining its poisoned light over bloodstained sand dunes. If he was already gone.

She and Varney and Cranswell were sitting together, passing a bottle of whiskey back and forth. Greta's hand was twined with Varney's; neither of them seemed to notice. Every now and then one of them would draw breath as if to speak, and then stop, and exhale: there was simply nothing more to say.

When the voice came in her head, it felt very far away, dim and faint, as if behind a wall of some deadening insulation, and it took Greta a little while to realize something was calling her name, and a little longer to care.

*Go away*, she thought at the voice. *Leave me alone.*

*Greta, listen to me!* It was familiar, somewhere beyond the numbness. It was a voice she knew. *Greta Helena Magdelena Helsing, will you bloody well pay attention?*

*Go away*, she said again. *I don't want you. I don't want anything.*

*This isn't about you!* the voice shouted, louder now, the volume knob turning up inside her head. *Have your hopeless despair fit later, if there's a later to have it in, you are needed NOW!*

Greta blinked. *Fass?* she asked.

*Who else would it be? Faust needs your help down here right now, you and Anna and Nadezhda, we've got wounded angels needing treatment and half the bloody hospital staff is incapacitated, stop wallowing and do your job.*

*My job*, she said slowly. She had thought there would simply not be anything left for her to do, that she was over, that her usefulness on the skin of the world was a thing past and completed and done with, like the rest of her, and it had felt freeing; this, now, was like being wrenched back to life. Pulled from some dim endless lake and pounded, slippery and shivering, back to life and breath and function. *My job.*

*I'm sending someone up there to fetch you*, Fastitocalon said. *Call the others. Tell them to expect us.*

Just like that, she was alone again inside her head. Greta sat up slowly. Beside her, Varney and Cranswell stirred.

"I think it's not over yet," she said. "I think there's—something left to do."

"Like what?" Cranswell asked.

"Fass says they need me in Hell. In the hospital. For—I don't know what's going on, he said something about wounded angels—"

"*Angels?*" said Varney. "In Hell?"

"I don't know," said Greta. "But . . . I have to go."

She fished out her phone, which still—improbably—had over half its battery left (when had she had a chance to plug it in, what day was it, how long had this been going on?) and dialed Nadezhda in London. Under the dregs of stirring adrenaline she had begun to feel something else, a small and terrible bloom of hope, but as the ringing went on and on, it began to wilt—

"Greta?" said the voice on the other end, her friend's voice but nothing like her friend: she'd never thought Nadezhda Serenskaya could sound so small and frightened. "Greta, is that you, is—where are you?"

"Still in France for now," she said. "Dez, are you even slightly close to okay?"

"No," said Nadezhda, "but—is—did it . . . rain there, too?"

"Yes," she said. "Is that star—"

"*Yes*," said Nadezhda. "We're in the downstairs bathroom, it's the only room that hasn't got a window other than the cellar, and the cellar's flooded—God, that light touched me and I wanted to die, Greta—"

"I know. It's awful. But I need your help," she said. "You and Anna. Right away. Don't ask questions I can't answer, but we're all three of us needed to help out at a—field hospital."

"What field? What—which war?"

"Possibly the last one," said Greta. "Stay there, all right? I'll come for you."

"*How?*" Nadezhda almost wailed.

"How's not a useful question," Greta said. "Do you trust me?"

"...Yes," said the witch, sounding heartbreakingly tired.

"Then trust me," said Greta, and hung up. She slipped the phone into her pocket and went to talk to Sister Brigitte, who had managed to get most of her remaining staff to calm down a little; there was no more weeping, at least, although the constant muttering of prayer had not ceased.

"There's no good way to say this," she said. "I have to leave. I—I'm needed elsewhere."

Brigitte just nodded. "I am afraid none of us can come with you."

"I know," said Greta, "and I would never ask that of you. Thank you so much, for all your work, throughout all of this"—she couldn't find a word to encompass everything they'd gone through in the past few days—"throughout. It's been a pleasure working with you and your staff."

"Likewise, Doctor," said Brigitte, and held out her slim dark hand exactly as she had when Greta arrived, unsure of herself and so excited to be there. "You are not as skilled as Dr. Kamal led us to believe. You are a great deal more."

Greta felt herself blush, which was faintly surprising: she hadn't thought she retained sufficient emotional capital. "Thank you," she said, and shook her hand firmly. "That means a lot."

Brigitte nodded again. "If you are needed, then go. We are—as well as we can be here, and my staff and I are capable of managing the patients." She did not add, *Not that we'll need to for very long*; she didn't have to.

"Yes," said Greta quietly, and turned away without saying

good-bye, certain she would never see Sister Brigitte again. The others were waiting for her; they got up as she arrived.

"Varney, Cranswell," she said, "I don't know what's going to happen next—"

"We're going with you, of course," said Cranswell. The level in the whiskey bottle had substantially declined. "Fuck sitting around here waiting for locusts, or boils, or whatever's next."

"And to borrow a phrase, fuck *not being with you*," said Varney, enunciating with exquisite clarity. He so seldom cursed that it was always effective, and Greta wrapped her arms around him and buried her face in his chest and *clung*.

She didn't let go even when the demon Fass had sent appeared to flip them; in fact, Cranswell simply wrapped *his* arms around the both of them, and it was noticeably less disorienting to be translocated in close contact with other people. Once the fizzing sparkles around the edges of her vision had died away, she found herself in the foyer of what could have been any high-end hospital on Earth; one curved wall was entirely window, looking out over a fantastical landscape she had only heard described, and she realized they must be inside one of the eight towers of Dis. Somewhere beyond all the emotional exhaustion of the past forty-eight hours, Greta was conscious of a distant but vast excitement.

She unwrapped herself from Varney and Cranswell, looking around. A few moments later another group of people popped into existence: Nadezhda, very white, the mass of her hair for once subdued in a tight knot, and Anna, short and sturdy and also pale enough for the spray of freckles to be visible over her cheeks—and Hippolyta, clinging to Nadezhda's hand and looking as if she was about to be sick.

A moment later Greta was hugging her friend as tightly as she dared. "Dez," she said, "Dez, thank you for coming, it's—I'll explain everything later. Come on, we have to find Dr. Faust—"

"This is Hell?" Nadezhda asked, her eyes still too wide.

"Nor are we out of it," said another voice, and they all turned to see a stocky man in a surgical gown liberally spattered with what looked like gold paint. The woodcuts didn't really do him justice. "Johann Faust. You're Helsing?"

"I'm Helsing," said Greta. "This is Nadezhda Serenskaya, she's a witch, helps run my clinic, and Anna Volkov, mostly human and part rusalka, who's my nurse practitioner."

"Come with me," said Dr. Faust, turning on his heel. "Your friends can wait somewhere comfortable, I'll get someone to see to them, but I need all three of you to scrub in right away. How much did Fastitocalon tell you?"

They were hurrying to keep up as he led them back through swinging doors into what looked like any active trauma center in any major hospital Greta had ever seen, except for the—enormous white wings attached to most of the visible patients, or the gold paint splattered everywhere. "Nothing at all," she said. "Only that you needed backup."

"Short version: War in Heaven with a bunch of invading angels, our lot's getting absolutely destroyed, Sam's sent demons up to do a bit of smiting back, they're evacking casualties down here for emergency treatment, which is a hell of a strain on our resources purely for numbers' sake, but I'm also dealing with the compounding factor of most of my staff being extremely allergic to angels and thus not a lot of use. We've started to get wounded demons as well, but the majority of the casualties are angelic in origin."

"Ah," said Greta. He had led them back to a scrub station and was removing his soiled gown; Greta took off her somewhat bedraggled white coat as well. She looked down at the ring on her third finger, remembering how it had *expanded* the last time she'd had to take it off to scrub, and shrunk to fit again as soon as she put it back on; this time was no different, the metal heavy and blood-warm, feeling almost alive.

She slipped it into her pocket and began washing her hands and forearms, while Faust did the same. Beside her, Anna and Nadezhda, also scrubbing, were muttering to each other in Russian. "You really want me to do emergency surgery?" Greta said to Faust. "I have to say it's been a long time since I did my surgical rotation; mostly what I handle is minor outpatient stuff."

"I don't care, you're apparently basically competent and not violently allergic to angel dander; that's the best I can hope for right now," said Faust. "I have a couple of vampires doing triage and patching up the simpler cases, and what's left of my staff is handling the rest, but I can't do all the surgery myself and some of this trauma's extensive. It's all sharp-force trauma, stab and slash, nobody up there is using projectiles:

they're just hacking at each other with swords from what I can make out. Gloves and gowns," he added to an assistant, who helped the four of them get ready.

"Doctor?" asked Anna, apparently over the initial shock of the situation. "I'm not a surgeon, I'm a nurse practitioner, I'm not qualified—"

"Do the best you can," said Faust. "That's all I can ask. We need all the help we can get."

# CHAPTER 16

Varney watched as Faust led the women away, past the swinging doors into the noise and clatter and chaos beyond, and thought he might have some idea what the mummies had felt like when Van Dorne did her little trick: a kind of awful drawing *strengthless* feeling, a heaviness in his chest threatening to pull him off balance, shot through with a leaden certainty that he would never see Greta Helsing again.

*At least I gave her the ring*, he thought, not really aware that he was swaying. *At least I did that much.*

"—Varney?" someone was saying, and there was a hand on his arm. He opened his eyes, not having been aware of closing them, and found Cranswell and the blonde woman staring at him. What the hell was her *name*, it was something entirely improbable for an American, he couldn't remember—

"Varney," Cranswell said again, "you should sit down."

"I'm fine," he said, straightening up, despite the awful weight in his chest.

"You're not even close to fine," said the woman. "Fuck if I am, either, but you look awful. You went *grey.*"

Varney blinked at her. "...Decay of the system," he said vaguely. "I want renovating."

"What you want is some goddamn blood," said the woman. "And I want a lot of scotch. I'm betting you do, too, August."

"Yeah," said Cranswell, without taking his hand off Varney's arm. It felt strange, that touch. Strange, but not unwelcome. "Yeah, I was just getting started topside, with the fucking Star Wormwood and all."

"Hey!" the woman called to a passing demon. "You, with the cool horns, where's the nearest bar that serves virgin blood and single-malt?"

"What, *together*?" said the demon, who looked entirely nonplussed at being addressed by a random living human. It also clearly had places to be in a hurry, and was carrying a clipboard. "*Eww.* You want Grakkar's place, first floor, Tower Two," and it went on its way.

"There, see? You just have to ask the locals," she said. "Lean on me."

Varney was about to insist that he was absolutely *fine* and could walk unaided when some of the color washed out of the world for a few moments, dizzying. A sturdy shoulder inserted itself under his arm, and he had to admit he was grateful for it. "When'd you last have anyone to drink?" she asked as they walked to the elevator bank, Cranswell on his other side.

"I can't remember," he said. "I did go down to Marseille but—couldn't find anyone suitable, at least not right away, and I didn't want to leave Greta for very long, and how is it that you know so much about vampyres, miss?" All he really knew about her was that she was with Nadezhda Serenskaya and had been working at the clinic.

"Oh, I like reading the classics," she said, and grinned when Varney groaned.

Grakkar's turned out to be the equivalent of a semi-classy local bar, not very crowded—but the patrons who *were* there had their collective attention on the three TVs mounted around the room. The three of them got stares as they walked in, but not for long: they weren't as interesting as whatever was on.

Varney subsided gratefully into a booth, rather than trying to find somewhere at the bar itself, and closed his eyes. "Thanks," he said in general. "I wonder if this place takes credit cards."

"We'll have to find out," said the woman, whose name he absolutely could not ask at this point—was it Athena or something?—"I'll get the first round in."

Varney just nodded, eyes shut. He really had pushed it too far, in the last several days: he hadn't felt like this in centuries, the kind of exhausted and weak where standing up straight was an achievement. Nor was he actually expecting the place to have virgin blood on tap, so that when the heated glass was set down before him and the scent hit him like a blow, arousing *desperate* thirst, he opened his eyes and stared at it in honest puzzlement.

Dark red, real, warmed to living blood-heat, *the real thing*—he could smell it, there was a definite difference with virgin blood, this was the thing itself, and Varney took the glass in both hands and downed its contents in three huge swallows. It went down like silk and spread gorgeous, impossible warmth through his whole body, driving back the heaviness, even lessening the general despair a little. It took him a moment or two to remember his companions, and his manners, and—

"Could I have some more," he said, and the woman and Cranswell, across from him in the booth, grinned at one another.

"Coming right up," she said. "I suspect, actually, you can get a glass of pretty much *anything* in this place if you ask real nicely, including liquid nitrogen or motor oil," and returned to the bar to order him another.

"*Are* you okay?" Cranswell asked, hands around his own glass. "You look way better, but—"

"I will be," said Varney. "Thank you. So much."

"What are friends for," said Cranswell, "and also this is way better than sitting around in some godawful—uh, excuse me, terrible waiting room while everybody else plays *M*A*S*H: Paradise Lost.*"

The woman came back—*Hippolyta*, his mind finally supplied, all his thoughts less sluggish now with proper blood inside him—and set down a second glass. Varney sipped at this one, savoring it, warming from the inside out. "Thank you," he said. "What—*is* that they're watching on the television?"

"Looks like cable news to me," said Cranswell. "HNN."

In fact, it was *ENN*, according to the chyron at the bottom of the screen. Erebus News Network. Varney directed his attention more closely, and stared at the words scrolling across the chyron. *Active combat in Heaven continues as casualties mount on both sides...still no clear explanation for the initial invasion...preliminary modeling suggests interreality rift...*

"Um," said Cranswell. "Shit. Remember Djehuty being all, like, 'this magic is from some other universe'?"

"Was the spell trying to let something *in*?" Varney asked, staring at the screen. "Is that what it was for?"

"What are you guys talking about?" said Hippolyta. "What spell?"

"...Okay," said Cranswell, "this is gonna be kind of a long story."

"You're *sure* you want me doing this?" Greta asked, standing by the OR table. Faust paused in the doorway.

"You going to keep asking stupid questions?" he said.

"Look, I've never *done* trauma surgery," she said, "I sew up cuts and set bones, the worst thing I've done in months was an emergency appendectomy on a were-something, and that was only because they refused to listen to their boyfriend and didn't come in until the thing was ready to pop—"

"One of your vamp friends told me you dealt with a punctured lung in the middle of a battle," said Faust. "I suggest you shut up and get on with it. In here," he added, moving aside for aides to roll a gurney in, and was gone.

*Fuck*, thought Greta. "Okay," she said out loud to the people shifting her winged patient to the table. The angel was unconscious, covered in gold—*blood, that's angel blood*, she made herself think—and they'd already intubated. Not good. Neither were the monitor readouts on the screens once the leads were applied. "Talk to me. What do we have?"

"Single sharp-force injury to the left chest, hard enough to crush," said one of the aides, a demon who was clearly having some difficulty with the allergen but still functional. "Dyspneic on arrival, weak pulse, improved a lot once we intubated. Looks like a blow from a bladed weapon, multiple depressed rib fractures, left-side hemothorax. The right wing's broken in three places, but—"

"Never mind the wing for now, as long as it's not bleeding," said Greta. "Do we have imaging? Someone get me ultrasound, and—oh, hell, what do you do for blood transfusions for these poor bastards, you can't have angel blood lying around—"

"Dr. Faust's come up with something," said one of the aides hurriedly. "It's—it's actually lake water run through a bunch of filtration and processed in the MRI scanner to adjust its pneumic signature—it's better than nothing—"

"Get me at least three units," Greta said, cutting him off. "I want him closer to hemodynamically stable. Start running the replacement stuff into him right away—thanks—" She took the ultrasound wand somebody handed her, ran it over the angel's wounded side, looking at the black-and-white display screen on the machine they'd rolled over. It wasn't possible to tell what kind of bleed was causing the hemothorax, not on ultrasound, but the fact that the angel wasn't already dead suggested it wasn't arterial. "Okay. I want that hemothorax relieved, give me a 14-gauge." She held out her hand, not looking away from the damaged chest wall, and was faintly gratified when the capped needle and syringe were placed into her palm almost at once.

This she knew how to do, but hadn't done in years: easing the needle in over the rib, pulling back on the plunger until that incredibly strange golden blood appeared; threading the cath down over the needle, watching the gold flow through the tube, letting the blood out from the pleural space, allowing the angel's lung to reinflate. The numbers on the monitors changed almost immediately once she'd let off most of the blood, and Greta sighed. Good. He'd need more work to repair the wing, but at least he'd probably live long enough to *get* it.

"Okay," she said. "Keep an eye on him, have someone sort out that wing, keep him stable, he'll probably do. Who's next?"

It was a little impressive just how quickly they were able to wheel one patient out and the next one in. Greta stood up straighter as they brought her another wrecked angel.

"Oblique fracture, right femur, internal bleeding," said the orderly without her having to ask, as they transferred the angel to her table. It was obvious that a sharp end of bone had nicked some serious blood vessels; one thigh was swollen, a deep cut across it gaping open with the internal pressure. They'd put a tourniquet high on the leg, as high as possible, which was why the angel was here instead of wherever they were using for a morgue, and this one was semiconscious, making little choked sounds of pain.

"I need one of you to be my anesthetist," she said. "Who's most qualified?" The nurses and the aides and the volunteers all looked the same, gold-splattered scrubs and gowns, masks and caps. One of them came forward.

"I'm a nurse," he said, "not an anesthetist, but I might be the best you've got, Doctor—"

"Good. Get going. I want Versed, and then IV propofol, whatever you've got that pretends to be propofol, and oxygen, and watch his sats. If you can hear me," she added to the angel, "I know it hurts, we're going to fix that, and sort out your leg: you're safe here, you're among friends."

"Who...?" it managed.

"I'm a doctor," she said, and for a moment felt as if she might know what it was like to be only what she was, a thing that fixed, not a person with a tiresome personal life: a thing that repaired, the way some of the mummies were Things That Coded. "I'm here to help."

The nurse had fetched the appropriate drugs and was beginning to inject them into the angel's IV, and it gave a little sigh and closed its eyes again; she watched on the monitors, but the vitals were still steady, if less than great.

"Okay," she said, "let's get on with it," and thought absurdly, *Let's fix a femur*, and reached out for a pair of forceps already clamped on a pad of gauze soaked with topical antiseptic. Now that she'd gotten somewhat settled, she was getting used to reaching out a hand and having someone put the tool in it, and *that* was a kind of luxury she'd seldom had before—except at Oasis Natrun—no, she wasn't going to think about that. At all.

She was going to bloody well get on with it. Like Faust had said. Do the job that is in front of you, and do it to the best of your ability, and do it until you can't do it anymore, and then—get out of the way.

Nobody was paying any attention to Zophiel.

Once the host of Heaven had marched off, flaming swords in hand, the rest of the inhabitants had gone into a sort of jubilation, singing and playing their harps and praying and—not paying any attention to Zophiel. He slipped past a knot of angels on their knees and made his way through the palace to find Amitiel still standing on the other balcony: standing with his wings folded tightly and his arms wrapped around himself. Zophiel noticed with a kind of horror that his halo was tilted ever so slightly out of true.

"Why don't I feel joy?" Amitiel asked, looking up at him with blank golden eyes. "Everybody else is—triumphant?"

"I don't know," said Zophiel, and—because no one was paying attention—wrapped his arms and his wings around Amitiel and held him close. *That* was the only thing that felt completely right, the only thing that had seemed to fit, ever since their return.

"They're killing the other angels, aren't they," Amitiel said into his shoulder. "On the other side."

"They're killing *false* angels," said Zophiel, but even he didn't sound as if he was entirely sure. "It's all right to kill false angels, they're profane."

"What do they look like?"

"I don't know," said Zophiel. "I've never thought about it."

"The demons looked like—people," Amitiel said. "On the wrong Earth."

"Do you—" He stopped, stroking Amitiel's curls. "Would it help if we went to see the battle?"

"Can we do that? Are we allowed?"

"I don't know," he said again. "Let's find out."

Varney had moved on to whiskey after the second dose of blood. Cranswell watched him watching the TV, the picture reflected in his eyes, and wondered if they'd feel it when the world actually got around to ending: would it hurt?

The ENN anchor was looking somewhat exhausted, but their hairstyle was pristine; Cranswell thought that was a function of being a news anchor: you developed natural resources of hairspray. He could remember the morning after the Gladius Sancti thing, sitting in the Savoy, watching a different but practically interchangeable anchor blithering about the state of the city on a different but practically interchangeable TV.

Beside him, Hippolyta was on her third large scotch, which didn't seem to be having much of an effect. "I guess there's one good thing about all this," she said. "You guys don't have to figure out how to return that stone tablet thing you stole."

"I hadn't thought of that," Cranswell said. "You've got a

point, though. Also we don't have to explain about Van Dorne vanishing, on account of everyone else is gonna vanish, too."

"What do you think is happening up there?"

"On Earth? No fucking clue," he said. "I remember there's supposed to be locusts and boils and darkness and—wait, no, that's the plagues, isn't it?"

"They're practically the same," said Varney without looking away from the TV. The chyron now read, *Nacreous Gates secured in joint advance between infernal and divine troops, active combat continues with mounting casualties.* "John of Patmos, while a thoroughly creative thinker, was undoubtedly inspired by earlier works."

"Figures you'd know it," said Hippolyta.

"He did get the order wrong," Varney said. "Unless the seven seals and the horsemen and so on happened somewhere else. In Revelation, it goes seals, horsemen, trumpets, and the bloody rain and hail are supposed to have fire mixed in with them. And a mountain is hurled into the sea, and *then* we get Star Wormwood. Clearly whatever runs this version of reality hasn't done its reading."

"We should complain," said Cranswell. "Send a sharp letter."

" 'I want my expectations managed with more integrity,' " Varney said, and took a sip of his drink. "No, that's Edmund; he writes the sharp letters. Wrote, I mean. I suppose it's a mercy that the Walkie Talkie building is getting destroyed along with the rest of it; he won't have to complain to the *Times* about dreadful architecture any longer."

"What do you suppose he's doing?" Cranswell asked. "Ruthven, I mean. And Grisaille. They're down here, too, right?"

"Probably same as us," said Hippolyta, and drained her glass. "If they have any sense at all, I mean. Time for another round."

At some point, Greta had lost count of how many casualties she'd seen: it all turned into body after body to be repaired, golden blood vessel after golden blood vessel to be clamped, bone after bone to be set, endless sutures: there had never been a time when she *hadn't* been covered in golden blood, when she hadn't had open wounds under her hands, when she hadn't been barking out orders: all the world had shrunk to the operating table in front of her, the angel to be fixed before she could get to the next one in line. Briefly, near the beginning, she'd thought of Nadezhda and Anna in the other ORs, wondering how they were holding up, but she simply hadn't had the attention to spare for following that train of thought for very long.

They kept running out of blood replacement and someone was busy flipping back and forth from the imaging scanner, which was running at full power, a twenty-desmarais mirabilic field reversing polarity six times a second, turning the lake water into a pneumic-neutral substance the angels' bodies wouldn't reject that still carried a healing charge. Someone else was busy spinning suture thread out of raw firmament and cycling the autoclave over and over to sterilize tray after tray of instruments.

She didn't know how long she had been working, and it did not matter, except that she began at some point to lose her voice, and that was distantly annoying; all she was really aware of was the *line* of broken angels, waiting for her, waiting for Dez or Anna or Faust, waiting for help, and the one under her hands was trying very hard to die and she was trying very hard not to let it and someone touched her shoulder, someone a long way away said her name, said, *Greta, stop, they're dying too fast, there's too many, the ones waiting in line are already dead, we've done all we can do—*

"Fuck you," Greta snarled, "I am not giving up," and the monitor squealed its awful single note and *no, fuck this, fuck everything,* the chest was already open and she had never held a hot and lifeless heart between her hands before but she was doing it now, pressing and releasing, pressing and releasing, *oh, beat for me, you stupid thing, beat, beat, beat, beat, beat,* and over it all that blank idiot squeal, like a skewer going through her skull from ear to ear—

"Greta," whoever it was said again. "Greta, it's over."

That squeal. It wasn't the sound of desperation. It was the sound of despair.

"I know," she said, barely audible, and her hands inside the angel's chest went still.

In Samael's command center, the blue-glowing projection of the rift had changed in real time, reflecting the transformation overtaking it; the scale had had to change, zooming out farther and farther to be able to show the whole thing as it grew. On the main screen the video feed was half-obscured with blood, showing several crumpled bodies under a blanket of dust; it shook from time to time. All of the demons watching had fallen silent.

In the world above, the boiling seas hammered what was left of the coastline with hundred-foot waves; the cities burned, the deserts turned to glass and cracked wide open, every volcano on Earth—even those that had been extinct for thousands of years—erupted at the same time; from the International Space Station, astronauts and cosmonauts alike watched in silent horror as the blue of the planet's oceans turned a deep and terrible red. Vast clouds of smoke blotted out the view of continents and islands. The awful light of the single remaining star crawled on their skin. Nuclear stockpiles went off one by one, scything away the remains of half the planet's population in a series of unthinkable blasts. The ocean's burden of shipwrecks rose to the surface, crewed by dead men, sailing before poisoned wind.

In Heaven, Amitiel and Zophiel peered through the shifting, changing, shimmering discontinuity that was the rift, into a smoky, dusty, reeking *strangeness*: through the smoke they could pick out what looked like ruined battlements, heaps of—

"Those *are* angels," said Amitiel softly. "Dead ones."

Before Zophiel could stop him, he closed his eyes and stepped *through* the rift, into the other world. Zophiel said something under his breath that he absolutely should not have known how to pronounce, took a deep breath, and stepped through to follow him.

The smell hit him at once, an awful combination of burning

and blood—and yet somehow being here felt familiar, despite everything, even without the constant comfort of *their* God's attention. He thought dimly that they had lived here for so long, on this world's Earth, that they had grown used to it; was trying not to think that it felt more like *home* than their own Heaven.

Amitiel was walking slowly toward the pile of bodies. Golden ichor was everywhere, splashed on the ground, soaking the angels' robes, staining the white feathers of their wings.

"Don't," said Zophiel. Amitiel ignored him, reached down to touch the nearest body.

"It's still warm," he said wonderingly. "I think it's alive—"

"*Don't,*" Zophiel said, too late: he'd already bent to roll the angel onto its back.

The golden eyes stared sightlessly past Amitiel. The gold-clotted insides slithered out of the gaping wound from neck to abdomen with a slick *plop* Zophiel could have done without, and he was only just in time to catch Amitiel before he fell, holding him while he was helplessly, violently sick.

"Is it one of ours?" he managed when it was over. "Zophiel, is it one of ours or theirs?"

Zophiel let go of him long enough to reach out gingerly and touch the angel's wing. It felt—exactly like an angel's wing should feel.

"I don't know," he said slowly, numbly. "Amitiel... I can't *tell.*"

* * *

In Grakkar's, every pair of eyes was fixed on the television screens, watching frozen as the numbers of dead grew higher and higher. Every pair but one.

Sir Francis Varney looked into the depths of his glass, swirled the amber liquid, looked *through* it and through time. All the mobs, all the desperate flights through the darkened countryside, all the gasping fainting damsels, the death and turning of Clara Crofton, the lies and the thievery and the slow sinking decay, dying over and over, gunshot after gunshot, breathing his last in a country inn's bedroom, waking to the touch of moonlight; all of the things he had done, and done to others, and had done to him, over the centuries. It had been a very long, and very strange, life; and in it there had been nothing close to sustained pleasure, nothing close to joy, until the very end. Until he'd woken from agonized fever-dreams to find a human bending over him with gentle hands.

He'd snapped at her, raw instinct, and wanted at once to sink into the floor and disappear, and she had not run away; had not run away at all, was—still *not running*, even now.

Varney had said it to her, more than once, in the beginning: what he was could never be forgiven for its very nature, he was a damned and unholy creature doomed to eternity outside the sight of God forevermore. He had long ago—so long ago—given up all hope of absolution, turned his face away from forgiveness.

*Forever is not long at all*, he thought now, and drained the glass. He'd told the others about Revelation a little while ago, and the language of that book still resonated in his mind; brought with it other language, other words, graven so deep in memory that even now they came back to him, so many centuries after he had lost the privilege of pronouncing them and hoping to be heard. He thought of Tefnakhte, back in the world, asking for help in a language dead for thousands of years, begging a god for answers that did not exist, asking the questions anyway.

There was nothing else to do in all the world, all that was left of it. No other options, no more last chances, no one left to appeal to, except one.

*I can't do this*, he thought. *I've forgotten how. Even if I could, and somehow avoided being struck by righteous thunderbolts for daring to try, nothing would deign to hear me.*

And then, with a mental sigh: *One can always do what one must.*

Sir Francis Varney brought his hands together, closed his eyes, and began to pray: not for absolution, not for forgiveness, but simply for *help*, at the end of all things.

The citadel of Heaven was breached; white fire roared from a hundred jewel-framed windows, crazed and cracked the blocks of solid ruby that crowned the battlements where they had not been knocked down to heaps of choking rubble. Fighting still went on within the citadel itself, shouts and cries and the clang of sword on sword, the duller thump of metal into flesh. In the space between the Nacreous Gates—sixty feet tall and made of solid pearl—and the entry into the citadel itself, bodies were heaped up in untidy piles: white and gold, red and black, angel and demon alike. The agate cobblestones were slick and sticky with their mingled blood. Crushed-jewel dust and acrid smoke stung the eyes and throat.

Amitiel and Zophiel wandered through the ruins, hand in hand, golden eyes blank. Both were covered in dust, the hems of their once-white robes a muddy gold-and-scarlet mess.

"The towers are gone," Amitiel said quietly, looking up at where the three great central towers of the citadel should have been, gleaming with jewels, their white and gold banners proud and magnificent. The great golden bell that should have hung at the very top of the central tower would never sing again. "How did they bring down the towers?"

"I don't know," said Zophiel. "I—it was never my thought to wonder how the Archangel Michael achieved his victories. I just knew he did, and that it was righteous."

Amitiel started walking again, toward the crumbled wreckage of the citadel gateway, and drew Zophiel with him. Both of them had been sick now, more than once, and the awful taste of sour ambrosia and nectar coated the inside of Zophiel's throat. He had never experienced *despair*: never understood the concept, even, but as Amitiel led him inexorably through the streets of the citadel, past fires, past the rubble of ruined stone and ruined bodies, toward the faint but growing sound of battle—he thought perhaps he might be getting some idea.

* * *

Hell: Samael's command center. The last of the live video feeds had gone to blind idiot static; all they had was audio, and none of that was anything they wished to hear.

Fastitocalon came around the table to Samael, put a hand on his shoulder. The Devil was sitting halfway down the long pearl table, watching the screens with a completely expressionless face: outside, it was raining steadily, a soft grey endless rain, on and on, like tears.

"'Why,'" Fastitocalon said softly, "'all our ranks are broke.'"

Samael looked up at him, and the blank red eyes turned their ordinary butterfly-blue. "'The devil take order now,'" he said with the hint of a smile, and covered Fastitocalon's hand with his own. "We tried, Fass. We tried. That has to matter a little, doesn't it, in the end?"

"I'm glad I was here. If it has to be over—well, I'm *tired*, Sam, I've been tired since Paris, I don't know how much longer I would have been useful to you, but—I'm glad I *could* at all."

Samael sighed. "So am I. I wish I had acted sooner. None of my people could have worked harder, done more; this isn't on them."

"It's not on anyone, really," said Fastitocalon. "Except perhaps Asmodeus and his inability to do his job. And don't say you should have noticed that; so should we all."

"'Upon the king,'" Samael said with a wry, crooked smile, "'let us our lives, our debts, our over-careful wives, our children, and our sins lay on the king; we must bear all,' as well you know, and don't chop logic with me in the middle of the bloody eschaton."

Fastitocalon squeezed his shoulder. "I'm glad I was here," he said again, more softly, and outside the grey curtains of rain lightened a little, for a while.

In Tower Three, there was no silence; the chaotic combination of monitor tones and the cries of wounded creatures filled the air as comprehensively as the reek of blood and other, more unpleasant things. They had stopped receiving casualties some time ago. Either there were no more wounded to bring down for treatment, or there was no one left to bring them.

At one end of the bloodstained ward sat five people, very still, with the blank stares of the traumatically exhausted. The worst of the blood had come off with their disposable gowns, but some of it had soaked through to what they'd been wearing nonetheless.

Grisaille sat with his hand in Ruthven's, their fingers laced together. Nadezhda, Anna, and Greta shared a couch. None of them spoke. None of them made a sound at all, despite the slow and continuous flow of tears down their faces.

Greta was somewhere a very long way away, being slowly crushed between two unyielding objects, squeezing her chest; she could not breathe and did not care, because nothing mattered at all anymore: nothing was left to matter, everything was *over.*

*I wish Varney was here*, she thought vaguely, at a distance. *That does matter, a little, at the end of it.*

* * *

And in Grakkar's the bartender was no longer bothering to charge for drinks. Many of the demons who had been here when it began were already passed out, beyond the reach of terror or anticipation; most of the others were on their way. Beside Varney, Cranswell had put his head down on the table. The woman Hippolyta was snoring faintly.

Varney paid no attention to any of them, or to the fact that the TV news anchor had finally been replaced with a screen that said STAND BY. He was lost inside a place in his own head he had not visited for centuries, a place he had long thought walled up and locked away, completely inaccessible; but it had been there waiting for him as if expecting his return: dark, and musty, and smelling of lilies and damp stone.

At first it had been just reciting the words, sunk into his mind so long ago that even unspoken he had remembered them ever since: repeating them like a spell: *Our Father who art in heaven, hallowed be thy name, thy kingdom come, thy will be done*, over and over until the words themselves lost all meaning and became nothing but syllables, incantation. Varney had expected—he wasn't sure what—pain, violent resistance, a thunderbolt expressing disgust and displeasure that such a thing as he should dare, but at first there had been simply nothing: the blank silence inside his own mind, listening to himself go on and on and on in an empty room, talking to the walls.

And then—some unknowable time after he had begun—*something began to listen*.

The space inside Varney's mind was different now. Larger. Less like a shut-up closet. *Warmer* somehow. He realized he had lost the thread: *andforgiveusourtrespassesaswe... as we...*

There was no reply, but that sensation of space and warmth increased slightly, like a prompt. Whatever was listening was paying attention. That was too frightening to think about for very long, so Varney plunged ahead, not knowing if this was the worst idea he'd ever had in a life marked by terrible decisions, and said, *Please, if you're there, if you're listening, please, is this what you want to happen, is this how it's supposed to go, is this right?*

The words dropped into that warm and waiting silence—and a moment later came back:

*is this what you want to happen*

*is this how it's supposed to go is this what you want is this right is this right is this*

*right is this right*

*is this right*

*is this*
*is this*
*is*

It echoed and re-echoed inside Varney's skull, sounding vast and strange and quite unlike his own voice, and with the echoes a series of awful, unspeakable images he could not remember seeing. The seas clotted and boiling, the sky dark but for that terrible star, a fiery mountain crashing into the waves; cities on fire, vast nuclear explosions, the destruction of Earth in a sequence of shutter-click visions—*had that happened, was that already happening, was everyone on Earth already dead or wishing that they were, all Greta's mummies so much bitter ash on that wind, all our friends, all our enemies, all the world gone up in flames*—and then the images changed, showed him somewhere all white and gold and jewel-hued, impossibly beautiful, and a moment later that same white city laid waste, fire and battle and the screams of dying men—

—no, not men, *angels*, those were *angels* and this was war in Heaven—

*Is this right*, said his own voice, far away now, a still-reverberating echo that would not die. *Is this what you want is this what you want is this*—

And there was a sense of titanic breath being drawn, something unimaginably vast preparing to speak: Varney felt as if he should hang on to something to prevent being pulled off his feet by a gale-force wind rushing past him, but his hair did not even stir. The intangible wind died away, followed by a pause long enough that Varney thought he might actually go mad waiting for it, and then a voice he did not so much hear as *feel*, inside his mind, inside his bones, the hollow spaces of his body, said:

# NO.

One word, but it seemed to go on forever, gorgeous and clear and ringing and somehow *warm*, like brandy, like the glow of polished brass. When it began to die away, Varney found himself reaching for it, wanting so much to go on listening, wanting to hear more, and it was terrible and wrenching to find himself being drawn back out of the place inside his mind where the voice had come, being shaken back to consciousness, to awareness, someone's hand on his shoulder, someone saying his name. For a moment he had to cover his face with his hands to hide his naked distress at the *lack* of that voice. It had felt like—thrall.

"Varney," someone was saying, "Varney, wake up, wake up, something's *happening*."

# CHAPTER 17

For the people on Earth—a few had survived, at least for now, in dark places under the surface, and were hiding in the darkness feeling the rock shaking all around them and hearing small gobbling-chuckling voices in the creak and squeal of uneasy ground—there was no word spoken: no one would remember hearing "no" at all, only a word, or something like a word, which they could not recall. All those who had survived long enough to hear it, however, heard it very well: a voice that seemed to come not from the air or the ground, but from within their own minds: vast, huge, the voice of something unimaginably large, unimaginably powerful, *whispering* so as not to burst their eardrums with its lightest tone.

A voice, and within that voice, around it, in its harmonics and its overtones and its echoes, more beautiful than they had ever heard, music. Some would remember it as a single note, hanging pure and glass-clear and perfectly sustained until it began to fade—a note that they would spend the rest of their lives trying to reproduce in some way, trying to hear again that ringing clarity, that sweet clean perfection of tone. Some would remember it as the swell and joy of choral music, massed voices raised together in complex and gorgeous harmony. Some would hear song and some would hear instruments and some all of it together, and in the music, woven through the music, *part* of it, a sweetness unimaginable in its warmth and peace: a feeling like being cupped in the palm of some huge incomprehensible hand, held with such care it took the breath away.

None of them could remember, either, how long it had lasted. It felt like—moments, hours, years, decades, caught in the warmth and care of that regard, suffused with the sweetness of music; afterward there would be endless, endless arguments, and for once on the skin of the world all sides would be *right*. It did go on for decades; it was over in a sweet, passing, piercing moment; both were true.

But when it ended, when the last echoes of it were no longer even imagined, faded to nothing at all, the people hearing it woke from dreamless sleep to find themselves at home, at work, in their cars, in their airplanes, wherever they had been when the world closed around them like a fan snapped shut and everything had turned to fire. All systems back to green across the board. Trucks had never shifted from their lanes; nuclear plant workers had never been toppled by earthquakes into spent-fuel pools; planes had never even veered off course. Those who had been conscious at the end of it could remember almost nothing; those who had seen their death coming, stared it in the face, recalled only a vague and improbable nightmare. In the space of time taken up by that voice's music, the world had—healed itself, or woken from a nightmare of its own, and spun gently on in its diurnal course exactly as it always had and always would.

*What was that*, people would ask in the months following, *what happened, what just happened, why do I have strange dreams*, and after a little while a quasi-scientific explanation to do with climate change and gas emissions and collective hallucination and volcanic smog would be patched together—and unlike other patched-together excuses for the unscientific statement *we don't know*, would be globally accepted.

"—something's happening, Varney," the voice said again, and he blinked his eyes open, stinging with tears for the loss of that music, that voice, that *regard*, and found Cranswell staring into his face.

"What—" Varney began, and hated the sound of his own voice, raw and unbeautiful and ordinary compared to the echoes in his mind. "Aren't you drunk?"

"I was," Cranswell said, "like everyone else in this joint, but—did you *hear* something just now? Some kind of music, or someone saying something?"

Varney straightened up. The demons who had been draped over various chairs and tables seemed to have somehow sobered up, but several of them were hugging one another in a way that made Varney slightly embarrassed to have observed. He realized that, for once, no part of him was hurting. That he felt... better than he had in centuries.

The music was gone but something of that warmth and sweetness remained, caught inside him, and he thought—looking at the expressions on everyone's faces—that it had caught inside them as well, was still warming them, a kind of unfocused but gorgeous *care*. A sense of being seen, and not in the observed-and-judged way: a feeling of being somehow *understood*.

Someone turned the TV back on—it had gone off, Varney didn't remember that—and the STAND BY sign was still there, but as he watched, it shivered and turned to the familiar ENN news desk, empty. After a moment the anchor reappeared, and appeared to have been crying but was currently making a valiant attempt to pretend this wasn't true.

"—hello," they said, swallowed hard. "I don't—know what to say, this is the first time in my career I don't know what to say, but—everyone—look outside, stop watching this network and just look outside—"

They fumbled at something in their ear, set it down on the desk, turned to look at something other than the camera. "I'm sorry, I—I—can't do this right now, can someone please take over—"

The screen went black for a moment and then WE ARE EXPERIENCING TECHNICAL DIFFICULTIES popped up, and Varney found he was suddenly, actually, amazingly still able to laugh.

"What?" said Hippolyta, who had woken up and was blinking at the two of them. "Why don't I feel like shit?"

"I don't know," said Varney, pressing a hand to his chest, "but—what are you waiting for, let's go and see what's happening outside?"

*Greta*, he thought, and something of that last echo of the voice's sweetness, its warmth, rose in a tide inside his mind: he was suddenly, completely certain that Greta was all right. That—all of them were, somehow.

What had just happened to Varney—and somehow *because of Varney*, to the rest of the world—was far, far too huge to contemplate, and so with the peculiar and selective practicality that had largely kept him alive despite himself, he simply placed it aside on a mental shelf to think about *later*. It seemed as if there might *be* a later, after all.

Zophiel came back to himself slowly, regaining awareness little by little of his surroundings, of the weight of Amitiel in his arms. He wasn't sure what had just happened, only that it was *wonderful*.

There had been—fighting, hadn't there, and dead angels, and bitter harsh smoke that burned in his chest and stung tears from his eyes, and he had—been holding Amitiel, the other angel's face pressed into the cup of his shoulder, as the cracked and spalling jewel cobblestones shook beneath their feet and the crystal vault of Heaven rang and chimed out of tune, harsh—thinking: *We did this, we made this happen, this is all our fault*, wanting it to be *over*—and then all the world went pure and blinding white.

He blinked, the edges of things beginning to come back into focus. In his arms Amitiel stirred, raised his head, tearstained and uncertain and still so beautiful.

It was like *coming in from the cold*. All around him, Zophiel could feel the *rightness* again, and had not even known that it was missing, had not known he was without something so basic to an angel's nature that its absence felt numb and dizzying—*how could I not have known*, he thought, *how could I not have realized it wasn't there*—

"It's Him," said Amitiel in a tiny voice, and although his eyes were still suspiciously bright, the lashes drawn into heavy points with faintly golden tears, he smiled: tremulous, dawning, brilliant as sunrise. "It's Him, Zophiel."

"I know," said Zophiel, soft and wondering. They were standing in the vast courtyard between the gates and the citadel, and—the citadel was *there*, the highest tower halfway to the crystal sky, the battlements unscathed, the air innocent of dust and smoke. All around them stood other angels, blinking in the clear light, looking around themselves at the restored beauty of Heaven.

"But we're in the wrong world," said Amitiel. "Aren't we? I—walked through and you came with me into the other world, and—there was a war—dead angels—"

"I think," said Zophiel slowly, "I think wherever we are, we *are* in the right world. Or—we're allowed to be." He could still hear the echoes of a voice that was not a voice at all, but music; he could still feel the unutterable sweetness of that attention, that care. Of being *seen* and understood, all his deeds and misdeeds held up for inspection and acknowledged and recorded on some celestial ledger.

"What are we supposed to do now?" Amitiel asked, still smiling, but the uncertainty was in his tone as well as his words.

"I don't know," said Zophiel, and was a little surprised to find he didn't *mind* not knowing; that he didn't have to dread the future, whatever it held. "As long as I have you," he added, "it doesn't matter."

All around them the other angels were beginning to talk, laughing and crying and embracing one another, and Zophiel smiled helplessly, and bent to kiss Amitiel just once, lightly, on the mouth.

*Lips are soft*, he thought, wonderstruck. *I didn't know that, there's so much I don't know, but maybe I'll be allowed to find it out*, and then Amitiel was kissing *him*, and Zophiel felt as if he might come apart with simple glass-clear *gladness*.

In Tower Three, the hospital was silent. The cries and moans of wounded angels, the urgent orders and demands of the nurses, the squealing of monitors all vanished to nothing under a huge empty calm silence.

Greta, numb with shock and horror and despair, thought *there was silence in heaven for the space of half an hour* before the wave of intensely beautiful music washed over her. Afterward she wouldn't be able to describe it with any clarity: a kind of synesthetic pleasure, warmth and sweetness and care all at once, like a hot bath for the mind; the closest she could come was *thrall*, and this held none of that deliberate influence, it wasn't directional, it simply *was*.

Nor did she know how long it went on, the echoes ringing in her mind, before she found herself back in the little ready room in the hospital, entirely clean of golden blood. The shock of realizing that nothing hurt was enough to make her dizzy: all the exhaustion, all the pain from hours of desperate work, had vanished with the blood.

She blinked, looking around at the others, who were also—*waking up* wasn't the right phrase, but something like it. Grisaille and Ruthven were staring at one another.

"What just happened?" said Grisaille.

"I don't know," said Greta, "but I'm not arguing," and she got up, swaying only a little, and went to the door, not knowing what to expect: had that all even *happened*, had they simply hallucinated the entire godawful business—

Oh. They hadn't imagined it.

There *were* angels everywhere, lying on cots and stretchers, but as Greta watched, they were sitting up, prodding their chests experimentally, staring around at the controlled chaos of the emergency ward. The mess of blood and broken feathers that had splattered the floor and walls was gone as if it had never existed. The doctors and nurses were also staring around and blinking, but as she watched, they began to pull themselves together and start checking their patients over.

"Well, that's one way to sort out the situation," said Faust beside her; Greta jumped a little. "Never thought I'd get to see it myself, but it's not exactly unheard of in the literature—Take it easy," he added to an angel who was attempting to get up and looking rather dizzy. "You'll feel right as rain in a few minutes, but don't push it."

The angel stared at him. "Who are you?" it said in a beautiful bell-like voice that reminded Greta of Samael. "Where am I? What happened?"

Faust counted with his fingers: *one, two, three.* "Splendid," he said, "the classic-question trifecta. I'm a doctor, you're temporarily in Hell, and that was the use of the *vis vires divinus* if I'm any judge."

"The what?" said Greta, about as confused as the angel looked.

"Him upstairs," said Faust, nodding at the ceiling. "Getting involved. He's done it before, of course, but it's been a good long while since anybody's heard from Him; someone must have finally yelled loudly enough on the correct wavelength to get Him to pay attention. The rest of you doing all right?"

Greta nodded. "I think so."

"You were bloody good back there, by the way. Thanks for your help."

"I didn't do enough," she said. "I lost so many."

"We all did," said Faust. "No one could have done more, Helsing. It wasn't a situation we could win, but we did the best we could, all of us." He clasped her shoulder briskly, not unkindly, and gave her a brief smile. "My people can mop up from here. Go and find your friends and do a bit of celebrating, why don't you."

She was about to protest automatically, and then had to stop and laugh. "Okay," she said. "Thank you."

"Don't mention it." He nodded, turned away, and a moment later was abjuring another angel to lie still until the dizziness wore off: a short, businesslike figure in a black gown, bustling along the ward, entirely unfazed by the situation. Greta envied him that unflappable calm, and it took her a little while to remember where she'd seen it before—and the realization brought with it no surprise: he reminded her of her own father, years ago.

"Do *you* know what's going on?" Grisaille asked, joining her; a moment later Ruthven, Anna, and Nadezhda followed. "Nobody seems to be perforated anymore."

"I'm not sure," said Greta, "but I want some fresh air, and to find the others."

"Yes *please*," said Nadezhda. Greta noticed with some amusement that her hair was slowly coiling itself around her earrings again: it must have gotten over the shock. "Right now," Dez added, and a pang went through Greta's chest: she was obviously missing Hippolyta about as much as Greta missed Varney, which was to say *like a limb*.

"Come on," she said. "Let's get out of here."

Varney and the others joined a stream of people walking out of the bar, heedless of whatever their tab might have been; unable to resist the pull of curiosity—

—they were not alone; demons were flowing out of the other towers, out of the businesses circling their bases, out into the vast empty space of the plaza with its central fountain, all of them looking up in wonder and awe, because *it was snowing in Hell*, and it was snowing *gold*. Soft flakes of glittering, glowing gold, dropping out of nowhere, out of the arched vault that formed the sky of Hell.

Already the white stone of the plaza was gilded, the snowfall soft but steady. People were holding out their hands, lifting their arms to catch the snowflakes; they touched Varney's upturned face in tiny soft kisses, *warm*, not at all the chill of ordinary snow. They were giving off a gentle golden light. It didn't seem to matter that this made no sense; it didn't matter at all.

He was dimly aware of Cranswell and Hippolyta nearby, talking, possibly talking to him; all he could think was *how beautiful it is, how beautiful*, the strangest and loveliest sight of his long life; his mind was still trying to comprehend what had just happened to him, what he had—done, or tried to do, or asked for, the vast and unutterable *weight* of that, but in the face of the falling golden snowflakes, thoughts refused to stay together, scattered and sparkled like motes of gold themselves.

*How beautiful*, and then Varney heard his name, distant, somebody calling his name. A voice he knew.

That was enough to shake him out of his daze, and he turned to see Greta Helsing threading her way through the crowd; and a moment later he had closed the distance to her, taken her in his arms, and hugged her off her feet, burying his face in the sweet and familiar scent of her hair. "*Greta*," he said, muffled, and did not know if he was crying or not, or if *that* mattered.

She was holding him so tight his ribcage creaked. "Varney," she said, sounding a little choked herself. "*Francis.* I thought I'd never see you again."

"So did I," he said, his lips against her neck, aware of the blood pulsing rapidly, so near, so very near, warm and bright and alive, and felt nothing but joy. "... Say that again?"

"What?" she asked.

"My name. It's... it sounds nice."

Greta pulled back enough to look him in the face. Golden snowflakes starred her hair, glittered in her eyelashes, and his chest hurt with a deep, sweet ache. *How beautiful*, he thought again. "Francis," she said, reaching up to take his face between her hands—clever hands, *kind* hands—"I love you," and drew him down into a kiss.

All around them the host of Hell was laughing, crying, dancing, holding one another, as the golden snowflakes fell. Ruthven and Grisaille and Nadezhda and Hippolyta were clinging to each other silently; beyond them, Cranswell and Anna were dancing terribly, both unable to do anything but smile as they waltzed. The snow fell over the whole of Dis, over the distant smudge of Oldtown on the far shore of the lake; gilding each surface in light, the dome of the Spa glowing gently, the white stone of the plaza a drift of gold, bringing with it something of that feeling of peace and sweetness. Every being in Hell that could think was aware of—respite. Of having been spared an ending, and allowed a future.

* * *

On the sixtieth floor of Tower Six, Samael stood looking out of the floor-to-ceiling windows of his conference room and quondam command center, the monitors and projectors abandoned now. Only he and Fastitocalon remained.

He was standing with his hands clasped behind his back, white wings mantled, looking down at the celebration in the plaza with a faint little smile on his face. Fastitocalon came to join him. On the other side of the glass, the points of falling golden light slid softly down the window, soundless, like a series of tiny caresses.

"They'll be expecting an announcement," said Samael.

"In a minute," Fastitocalon told him. "Is it—can you *feel* this happening?" He gestured at the snow. "Because it's not you doing it."

"No," he said. "It's not." For a moment there was an ache in his voice so deep it echoed. "And you know that I feel *everything*."

Fastitocalon winced. "What are you going to tell them?"

"The truth, or a simplified version of it," said Samael. His wings settled, the feathers rustling slightly. "Without the damaging political detail."

"There's going to be a lot of cleanup to do," said Fastitocalon, absently rubbing his chest. "Have we made contact with Above?"

"Not yet," said Samael. "I have no idea what's going on up there, and I'm giving them a little longer to catch their collective breath before they have to deal with us."

"'Deal with us,'" Fastitocalon repeated sourly, "they ought

to be thanking you. You bloody well saved who knows however many of their people, and you didn't have to do that."

"Yes I did," said the Devil, and looked sideways at him. His eyes were the brilliant, shifting blue of a butterfly's wing, of the glow in the depths of a moonstone. "You know I did, Fass."

"...all right," said Fastitocalon, and sighed. "Yes. I know."

"What I *don't* know," said Samael in a slightly different tone of voice, "is what actually flipped the switch. There had to have been some kind of—catalyst, or something, that was finally enough to get His attention and His intervention."

"What kind of deity takes an eighty-year nap and lets reality fall apart to the point where large holes appear in it," said Fastitocalon. "I mean, part of the whole business is that He's supposed to be watching everyone all the time, right?"

"That's ineffability for you," said Samael. "Everything *might be* happening for a reason, or it might not, and that's all in His plan, presumably. Perhaps all this mess was supposed to happen. Perhaps he intended the whole thing."

"The rift is gone as if it never existed," said Fastitocalon. "Everything's been... undone. All the damage erased, no sign of anything ever happening. I'm willing to bet the mortal world is going to have no memory of any of this."

"They won't be *allowed* to remember," Samael said. "That much trauma is—well, too much for humans to bear and still function."

"Unlike us," said Fastitocalon drily. "Presumably the next universe over is going to try to find another way through at some point, unless they've given it up as a bad job or been told off by *their* version of Him, who seems like a rather more smite-y version than the one we've got. Ours is back online, though, either way," he added. "Even I can feel that."

"He's awake," Samael said. "And judging by the light show, approves of our performance. But I still don't know what the trigger was, and that's going to itch at me until I find it."

"You will," said Fastitocalon, rubbing at his chest again. Samael glanced at him.

"Are you all right? You said something, before the end, about being tired—"

"I was," Fastitocalon said. "I've—the treatments in the scanner did reset my signature most of the way, so I was in better shape than I've been in centuries, but I had to use a *lot* of energy stapling Paris back together, and I never really got it back. I—think I have now. Nothing seems to hurt."

"Well, good," said Samael. "I still want Faust to look at you. Oh, damn," he added. "I need to get down there and see what the status is; if the evacuated angels made it through that and didn't get raptured, they'll want repatriation. I'll have to organize it."

"I'll come with you," said Fastitocalon. "You can go live from there afterward, to make the announcement. It'll look even better with the hospital behind you."

Samael nodded. "You were right, there's going to be a lot of cleanup to do, and I need all my Council of Nine confirmed and on board with it. How'd you like to descend to full archdemon status and be given the responsibility for rebuilding M&E?"

Fastitocalon stared at him. "Really?"

"Really. You're far better at it than Asmodeus ever was, you don't wear an insufferable and endless variety of crowns, you don't foment political unrest, and I can trust you to do the sums right the first time. I know there isn't much I can do to make up for those centuries of exile on Earth, but this might be a way to start."

"Yes," said Fastitocalon simply. "I would love to. It's... been a long time since I had a purpose. Or a home."

"Come here," said the Devil, and drew him into his arms, wrapping the white arches of his wings around them both for a long moment. When he let go, he was smiling. "You *are* home, Fastitocalon. Hell welcomes you back with open arms."

"Well," said Fastitocalon, eyes suspiciously bright. "In that case, let's get to work."

It was evident that Hell needed very little excuse to throw a party, and even less notice. In about half an hour from the beginning of the snowfall and the initial rush to the plaza, cocktail tables had been set up around the central fountain, which had unaccountably stopped running water and started running champagne, and demons in white jackets were carrying trayfuls of glasses to distribute to the crowd. Greta was halfway down her first drink and feeling slightly, pleasantly high when a huge swath of one of the towers' glass facades lit up like a giant LED screen, showing Samael in his winged form with the very familiar sight of the hospital behind him. In the background they could see angels being examined, and it was impossible from this distance to tell them apart from the white-winged golden-haired figure of the Devil, save for the faint glow of halos here and there.

The hush that rippled through the crowd was almost immediate and absolute; she heard one or two people whisper, *He's making an announcement*, and thought to herself that stating the obvious was not a trait reserved solely for humankind.

On the screen Samael looked—not *tired*, she thought, but faintly melancholy, as if he were missing something he knew he could never get back. When he spoke, however, he sounded both confident and brisk. "May I have your attention, please."

Utter silence, save for the splashing and fizzing of the fountain.

"We are continuing to examine the details of what's just happened," he said. "What we know so far is this: the attack by an external universe upon a vulnerable point in ours caused a chain reaction that initiated the Armageddon sequence, while also establishing a state of war in Heaven, whose leadership called on me for aid. Which we provided."

Another pause, and it felt like he was looking directly *at* Greta, that he'd picked her out of all the thousands of people in the plaza, when he continued. "I cannot clearly enough state my pride in every last one of the responders. Those who volunteered to fight, those who ran logistics, those who kept order—and I am immensely proud, too, of the citizenry of Hell. This was a crisis of proportions not seen since the Harrowing, and you faced it unblinking. I know you did, because *I know you all*."

A sigh went through the crowd; evidently that struck the demons as caring rather than creepy. Samael smiled a little. "We are not out of the woods yet. The—intervention—that stopped the sequence and reversed the damage is obviously divine in origin, although the details remain to be clarified. I have not yet ascertained the current conditions in Heaven, but if we are called upon to provide assistance in rebuilding, I will ask again for volunteers.

"As you can see behind me, our Erebus General Hospital opened its doors to casualties of war, regardless of affiliation. I want to thank, as well, those visitors who volunteered their skills and aid to the medical team. You were desperately needed, and you rose to the task."

Greta couldn't help feeling a swell of pride. She knew exactly what the Devil was doing, and thought she ought to mind the manipulation more; but the warm sense of being appreciated was undeniable.

"We have with us fifteen remaining citizens of Heaven who, as soon as Dr. Faust pronounces them fit, will be returning to their home. Once that is done, I proclaim three days of holiday in celebration.

"Thank you," he concluded, still audible over the immediate roar of appreciation that had followed *celebration*. "Thank you all," and the screen vanished; the building facade was again simply half-mirrored glass.

"He's good," said Anna. "I know from propaganda, and he's *good*."

"The snow is stopping," said Cranswell, looking up, and stuck out his tongue to capture one of the last flakes as it drifted down. "I think maybe things are about to get a bit infernal round here. Why do these taste sweet?"

"Why are they sparkling gold?" said Grisaille, who had snowflakes starring the long fall of his hair and was already on his second glass of champagne. "Why is anything the way it is? I think I've gone mad."

"I wouldn't blame you," Nadezhda said. "On the other hand, we're in Hell, and they're throwing a three-day party: if anywhere's a good time and place to go mad, this might fit."

"I haven't had a proper debauch in *ages*," said Ruthven, smiling. "Go with it. *Let us condole the knight—*"

Greta remembered a sitting room in the Savoy, in another world, after a completely different kind of fight, and finished the quote for him: "*for, lambkins, we will live.*"

"Or at least drown in a fountain full of vintage Krug," said Ruthven, "which is a perfectly demonic way to go. Where'd I put my glass?"

It turned out human—or vampire—laughter was indistinguishable from that of demons, even in a vast and noisy crowd.

In a white-and-gold office with a ceiling painted deep blue with gilded stars, Amitiel and Zophiel stood before a desk and tried not to anxiously ruffle their feathers.

The angel behind the desk had a *pencil* tucked behind

its ear, startlingly ordinary, and a ledger lay open before it. Zophiel watched it running a fingertip down the columns until it came to two entries made simply out of asterisks.

"There we are," it said. The nameplate on its desk read PRAVUIL; when they had been taken into the citadel and told they must see the recording angel, Zophiel had immediately feared the worst. This Pravuil was not actually very terrible at all.

Yet.

"Two entities that aren't on the list. Two visitors," it—he—said. "I'm assuming you're from the, ah, other side. We need to ask you a few questions."

"We didn't mean to," Amitiel blurted out, and then huddled against Zophiel's shoulder. Zophiel put an arm around him. He wasn't sure that was allowed, but Pravuil didn't seem to be paying much attention to inappropriate physical behavior; he closed the ledger, folded his hands upon it, and looked at them with blank and golden eyes.

"Didn't mean to do *what*?" he asked.

"To—make all this happen, to—break things, to make angels *dead*," Amitiel managed, beginning to sniffle. "Well, I mean, we *did*, that was what we were sent to do, but—"

"But we didn't understand what we were doing," said Zophiel miserably. "It's still our fault. We caused reality to become extremely fragile on purpose, so that our armies could—invade and destroy the, um, the false Heaven—we were sent to this Earth to prepare the way—"

He thought he was going to be sick again; *guilt* rose in his throat and he held Amitiel close, waiting for Pravuil to tell them what punishment this world's God decreed for creatures such as themselves. The angel's eyes had widened, but narrowed again, and he said, "Sit down before you fall down, both of you, and start from the beginning. I think you'd better tell me everything."

It was a Hell of a party.

Greta *thought* she could remember seeing multiple otherwise-respectable individuals dancing on tables with lampshades on their heads, but her recollection was definitely hazy. It was still going on a day later when Ruthven went in for a scan to determine if he was still carrying the curse; they had to fight their way through a writhing mass of happy drunken demons to get to the hospital, and even inside, the noise of music and raised voices was still audible.

She was accompanying him both as his doctor and as a fascinated observer; the mirabilic resonance scanner was one of the things she'd wanted desperately to see ever since she'd heard of it, and Faust was willing to let her have a look. The imaging center was on another floor of the tower from the emergency room.

"You'll have to remove all jewelry," said the tech who met them at the front desk. "Enchanted or otherwise."

"I know," said Ruthven. "I vividly remember the last time I did this. Let's get it over with?"

"Of course," said the tech, and led them into the back. Greta was expecting something like an ordinary MRI, possibly sleeker, but the thing awaiting them was both bizarre and gorgeous, a raised horizontal cylinder of *totally transparent material*, clear as glass. She could see right through it to the other side of the room.

"This won't take long," said Faust at the controls. "We're not doing diagnostics, just checking his signature for interference. I have a feeling it's been reset with everything else, since all the damage seems to have been undone, but I want to make sure."

Greta nodded, and went to look over his shoulder as Ruthven, in a hospital gown that he somehow managed to make *stylish*, lay down on the machine's couch and slowly slid inside the cylinder. They could see him close his eyes. "Does it hurt?" she asked Faust.

"Nope. Feels a bit tingly, that's all, and it makes some noise." He entered a series of commands, and Greta stared as the transparent cylinder of the scanner lit up with a moving pattern of light. It looked a little bit like the grey glass communication devices Fass had used to collimate his magic back in Paris, with faint holographic color hovering inside the glass itself.

On the screens an image was beginning to form as the light pattern shifted and moved down the bore of the cylinder from Ruthven's head to his feet. The image looked a little like a wire-frame model of Ruthven himself, with something like magnetic field lines surrounding it. "Mm," said Faust. "Good. Looks fine to me so far."

"What are those lines?"

"Mirabilic fields. I can show you his earlier scans, they were a mess, but this is nice and clear, no sign of any residual curse damage. I think he'll be fine to return to Earth." Faust did some more typing, and the light patterns shifted and made their way back up the cylinder before cutting out altogether. Inside it, Ruthven turned his head to look at them through the observation window, eyebrow raised, and Greta gave him a thumbs-up; the relief on his face was very clear even through the slight distortion of the scanner's wall. It was relief she shared.

"One day," she said, watching as the couch slid back out of the scanner, "I will actually understand how this stuff *works*, but this is not that day."

"I can give you some reading material," said Faust. "Did Fastitocalon tell you about mirabilics?"

"Not much. I mean I sort of get the idea, magic's like physics, but beyond that, I'm pretty much lost."

"I'd start you off with the intro texts," he said. "You can take them with you and expand your mind in all your copious free time."

Greta laughed. "I have so much of it. I wonder what's been happening up there."

"Probably business as usual," said Faust. "It looks to our surface ops like everything's back the way it was before this whole mess happened. No one on top seems to have much if any memory of the entire sequence, which is to be encouraged. Your patients should be fine."

"I can't wait to get back to it," she said. "I've had enough emergency surgery to last me the rest of my *life*. I want to go back to repairing people in a less dramatic fashion."

"You did a bang-up job," said Faust. "Under extreme conditions. I was impressed, or at least I was afterward when I had the ability to think. You *and* your friends."

"I was happy to," she said, meaning it. "But I'm glad I don't have to do that again."

"Do what?" Ruthven said, rejoining them, tying his tie. He had gone shopping with Nadezhda and Hippolyta and Grisaille up and down the famous Plutus Boulevard, and was currently arrayed in a new and very nice grey suit with a faint shimmer to it. Greta was still wearing the clothes she'd arrived in, although they had been cleaned while she slept off the party in a hotel room.

"Staple bits of angels together," she said. "You're good to go, apparently."

"I am *so* pleased to hear it," said Ruthven. "Um. How do we get home?"

"Someone'll flip you," said Faust. "Sam will probably want to say good-bye, and he can arrange it. Off you go."

"Thank you," said Greta simply, and took the hand he offered her. "Thank you so much. For everything."

"Just doing my job," said Faust, and gave her his rare and narrow smile.

They had arranged to meet up with the others in the lobby, and the look of relief on Grisaille's face when he saw Ruthven smiling was almost comical. "Can we go home?"

"We can," said Ruthven, and nearly lost his balance when Grisaille launched himself into a thoroughly enthusiastic hug.

"I want to spend a hundred years *not leaving London*. I've had enough of travel for a while."

"Fuck traveling," said Grisaille. "In fact, fuck everything except your house. I like your house and plan to stay in it like a hermit crab inside its shell for the foreseeable future."

"Good to have plans," said Greta. "Let's get out of here."

Samael did, in fact, want to see them before they left. He spoke to them individually. Varney was last; he spent the time while the others talked wandering slowly around the Devil's enormous office, which was all in shades of white. Even the books on the shelves were bound in white; it was a little hard on the eyes after a while. From here the view out over the lake was outstanding, however, and Varney watched tiny sailboats, miniaturized by distance, scudding back and forth through the dancing flames.

"Sir Francis?" said Samael. Varney turned from the window, came back over to his desk, half an acre of white carpet away.

"How may I be of assistance?" he said.

"So far we haven't been able to determine exactly what was the catalyst which prompted divine intervention. I'm trying to find out if anyone has any information that might be of use in tracking it down."

Varney could feel his face heat up ever so slightly in a faint flush. He had deliberately been avoiding the subject, trying not to think about it: he didn't *know* if what he had done in daring to pray for the first time in centuries had actually been the triggering factor that undid Armageddon, but—

"Sir Francis?" said Samael, head tilted. The blue eyes were hypnotic, hard to look away from. Not for the first time he thought that the Devil had his own version of thrall.

*He's going to find out, somehow, eventually*, Varney thought, and closed his eyes for a moment. "My lord," he said, "it might be simpler if you had a look yourself, instead of relying on my limited powers of description."

"*That's* not ominous," said Samael. "All right. Hold still, this won't be fun but I'll try to be quick."

Varney opened his eyes, nodded, and was almost prepared for it when the feeling of Samael *inside his head* slammed into him: a searchlight looking through his eyes into the thoughts behind them, brilliant and glaring and merciless. His recent memories were called up, flipped through the way a man might flip through a book searching for a particular passage, back, back, further back, until he was once more in the bar with desperation thick in the air, closing his eyes, reaching inside himself for that small quiet emptiness he had not touched for so many centuries, beginning to *pray*, daring to try despite the fear, *because* of the fear, how it had turned into almost a nonsensical chant before that strange, impossible feeling of *listening* began—how he had asked the question, *is this what you want*, and received an answer—

The searchlight cut off; Varney steadied himself on the edge of the desk, blinking. Samael was looking at him with a completely unreadable expression.

"I think," Samael said after a long moment, "that we all may possibly owe you an enormous debt of gratitude. None of us *thought of that.* At all. Didn't even occur to us to try, because—well, we were all so damned sure that nothing out there would hear it. That Himself was out of range, or out of interest, that we were on our own."

"It was the only thing I *could* think of to do," said Varney, remembering again Tefnakhte and the stela, sending out his request for information, for assistance. "I—expected to be punished for daring, but it seemed as if I would be punished, anyway, with everybody else."

"Which seems eminently reasonable," said Samael. "*Thank you* is inadequate. Ask me for anything you like, and it will be yours."

"I want to go home," said Varney, "and marry my fiancée, and repair my roof and care for our monsters and—no offense, your lordship—try to forget this ever happened."

"None taken," said Samael with a wry smile. "Forgetfulness, at least, I can grant. I have a whole river's worth of it at my disposal." He held out his hand, palm upward, and a small blue glass bottle appeared in it.

Varney stared. The fluid inside was heavy, syrupy, and looked a bit like liquid pearl. "Is that—" he began.

"Pure Lethe," said Samael. "One drop of this will fade recent memory; three will remove it; five will remove farther back. Use with caution." He held out the bottle. After a moment Varney took it, not surprised at how heavy it felt despite its size, and slipped it into his pocket.

"Thank you," he said. "I—appreciate it."

"The very least that I could do," said Samael. "And now I

will have somebody escort you home, or wherever on the skin of the world you choose to go, at your command."

"Dark Heart," he said. "No one calls it Ratford Abbey; it's Dark Heart House."

Samael nodded and got up, gesturing for Varney to precede him. The others were waiting outside the office with a couple of Samael's staff. Greta took Varney's hand, and he squeezed her fingers gently, not sure what he wanted to do with the bottle, not sure of very much at all except that he was very tired of magic and adventure and peril, and wanted to be home.

"Thank you," Samael said to all of them, "and good luck," and the staffer demons took their hands and the world twisted into the sideways disorienting whiteness of translocation and this time Varney welcomed it with all his heart.

# CHAPTER 18

Greta had never in her life been so utterly glad it was raining.

You didn't really notice the lack of a proper sky in Hell—the mind sort of bounced off it, a protective reaction to limit the shock—but, oh, it was *so* lovely to look up and see clouds, to feel the rain on her face, feel the movement of air again. To *smell* it, the scent of wet earth, green things growing, *alive* and real and blessedly ordinary.

They were standing hand in hand on the terrace of Dark Heart House, its pale stone darkened with the rain. The demon who had brought them had said polite good-byes and popped out of existence again—nobody seemed to be particularly worried about translocation destabilizing anything, which was a nice change—and they were still standing here getting wet, and she didn't know what to do with how glad she was to be back.

Varney didn't seem to mind the rain, either, standing with his face turned up and his eyes half-closed, smiling his infrequent but rather lovely smile. They might have stayed there indefinitely had Emily not come out onto the terrace and demanded to know what they were doing there, weren't they supposed to be in France, why were they standing in the rain—and a moment later her questions were cut off because Greta was hugging her very tight.

"Come *inside*," Emily said when she got her breath back, "you're soaked, c'mon, I made tea a minute ago," and when Greta let her go, led them through the French doors into the blue drawing room.

It had not been all that long since Greta had visited Dark Heart, but every time, she was struck anew by how beautiful the great old house was becoming under Varney's reawakened care. How beautiful it once had been, its lovely bones, and how his refurbishment was bringing that latent grace and style back to the surface after decades of near-abandonment. This room had been completely gutted, the ruins of the silk wallpaper drooping in long tatters, the marble mantelpiece cracked, the ceiling plaster damp and bubbled, and now it was simply, elegantly appointed in a way that was not identical to the original but an evolution thereof. The clutter of Emily's veterinary textbooks and notes didn't subtract from the elegance; they made it feel more like home.

Greta drifted over to the new banded-fluorite fireplace, blue and violet and white, and held out her hands to warm them over the comfortably dying fire. A couple of hairmonsters were sprawled on their sides in front of the fire like hunting dogs, and wuffled at her when she bent down to stroke them. She couldn't stop smiling. Varney was watching her—she could feel the weight of his eyes, a pleasant touch—and she thought again how right he and this house were for each other. He *fit* here.

Reality was still there, waiting for her, when she straightened up. She'd have to call the spa and tell them she'd be returning to continue her job in—*a few days*, she thought, *please, I want a few days of this, of* here, *before I go back to work—I* was *called away on an emergency, like I told Brigitte, that much was true, I hope they can cope without me a little longer—*

"Why didn't you call and tell me you guys were coming back?" Emily asked, returning with a tea tray. "I mean, not that I was having crazy house parties while you were away, I was *studying*, but I could have got stuff ready for you—wait, did something happen?"

The question was entirely reasonable given the circumstances, but Greta looked away from the fireplace to look at Varney for a moment before bursting into laughter. *Did something happen*, she thought. Varney was laughing, too, helplessly, and half-fell into a chair, a hand over his eyes. Emily stared at him, and then at Greta, and back at Varney.

"*What?*" she demanded. "What's so funny?"

"Did something happen," Varney managed, "yes, I think it's safe to say that," and dissolved into mirth again. Emily scowled at him, hands on her hips, and blew a strand of hair out of her face.

"Okay, whatever, you're both apparently nuts," she said. "Do you want tea?"

In the Embankment house, Ruthven and Grisaille had said their own good-byes, to the demon and to Nadezhda and the others, and were in agreement that the house had way too many stairs; they had just negotiated the staircase and achieved their bedroom. Grisaille let go of Ruthven and flopped face downward onto the duvet, with a creak of springs.

"I am never leaving this bed again," he said, muffled by the covers. "I am amalgamated with this bed. This bed and I have achieved spiritual oneness. I am it and it is me."

Ruthven smiled. "I shall have small wheels attached to it, so I can push you around like the world's largest and least innocent infant in a mahogany pram."

"Quite right," said Grisaille, and then, "Why are you all the way over *there*, it's insupportable," and Ruthven didn't even stop to take off his shoes before flopping on the bed beside him and taking him in his arms.

At Oasis Natrun, Sister Brigitte put down the telephone and turned to Tefnakhte. "She'll be back in a week," she said. "It must have been rather a significant emergency. She sounded all right, at least."

"Good," said Tefnakhte. "And—I rather think it was."

He could remember some of it, and didn't want to. Where the humans had a vague blank space in their memories, mummies were creatures of memory, recorded history, and the thing that had washed over the world and wiped away the images of horror had left a faint stain in his mind. There had been—blood, and hail, and a terrible star from a book of magic that was not his own, and then he lost coherent sequential memory; it all blurred together in a sickening pulse of fear and pain.

Brigitte was looking at him, head tilted. "Are you all right?" she said. "You're not—having an attack?"

"What? No," he said. "I'm fine. And we don't have to worry about the attacks anymore; remember, that stopped with Van Dorne—you weren't there, that's right, you didn't see. Be glad of that."

Brigitte frowned. "I can't *remember*; she was... there, and then she wasn't, and the stela wasn't, either."

They had discovered that the Hermopolis Stela was missing not long after the world came back. There was no sign of it anywhere in the facility; they searched every room, every hiding place, any possible location it could be. It had simply vanished without a trace.

It had been Tefnakhte and Nefrina, the IT specialist mummy here to have her tendons replaced, who had thought to look it up on the Internet and see if there was anything in the news about it being found somewhere, and oddly enough, there didn't seem to be any mentions at all of it having been stolen in the first place. They looked through all the news sites back to before the robbery, and there simply was nothing there. Leonora Van Dorne's disappearance *had* hit the news; she was sufficiently rich and well known that her sudden vanishing was worth talking about. There were multiple theories floating around the Internet: she'd been kidnapped, she'd been killed, she was on the run from something. But the stela wasn't there.

The patients argued about it in between playing board games in the sunroom. Antjau was finally well enough to get up and join the others, but didn't say much; Nesperennub insisted that the stela had returned itself to its origin once its work was done; it was sacred to Thoth, and Thoth did not like disorder, or loose ends. Maanakhtef, who was hardly limping at all now, thought that some enterprising local had stolen it during the—strange dream everyone had had.

It wouldn't be until Tefnakhte and Nefrina spent enough time on the Metropolitan Museum of Art's website to check the gallery map and look at the images of the room that popped up that they discovered the stela and its plinth simply weren't there. The Metternich Stela stood alone in its narrow glass case.

The Hermopolis Stela wasn't on the Met's catalog list. It wasn't on the Internet, either. There were no references to it in any of the literature they skimmed. There were no pictures of it, even low-res Pinterest JPEG files. There were no references to it in any of Oasis Natrun's books. It didn't exist.

Tefnakhte thought that it was part of the *forgetting*. He couldn't forget it, of course: he'd used it to perform the spell to summon Thoth, which was written in the book of his heart, never to be erased; but the humans, well, the humans were so ephemeral these days.

* * *

After they'd had tea, and Greta had redirected Emily's inquisitive focus to learning about the work she was doing over at Oasis Natrun—the account of having to rebuild most of Maanakhtef's left side fascinated and grossed Emily out at the same time—Greta made her apologies and left the two of them alone with the hairmonsters, trudging up the grand staircase to Varney's huge bedroom. After the—crisis, afterward, when everything woke up to find itself repaired, she had thought the sleep debt might have been wiped out with all the rest of the chaos, but apparently partying with demons was a really great way to get *exhausted* all over again.

It was difficult to bother taking off her clothes, but the grandeur of the bedroom almost required it; one didn't crawl beneath the covers in a vast canopied bed like this one wearing jeans, a somewhat battered shirt, and an even more battered white coat that still read MEDICAL DIRECTOR over the left breast. The last time she'd stayed down here, she had left some things, and it took her only a few minutes searching in drawers to find an actual nightgown.

After that, she barely remembered pulling back the covers, let alone lying down: she was *gone*, sunk away from consciousness like a stone into water, so deep she could not dream.

Varney found her like that a little while later, and stood for a time by the edge of the bed, looking down at her, at the face he had grown to love long before he could admit it even to himself. It was a pale, pointed little face, relaxed in sleep, but the faintly pink lines where worry-wrinkles habitually formed were still visible. He thought he could picture what she'd look like as an old woman, and his chest hurt sharply, vividly, at the idea.

Asleep, she looked almost frighteningly fragile. Like one of the maidens he used to terrify in the night, so vulnerable, so defenseless; but Varney knew that the fragility was false.

*One can always do what one must*, he thought again, and knew that it was the same for her as it was for him: there was no particular valor in the act of doing what must be done, because it needed doing, and he happened to be at hand.

He turned away, walked over to the window, looked out over the ornamental lake—smaller than it had been, but still brimful—and at the rolling parkland and the woods beyond. Varney remembered this view yesterday, a century ago, two centuries: the trees had changed but the contours of the landscape remained the same; time's blurring brush had not altered the bones of the land itself. What had changed was—everything else. What had changed was him.

He took the little blue glass bottle from his pocket, watched the pearly liquid swirl. *I want to forget this ever happened*, he had told Samael. Here was forgetfulness enough to wipe out all the horrors of his past, all the things he had done in his long and fruitless life, all the hurt he had caused and the pain he had inflicted and the loss he had forced upon people whose only crimes had been being in the way of something Varney wanted. Here was a blank curtain falling on a bad and venal play, its characters unsympathetic and its plot both unpleasant and dull. He could, if he so chose, wipe it all away, and—have to hope that he would fall in love with Greta all over again, and build a new Varney for a new and brighter world.

The stuff in the bottle was both heavy and *cold*, chilling his hand. After a little while he set it down on the window-sill, and thought without realizing he was thinking it: *What should I do?*

And again, just as unexpected, extraordinary, the sense of *something listening* was back. Inside the quiet empty place he had only recently discovered was still present deep inside himself, something was listening, and heard him very well.

Absurdly, Varney thought, *Should I be kneeling now, I don't know how to do this, I don't know* how *to pray, I just asked questions*, and there was not so much an answer as a drawing back: an invitation to speak words into that emptiness, and have them be heard. He shut his eyes—it was easier to concentrate, not looking at that small and somehow terrible bottle—and let himself float in the darkness, heard his own voice inside his mind, not realizing he had already begun.

It was full dark when he came back to himself, blinking, to find his feet and back aching, his muscles stiff and numb from standing still for hours. Greta was beside him, pale in the dimness, her hair and her nightgown the same shade of silver-gilt. "Varney?"

"I'm sorry," he said. "I was—thinking?"

"How long have you been standing there?" she asked softly. "Come to bed, it's cold, you must be frozen. What's wrong?"

"Nothing," he said, sounding vague even to himself, and then cursed and reached for the windowsill to steady himself when he tried to take a step and his aching knees threatened to give out. Instantly there was a narrow shoulder insinuated under his arm, a hand on his waist, warm and living and real.

"Lean on me," she said, and he did, and together they made their way back to the bed: deliciously sleep-warm and huge and welcoming. Varney got out of his clothes without the usual flicker of shyness and embarrassment; perhaps he'd burned up his store of that somewhere in the recent series of events. It felt...perfectly ordinary, to undress, to climb into bed mostly unclothed next to a living woman, as if he was supposed to do any such thing.

When they were comfortably settled, Greta leaned her head against his shoulder and said softly, "What were you thinking *about*, that you were so far away?"

"Forgetting," he told her. The space inside his mind where listening happened was empty now, but a comfortable emptiness, not a yearning void. "Whether it's better to forget terrible things, or to keep the knowledge that they happened so that they don't happen again."

"That bottle on the windowsill," said Greta. "Is that what I think it is?"

"Lethe water," he said. "Samael—gave it to me. As a gift."

Greta nodded against him, and was still for a while. When she spoke, her voice was quiet. "Do you *want* to forget it all?"

"Yes and no," said Varney, still conscious of an uncharacteristic sense of calm: it seemed to be *acceptable* to say these things, out loud, to talk about his own wants and failings without the constant lapping weight of melancholy and the tide of memory bringing with it bitter and self-excoriating wrack. "I would . . . like to erase certain parts, and keep others, and I don't think it works that way. All the things I should like to forget are long past the recent times, and I can't destroy those memories without destroying the good ones that came afterward, and those I do not wish to lose." He curled an arm around her shoulders; she was so *warm*, delicious, intensely pleasing to hold. "I would not want to forget you."

Greta rested a hand on Varney's chest. In the dimness the jewels in her ring caught whatever light there was and held it, a tiny row of colored sparks. "That's the problem, isn't it. You keep getting farther and farther away from the old and awful stuff, every moment, every breath, every word."

"Yes," he said. "And it becomes harder and harder to countenance erasing the good to get to the bad."

"There's probably a metaphor in there," said Greta. "This isn't *we must pass through bitter waters to reach the sweet*. You've done that, Francis. Your whole life's been bitter water, and—now you're out of that. It's over and done with. You can be who you are now, not what you were then."

Somewhere inside his own mind Varney was astonished at the fact that he was able not only to have this conversation at all but to laugh, a little, and rest his cheek against the pale silk of her hair. "It is convenient," he said, and heard himself say, "that the people who actually remember any of those events are all dead, and getting deader all the time, as it were."

She laughed, too. "I might want to take a nip out of that bottle from time to time myself, but—despite how bloody awful so much of this has been, I don't want to lose it all, either. There were some amazing moments, in amongst all the bad."

"We can keep it under the bathroom sink," said Varney, "with the spare shampoo, and no one will be the wiser," and that made her laugh more, and then he simply had to kiss her; there was no choice in the matter at all.

When he pulled back, he was aware, very aware indeed, of the warmth of her, the sweet weight against his side, all the places that they touched; and he was enormously glad of his strange newfound ability not to go to pieces, because *desire* washed through him like a tidal bore and, oh, he *wanted*, wanted things he should not have, and—

"...when do you want to get married?" he asked, not quite steadily.

"Now," said Greta, still pressed close to him. "Right now, in this bed. One of the little brown bats in the roof colony can officiate, or a mouse, I'm sure it's allowable protocol."

"We should have asked Samael to do it," he said, definitely unsteady now, and heard himself make a soft and helpless sound as Greta's hand on his chest slipped lower and lower. "He did say I could ask for anything—*oh*—"

"What did you *do*, Varney?"

It was so difficult to concentrate enough to talk. "Saved the world, I think—"

"In that case," said Greta Helsing, smiling in the dark, "you deserve rather more of a reward," and shortly afterward Varney's ability to string words together in any semblance of order vanished like a blown-out candle flame, and all there was, was joy.

And so, ten days later, there *was* a wedding: officiated not by bat or mouse but by the perfectly inoffensive local vicar—and for once the British weather had relented, and allowed them to hold it outside, on a clear and lovely autumn day.

Greta was amazed all over again at how fast things happened when you threw money at them; Varney had called Ruthven, and the latter had slipped into accelerated event-planning mode, and she had found herself taken to town and made to try on a lot of silly dresses until she found one she actually absolutely loved; there were absurd appointments for cake tasting ("It tastes like cake," she had said, and Ruthven had *sighed* at her) and the dress had to be altered to fit, and everybody had to be rung up and invited and told to arrive at such and such a time, Fastitocalon had to be invited to give her away (and Ruthven had sulked about it until she said, "I've got two arms, haven't I, you can both walk with me") and so much of it seemed to happen at once, *around* Greta, a whirlwind of activity. She herself kept out of Ruthven's way except when he needed her to do something, and spent the time with Emily and the monsters—and Varney, when he could be spared from the wedding effort.

It had all seemed somewhat unreal to her, bemusing rather than exciting—until the day actually came, and she had to excuse herself right before walking down the aisle to swallow one of Emily's anti-anxiety pills and something for her stomach. As soon as it began, though, the crawling stage-fright lifted from her like a cloak.

Afterward she would remember the whole thing in a series of images, beads strung together on a thread, each a turning jewel: taking Ruthven's and Fastitocalon's arms and stepping between them out of the house on that long walk across the terrace and up the grassy slope to the old stone summerhouse draped with garlands of peach roses; passing between the rows of chairs, face after familiar face turning to follow the bridal party as they went. Almost everyone they'd invited had been able to come, and in many cases had their travel paid for by Varney and Ruthven; she was enormously pleased to catch a glimpse of several of her mummy patients in the throng. Sheelagh Montrose the banshee, Krona the barrow-wight, St. Germain the wolf, Ruthven's vampire friends from Paris, practically everyone Greta knew and *liked* was there to watch this moment. Even the psychopomps were there, Crepusculus Dammerung looking absurd in a dinner-jacket and grinning at her, Gervase Brightside actually smiling for once.

Having Ruthven and Fastitocalon flanking her felt *right* in a bone-deep way, the solid comfort of their presence giving her something to hold on to. And looking up the grassy aisle between the rows to see Sir Francis Varney in deep grey, Grisaille and Cranswell beside him, closing the distance, her heart beating too fast, felt a little like walking up to the edge of some unknown precipice: exciting and dangerous at once.

After that, it all happened very fast. Taking her place next to Varney, with Nadezhda and Hippolyta and Anna and Emily arrayed beside her, listening to the murmured speech of the vicar and the solemn recitation of the vows, feeling the strange lovely weight of her wedding band warming to blood-heat, all of it blurred together until the moment when Varney lifted her veil, took her face in his hands, and kissed her as his living wife; with that, she had taken the last step over that precipice into clear air, and was not falling but *flying*.

Through the applause she thought, *How strange it is that all of this should have happened so quickly; I have only known him for a little over a year.*

*I want to make up for lost time.*

Looking out over her friends, her family, the people she had met and worked with and loved and cared for, saved and been saved by, Greta thought how utterly fortunate she was to be what, and who, she was. All her life she'd been aware of existing in the strange liminal space between the ordinary world and the one her patients inhabited, not quite wholly in either one, and resigned to loneliness. Now the borders of that space seemed to have expanded, drawn back like stage-curtains to encompass not just Greta but the people she loved, and who loved her.

The old golden stone of Dark Heart House glowed against the copper beeches that had given it its nickname, the rolling green parkland stretching away to the woods on the other side of the valley. The house had stood there for six centuries, while the world around it shifted and changed and moved on; she thought now, looking at it, that it could stand for six more.

*Home*, she thought. *That's home.* Not the flat in Crouch End where she'd lived for so many years, in her other life.

The crowd of their guests was mingling now, wandering down toward the house, where champagne and canapés had been set out in the great hall. Varney smiled down at her. "Shall we? I'm sure Edmund is going to want to make a speech, and he'll mind if we're not there to listen."

Tomorrow she would go back to Oasis Natrun, and her job; there would always be the job, the need, the work and care of it, but for now—just for now—Greta took the arm her husband offered her, and let him lead her home.

# EPILOGUE

The setting sun struck fire from the windows of Oasis Natrun, turning the distant sea into a sheet of gold; above it the sky shaded from lemon-yellow through a delicate green to the deepest of blue scattered with stars. Greta Helsing stood on the terrace's balcony, watching the spa's helicopter dwindling with distance as it bore a departing patient to the airport: Mr. Antjau, officially cured, carrying the jar containing his lungs in a crocodile-skin travel case.

She leaned her elbows on the railing, pleasantly tired, and was not at all surprised when Varney came to join her, drinks in hand. He was spending a week at the spa, ostensibly so that Tefnakhte could tutor him in Egyptian, but also because of evenings like this one: pale gold and deepening blue, the air like wine.

"Thanks," she said, taking the glass he offered, clinking it with his. "I keep thinking the sunsets can't get better, and I keep being wrong."

Varney slipped an arm around her waist. "Dark Heart isn't much for spectacular sunsets," he said mildly. "I ordered you dinner in an hour."

She smiled. "I should be doing work, not lazing about and eating gourmet food."

"You've *been* doing work all day," he said. "I watched you. That infestation case this morning was remarkably nasty."

"One of the worst I've seen, but she was under the sterilization linac within half an hour of checking in, and that thing works like—well, like magic." Greta sipped her drink. It had been a relatively slow day, after dealing with poor Ms. Akhetbasaken's dermestid beetle problem; a couple of routine daily exams, one replacement finger, one partial rewrap. The spa's clientele was growing. "Which reminds me, I need to actually set aside some time to concentrate on reading Faust's book; I got halfway through the first chapter on introductory mirabilic principles before I had to go and fix somebody's kneecap, and it's all gone right out of my mind. How's the Egyptian coming along?"

"Slowly," said Varney. "I've read a lot of it in translation, and it's slightly infuriating just how long it will take me to be able to read Egyptian poetry to you. They're fragments, but they're beautiful nonetheless."

Greta smiled, leaning against him, shoulder to shoulder. "You could do it in French."

"All the French poetry I know is extremely depressing," said Varney, "which I should imagine comes as no surprise. I *will* master Egyptian if only to be able to tell you beautiful things."

"And to help with the patients when you're here," she said. "It really does make a difference having you recite the spells along with Tefnakhte. There's a unique quality to your voice that seems to act as a force multiplier."

" 'Mellifluous,' " Varney said, and made a face.

"Precisely. I'm thinking of doing a paper on the effects of auditory spells on patient outcomes; I don't think it's been studied before. I might use that to open the conference, in fact."

Varney sighed. "I suppose I could—I don't know, have my voice recorded and analyzed, if it will make you happy, and that reminds me, I've got to hurry up and get the last bit of the roof finished before your learned friends are scheduled to arrive."

"You've got time," said Greta. "It's not until next year, and I haven't decided if I want to hold it in a different place each year or if it should stay at Dark Heart. There aren't that many mummy specialists worldwide, it's such a niche area; I think we can all fit into the great hall without getting too friendly with one another."

Varney nodded, sipped his drink. "I'm proud of you," he said after a moment, slightly awkward. She turned to look at him.

"For what? Dealing with those beetles wasn't much fun, but it's hardly the first time I've had to manage."

"For—everything," he said, flushing very pale pink. "For all of the work you did in Hell, and—coming back here after that and *still* doing your job, and organizing conferences and studying magic and being patient with people who don't strictly deserve it, and—"

Greta smiled. "You do know," she said, "that I'm able to do my job because it must be done, but do you also know how much easier *everything* is when I don't have to do it alone?"

Varney's blush deepened. She covered his hand on the balcony railing with her own, the dying sun catching in the stones of her ring. "I mean it, Francis," she said. "Everything is better with you. Simpler. I can do more because I know there's someone there to catch me, somebody I trust to help when I need it. I didn't know how badly I needed it before."

"I will *always* be there to catch you," he said. "That at least I can promise."

"And I will be there to help." She set down her glass. "It's what I'm for, when you get right down to it. I—can't believe it's only a year and a bit since I met you; it feels like forever."

"Forever's not long at all," said Varney. "But it'll do, for now."

He took her hand in his, and together they watched as the vault of the sky above them slowly came alight with stars: a hundred, a million stars, diamonds scattered across a vast and endless blue. Greta thought of golden snowflakes falling in Hell, lit with the moving opalescent glow of the burning lake; thought of jeweled battlements in Heaven, white-winged angels, Samael, almost indistinguishable from them save for the color of his eyes; thought of all the mummy bones she had repaired, the architectural structure of muscle and tendon and ligament replaced with new materials, the time she had spent just sitting with her patients, listening, understanding, *learning*. Thought of the books she had read and the books she would read, how much more there was to learn, how she never wanted to *stop* learning, all the days of her life, with him beside her. How she never wanted to waste a single moment.

*Varney was right*, she thought, looking up at the stars: *forever would do, for now.*

THE END

# ACKNOWLEDGMENTS

This series would never have happened without the encouragement and support of a great many people. First and foremost, my wife, Arkady Martine; Stephen Barbara, best of agents; Emily Byron and Sarah Guan (and Lindsey Hall), my editors; Ellen Wright, my publicist; Laura Schlitz, who told me not to stop, and Jane Mitchell, who first led me to some of the places Greta explores; Melissa Bresnahan, who asked what happened next; Dr. Kevin Ferentz, who prevented me from getting *too* much of the medicine wrong; and everyone else who came along with me on this bizarre, intense, and absolutely incredible three-year journey.

# extras

# meet the author

*Photo Credit: Emilia Blaser*

Vivian Shaw wears way too many earrings and likes edged weapons and expensive ink. She was born in Kenya and spent her early childhood in the UK before relocating to America at the age of seven. She has a BA in art history and an MFA in creative writing and publishing arts, and has worked in academic publishing and development while researching everything from the history of spaceflight to reactor design to mountaineering disasters to supernatural physiology. In her spare time she draws, sews, makes jewelry, collects vintage cookbooks and fountain pens, and writes fanfiction (pen name: Coldhope). She lives in Baltimore with her wife, the author Arkady Martine.

## if you enjoyed
## GRAVE IMPORTANCE
### look out for
# THE UNLIKELY ESCAPE OF URIAH HEEP
### by
## H. G. Parry

*For his entire life, Charley Sutherland has concealed a magical ability he can't quite control: He can bring characters from books into the real world. His older brother, Rob—a young lawyer with a normal house, a normal fiancée, and an utterly normal life—hopes that this strange family secret will disappear with disuse, and he will be discharged from his life's duty of protecting Charley and the real world from each other. But then literary characters start causing trouble in their city, making threats about destroying the world... and for once, it isn't Charley's doing.*

*There's someone else who shares his power. It's up to Charley and a reluctant Rob to stop them before these characters tear apart the fabric of reality.*

# I

At four in the morning, I was woken by a phone call from my younger brother. He sounded breathless, panicked, with the particular catch in his voice I knew all too well.

"Uriah Heep's loose on the ninth floor," he said. "And I can't catch him."

My brain was fogged with sleep; it took a moment for his words to filter through. "Seriously, Charley?" I said when they did. "Again?"

"I've never read out Uriah Heep before."

"True, but—you know what I mean." I rubbed my eyes, trying to focus. The bedroom was pitch black and cold, the glow of the digital clock the only fuzzy source of light. Next to me, I heard Lydia stir and turn over in a rustle of sheets. I had a sense then of being suspended between two worlds: the sane one in which I had fallen asleep, and Charley's, reaching to pull me awake through the speaker of my phone. It was a familiar feeling. "That's Dickens, isn't it? You know you and Dickens don't mix—or... mix too well, or whatever it is the two of you do. I thought you were sticking to poetry lately. Those postmodern things that read like a dictionary mated with a Buddhist mantra and couldn't possibly make any sense to anyone."

"There is not a poem on earth that doesn't make any sense to anyone."

Even half-asleep, I could recognize an evasion when I heard it. "You promised. You promised it wouldn't happen again."

"I know, and I meant it, and I'm sorry." He was whispering, presumably trying not to alert the security guards roaming the university campus—or perhaps not to alert Uriah Heep. "But please, *please*, Rob, I know it's late and you have work tomorrow, but if they find him here in the morning—"

"All right, all right, calm down." I forced exasperation out of my voice. There were times when he needed to hear it, and times when it would only tip him over the edge, and right now he sounded dangerously close to the edge. "You're in your office? I'm on my way. Just try to keep an eye on him, and be down to let me in the building in ten minutes."

He sighed. "Thank you. Oh God, I really am sorry, it was only for a second..."

"Ten minutes," I told him, and hung up. I sighed myself, heard it go out into the darkness, and ran my hand through my hair. Oh well. It wasn't as though I was *surprised*.

"It's my brother," I said to Lydia, whom I could sense watching me with sleepy concern from the other side of the bed. "He's having a crisis."

"Is he all right?"

"He'll be fine." Lydia didn't know the form my brother's crises took, but it wasn't the first time he'd phoned me with one. It wasn't even the first time in the middle of the night. I had no idea who used to help him while he was living in England, but since he'd come to Wellington, I seemed to be on speed dial. "He just needs some help with a problem. You know how he is."

"You've got a trial this morning," she reminded me.

"I know," I said. "I'll make it. Go back to sleep."

"You can't fix all his problems for him. He's twenty-six."

"I know." She was right; he did need to learn to deal with these things himself.

Uriah Heep, though. I'd never read Dickens myself, but I'd learned to have an instinct for the names, and that one didn't sound promising.

My brother works as a lecturer at Prince Albert University of Wellington, which I can, as I promised, drive to from my house in about ten minutes, provided I stop only to pull on a pair of shoes and shrug on a coat over my pajamas. It's a tricky road in the dark, skirting the central city and winding up into the foothills of Kelburn. I missed a turn, and found myself on the wrong side of the botanic gardens. Wellington's like that. The city itself is nestled between the harbor and the hills: too far one way, and you hit the ocean; too far the other, and you're facing a wall of impenetrable forest sloping up into the clouds. It's not a good place for my brother, whose relationship with "too far" has never been a healthy one.

The campus is perched halfway up the Kelburn hills, a tumbling assortment of buildings on either side of the road connected by an overpass. They're old buildings, by New Zealand standards, but they probably don't seem that way to Charley. Until three years ago, he'd been at Oxford, where referring to a building as old meant someone was studying in it a thousand years ago. I'd been there on a family visit once, and had felt the dust-stifled weight that comes from centuries of scholarship and ancient stone. I wasn't certain I liked it. It felt too much as though it had come from the pages of a book. The Prince Albert campus, just over a hundred years old, still feels as if it was built by people. Most of its office blocks started life as a settler's house, and even its grandest buildings are infused with the labor of Victorian colonials re-creating England in basic scaffolding. When I think of Oxford, I think of the still peace of the summer air; here, the air is never still, and rarely peaceful. That particular night, it was raining lightly, and the streetlights caught the drops in a mist of silver. When I got out of the car, the haze clung to my face and stung like ice.

I think Charley had the door to the English department open before I could even knock. In the light spilling from the corridor behind him, I could see his eyes huge and appealing, his unruly mess of dark curls and baggy sweatshirt making him look smaller and younger than he was. He's very good at that. It didn't mean I wasn't going to kill him this time—I was—but maybe not when he was completely beside himself with worry.

"He got away from me," Charley said immediately. As usual in a crisis, he was talking almost too fast to be understood. "I tried to stay with him, but I had to call you, and... and my cell phone was in my office, so I had to go there, and then once I called you I tried to find him again, and he..."

"Hey, slow down." My left shoe had a hole in it I hadn't noticed until I ran through the puddles. I could feel my wet sock squelching inside it now. "Take a breath. He has to still be in the building, right? He hasn't got a card to swipe out, and the building locks down after dark?"

"That's right," Charley confirmed. He took a deep breath, obediently, and released it. It didn't help. "Unless he breaks a window, or someone left one open—"

"Any sign of that?"

"No. And I've looked in every room. But I can't find him."

"We'll find him," I assured him. "Don't worry. It's only some nasty Victorian with no eyelashes." I'd Googled the character on the way here, which might have contributed to the wrong turn I'd taken. Apparently he was an ugly redheaded clerk who tries to ruin the lives of the main characters in *David Copperfield*. Also, there was a rock band named after him, which sounded cool. "Not like that time you brought Dracula out of *his* book, when you were eight."

"Vampires have weaknesses," Charley said darkly. "Stoker wrote them in. People are far less predictable."

I couldn't argue with that. "Come on. Let's start in your office."

I'd never been in Charley's office before, but it was exactly how I'd pictured it: complete chaos. Mugs littered the desk and peered out from bookshelves, books spilled from every nook and cranny, and the computer was buried beneath pages of scribbled notes. The battered armchair by the window was the only thing clear of clutter, because it was obviously where he sat in order to clutter everything else. It was a Charley-shaped hole in the mess, like an outline at a police crime scene.

There was no sign of a wayward Dickensian villain, but I could smell the faint tang of smoke and fog that I'd learned to associate with Dickensian England, amid the more usual smells of books and stale coffee.

"What were you doing here at four in the morning, anyway?" I asked. I was out of breath: we'd climbed the stairs to the ninth floor so as not to alert Uriah Heep of our coming. The elevators were notorious for breaking down in this building anyway. I remembered that from my undergraduate days, although my classes had usually been at the law campus in the central city.

I'd never been in the English department, and right now it was eerie in the dark. Reception was locked off, and the corridors were a labyrinthine world of shadows.

"I was finishing an article," Charley answered. "Well, I was starting it, actually. Someone wants it by next week, for an anthology. And I just—I don't know, I'd actually proposed something about the autobiographical form in *David Copperfield* and *Great Expectations*, but I became very interested in how Uriah Heep was functioning as a scapegoat for middle-class anxieties in *David Copperfield*, and the means by which he's constructed as a threat to the social order, and I was reading and thinking about him quite closely—"

"And he sprang off the page," I finished grimly. I'd heard it before. "You couldn't just put him back?"

"He was too fast. He knew what I was going to do, and he wasn't going to let me."

I shook my head. "You shouldn't be here in the middle of the night."

"I got caught up." He sounded apologetic. "Anyway, it's better to work when no one's around, in case something like this happens."

"I suppose, but you know it's more likely to happen when you're tired. And *definitely* when you're caught up."

"I didn't mean it."

"Never mind." I picked up a paper from the top strata covering the desk, filled with the least legible version of Charley's handwriting. *LOOK AT pg. 467,* it began. *Model clerk—model prisoner—Heep is his own parody—becomes what people expect him to be—commentary on 19thC hypocrisy—fear of* squiggle squiggle—*shape-*squiggle—squiggle *David's own* squiggle—*like Orlick and Pip from GE—Fitzwilliam writes on this in* squiggle—"You say you were thinking about him as a threat to the social order?"

He nodded unhappily.

The figures Charley summons from books are always colored by his interpretations. Charley calls it postmodernism at work. The last thing we needed was for this latest one to be colored by danger, however theoretical.

"All right." I tried to think. It was hard, when I had been sound asleep twenty minutes ago. Unlike Charley's, my brain doesn't work well in the hours before dawn. "You know this character. Where would he go?"

"I don't know. He doesn't go near an English department in the book. I suppose we just have to look for him."

"Charley—!" I bit back a surge of temper just in time. It was more than temper, really. I hated this. I'd always hated this, but I hated it more now, here, in my city.

I looked out the office window. Beyond the campus, the ground dropped away dramatically, and Wellington spread out like a blanket. Down in the distance, I could see the glittering lights of the central city, and past them the long curve of the harbor and the dark of the ocean. Outside the mess my brother worked in, it all looked impossibly clean and young and bright.

"Do you think we should check the library?" Charley asked.

I forced myself to focus. "Would he *want* to get to the library? Is that where you think he'd go?"

"Possibly. I have no idea where he'd go."

I pinched the bridge of my nose. "Charley, I have a big trial coming up in a few hours. I'm expected at the courthouse at nine. It's my job. There are people depending on me. I can't just keep looking all night!"

"I said I was sorry! I knew I shouldn't have called you."

"You shouldn't have had to!" So much for keeping exasperation out of my voice. I had never been very good at that. "How many times does it take? Just keep your thoughts under control when you read a book! It shouldn't be so hard!"

"Maybe you should go. I can deal with this myself. It's not your problem."

"It *is* my problem, though, isn't it? It's always my problem. You make it my problem when you bring these things into my city and into my life."

"I didn't mean to."

"It doesn't matter what you mean! It's what you do. It's what you always do."

"I said I would deal with it myself," Charley said. His face had hardened. "I shouldn't have asked you to come here. Just go home, Rob. I mean it. I don't need your help."

I might have gone. I don't think I would have—I hope I wouldn't have. But I was furious, and I could already feel fury pushing me to say and do the things I tried to avoid. It just might have propelled me out the door.

Except, just for a moment, I looked at Charley again. There was something there, in the tilt of his head and the lines of his face, that I'd never seen before. Something hard, and cunning. There was a glint in his eyes that could almost have been malice.

All at once, Charley's notes flashed up before my eyes, and I felt cold.

Shape-squiggle. If my brother's handwriting hadn't been so terrible, I might have worked it out sooner.

As I said, my brother's creations are always colored by his perception of them. Sometimes this is slight, and manageable: a shift in personality, or a blurring of appearance. But some colorings are deeper and stranger, and the deeper he gets into literary theory, the stranger they become. Traits that are metaphorical in the text become absurdly, dangerously literal. A shy character may come out invisible. A badly written character might come out flat. The Phantom of the Opera walked in a little cloud of darkness, and all Charley could say about it was that it was a half-baked theory about pathetic fallacy and his concentration slipped.

Dickens, as far as I know, has no shape-shifters in his books. But somehow, Charley's Uriah Heep had come out as one. And he had been standing in front of me from the moment I entered the building.

"Where's my brother?" I said slowly.

The thing that wasn't Charley looked confused. He did it well—he got the nose wrinkle just right—but it didn't matter. I knew now. "What are you talking about?"

"You weren't down at the door because you were waiting for me." I could feel the pieces start to fit, the way they did on a good day in court when a hostile witness said just the wrong thing at the right time. "You were down there trying to get away before I arrived. Sometime after Charley called, you took him out of action somehow and stole his key card. But I arrived too soon, didn't I? You had to let me in, and bluff it out. That's why you told me to leave; that's why you're trying to provoke an argument. You need me to storm out and leave you here alone, so you can get away."

He shook his head. "Rob, you can't possibly..."

"You should have known me better than that," I said. "Or Charley should—I suppose you know me from his memories. I wouldn't leave him in danger just because he was getting on my nerves."

"You've done it before," Charley said. My stomach twisted, because I knew what he meant.

"Yes, I have," I admitted. "And that's why I'd never do it again. Where is he?"

I didn't wait for the impostor to lie this time. I pushed my way past him, out into the corridor. "Charley!"

The corridors were lit only by the light spilling from Charley's office. It might have been my imagination, but I thought I heard a faint sound in response.

"Very well." The voice from behind me wasn't quite my brother's anymore. I turned around quickly, and the face wasn't my brother's either.

For the record, Uriah Heep is a very ugly character. He had a face like a skull—cadaverous, I think the Internet had said—and a skeletal body to match: tall, pale, thin, with red hair shaved far shorter than I'd thought the Victorians went in for, and reddish eyes without eyebrows or eyelashes. His jeans and sweatshirt had changed with him to a black tailcoat, funereal garb. His limbs twitched and writhed, apparently without his input; I thought, inexplicably, of the branches of the tree at the back of our childhood house. I was more interested in the knife in his hand. It was a modern box cutter, and he held it like a dagger in my direction.

"I should have known better, Master Robert," he said, "than to think my umble self could fool a gentleman of your station and fine schooling. Do forgive me, won't you, Master Robert? It was on account of my being so very umble and unworthy."

"Don't give me all that." I mastered my shock, and hardened my tone. "I don't even like Dickens. Where's my brother?"

"Oh, you mustn't think I've hurt Master Charles," Uriah said, with a laugh like someone grating iron. His voice was honey and rusty nails. "No, no, someone in my umble position—"

"God, literary critics must have a field day with you," I groaned.

I saw it then: a flash of hatred, right across his face. And then, all at once, the knife was at my throat, and I was against the wall of the corridor opposite, a bony hand on my shoulder holding me there. It was so quick, I didn't even have a chance to flinch. The blade touched my neck; it stung, but didn't cut. My heart was beating so loud and fast it filled my entire body.

"I never asked for this," Uriah hissed. "I never asked to be poor, and ugly, and the villain of the piece. I never wanted to be obsequious, and insincere, and deadly. I never wanted to fall in love with a woman that was always destined for the hero of the novel."

"I'm sure you didn't," I managed. It was my best attempt at conciliation. It might have been better to keep quiet. "But that's not our fault."

"Master Charley brought me out." His face, inches from mine, melted from the shadows. "And now he wants to put me back in. In my place. Just as everybody's done, all my life. Well, I won't go, do you hear me? I won't. This world out here—it hasn't been written yet. For all I know, I can write it for myself. I don't have to do what the story says. I can do whatever I want."

I couldn't help but laugh at that. "You've got a lot to learn about the world out here, don't you?"

The blade dug deeper. A thin drop of blood was suddenly warm on my throat, like a shaving cut. Whatever Charley had managed to do to Uriah Heep, he was no longer merely a nasty Victorian with no eyelashes.

"Look, fine." I tried to speak very carefully, without my voice trembling. "Go, if you want. Just tell me where my brother is."

"Why should you care? I've seen you, you know, in his memories. You don't like him. You wish he'd never come here."

"That's not true," I said.

"Yes, it is." Uriah shook his ugly head. "You'll be better off without him anyway, with what's coming. He's going to be right at the heart of it. Stay out of it, keep your head down, and don't look too closely at what's going on, that's my umble suggestion, Master Robert."

Curiosity momentarily overcame my fear. I frowned. "What do you mean?"

"Just what I said, Master Robert. You stay out of it. It don't concern you. And you won't want it to."

"What doesn't concern me?"

“The new world,” he said. “There won’t be a place for you in the new world.”

Down the corridor, one of the doors burst open. I turned toward the sound on instinct before I had registered what it was. My brother came out.

It was definitely my brother this time. He was wearing the same clothes as the Uriah Heep version of him had been—maybe those were all the clothes of our world that thing had known well enough to copy. His hair was the same mess of curls in need of a haircut. But I had been right. He did look different. His face was softer, and less sure of itself, and his eyes lacked that touch of cunning I’d seen in the copy. I suppose in a Dickens novel evil is real, and it shines out.

He stopped short at the sight of us. The knife was still at my throat, even though Uriah Heep turned to look at him at the same time I had. Then he raised his head.

“Let him go.” His voice had that touch of an English accent I’d noticed at odd times since he returned from overseas. “I’m here now. It’s over.”

“With all due respect, Master Charley,” Uriah said, “you were here at the start. I tied you up and put you in a cupboard.”

“Well,” he said rather weakly. “I’m back again.”

I took a chance then. Uriah was looking the other way; even had he not been, my heart was now beating so fast I couldn’t have held still a moment longer. I grabbed Uriah’s wrist and wrenched the knife away from my throat.

Uriah lunged forward with a hiss. But I was prepared for his wiry strength this time, and adrenaline was flooding me with strength of my own. I kept a tight grip on his wrist, twisting it farther away from me; at the same time, I grabbed his other arm and clung on for grim life. It really was like holding a writhing skeleton. His bones stood out through his clothes, and his unearthly wail was that of a specter. The knife clattered to the floor.

"Now!" I snapped. "Put him back!"

"No!" Uriah cried. There was hatred there—seething hatred—but also real despair. It made me feel sick, despite myself. "You have no idea what it's like in that book. They always win. *They all hate me and I hate them and they always win!*"

"I know," Charley said. He sounded unhappy too. "I'm truly sorry."

He reached out and touched Uriah on the shoulder, and deep concentration swept over his face. And suddenly my hands were closed around nothing at all. There was a flare of light, and between one heartbeat and the next Uriah Heep had vanished. His screams lingered even after the sound of them had faded, like the smell of Victorian smoke and fog still clinging to the air.

Lydia was right. I really did need to start letting Charley sort these things out for himself.

**if you enjoyed**

**GRAVE IMPORTANCE**

**look out for**

# THE DEVIL YOU KNOW

## Felix Castor: Book One

**by**

## Mike Carey

*Felix Castor is a freelance exorcist, and London is his stomping ground. The supernatural world is in upheaval and spilling over into the mundane reality of the living, and his skills have never been more in demand. A good exorcist can charge what he likes—and enjoy a hell of a lifestyle—but there's a risk: Sooner or later he's going to run into a spirit that he can't handle.*

*After a year spent in "retirement," Castor is reluctantly drawn back to the life he rejected and accepts what should be a simple exorcism case—just to pay the bills. Trouble is, the more he discovers about the ghost, the more things don't add up. This new case is rapidly turning into the "Who Can Kill Castor First Show," with demons, were-beings, ghosts, and a ruthless East End gang boss all keen to claim the big prize.*

*But that's business as usual; Castor knows how to deal with the dead. It's the living who piss him off.*

# CHAPTER ONE

Normally I wear a czarist army greatcoat—the kind that sometimes gets called a paletot—with pockets sewn in for my tin whistle, my notebook, a dagger, and a chalice. Today I'd gone for a green tuxedo with a fake wilting flower in the buttonhole, pink patent-leather shoes, and a painted-on mustache in the style of Groucho Marx. From Bunhill Fields in the east, I rode out across London—the place of my strength. I have to admit, though, that "strong" wasn't exactly how I was feeling; when you look like a pistachio-ice-cream sundae, it's no easy thing to hang tough.

The economic geography of London has changed a lot in the last few years, but Hampstead is always Hampstead. And on this cold November afternoon, atoning for sins I couldn't even count and probably looking about as cheerful as a *tricoteuse* being told that the day's executions have been canceled due to bad weather, Hampstead was where I was headed.

Number 17, Grosvenor Terrace, to be more precise: an unassuming little early Victorian masterpiece knocked off by Sir Charles Barry in his lunch hours while he was doing the

Reform Club. It's in the books, like it or not; the great man would moonlight for a grand in hand and borrow his materials from whatever else he was doing at the time. You can find his illegitimate architectural progeny everywhere from Ladbroke Grove to Highgate, and they always give you that same uneasy feeling of déjà vu, like seeing the milkman's nose on your own firstborn.

I parked the car far enough away from the door to avoid any potential embarrassment to the household I was here to visit and managed the last hundred yards or so burdened with four suitcases full of highly specialized equipment. The doorbell made a severe, functional buzzing sound like a dentist's drill sliding off recalcitrant enamel. While I waited for a response, I checked out the rowan twig nailed up to the right of the porch. Black and white and red strings had been tied to it in the prescribed order, but still... a rowan twig in November wouldn't have much juice left in it. I concluded that this must be a quiet neighborhood.

The man who opened the door to me was presumably James Dodson, the birthday boy's father. I took a strong dislike to him right then to save time and effort later. He was a solid-looking man, not big but hard-packed, gray eyes like two ball bearings, salt-and-pepper hair adding its own echoes to the gray. In his forties, but probably as fit and trim now as he had been two decades ago. Clearly, this was a man who recognized the importance of good diet, regular exercise, and unremitting moral superiority. Pen had said he was a cop—chief constable in waiting, working out of Agar Street as one of the midwives to the government's new Serious Organized Crime Agency. I think I would have guessed either a cop or a priest, and most priests gratefully let themselves go long before they hit forty; that's one of the perks of having a higher calling.

"You're the entertainer," Dodson said, as you might say "You're a motherless piece of scum and you raped my dog." He didn't make a move to help me with the cases, which I was carrying two of in each hand.

"Felix Castor," I agreed, my face set in an unentertaining deadpan. "I roll the blues away."

He nodded noncommittally and opened the door wider to let me in. "The living room," he said, pointing. "There'll be rather more children than we originally said. I hope that's okay."

"The more the merrier," I answered over my shoulder, walking on through. I sized the living room up with what I hoped looked like a professional eye, but it was just a room to me. "This is fine. Everything I need. Great."

"We were going to send Sebastian over to his father's, but the bloody man had some sort of work crisis on," Dodson explained from behind me. "Which makes one more. And a few extra friends..."

"Sebastian?" I inquired. Throwing out questions like that is a reflex with me, whether I want answers or not; it comes from the work I do. I mean, the work I used to do. Sometimes do. Can live *without* doing.

"Peter's stepbrother. He's from Barbara's previous marriage, just as Peter is from mine. They get along very well."

"Of course." I nodded solemnly, as if checking out the soundness of the familial support network was something I always did before I started in on the magic tricks and the wacky slapstick. Peter was the birthday boy—just turned fourteen. Too old, probably, for clowns and conjurors and parties of the cake-and-ice-cream variety. But then, that wasn't my call to make. They also serve those who only pull endless strings of colored ribbon out of a baked-bean tin.

"I'll leave you to set up, then," Dodson said, sounding dubious. "Please don't move any of the furniture without checking with me or Barbara first. And if you're setting up anything on the parquet that might scratch, ask us for pads."

"Thanks," I said. "And mine's a beer whenever you're having one yourself. The term 'beer' should not be taken to include the subset 'lager.'"

He was already heading for the door when I threw this out, and he kept right on going. I was about as likely to get a drink out of him as I was to get a French kiss.

So I got down to unpacking, a task that was made harder by the fact that these cases hadn't moved out of Pen's garage in the last ten years. There were all sorts of things in among the stage-magic gear that gave me a moment's—or more than a moment's—pause. A Swiss Army penknife (it had belonged to my old friend Rafi) with the main blade broken off short an inch from the tip; a homemade fetish rigged up out of the mummified body of a frog and three rusty nails; a feathered snood, looking a bit threadbare now, but still carrying a faint whiff of perfume; and the camera.

Shit. The camera.

I turned it over in my hands, instantly submerged in a brief but powerful reverie. It was a Brownie Autographic No. 3, and all folded up as it was, it looked more like a kid's lunch box than anything else. But once I flipped the catches, I could see that the red-leather bellows was still in place, the frosted viewfinder was intact, and (wonder of wonders) the hand-wheeled stops that extended the lens into its operating position still seemed to work. I'd found the thing in a flea market in Munich when I was backpacking through Europe. It was nearly a hundred years old, and I'd paid about a quid for it, which was the whole of the asking price, because the lens was cracked right the way across. That didn't matter to me—not for what I principally had in mind at the time—so it counted as a bargain.

I had to put it to one side, though, because at that moment the first of the party guests were shepherded in by a very busty, very blonde, very beautiful woman who was obviously much too good for the likes of James Dodson. Or the likes of me, to be fair. She was wearing a white bloused top and a khaki skirt with an asymmetric hang, which probably had a designer name attached to it somewhere and cost more than I earned in six months. For all that, though, she looked a touch worn and tired. Living with James Supercop would do that to you, I speculated; or, possibly, living with Peter, assuming that Peter was the sullen streak of curdled sunlight hovering at her elbow. He had his father's air of blocky, aggressive solidity, with an adolescent's wary stubbornness grafted onto it. It made for a very unattractive combination, somehow.

The lady introduced herself as Barbara in a voice that had enough natural warmth in it to make electric blankets irrelevant. She introduced Peter, too, and I offered him a smile and a nod. I tried to shake hands with him out of some atavistic impulse probably brought on by being in Hampstead, but he'd already stomped away in the direction of a new arrival with a loud bellow of greeting. Barbara watched him go with an unreadable, Zen-like smile that suggested prescription medication, but her gaze as she turned back to me was sharp and clear enough.

"So," she said. "Are you ready?"

For anything, I almost said—but I opted for a simple yes. All the same, I probably held the glance a half moment too long. At any rate, Barbara suddenly remembered a bottle of mineral water that she was holding in her hand and handed it to me with a slight blush and an apologetic grimace. "You can have a beer in the kitchen with us afterward," she promised. "If I give you one now, the kids will demand equal rights."

I raised the bottle in a salute.

"So...," she said again. "An hour's performance, then an hour off while we serve the food—and you come on again for half an hour at the end. Is that okay?"

"It's a valid strategy," I allowed. "Napoléon used it at Quatre Bras."

This got a laugh, feeble as it was. "We won't be able to stay for the show," Barbara said, with a good facsimile of regret. "There's quite a lot still to do behind the scenes—some of Peter's friends are staying over. But we might be able to sneak back in to catch the finale. If not, see you in the interval." With a conspiratorial grin, she beat her retreat and left me with my audience.

I let my gaze wander around the room, taking the measure of them. There was an in-group, clustered around Peter and engaged in a shouted conversation that colonized the entire room. There was an out-group, consisting of four or five temporary knots spread around the edges of the room, which periodically tried to attach themselves to the in-group in a sort of reversal of cellular fission. And then there was stepbrother Sebastian.

It wasn't hard to spot him; I'd made a firm identification while I was still unfolding my trestle table and laying out my opening trick. He had the matrilineal blond hair, but his paler skin and watery blue eyes made him look as if someone had sketched him in pastels and then tried to erase him. He looked to be a lot smaller and slighter than Peter, too. Because he was the younger of the two? It was hard to tell, because his infolded, self-effaced posture probably took an inch or so off his height. He was the one on the fringes of the boisterous rabble, barely tolerated by the birthday boy and contemptuously ignored by the birthday boy's friends. He was the one left out of all the in-jokes, looking like he didn't belong and would rather be almost anywhere else—even with his real dad, perhaps, on a day when there was a work crisis on.

When I clapped my hands and shouted a two-minute warning, Sebastian filed up with the last of the rear guard and took up a position immediately behind Peter—a dead zone that nobody else seemed to want to lay claim to.

Then the show was on, and I had troubles of my own to attend to.

I'm not a bad stage magician. It was how I paid my way through college, and when I'm in practice, I'd go so far as to say I'm pretty sharp. Right then I was as rusty as hell, but I was still able to pull off some reasonably classy stuff—my own scaled-down versions of the great illusions I'd studied during my ill-spent youth. I made some kid's wristwatch disappear from a bag that he was holding and turn up inside a box in someone else's pocket. I levitated the same kid's mobile phone around the room while Peter and the front-row elite stood up and waved their arms in the vain hope of tangling the wires they thought I was using. I even cut a deck of cards into pieces with garden shears and reconstituted them again, with a card that Peter had previously chosen and signed at the top of the deck.

But whatever the hell I did, I was dying on my feet. Peter sat stolidly at front and center, arms folded in his lap, and glared at me all the while with paint-blistering contempt. He'd clearly reached his verdict, which was that being impressed by kids'-party magic could lose you a lot of status with your peers. And if the risk was there even for him, it was clearly unacceptable for his chosen guests. They watched him and took their cue from him, forming a block vote that I couldn't shift.

Sebastian seemed to be the only one who was actually interested in the show for its own sake—or perhaps the only one who had so little to lose that he could afford just to let himself get drawn in, without watching his back. It got him into trouble, though. When I finished the card trick and showed Peter his pristine eight of diamonds, Sebastian broke into a thin patter of applause, carried away for a moment by the excitement of the final reveal.

He stopped as soon as he realized that nobody else was joining in, but he'd already broken cover—forgetting what seemed otherwise to be very well developed habits of camouflage and self-preservation. Annoyed, Peter stabbed backward with his elbow, and I heard a *whoof* of air from Sebastian as he leaned suddenly forward, clutching his midriff. His head stayed bowed for a few moments, and when he came up, he came up slowly. "Fuckwit," Peter snarled, sotto voce. "He just used two decks. That's not even clever."

I read a lot into this little exchange—a whole chronicle of casual cruelty and emotional oppression. You may think that's stretching an elbow in the ribs a touch too far, but I'm a younger brother myself, so the drill's not unfamiliar to me. And besides that, I knew one more thing about birthday boy than anybody else here knew.

I took a mental audit. Yes. I was letting myself get a little irritated, and that wasn't a good thing. I still had twenty minutes to run before the break and the cold beer in the kitchen. And I had one surefire winner, which I'd been meaning to save for the finale, but what the hell. You only live once, as people continue to say in the teeth of all the evidence.

I threw out my arms, squared my shoulders, tugged my cuffs—a pantomime display of preparation intended mainly to get Sebastian off the hook. It worked, as far as that went; all eyes turned to me. "Watch very carefully," I said, taking a new prop out of one of the cases and putting it on the table in front of me. "An ordinary cereal box. Any of you eat this stuff? No, me neither. I tried them once, but I was mauled by a cartoon tiger." Not a glimmer; not a sign of mercy in any of the forty or so eyes that were watching me.

"Nothing special about the box. No trapdoors. No false bottoms." I rotated it through three dimensions, flicked it with a thumbnail to get a hollow *thwack* out of it, and held the open end up to Peter's face for him to take a look inside. He rolled his eyes as if he couldn't believe he was being asked to go along with this stuff, then gave me a wave that said he was as satisfied of the box's emptiness as he was ever going to be.

"Yeah, whatever," he said with a derisive snort. His friends laughed, too; he was popular enough to get a choric echo whenever he spoke or snickered or made farting noises in his cheek. He had the touch, all right. Give him four, maybe five years, and he was going to grow up into a right bastard.

Unless he took a walk down the Damascus Road one morning and met something big and fast coming the other way.

"O-o-okay," I said, sweeping the box around in a wide arc so that everyone else could see it. "So it's an empty box. So who needs it, right? Boxes like this, they're just landfill waiting to happen." I stood it on the ground, open end downward, and trod it flat.

That got at least a widened eye and a shift of posture here and there around the room—kids leaning forward to watch, if only to check out how complete and convincing the damage was. I was thorough. You have to be. Like a dominatrix, you find that there's a direct relationship between the intensity of the stamping and trampling and the scale of the final effect.

When the box was comprehensively flattened, I picked it up and allowed it to dangle flaccidly from my left hand.

"But before you throw this stuff away," I said, sweeping the cluster of stolid faces with a stern, schoolteacherly gaze, "you've got to check for biohazards. Anyone up for that? Anyone want to be an environmental health inspector when they grow up?"

There was an awkward silence, but I let it lengthen. It was Peter's dime; I only had to entertain him, not pimp for him.

Finally, one of the front-row cronies shrugged and stood up. I stepped a little aside to welcome him into my performance space—broadly speaking, the area between the leather recliner and the running buffet.

"Give a big hand to the volunteer," I suggested. They razzed him cordially instead—you find out who your friends are.

I straightened the box with a few well-practiced tugs and tucks. This was the crucial part, so of course I kept my face as bland as school custard. The volunteer held his hand out for the box. Instead, I caught his hand in my own and turned it palm up. "And the other one," I said. "Make a cup. *Verstehen Sie* 'cup'? Like this. Right. Excellent. Good luck, because you never know..."

I upended the box over his hands, and a large brown rat smacked right down into the makeshift basket of his fingers. He gurgled like a punctured water bed and jumped back, his hands flying convulsively apart, but I was ready and caught the rat neatly before she could fall.

Then, because I knew her well, I added a small grace note to the trick by stroking her nipples with the ball of my thumb. This made her arch her back and gape her mouth wide open, so that when I brandished her in the faces of the other kids, I got a suitable set of jolts and starts. Of course, it wasn't a threat display—it was "More, big boy, give me more"—but they couldn't be expected to know that look at their tender age. Any more than they knew that I'd dropped Rhona into the box when I pretended to straighten it after the trampling.

And bow. And acknowledge the applause. Which would have been fine if there'd been any. But Peter still sat like Patience on a monument, as the volunteer trudged back to his seat with his machismo at half-mast.

Peter's face said I'd have to do a damn sight more than that to impress him.

So I thought about the Damascus Road again. And, like the bastard I am, I reached for the camera.

---

This isn't my idea of how a grown man should go about keeping the wolf from the door, I'd like you to know. It was Pen who put me up to it. Pamela Elisa Bruckner—why that shortens to Pen rather than Pam I've never been sure, but she's an old friend of mine, and incidentally the rightful owner of Rhona the rat. She's also my landlady, for the moment at least, and since I wouldn't wish that fate on a rabid dog, I count myself lucky that it's fallen to someone who's genuinely fond of me. It lets me get away with a hell of a lot.

I should also tell you that I do have a job—a real job that pays the bills, at least occasionally. But at the time currently under discussion, I was taking an extended holiday, not entirely voluntary, and not without its own attendant problems relating to cash flow, professional credibility, and personal self-esteem. In any case, it left Pen with a vested interest in putting alternative work my way. Since she was still a good Catholic girl (when she wasn't being a Wicca priestess), she went to Mass every Sunday, lit a candle to the Blessed Virgin, and prayed to this tune: "Please, Madonna, in your wisdom and mercy, intercede for my mother though she died with many carnal sins weighing on her soul; let the troubled nations of Earth find a road to peace and freedom; and make Castor solvent, amen."

But usually she left it at that, which was a situation we could both live with. So it was an unpleasant surprise to me when she stopped counting on divine intervention and told me about the kids' party agency she was setting up with her crazy friend Leona—and the slimy sod of a street magician who'd given her an eleventh-hour stab in the back.

"But you could do this so *easily*, Fix," she coaxed over coffee laced with cognac in her subterranean sitting room. The smell was making me dizzy—not the smell of the brandy, but the smell of rats and earth and leaf mulch and droppings and Mrs. Amelia Underwood roses—of things growing and things decaying. One of her two ravens—Arthur, I think—was clacking his beak against the top shelf of the bookcase, making it hard for me to stick to a train of thought. This was her den, her center of gravity—the inverted penthouse underneath the three-story monstrosity where her grandmother had lived and died in the days when mammoths still roamed the Earth. She had me at a disadvantage here, which was why she'd asked me in to start with.

"You can do real magic," Pen pointed out sweetly, "so fake magic ought to be a doddle."

I blinked a couple of times to clear my eyes, blinded by candles, fuddled by incense. In a lot of ways, the way Pen lives is sort of reminiscent of Miss Havisham in *Great Expectations*: she only uses the basement, which means that the rest of the house apart from my bedsitter up in the roof space is frozen in the 1950s, never visited, never revised. Pen herself froze a fair bit later than that, but like Miss Havisham, she wears her heart on her mantelpiece. I try not to look at it.

On this particular occasion, I took refuge in righteous indignation. "I can't do real magic, Pen, because there's no such animal. Not the way you mean it, anyway. What do I look like, eh? Just because I can talk to the dead—and whistle up a tune for them—that doesn't make me Gandalf the bastard Grey. And it doesn't mean that there are fairies at the bottom of the sodding garden."

The crude language was a ploy intended to derail the conversation. It didn't work, though. I got the impression that Pen had worked out her script in advance for this one.

"'What is now proved was once only imagined,'" she said primly—because she knows that Blake is my main man, and I can't argue with him. "Okay," she went on, topping up my cup with about a half-pint of Janneau XO (it was going to be dirty pool on both sides, then), "but you did all that stage-magic stuff when we were in college, didn't you? You were *wonderful* back then. I bet you could still do it. I bet you wouldn't even have to practice. And it's two hundred quid for a day's work, so you could pay me a bit off last month's chunk of what you owe me..."

It took a lot more persuasion and a fair bit more brandy—so much brandy, in fact, that I made a pass at her on my unsteady way out the door. She slapped off my right hand, steered my left onto the door handle, and kissed me good night on the cheek without breaking stride.

I was profoundly grateful for that when I woke up in the morning, with my tongue stuck to my soft palate and my head full of unusable fuzz. Sexy, sweet, uninhibited, nineteen-year-old Pen, with her autumn bonfire of hair, her pistachio eyes, and her probably illegal smile would have been one thing; thirty-something Earth Mother Pen in her sibyl's cave, tended by rats and ravens and Christ only knew what other familiar spirits, and still waiting for her prince to come, even though she knew exactly where he was and what he'd turned into—there was too much blood under the bridge now. Leave it at that.

Then I remembered that I'd agreed to do the party just before I made the pass, and I cursed like a longshoreman. Game, set, and match to Pen and Monsieur Janneau. I hadn't even known we were playing doubles.